The Lagahoo's Apprentice

The Lagahoo's Apprentice

RABINDRANATH
MAHARAJ

Alfred A. Knopf Canada

PUBLISHED BY ALFRED A. KNOPF CANADA

Copyright © 2000 by Rabindranath Maharaj

All rights reserved under International and Pan-American Copyright
Conventions. Published in 2000 by Alfred A. Knopf Canada,
a division of Random House of Canada Limited, Toronto.
Distributed by Random House of Canada Limited, Toronto.

Knopf Canada and colophon are trademarks.

Parts of this novel appeared in different form in
The Ottawa Citizen, lichen and *Matrix*.

Canadian Cataloguing in Publication Data

Maharaj, Rabindranath
The lagahoo's apprentice

ISBN 0-676-97247-0

I. Title.

PS8576.A42L23 2000   C813'.54   C99-932756-9
PR9199.3M344L23 2000

First Edition

Printed and bound in the United States of America

10 9 8 7 6 5 4 3 2 1

To Uma and Hari

The now, the here, through which all future plunges into the past.

JAMES JOYCE

PROLOGUE

I never believed Cane was a lagahoo, a haunted creature
that emerges from the shadows of midnight, its approach
signalled only by the clanking of the chains wrapped
around its ankle. Cane lived alone in a small house almost
concealed by sugar cane, not the plantation variety but
tough, woody bon-bon that loosed a fine mist of pollen in
the ruffling of the humid afternoon breeze, so that his
house always seemed lightly powdered with dust.

In Agostini Village, doors and windows were usually
left open. Verandas were extensions of the living rooms,
with chairs, tables and couches neatly arrayed in every corner. Neighbours dropped by to exchange gossip, kicking
away the dogs sniffing at their boots. But no one I knew
had ever spoken to Cane or could provide an accurate description. Rumours arose because of his reclusiveness and
the notion that he had something to hide. In time, gossip
thickened these rumours into stories. In the afternoons, on
my way home from the Ecclesville government school,
staring at the house and imagining that I could glimpse
Cane peeping from a window, I reflected on the stories.

There were several. He was the great-great-grandson of
a maroon, a runaway slave who had murdered an overseer.
He was a Madrasi, shunned by the other Indians because
of his colour and caste. He was a white man, driven into
seclusion by the Black Power riots of the nineteen-sixties.

His daughter had been raped; he had exacted revenge. He was the last pure Carib, the aboriginal people decimated first by the Spanish, then the French and British colonizers.

Of all the stories, I preferred this last one, that he was a man forced into isolation because he was so different from everyone else, the last of his tribe. But when I asked my father about Cane's heritage, while he was arranging tins of condensed milk and shifting pans of brown sugar and rice on the shelves of the shop, he said absent-mindedly that Cane was from Venezuela. He must have continued to think about my question, because the next day he told me that people who live alone do so for a reason. My mother, sitting on her stool with an elbow on the counter, glanced at me sternly and cautioned that it was best to leave these people alone. I knew she was thinking of my little adventure three years earlier, when I had packed my canvas school bag with pens, markers and plastic beads taken from the shop, and set out to visit the Caribs on the outskirts of the Guanapo forest bordering Agostini. Mr. Tribhawan, a coffee farmer who lived close to the forest, found me and escorted me back to the shop. My mother was not impressed with my explanation that my standard three teacher, Mr. Palloo, had earlier in the week recited a poem about the aboriginal Indians who lived here before the arrival of Columbus; my father explained that the Caribs were not true aboriginals because they had, over the years, intermarried with all the other races in the island and that they were no longer interested in shiny beads.

I usually trusted my father, but I hoped he was wrong about Cane. From Venezuela! Venezuela, just half an hour from Trinidad, and inhabited by dusty, khaki-clad mestizos with hands calloused and scabbed from hacking away at the jungle.

I had never been impressed with Venezuela: it was too close and accessible and in my imagination, too parched and plain.

Each morning, I stared through the tangle of cane. In the afternoons, I knelt at the bank of the drain, really a roadside canal, and pretended I was catching the multi-coloured guppies that darted beneath the reedy plants in the brackish water. I saw that beyond the bon-bon, Cane's front yard was ablaze with blood-red dracaena, the "bound" plant used to demarcate the boundaries between properties.

The house had no veranda, and the teak logs had rotted away in places, but no repairs had been made. Leafless love vines trailing from the tangled roots of a silk cotton tree had sewn shut a wooden jalousie. A semp flew in and out of a hole in the aluminium roof. I thought of throwing a small rock on the roof to rouse the old man from the house but was afraid it would fall through one of the holes. Once, a small frog jumped from the water and landed on my shoulder. I fell backwards. The breeze bent the cane stalks and the blacksage at the side of the house and fluted through the aerial roots of the silk cotton tree, sounding like gently piped laughter.

Two months before my common entrance exams, on a day of pelting rain, through the dancing stalks I thought I saw a man standing outside the front door. I was rushing home, trying to protect my book bag with its prized notes by clasping it against my chest, and soon I had convinced myself that I had seen nothing, only a shadow created by the rain, but the next evening I saw him again. He raised a hand and passed it before his face as if wiping cobwebs from the air.

I could barely wait for the next day at school. While we were copying notes from the blackboard about the past governors general of the island, I passed a message to Sam, who grabbed this rare opportunity to whisper into Sally's ear. She sucked her teeth and tossed her head, her stiff pigtail almost knocking Sam over. Mr. Philip turned around, placed his chalk on the table and dusted his hands. He summoned Sally to the front and although I could not hear what they were saying, I saw him glancing at me. When Sally returned to her seat he took the duster, cleaned the board and wrote in long, flourishing sweeps, "Mystery solved by local boy." He took a step forward, and leaned over the table. "Today, we going to leave these governors general aside for a minute. In any case, these fellas dead and gone a long time now." He paused for the outburst of laughter. "Today, we going to deal with one of our own local superstar who somehow manage to convince Cane to step out from his house and wave at him." His voice, harsher now, cut through the laughter. "This man, descended from generation of proud freedom fighters and chieftains before that . . . this noble man forget all that, and start waving to everybody all of a sudden. Oops, sorry, pardon me. Not everybody, just Stephen Sagar. Smart, show-offy Stephen Sagar." There was no laughter this time. "Stephen Sagar, stand up right now. When was the abolition of slavery?"

"Eighteen thirty-four, sir."

My correct response inflamed him. "Good. Very good. Now tell me who build the pyramids? Where was the cradle of civilization? What colour was Moses? Why did Jesus refer to everyone as a brother? What was *his* colour?"

After school, stinging more from Mr. Philip's disbelief than from his tamarind rod, I stepped over the drain, parted the long, sharp leaves and saw Cane standing by the door.

Observing him for the first time at this close range, I saw why he had been mistaken for an African, a Madrasi and a white man. His white hair was cropped close to his skull and he had the dull, weathered face of so many old people: features set in stone but smoothed by time.

Something glittered in his palm. He pushed out his hand as if beckoning. I took a step further. He turned over his palm like a magician and a watch dangled from a silver chain. Then he turned slightly and tapped open the door.

When I peeped inside I saw a room full of clocks. Brass-framed, bell-topped, glass-panelled, circular-cased, swan-necked clocks. The frames were mostly wooden and some had been dismantled with the dials and finials and faces strewn about on a long, rectangular table. There was a strong odour of methylated spirit and varnish. On a narrow shelf—a ledge really—were small jars and containers, masking tape, steel wool and tweezers, compasses and clamps.

"Do you make clocks?"

He stepped away from the door and glanced into the room. "I keep time." I wasn't sure whether he was joking but, just in case, I remained serious.

During the following weeks, I resisted telling Sam or anyone else at school of my daily visits to Cane's house, though at times I was on the verge of blurting out something about the way he looked hunched over his table, tapping some mechanism and explaining as he worked that it was the gear wheel or the pawl pivot or the ratchet wheel, twisting and turning the clock in his hand, opening his jars and patiently staining the wood.

I usually left while he was polishing, and the next day he would show me the finished clock and explain, once more, the entire process. He worked slowly and methodically, and

before he disassembled a clock or watch he would scruti-
nize it as if memorizing the arrangement. Occasionally, he
made sketches on sheets of brown paper.

In school, while Mr. Philip was lecturing about the
number of slaves that died during the middle passage or the
contempt heaped upon the indentured Indians, my mind
would drift back to another kind of lesson. *After you open up
a watch, always make sure you clean it with benzine. Anneal
the new dial by heating the copper and then dashing it in cold
water.* The magical words I had heard in the old house
remained with me. *Tourbillions, bezel, karrusels, escapement.*

The only times Cane was silent, his forehead furrowed
in concentration, was when he was working on a triangular
clock with a brass handle. This was the clock that usually
occupied him when I came in the afternoons. He would
continue working on it for about ten or fifteen minutes,
then carefully place it on a wooden chair. Sometimes, while
he was polishing another clock, he would glance in the
direction of the chair.

He began spending more time on this clock, sanding
the dark mahogany and the pateras on the sides, smoothing
the pores with paste filler, wiping off the residue with his
thumb, then sanding it once more. Although I was reluctant to disturb him, I missed the patient explanations and
the magical words. One afternoon I left after just five minutes or so. The next day, he was sitting on the chair with the
clock on his lap. He looked sad and exhausted. I didn't
know what to say.

"Is a special clock?"

I thought that he had not heard the question and perhaps he did not want to be disturbed. As I was about to
leave, he said, "It is a pendule d'officier." He told me that it

was designed by a man from France named Abraham-Louis Brequet, and during the campaigns of a brilliant general who later became an emperor it was transported from skirmish to skirmish so that after a while it became known as an officer's clock. Pendule d'officier.

"Are you finished with it?"

He shook his head. "I am building this clock for somebody very special. A woman."

I found this strange but I said nothing.

"It's taken me a very long time."

"Will she come for it?"

He seemed to be thinking of the question. "It is my wish," he said finally, speaking in his careful English.

As Cane continued his restoration, I began spending less time there, not only because I felt he did not want to be disturbed but because my common entrance was only a month away, and Mr. Philip, for an additional fee, had extended his lessons for another hour. Occasionally, I imagined this special woman and her surprise when Cane presented the clock to her. Three weeks before my exams, deluged with notes and lessons, I stopped visiting entirely. Mr. Philip had forgiven my earlier transgression and he was offering, free of charge, additional lessons—another two hours—to me and Allison, a girl with tightly pulled braids and a perpetually startled expression. We both knew that Mr. Philip's only real concern was the prestige of having a student win one of the scholarships offered each year to the top fifty students on the island, but we were flattered by the nervous attention he threw our way.

Each night, my mother forced me to drink a mixture of eggs and orange juice, and in the morning I rushed off before another dreadful mixture could be prepared. On the day of the exam, I was inexplicably relaxed. Perhaps I was relieved that my torment was over. I ticked off the little blocks quickly and handed in my papers fifteen minutes before the stipulated time. I saw Mr. Philip glaring at me, but I didn't care. My vacation was about to begin.

On my way home, I jumped over the drain and parted the long pointed leaves. There was no answer when I knocked on the door and I thought that Cane had gone to his special woman, carrying his gift. Then I heard a faint chink, like a knife hitting a saucer. I pushed open the door. Cane was sitting on the wooden chair. He turned his head to me and I was startled by the dryness of his face. He looked pale and powdery, as if he too were covered in dust. Because he was sitting on his chair, not saying anything, I told him, "I had my exam today." He nodded, as if he knew that. "Where is the clock?" He reached into a cardboard box by his feet.

It was the most perfect thing I had ever seen. Even in the dull light, the dark mahogany glowed like the skin of a snake in the moonlight. The dial and the Roman numerals glittered as if they were polished in gold. "How does it look?" His voice sounded old and tired.

"Perfect. You going to give it to the lady now?"

"It is my wish." He passed a finger over his white knotted beard, his head bent over the clock. "But she is dead."

"Dead?" I was only eleven years old at the time and confused by this revelation. "Then why you spend all this time fixing it up?"

"Why?" He leaned back on the chair, stroking the clock as if it were a pet. Then he unclasped the hinge, opened the glass case and spun the dial anticlockwise. And turning the dial, he told me. "I have sent it back to two days ago. Now look around the room. Do you see any change?"

"No."

"If I continue spinning it back, I could set it back one week. You think you will see any change then?"

His voice was exhausted. I shook my head.

"Exactly. What is gone is gone. You could never bring it back no matter how much you want to. But"—he hesitated as if searching for the correct words—"everybody who go away leave a little trace of themself." He held up the clock by the handle, allowing it to swing slightly. "This little trace is inside here."

"Inside the clock?"

"I rebuild this clock exactly the way she would have wanted me to. I know the exact colour she would want the case to be and the exact size and shape of the dial. Even the sound of the time ticking away. Every single day, I imagine her sitting right next to me, telling me what to do. Explaining what she liked and what she wanted changed. So you see"—he leaned forward as if he were about to whisper a secret—"every time I look at this clock, I see some part of her." He blew softly on the shiny surface and wiped away the film with the back of his palm. "Even her shape."

I had never previously considered the element of craziness in Cane's obsession, but this was the sort of thing that would ripple around the playground, confirming old rumours and, through peals of derisive laughter, creating new ones. Cane must have seen the flicker of disbelief on my face because he got up and walked to the door. My last glimpse of him was standing by the door, cradling the clock in his hands, his eyes dark and hollow, as if he were wearing the Carib mask I had seen in our *Royal Reader* textbook.

Two weeks later, when I was enjoying my break from school in the cricket grounds and on the river banks, a customer in my parents' shop mentioned that the crazy man who lived in the cane patch had left the village. It was late in the evening, but I ran down the road, jumped across the drain and pushed open the door. Neither Cane nor his clock was there.

Throughout the years that followed—my success in the exams (but not in the scholarship), my seven years at Presentation College, my job at the warden's office in Rio Claro, the sessions in the village rumshops, the liberties with a number of young women, leaving for Canada when I was nineteen—there was one regret that stayed with me. I regretted not asking Cane whether the person whose shape he saw in his clock was his wife, his mother or his daughter. Or some other special woman.

One

ONE

Some nights when the moonlight fretted between the dead leaves, and the only sound was that of my boots padding the hardened snow, I saw the shape of a woman stretched languorously in the fork between branches as if awaiting a special visitor. But too much time had passed and her pose, empty of expectation, was now a tired reflex: an obligation into which she had wilted.

I saw her in the pallid light, raising a hand wearily as I passed. Sometimes I stopped to stare at her hair stiffened into icicles, drooping down to her frozen clavicles, the fresh fall of snow like an emollient on her small breasts. During a terrible winter storm, I thought of her being pounded and thumped. The sidewalk was littered with the shoulders of trees and torn limbs in the storm's aftermath. I searched for her in the rubble, stepping over wooden splinters and icy fingers, but the woman I found was unfamiliar, her face moulded into features I no longer recognized.

Three months after the storm, the trees had regained their turgidity and foliar spurs were forming from the spiral of brown leaves. Old couples, released from winter's closeting, shuffled out of their apartments, straightening with each step. A squirrel scurried away from its mate and darted from branch to branch, as if canvassing its partner for attention. Rain soaked the ground, softening the trails and footpaths. I observed this renewal of the cycle and I thought: No change is permanent if we can find the beginning.

In the beginning, I believed in the mildly envious congratulations of my friends. My impending departure from Trinidad showed my recklessness, they said, my wild, adventurous spirit and courage. They recalled their own brief flirtations with sprawling, frigid lands where ice fell from beyond towering buildings and where men and women, bundled in their armour, walked with measured footsteps to houses with fireplaces and rugs and dogs that were more than pets; dreams shaped by the debris of postcards, movies, magazines and recycled conversations, and discarded in the end because romance was one thing but uncertainty quite another. Their congratulations were effusive because I had dared to step out of the circle of familiarity, and in many ways I was both hero and fool, deserving of both pity and admiration.

Luck, courage, boldness: I was deceived by the most fickle and insubstantial of fantasies, borne out during my first few years in Canada, until, granted the maturity of regret, I saw that it was fear, not romance, that had driven me away. I had glimpsed my future in pot-bellied men who spent their nights in bars and returned, bleary-eyed, the next morning for work. Men who would repeat with strangulated predictability the lives lived by their fathers, and expect no less of their sons. Violations enacted so often they took on the tone of a dogma; rituals granted grace because nothing else was acceptable.

How could I then, after sixteen years, return? The question remained with me during the lengthening days when those who shared the streets took their cue from the change of seasons and sprouted new complexions and unpacked their indulgences into terraces, lawns, backyards and parks. The letter from Trinidad, unsolicited and unexpected, read then tossed aside for three weeks, provided an excuse and from this excuse, examined methodically, sometimes desperately, an answer emerged early one morning. That same day, I told my wife, "I'm going back." She stared at me blankly but I saw the tightening of her lips, a prelude to the eruption of silence. I repeated the statement, too loud, not the balance for which I was searching.

She got up from the sofa with a flourish of her arms, and turned her back to me. "There's no way you're taking Vanita with you, mistah."

"It's only for a vacation."

She turned around. "I could care less." Then she strode into her room and I heard the tinkle of her bottles and vials.

Alone, once more, save for the lingering trail of her cologne, I reflected that loneliness has less to do with the absence of companionship than with the diminution of choices. Then I walked across the street to the community centre to get Vanita from her painting class.

She was just seven and I knew that the long periods of strained silence in the apartment bothered her. When I looked at her thin face and delicate features, I felt that she would either grow into an unhappy woman with a skewed view of the world, or that her frailties would fall away, one by one, and be replaced with a stubborn determination.

I visited her school and spoke with her teacher, Mrs. Mendelssohn, who remarked that she was sensitive and artistic, which I interpreted as a teacher's polite code for "weak." But when Mrs. Mendelssohn showed me her artwork, I saw disparate objects: houses, trees and figures standing apart but all connected by a thin, barely noticeable line. The impulse was even stronger in her stories. The final paragraphs always began with the phrase "Finally it was time." Fairies trapped in tiny flowers, princesses paralysed by evil spells, rabbits and squirrels lost in the forest. Then, in the middle of the crisis, *Finally it was time.* They all escaped.

About an hour later, I went into the bedroom. She must have heard the door opening because she rubbed her eyes and yawned sleepily. "Where's Mummy?"

"She went out."

"Oh." She looked away, to the window. A jet had left a line of smoke already diffusing into the blueness.

I sat on the bed. "I am thinking of going away for a while." She reached for her stuffed rabbit from the window ledge. *Thinking of going.* But she knew. She hugged her rabbit. "To Trinidad. Just for a few months. Maybe you and Mummy would like to come too."

She glanced hopefully at my face. "But I have my school. And Mummy has her work."

"School will be over in one month and your mummy could get leave from her work. You could join me there," I said stupidly.

Hope flickered and died. She hugged the rabbit forcefully against her chest. Outside, the line of smoke had separated into powdery puffs. "Okay, Daddy."

"Just okay?" I tickled under her chin and she smiled obediently.

During the week, I tried to persuade my wife to allow Vanita to make the trip. She was bewildered by my insistence, suspicion vitalizing her anger. I was again reminded why we had arrived at this state of mutual distrust, pretending to be nice in Vanita's presence and avoiding each other for the remainder of the day.

The onset of spring some weeks earlier had released me from the apartment, offered escape. I had fallen into the habit of taking early morning walks, when the air was cool and filled with the fresh scents of grass and flowers. For that hour or so, I felt surprisingly free, like a traveller in a strange land, and with a traveller's eye I noticed details that were lost when I passed that same area on my way from work. I saw the intricate designs on wrought iron gates and on bird feeders, some like miniature chapels suspended from the branches of maple trees. I observed robins and swallows nuzzling the grains and squirrels biting the newly emerging shoots of tulips and daffodils. On the decks and porches I saw hanging baskets with marigolds and petunias and Mediterranean clay urns, which, as spring progressed, blossomed with nasturtiums and fuchsias.

Now the gardens were in full bloom, some all blue and others red. None were alike. I felt like the solitary walker in the Wordsworth poem Mr. Philip had forced the class to memorize. "I wandered lonely as a cloud . . ." Once our teacher had revealed that he owed his good health to soups supplemented with flowers and I had leaned over to Sam and made a baa-ing goat sound. Now, on the day I was to leave, I wondered about the taste of the calendulas and the bee balms, lingering to get a whiff of their scent. Then, glancing at my watch, I saw that it was almost time to drop Vanita to school. Her mother would be gone in a few minutes.

I had tried again, the night before. "You haven't taken a vacation since you started working with the dentist. This will be a good opportunity to visit your old friends."

"I am quite happy with my friends here."

"And Vanita has never been to Trinidad. We could take her to the beach, the—"

"I will not allow my daughter to go into that hole. That deformed place. Ever! Do you understand, mistah?"

So much of what I had found cute and endearingly funny later began to grate. The word *mistah*, uttered with a tight, flashing smile. The umbrellas in the sun. Hurrying away in the malls whenever we noticed a group of people who might have been Trinidadian. Her skin-lightening creams, which left such a bitter taste in my mouth that I had to chart my advance with precision, like a general in a booby-trapped field. Once I asked her jokingly if her creams were anti-pheromones to ward off pests, to which she replied, "The poison only lasts a few hours. So you are safe." I found that funny and said something like, "Well, keep the antidote handy." But as time passed, my sense of humour began to desert me, or rather, to become dry and mean-spirited, like the self-conscious, blustering humour of ugly comics who make jokes about their families or their communities. I was growing into the kind of person I had always despised.

Fourteen years before, at the University of Waterloo, my professor in a travel literature course was a funny little man with pudgy red cheeks and a great swirl of hair brought from the sides to cover his bald pate. He was obsessive about his appearance, and while he was lecturing us on the heroic exploits of some nineteenth-century traveller he would be distracted by his reflection on the window and repack a few strands on the bald area. We made fun of him, Angie and I: at the way he would rise up on his toes when he was excited

by a particular traveller and the deep fake voice he slipped
into when he was boasting of his own bold wanderings.
Angie was a classmate; I have sometimes wondered about
the direction my life might have taken had I married *her* and
not my wife, but neither Angie nor I had any thoughts of
marrying then, and she soon vanished from my life. She was
a beautiful, long-legged woman who had left Canada when
she was four to accompany her parents to Tonga. Her parents had taught English there and occasionally Angie would
utter some made-up gibberish and claim it was a Tonganese
maxim. She said she lived in a village called Longa Donga
and invented bizarre sexual rituals, which, she maintained,
were practised by the natives. I invented equivalent Trinidadian customs. We called each other "Pervy" and sometimes
while the professor was crowing about one of his adventures
we would glance at each other and she would exaggeratedly
roll her eyes. Later, at night, I imitated the professor's deep
husky voice.

I was silly, immature, irresponsible, frivolous—words
with which I had grown familiar—but as time passed,
I longed for those carefree days.

I could not give up. I explained to my wife that the decision
to return was not an impulsive, fanciful idea plucked from
nowhere but was the result of an invitation issued by an ex-
politician, still powerful, about whom I had written an article. I brought out the letter from my briefcase and read
selected sentences. "I am desirous of having my biography
written by someone familiar with Trinidad but unaffected
by the hurly-burly of everyday politics." I stressed the word
"hurly-burly" and tried to make the letter playful rather
than reckless. "I feel you would be the ideal candidate."

She displayed no surprise and I knew that she had already read the letter. Eventually, I accepted her decision and resigned myself to the fact that I would have to make the trip alone. But I had always known that. Just as I had always known that I could never reveal the real reason for the trip.

When I left, my wife was at work and Vanita in school. I packed my light cotton T-shirts and jeans into my suitcase and my articles from *The Caribbean Crossroad* in my briefcase. In the pouch, I placed Vanita's letter with the list of items she wanted me to get her. Then I called a taxi. While I was waiting, I placed a note for Vanita beneath her pillow. *I love you*, written on a page from her notepad, the light pink paper edged with curling daffodils.

The driver, a young Sikh with a long austere face, drove slowly and indecisively. At every traffic light, he opened his glove compartment, produced a small green book and consulted a map with red and yellow squares. I glanced anxiously at my watch.

"Where are you going?" His English was perfect.

"To Trinidad."

"I had a friend from university who was from Trinidad. He lived in San-something."

"San Fernando?"

"Yes. His name was Latchman. He returned after he graduated. Said there was much scope for engineers there. Developing country."

"Like India? Maybe you will return some day too."

He was offended. He picked up his book and pretended he was studying the map.

Once, during our courting days at the University of Waterloo, I mentioned to my wife that ever since I'd arrived in Canada at the age of nineteen, I'd assumed that I would eventually return to a little village in Trinidad and build a school or a library. She had replied that she would return only if she were deported. What crimes are you contemplating? I asked. I could have told her something about being granted the opportunity for escape only once.

Just before he dropped me off, the Sikh said, "I have spent the last ten years learning to be a Canadian. Why would I want to return to that confusion?"

TWO

Airports are like huge washrooms: people bustle in and out, façades fall away, new disguises are contemplated. Almost sixteen years ago at the Pearson airport, I had been given a distorted picture of Canada as a land of impatient, disoriented immigrants. I now saw why. The place was crowded with teenaged Asian children elevated on platform shoes, towering over their drably attired parents; Middle Easterners brimming with religious devotion looking like smugglers and pirates from movies; a few Anglo-Saxon Canadians, newly returned, brandishing their tans like badges of merit; islanders rehearsing their swagger; and those who were impossible to categorize: gradations of colour so minute, it was impossible to distinguish Italian from Lebanese, Greek from Iranian.

But when I boarded the BWIA plane I was thinking of what the Sikh had said. The seats were filled with black and brown faces, men and women I might have seen walking morosely along some street in Toronto. Here they were chatting, laughing, gesturing, fussing over each other. Most of the men were accompanied by their wives and children. My seat was on the left side of the middle aisle. Across from me were two boys wearing UM stickers on their shirt pockets. Unaccompanied minors. Were their parents staying behind in Canada? One of the boys saw me staring and smiled. The other tugged at his brother's shirt and pointed to the window. They were both excited; perhaps their parents had gone ahead and now, skipping the last two weeks of school, the boys were joining them.

I opened my briefcase and withdrew Vanita's list from the pouch. Trinidadian shells. Trinidadian flowers. Trinidadian pictures. Trinidadian dresses. She had spelled the word as *Trindadan*. It was ten-thirty. I pictured her on her recess break, surrounded by a group of girls sharing her excitement as she boasted of her father who was visiting Trinidad and who would be back four months later, his suitcase stuffed with shells and pictures and flowers and dresses. She and her mummy might even join him in a few weeks. The fear that she had shuttered away so painstakingly was now laid to rest: she was part of a happy family.

I folded the page and placed it in my pocket. Maybe she never spoke about her parents.

A slim, middle-aged man in a striped brown suit and very dark shades walked stiffly down the aisle, opened the overhead compartment and shoved in two bags. His movements were so stiff, he could have been bandaged in duct tape beneath his clothing. He carefully lowered himself into the seat on the right, clicked on his seat belt, and surveyed his fellow passengers with a sniping distaste. His gaze finally settled on me, and we acknowledged each other with a brief "Hello."

He pulled a handkerchief from his jacket pocket, patted his cheeks and chin and stared straight ahead. Did he have a family? I watched the way he carefully folded his handkerchief, placed it on his leg, then clasped his fingers over it slowly, one by one. All his movements seemed distressed. "Are you returning for a vacation?" I asked him.

"No."

He had a thin, pointed upper lip, peaking at the centre, like those I had seen on babies and birds of prey. I refocused my attention on the two boys. One was offering the other gum from a pack. They chewed slowly, savouring the taste. The trip was an adventure for them.

The no-smoking light flashed and a woman I had not noticed before came from somewhere at the back of the plane and took the seat between the thin man and me. I couldn't see her face but she was wearing dark-green corduroy trousers, shiny at the knees and baggy around her ankles. I heard a soft, subdued cough, like a whimper, to her right. I closed my eyes. The plane taxied onto the runway.

When I opened my eyes about twenty minutes later, the woman had already unbuckled her seat belt and was reading a travel book. At the top of the page, I saw the words, "Departure with an Escort," which I thought was the title of the chapter, but when she turned the page, I saw another heading. Such a precise writer; every page titled.

I was reminded of my excuse for returning. I removed my briefcase from beneath my seat, opened it and read the letter written two months ago by Mr. Rampartap.

Dear Mr. Sagar,
While I am considerably flattered by your generous portrait of me in your esteemed newspaper, I am

nevertheless angry that I had to procure a copy of said newspaper by means better left unstated. However, the purpose of this missive is not to complain but to issue an invitation which I hope you will consider carefully in the coming weeks. As you alluded to in your portrait, my political experience has set me apart from these new breed of fly-by-night politicians. To put the offer in a nutshell, I am desirous of recording the events that comprised my political career but unfortunately, while I am or was the perfect political beast, I have never had the time to hone my writing skills. This is where you come into the picture. I am desirous of having my biography written by someone familiar with Trinidad but unaffected by the hurly-burly of everyday politics . . .

And so on. Compliments. Promises. Was I so bad a writer that he believed he could inveigle me into writing a flattering book he could parade to his friends and enemies? Two years ago, I had met him in the editor's office, and the only thing I can recall now from that ten-minute meeting was that he was thickset and had fluffy magisterial eyebrows over mean-looking eyes. He had misunderstood: the article, written hurriedly, was directed by the editor's demands and three other pieces, written in ornate, almost archaic English, were not from my paper but from *The Trinidad Guardian*.

I replaced the letter and glanced at the book the woman was reading. Another page, another title. Buried at the bottom of my briefcase were the other articles I had written. I withdrew a few.

The woman got up. I still had not seen her face. The cover of her book, left on the seat, was angled towards me.

I felt she wanted me to notice it. *The Valley of the Assassins*, by Freya Stark. A painting, or a photograph, of valleys and mountains.

I had developed the habit, usually after an argument, of staring at myself in the mirror. The face, staring back, always surprised me. An assured man, still boyish-looking, with satisfactory features. Confident, at peace with the world. But it was not me.

I looked at the book again. Photograph or painting? I leaned over to get a better view.

"It's about Persia." I jumped. She had returned from the other aisle. She sat and I saw her face. A severe-looking woman with high cheekbones, narrow-set eyes and thin, forbidding lips. None of this matched the image I had formed when, as she was leaving her seat, I had stared at the way she fitted in her tight corduroy trousers. "Would you like to look at it?" She held the book in her hand. I flipped through the pages until I saw "Departure with an Escort." At the bottom, I read: "To be treated with consideration in the case of female travellers is too often synonymous with being prevented from doing what one wants."

"My favourite writer. I wish I was as good."

"Are you a writer?" I asked.

"Like you?" She smiled, her lips curved, her eyes twinkled, and unexpectedly she looked the way I had expected her to. "I saw the articles with your photograph."

I changed the topic. "What do you write about?"

"Oh, I'm not really a writer. More of a publicist for a travel agency. I promote exotic destinations."

"Is that why you are going to Trinidad?"

"Yes, but I'm not sure Trinidad is exotic." A disapproving little cough came from the other seat. "I should have been there for the February Carnival, but I was in Spain."

"Do you travel a lot?"

"I'm always going down, landing in some faraway place." She said it so quickly that I felt she had used the sentence before. "Are you returning for a funeral?"

I laughed. "What gave you that idea?"

"Oh, nothing in particular. Do you travel a lot?"

"Only in my neighbourhood."

In those weeks before my departure, as spring shifted into summer, I had ventured farther each day. One morning, I saw a middle-aged man leaning over an antiquated urn. With his cherubic, reflective face, he looked like a mediaeval monk preparing for penance. He looked up as I passed. The next day I said hello and he told me he was building a Japanese garden, and asked if I was from South America, but then carried on about his garden without waiting for a reply. On successive days he asked whether I was Indian, Iranian or Arab, but he never seemed interested in my response. On impulse, I told him I was a guest, but he seemed neither baffled nor curious; he only explained the care he had put into his garden, which he called an ikebana. He said he was creating a special arrangement, a moribana.

"Well, I have no neighbourhood of my own. You're lucky."

The woman had turned away slightly and because she was silent, I asked her, "What are you going to write about concerning Trinidad?"

"I wouldn't know until I'm actually there. Any ideas?"

After a while, I told her, "I haven't been back for quite a while. It must have changed a lot since."

"Some places never change. That's their enchantment." She got up, and I half stood to allow her to move out to the aisle.

"Damn foreigners," he said when she was gone. "Always pretending to be so nice and friendly. Until they land back in they own country. I can't stand them."

"She's a publicist."

"Yes, I hear what she say." He tapped his shades. "Departure with a damn escort."

For a few minutes we sat in silence. Then he turned to me and asked, "Why you going back?"

"Pardon me?"

"Why you going back to Trinidad?" He removed his shades and wiped his eyes.

I was about to say for a vacation, but I figured he had seen the letter. "I plan to do some writing."

"You is a publicist too?"

Before I could answer, the woman returned, this time from the other side. The man pulled his feet out of the way, gazed at her bottom and frowned. She settled in her seat. "Cigarette break. I should have chosen the smoking section but I feel safer here in the womb of the plane. I had a bad experience. Over Afghanistan in a rickety little plane." Just then the plane shook and she grabbed my arm. I was astonished by her firm grasp. "Oh, I'm sorry."

"It's okay."

"I travel by train wherever it's possible. Are there trains in Trinidad?"

"Used to be. Transporting cane to the factories."

"Sugar factories. Slaves dancing during the Carnival.

Do you think there might still be these plantation houses where the masters lived? I've read that they had these magnificent balls." She removed her hand from my arm.

"I believe the plantation houses were converted into government buildings. Warden's offices and schools."

"I've seen that in other places. It's so sad, when you think of it." Turning to her book, she flipped through the pages, too fast to be reading. "I wish I could see Trinidad through your eyes. I wonder what I would see? Feast on your memories," she said seriously, as if quoting from a book. But without waiting for a response, she fished a pack of cigarettes from her purse. "It's a terrible habit. One of my vices." And she manoeuvred herself out into the aisle again.

"That woman have no blasted manners. Pushing she bottom straight in me face. And what was all that talk about slaves and masters? If you ask me she still hungry for them days. That is why all of them does be travelling about to these poor-poor countries." He patted his cheek with his handkerchief. "You know why I leaving Canada? For seven years I take all the licks they could dish out. Then at last I start to prosper. Little by little. Finally, I open up a small business. Selling goods from back home. Ice cream. People thought I was mad. But I sell other things too. Sweet-drink. Fish and meat. Vegetable that you couldn't get here. Doubles just like home with spicy chickpeas in it. The first year I lost nearly everything. The second year I cover back me loss. And the third year I make sixty-five thousand. Profit. I could have been a millionaire in five years' time. But as time pass that five years start getting longer and longer. And I will tell you why." He funnelled his handkerchief, pushed up his glasses and wiped his eyelids. "Every time I had a problem, a minor problem, mind you, the attitude of the government people was why the hell I complaining so much. What give me the right? And furthermore, if I didn't like it why the ass I didn't haul me mangy tail back to where I come from. You see, I had lost the right to complain, to get vex about anything. No matter how rich I get, I was still this damn outsider who couldn't appreciate how lucky he was. And watch youself, eh. I notice how she grab on to you hand. Take care she don't feast on you. Just another one of she vice."

The woman returned. "I think I will take a little snooze. You can have the book in the meantime." She leaned back. "Wake me when they are serving dinner."

I gazed at the cover of her travel book then turned to the last page: "Many delays there were and breakdowns in the very sight of the capital, but finally we did arrive that evening, and in a flowering garden amid the refinements of life, said goodbye . . ."

The day I was leaving Trinidad, Keith, a co-worker at the warden's office, had pushed a book in my hand, which I barely glanced at, because my parents were there at the airport with Varun, my younger brother, and later, on the plane, I was too excited to read, looking down from the window on places I had seen in atlases: Goat Island, Scorpion Island, Dragon's Mouth, Coral Cove. I read only a few pages of his book, *A Traveller's Guide to North America.*

I turned to the cover once more. The woman's head slid onto my shoulder. From the other side, I heard a soft whisper: "Careful! Vices! Feast!" I closed my eyes.

For the last few days, I had imagined that my trip was an escape into a familiar land but now, with this woman sleeping next to me, I felt lonely and sad, like a man who was going to a party long after the other guests had departed. My parents were dead, Varun was living in England, I had not communicated with any of my old friends, and worst of all, I was going alone. I pictured a man, well dressed, a gift in his hand, staring at the musicians packing away their instruments.

I gazed around, trying to read the faces of the other passengers, but most were asleep with blankets drawn across their necks. A beautiful stewardess with olive skin and light grey eyes walked down the aisle smiling sweetly at the sleeping passengers. She reminded me of the attractive mixed-race women I had seen in Trinidadian beauty pageants, or advertising soap and creams on the television set my mother had installed on an empty shelf in the shop. On weekends some of the women from the village would drop by to watch *Peyton Place*, and occasionally, after a cricket match, when my friends came to buy iceblocks or penny sweet-drinks, she would allow them to watch *Lassie* or *Lost in Space* or *Batman*, and the next day in the playground we would shout at each other, "That does not compute," or "Take that, you diabolical fiend," or "Run, Lassie, run."

This was the Trinidad I had re-created for Vanita and it was just as real as the island where horrible poverty existed alongside shameless displays of wealth, where respectable men and women would come to the warden's office with every imaginable scheme for child support or social assistance, where children were chased down the road by their parents, whip swishing the air. But the memory of my childhood friends was comforting. Perhaps I would meet one of them at a busy intersection and we would spend the rest of the day trading memories and ribbing each other in the old style.

Keith, though, would be just as thoughtful and reserved. We had corresponded regularly during my first year in Canada, but after a while the letters dried up. It was impossible to respond to his sincerity and earnestness—carefully expressed in his three-page letters—when my own idealism had been displaced by the excitement of life in my new country. In my last letter, I had told him that I didn't want to change the world, I just wanted to enjoy it. But he would have expected all that. Maybe he would be pleased to see how much like him I had become.

When I awoke, the woman's head was resting on my shoulder and her hand on my leg. The man had reclined his seat, but with his dark shades it was hard to say whether he was asleep or awake. The stewardess was wheeling a trolley down the aisle. "What would you like, sir? We have chicken and beef sandwiches."

"Chicken."

"And your companion?" she asked, indicating the sleeping woman.

I heard a little snort; he had been awake all the time.

I touched her arm and she snuggled her nose against my neck. "Another chicken sandwich." I unhinged her tray and the movement must have disturbed her because she opened her eyes and brushed a finger against her lip. She gazed distractedly at the food. "I had the strangest dream, that I was in Egypt and I was drunk from the heat and wine. I had the most wonderful guide."

"And?"

She looked at me and smiled. "You wouldn't want to know the rest. What's this?"

"Chicken."

"How did you know?"

"I guessed. There wasn't much of a choice really."

She ate silently, not looking at the sandwich. The man on the right had moved closer. I felt the warm squirt of clove and yolk on his breath. I flicked him a glance; his uneven moustache and pointed lip gave him a twisted, cynical smile.

The woman asked me, "If you started your book with this journey, on this plane, what would you write about?" To myself I thought, a woman whose face was unsuited to her body, until she smiled and you saw that she was as excited and frightened by this trip as she had been by the others she had told me about. Perhaps she, too, was running away.

She was looking at me intently, waiting for me to answer her question, so out loud I said, "About a woman who dreamed that somewhere in the desert she was making love to her guide."

She laughed and stood up. "You know what I'm going to do."

The moment she was gone the man said, "Making love in the desert, eh? I wonder who going to be she guide this time? You married?"

"Yes."

"Children?"

"A daughter."

"How old?"

He was irritating me. "Seven."

"Seven, eh? What you think she will say if she know what she daddy doing right now?"

I took a sip from the glass. "Her daddy is having a Coke. Just like he does when he is at home."

"Okay, but don't say that I didn't warn you. These foreign women does have only one thing on they mind when they heading down to these hot sweaty countries. And is the same bitches who you does bounce up two-three months later behind a glass window in a office, staring down at you and wondering why the ass you complaining so much. So why the madam not with you?"

"She couldn't get any vacation."

"I see. That will come in real handy if you bounce up any old craft, not so?" His chiding tone deserved a response, but he extended a hand. "By the way, my name is Goonai." His palm was soft and oily. "But you know what all these bitches does call me in Canada? Goon. *Mister* Goon, if you please. All of a sudden I come a big thug." I pulled away my hand and wiped it on my trousers. When the woman returned, he took off his shades, blew on the lenses and wiped them with his handkerchief. He looked at his watch. "We should reach in a hour time."

The woman got out her book and began flipping through the pages. The pilot announced that we were approaching Piarco Airport and the plane circled the island in preparation for landing. "I've never been to Trinidad before."

"Yes, I know."

"Did I say that?" After a while she said, "I imagine you have relatives in Trinidad?"

"Not any more."

She gazed out of the window. "A traveller without attachment is like a man—or a woman—living in an apartment without paying the rent." It was a strange observation and I felt that she had lifted it from one of her odd travel writers, but her voice was soft and sad.

"I will be at the Bel Air for a few days. Unfortunately, it's not free."

She smiled. "I'm going to the Hilton in Port of Spain. Is that close to where you are staying?"

"Not really. The Bel Air is in Piarco. Just a few minutes from the airport."

"How far away is Port of Spain from the airport?"

"About half an hour."

She placed the book on her lap and passed a finger over
the rounded glass crystal of her rose-gold Crawford. I felt
that I should say something, but then I heard his voice. "I
am going to Port of Spain. I intend to rent a car in the airport. I could carry you. Is no trouble at all."

"That's very kind of you," she said, looking at me.

"No trouble at all. In fact, I too going to the Hilton for a
few days," he lied. "Plan to do a little sightseeing. Beach.
Old-time buildings. Nice forest. Sugar factory. Train. That
is why I renting the car for a few weeks."

She was still looking at me. "It's very kind of you."

He waved his hand. "No trouble at all. Is my pleasure."

"Well, it was nice meeting you, Mr. . . ."

"Sagar."

"Perhaps we will meet again."

"It's a small island."

The wheels touched the tarmac and the plane shuddered. They walked towards the door. I remained behind to
avoid the rush. She looked back and waved. He placed his
hand on her shoulder and steered her away. From his jaunty
stride, I felt he would show her off to his friends and later
blow on his sunglasses and in a bored voice boast of these
foreign women who couldn't get enough of his charms.

THREE

With some people, familiarity, like fatigue, enforces a dull
sinking pleasure if only because of the simple uniformity
of events.

After sixteen years, it was my first night in Trinidad, the moment I had envisioned in so many variations. I waited for familiar cadences to seep into the room that smelled of moth balls and dirty linen. Crickets chirping madly, forsaken dogs pleading with their owners, drivers honking at no one in particular; a cavalcade of sounds given melody by the artful randomness. In this small room, the soft glow and the bare furniture cleverly chosen to make the space seem larger, all I heard was the hum and buzz of the overused air conditioner. But I shouldn't have complained; I had forgotten how hot the island was.

I had also forgotten the casual rudeness of the officials. After I disembarked, I stood behind dozens of fretting husbands and wives, their indignation stifled into quiescence for so long, now released, licensing them to shout and curse. They must have been thrilled. The immigration officer was unmoved by the annoyance directed at him. He had the contemplative scowl of a fading literary critic consigned to arcane, specialized texts, and it was easy to imagine him unbundling a mess of dog-eared books on his bed and cursing each time he reached for his dictionary.

"Holiday?"

"Yes."

"Where you staying?"

"At the Bel Air."

"I mean where you staying?"

"At the Bel Air."

He whirred through my passport, bending the pages. He repeated the action. The woman behind me inhaled through her clenched teeth, a sucking, impatient sound.

"You alone?"

"Yes."

"No family with you?"

"No."

"In other words, you travelling alone?"

"I suppose so."

He squinted at my passport. "You suppose so or you *know* so?"

"I am here for a holiday. I am travelling alone. I will be at the Bel Air for a few days."

The direct information puzzled, then angered him. He peered up at me. The yellow undersides of his eyes were irrigated with tiny veins, like the nervous scrawl of a drunk idler. The woman said, "This place will never change."

"Why that woman don't shut she old ass." He banged the stamp down, grazing a finger. "Next!" he shouted. "I don't have the whole kissmeass day, you know." As I was walking away, I heard, "These blasted fresh-water Yankee. Spend two months in a iceberg and come back here like if they own the place."

In the baggage area, I saw the woman and her new escort. In every mismatched couple, there is invariably some point of convergence: a gesture, the pitch of laughter, the concavity of a feature, the distance between footsteps, the synchronicity of the stride. And there *was* something quite intimate about the way they stood next to each other—he weighed down by the bags, leaning towards her, she staring ahead at the custom officials. I could have mistaken them for a couple whose marriage had dwindled to a benign boredom. Their point of convergence.

When I awoke the next morning, it was still dark outside. I opened my suitcase, straightened my jeans and T-shirts and read Vanita's letter. There was a black phone on the table, but it was too early to call Mr. Rampartap. I sat on the bed for about half an hour listening to the gaps of silence broken by the planes taking off and an occasional car leaving the parking lot. After the long flight and the extended wait in the departure lounge, the darkness and the silence were comforting, but completely different from the scene I had prepared myself for, the scene I had played and replayed in my mind so many times over the years.

In those visions I had seen my parents waiting outside the departure lounge, anxiously scanning the emerging families. In the car, my mother unpacking a bag of sweets for Vanita, my father driving slowly and every now and again glancing at me and waiting for some disclosure about my job and my house. In the back seat, Varun carrying on about his exams or some cricket match.

I got up from the bed and walked down the hall to the deserted lobby, to the right of which was a small café with beaded curtains rather than a doorway. The café was tiny, perhaps twice the size of my hotel room, and there were four tables, one at each corner. A couple in their late forties occupied one of the tables. Behind the counter, a young man with a thin, prematurely lined face was fiddling with a black-and-white television set. I rapped my knuckles lightly on the counter, expecting him to take my order, but he just continued with his adjustments, his lips pushed out in annoyance. Finally, I leaned over the counter and asked for a coffee. He slapped the set on both sides and grumbled some threat to it but didn't look up. "Gimme a minute or two. I trying to get this thing to work but she playing the fool this morning."

I went to the table adjoining a shuttered window. An old telescope was propped against the window ledge; and from the presence of this rusted telescope, the painting on the wall of a black woman with a bunch of bananas on her scarfed head, the rattan chairs, the bamboo counter and the ceiling fan with straw-patterned blades, I felt that the café had once been owned by a foreigner. The word used to describe it then would have been *cosy* rather than *tiny*.

The young man located a station with tolerable reception and stepped back, appraising a fuzzy man caressing a fuzzy woman. He reached for a huge thermos flask on a shelf, unscrewed the cap, shook and sniffed the contents. With a glance at the fuzzy lovemaking couple he pushed out his lips, this time approvingly, and dipped his nose in the flask. Finally, he poured a cup of coffee and brought it to my table.

"Oh, God." The woman at the table opposite stuck a thumb in her tummy and massaged.

The man seated at the table redirected his attention to his companion. He seemed vaguely amused.

"What's so funny, Poohoo?" the woman grumbled. "Goodness."

Poohoo pointed to the television. The woman moaned.

"I warned you about that roti last night. All that oil." He was on the verge of laughter.

"It's not the oil. It's the nastiness." I imagined her tongue curling in disgust. "Damn nastiness. There must be thousands of bacteria crawling inside me now." She shuddered.

Their accents were Canadian and their voices high-pitched in the manner affected by some Trinidadians I had met in Canada. Perhaps we had returned on the same flight. "Last night was a real horror movie. Remind me to buy some bottled water. I wonder if they sell it here."

"They didn't ten years ago."

"Nothing have changed. Goodness. It's so hot. Four weeks of this."

"It was your decision." Poohoo seemed unimpressed with her nausea. He pointed to a potted cactus with thick long leaves. "Remember that plant? It's called mother-in-law tongue."

A sliver of morning light intruding from the window fell on the television and the young man adjusted the contrast so that all the soap-opera characters were darkened. I found that funny. He changed the station once more. A government minister, relaxed in an open-necked shirt, was being interviewed by a pretty young woman. They were acquainted with each other and the conversation veered from all his official accomplishments to his kindness and his humility. The government minister smiled, tapped his teeth and tried to look modest. At the end of the interview, the young woman revealed she was his daughter. ("You are always bringing home your work, Daddy. It's as if you have adopted the whole island.")

Poohoo laughed loudly. "Only in Trinidad."

"Everybody so damn uncivilized. Did you see the people gawking at us in the airport?" She said *garking*. "No manners. Garking at everybody."

"You have to take things differently here, my dear." He seemed to be provoking her. "This is Trinidad, remember? The homeland." He laughed, then saw me staring and added, "The mosquitoes and sandflies like to suck nice, soft flesh. I hope you didn't forget to pack your sunblock and your insect repellent." He pinched his wife's arm. She slapped away his hand and he chuckled once more.

The woman, following her husband's gaze, noticed me watching and I looked away swiftly but not before I caught her scowling. She bent to her husband and whispered something. Perhaps she was saying, You see how these people start garking already. Goodness. Whatever she said sent her husband into another fit of laughter. For a minute, I imagined my wife and myself sitting at the table, planning our vacation. What would an observer have made of us? Would I have laughed at her preparations, her toiletries?

In the beginning, I did.

At the skin-lightening creams she daubed each night on her face and arms and shoulders. I was fascinated with this obsession, and I developed the idea that many dark-skinned women secretly bleached and abraded their skins to create more pallor. But when I mentioned it she didn't talk to me for a week.

I heard Poohoo telling his wife, "You up for Tobago? Remember?" Perhaps they had spent their honeymoon there.

"I hope it didn't change too much." I flicked a quick glance. Her expression had softened somewhat and there was a slight note of expectation in her voice.

I emptied my coffee in a metallic garbage bin, returned to my room and located Mr. Rampartap's number from my notebook.

"Hello." A female voice.

I explained who I was and that I had called Mr. Rampartap from Canada two weeks earlier, informing him of my visit. She told me to wait a minute, put down the phone and when she returned five minutes later, asked where I was staying. A car would be sent at nine.

On the table at the head of the bed was a glass of water and an old radio with a cracked grille. I switched on the radio. The newscaster was squawking about a police station that had been invaded by killer bees. He poked fun at the police, suggesting that it was the first bit of exercise they had had in years. He imagined them being stung repeatedly, their bellies and buttocks jiggling as they ran, danced and rolled on the grass. Then he revealed that two months ago, at a party hosted by a retired magistrate, a group of enterprising burglars had spiked the catered meal with *jakay*, a powerful herbal laxative. Then as the suffering revellers lined up by the toilet and rushed to the backyard garden they were robbed of their jewellery. The police, when they arrived, could barely suppress their amusement. The announcer had been one of the guests.

I tried another station. Indian music: sitar, tabla and, incongruously, a violin. I drifted off to sleep with the music, lugubrious and mournful, surging then receding to near silence, music of the parched plains and windswept valleys a world away, and I dreamed that a young boy, eleven or twelve, dusty after his one-hour trip from Presentation College, entered a shop fragrant with melting butter and rice fresh from the lagoon, where a man and his wife were listening to music that streamed from a gramophone. The woman hugged her son and left to prepare his dinner; the man waited for the boy to talk about the day's lesson or ask for help with his arithmetic or geometry homework. Few words were shared between this father and son. Years later, the son regretted that he had not broken with the tradition of silence and expressed his gratitude.

About an hour later, I was awakened by rough knocks on the door. I glanced at my watch. Eight-thirty. I slipped on my trousers, opened the door and saw a small man with thick, bushy hair, and a beard that seemed puny by comparison. "I come for you. Mr. Ram send me."

"Who?"

"Mr. Rampartap."

"Oh, I will be ready in five minutes."

"Throw in five more and is a deal." He grinned, wedged his tongue through a gap in his teeth and adjusted a drooping bit of gum.

"Five minutes on the dot," he said when I walked outside, although he was not wearing a watch. He walked with a limp, one leg resting then spinning into action, seeming to aim a kick at its healthy partner. He was literally dragging my suitcase. I felt some concern for him.

"I can carry the suitcase if you like."

"Nah. It not too heavy. By the way, what you have inside it? A car engine?" He laughed and spat out something green and gristly. "That is the first thing everybody does ask me." I had not asked him anything. He opened the trunk, stabilized himself on his good foot and heaved the suitcase inside. "They does ask me how the foot end up in this condition. One time, I tell a old lady from Joemany that it get cut off in a accident and this young doctor grab on to some deading fella who was in the same room in the hospital, saw out he foot and connect it to me. That time I was working in the airport. Was the biggest tip I ever get." He laughed and spat. "Just like the story about this one-foot fella who get a lady leg and anytime he had to go to the toilet to pee was real confusion because one foot want to stand up and one want to sit down. What you doing they?"

"Putting on my seat belt."

"I not going to ram the car 'gainst any bridge, you know."

"It's just a habit."

"Habit-grabit-rabbit." His minor annoyance faded.

"So what really happened to the foot?"

"Bicycle accident. Was only twelve years at the time. Doctor fella had to push in a piece of pipe. The next foot continue to grow but the pipe remain the same length. Bring up the fella who knock me down. Some rich hoity-toity from Valsayn. Get sixty thousand dollars. Still waiting for the money," he said cheerfully.

"How long ago was that?"

I regretted the question because he removed his hand from the steering and began counting on his fingers. "Twelve-toeteen years now. Problem was me and Mr. Hoity-toity had the same lawyer. Mr. Ram say that he will look in the matter for me but he too have he own worries."

"What sort of worries?"

"The usual," he said mysteriously.

The car emerged from the village of Piarco into Arouca. I knew that Trinidad, an oil-producing nation, had bene-fited from the investments made by Texaco, Shell and Amoco, but I was nevertheless astonished by the affluence. There were malls with Middle Eastern domes rising from a tangled profusion of glass and concrete; extravagant man-sions (the architectural eclecticism, confusing but impres-sive from afar, spoke of sudden wealth); a settlement of smaller houses painted in edible colours: chocolate brown, mint green, cherry red; squat concrete factories. Colour, confusion, imitation, display; in some ways a Trinidad I knew.

"So this is you first visit?"

"Yes."

"When you leave?"

"About sixteen years ago."

He whistled. "You leave as a little boy?"

"I was almost twenty."

"You still have family around?"

I shook my head. "I have a brother in England. My parents passed away."

"That is the way life is. My old man hanging on by the skin of he teeth. Doctor say rum eat up he liver. Old lady gone through. Nothing does ever remain the same. Had a time when you could sleep peaceable with all you door and window open but nobody doing that again. Look at all them new Honda and Toyota on the road. Some people does say that is drug money that buy all that."

"What about the oil?"

"It 'vaporate now. Everybody hook up in this drugs business these days. All the hoity-toity and them from Valsayn and Palmiste who does walk around with they snout up in the air like if them is preacher son. You don't know who to trust again because—" He stopped suddenly, sensing perhaps that he had gone too far. I noticed him drumming the steering wheel. "Everybody playing game here. It look like Mr. Ram is the only serious one around." He said this in a leaden, solemn manner and I felt it was a kind of requisite praise for his boss.

"What sort of games?"

"You shoulda be here for the Carnival. All them hifalutin people who don't have time of the day for small people does mess theyself up with grease and put on holey old clothes and play mas. All them hoity-toity woman and them from Valsayn wining up on everybody like if them is more *wajang*, bad woman, than anybody else."

"They get a chance to mingle."

"Mingle-pingle-dingle. Is a nice game if you ask me. I taking a li'l short cut here to buss out in the highway." There were small concrete flats built at precarious angles on the sloping land, a bridge constructed of thick planks and then just sugar cane.

"You were saying you didn't know who to trust again."

"Because according to the rumours, police and thief sharing the same room." He changed the subject. "Look on the other side across they." He pointed to a clearing in the cane the size of a playground, bordered by the road and on the far side by a tributary of the Caroni River. "That is way they does roast up all them dead people." Two men, their heads bowed, were staring at a mound of ashes in the centre of the cremation site. The taller of the two stooped and dusted the ground as if searching for something. He scooped a handful of ashes and walked to the bank of the river. He raised his hands, as in a religious ritual, and sprinkled the ashes in the brown water.

The bank of the Caroni River, where five years ago my mother was cremated. My younger brother had done most of the preparations for the funeral, and when he returned he wrote me a short, accusing letter. In the months that followed I composed a variety of responses, each more senseless than the last. I never posted the letters. Five months later my father died, and once more it was my brother who returned to perform the rituals, which by tradition was the obligation of the eldest son. He never bothered writing this time.

"Could you stop for a while?"

He braked suddenly, peeped in the rear-view mirror and reversed. I opened the door. "I will be a few minutes."

"Take you time. The day young." He lit a cigarette.

I walked towards the two men. The taller man, bespectacled, dusted his palm. "We will be finished in a little while." He spoke softly and he was smiling.

"A parent?"

"Brother. My younger brother." The other man, who I saw was also a brother because he had the same refined features, turned around. A solitary teardrop was running down his cheek. "And you?" the taller brother asked.

"No one. I was just passing through and I stopped."

"There's another cremation later today. I thought . . ." He turned to his brother, touched his shoulder. "Adesh."

Adesh was staring at the sprinkle of ashes as if he were seeing the imprint of a body. He stooped and picked up a tiny white bone. His brother touched his shoulder again. "Is time to throw the ashes in the river." I stood at the bank while they gathered up the ashes in a bucket and sprinkled them into the water. When they were finished, the taller brother told me, "He was just twenty-eight. In two months he would have presented his doctoral dissertation. He was researching the medicinal properties of marine plants." He smiled as if a memory had been dislodged. "He was very handsome. People said he looked like an Indian film actor." He closed his eyes briefly and I thought, How well he hides his grief. I felt we knew each other.

I walked slowly to the car, thinking of Varun lighting the oiled cotton, walking around the pyre, throwing the flowers into the fire and, in the absence of the elder son, performing all the rituals. Perhaps he had been scanning the crowd all the while, hoping for a message that I had arrived. How he must have hated me.

"Sorry to keep you waiting."

"I not in no hurry. We had to take the longer way because the bridge *kerketay*. Does happen every rainy season. Nobody tell the inginair fella that every year the river does flood. He done back in Canada or the States or wherever he spring up from."

We emerged into the highway with sugar cane on one side and marshy swampland on the other. Long-legged egrets and scarlet ibises were wading through the water lilies. At Chaguanas, he diverted into the Southern Main Road and into the Trinidad that I remembered. Narrow pavements with lazily strolling men and women. Wooden houses on stilts built a few feet from the road. Newer houses with ornate balusters, through which etiolated petunias and marigolds poked their heads. Small unkempt lawns embellished with religious flags, *jhandis*, and discarded automobile parts. Children running about in asphalt yards and around overweight men swinging solemnly in their hammocks. A shirtless child sliding down a banister. Two women, separated by a spare croton hedge, carrying on an animated conversation. An old man, his head pushed through a window, watching the women. A junction, with the aroma of *phoolorie*, *kurma*, and doubles wafting from the vendors' stalls.

On either side of the junction were two squat rumshops, almost identical concrete buildings with large wooden doors painted dark brown. But the clientele were different: from the one on the left came the sound of calypso music, and from the other chutney, a hybridized East Indian music I had heard a few times on the Caribbean radio programs in Toronto. The combination was jarring and unsynchronous—the calypso music was dominated by trumpets and the chutney by drums—but it was the Trinidad whose memory I had nurtured for so many years: a patchwork of random pieces and mismatched patterns held together not by tolerance and understanding but by a lacerating humour that both concealed and diffused racial grievances.

"This patch didn't change much, eh? 'Cepting for the burglar-proofing." A shortish man, his unbuttoned, over-sized shirt flapping like a cape, stumbled from the rumshop and walked unsteadily and slowly across the road. A vehicle coming from the opposite direction narrowly missed him, and the driver, his head pushed through the window, shouted a curse as he sped away. The driver was peeping in the rear-view mirror. I sensed he was disturbed by my silence. "Madhoolal is me name," he said. "Some people does call me Madhoo, some Hoolal and some just plain Lal. In school they used to call me Maddie. Use any one you like. Wifey still in Canada?"

"Yes."

"You think that safe? She alone they?" I was startled by the question, but then he said, "Supposing somebody hold she down in the night?"

"That doesn't happen much across there."

"Must be a nice place to live? Try to get a visa a few years aback but they don't want broko-foot people up they." He slowed, allowing an old woman to cross the street. "*Soucou-yant*. Still have a few of them left. I treat them nice just like everybody else." But a few minutes later, he shouted to a man bent over an open car bonnet, his slack pants low on his waist, "Pull up you pants, uncle. I don't want to see nobody bottomhole this time of the day." He glanced in the rear-view mirror, catching my smile. "So what work you was doing up in the cold?"

"I write for *The Caribbean Crossroad*, but was a teacher for a while at an adult centre."

"Teaching hard-back people like me? Them head too hard to learn anything. Like *banga* seed." He whistled a tuneless song. "You pong any of them?"

"What?"

"Over here, every week some teacher in the news for ponging somebody daughter."

"It's different there."

"Yeah?" He eyed me sceptically. "Is adults you just say, not so? That is real big woman as far as I concern."

I changed the topic. "I left the job to work for a newspaper."

"What sorta papers? With topless woman inside?"

I laughed. "A Caribbean paper."

"Allyou does get news about Trinidad up in the cold? All the drug dealing and thing?"

"We carry only the good news."

"Allyou don't want the white people to know how slack we is, eh?" He giggled mischievously. "So you going to put everything about Mr. Ram in the book?"

"Everything that's true."

"How you will know for sure?"

"Newspapers. Interviews. Mr. Rampartap himself."

"I wish you luck. In this place, everything is true and everything is lie."

"In what way?"

"You will find out for youself. You see them orange and grapefruit? They belong to Mr. Ram. He does employ nearly three-quarter of the village. Is the outsiders who causing all the trouble." Recalling his earlier evasiveness, I remained silent.

The road, bordered by fruit trees, was shaded by huge, gnarled immortelle and mahogany trees, and as we drove along slowly the morning shadows lapsed, shifted and reformed, creating the illusion of frolicking figures hiding among the bushes, leaping from the branches, following us from a distance. There was a sepulchral beauty about the trees, and I felt that if they could speak, they would talk of violation and betrayal.

"You see that silk cotton tree across they? The one with the big macco crab root? One day they find a fella prop up 'gainst one of them root. He coulda be sleeping or resting but he throat was slit. From side to side. We nearly reach. By the way, you know what the name of this estate is?"

I had a vague memory of the name: it was just one of many French and Spanish names, a legacy of the island's colonial past. But the question evoked a memory of Mr. Philip, his starched white shirt buttoned at the cuffs, his black face glowing with indignation, explaining that the Caribbean islands were routinely exchanged—he may have used the word *pawns*—during the peace treaties. "Carib, Arawak, English, Spanish, Dutch, French, Portuguese, Indian, African, Madeiran, Chinese, Lebanese, Syrian. A real mix-up broth. A callaloo." He repeated this litany several times, occasionally excluding a nationality or including another but we were never deceived by his enthusiasm because we knew he would soon launch into a spelling test. For this, he usually chose the Arawak and Carib names: Chaguaramas, Guayaguayare, Tunapuna. Once I raised my hand and asked him to explain the meaning of these strange names, and from the way he clapped the duster on the table's edge I knew he was annoyed. After class, while I was gathering my books from my desk, he clicked his fingers and summoned me to his table. For a while, he just stared at his texts piled on the tables and said nothing. I noticed the line of razor bumps on his cheeks. Then, looking at his texts rather than at me, he said, "I know you is an—," he paused and I thought he was about to say *intelligent* "—inquisitive fellow. I see you reading all these books from the library." He gestured

to the "library," a cupboard at the corner of the room. "But
sometimes we have to focus on the important things. Like
these Caribs, for instance." He reached for a text, flipped
the pages and tapped it back into the stack on his table.
Briefly, I wondered whether he had heard of my attempted
journey to the forest. "Although they are not true Caribs,
they still live by themself. Away from everybody else. You
ever see them advertising in the papers?" I shook my head.
"Or holding bazaars and inviting everybody from the
village? The real question is why. Why?" I waited for a clarification, but he seemed to have forgotten me. "So it's best
to focus on the things that are important," he repeated,
absent-mindedly.

This was an entirely unsatisfactory explanation, especially from a teacher, especially from *Mr. Philip*, and I was
sure that he just didn't know the answer to my question.
The next day, when Sam inquired about my detention,
Sorefoot Soogrim, a plump boy whose claim to fame was
his tendency to lick away the mucus running from his nostrils, said that Mr. Philip was afraid of the Caribs because he
had an illegitimate son with a woman living in the Guanapo
forest. Furthermore, Mr. Philip had been banned from visiting the boy, who scampered naked in the forest hunting
squirrel, agouti, tattoo and quenk. I wasn't sure whether I
should believe Sorefoot Soogrim because he had also spread
rumours that Sally, a classmate, was running around with
a taxi driver three times her age and that Miss Mary was a
soucouyant, who each night would slip out of her skin and
fly off as a ball of fire. But he might also have been seeking
revenge on Mr. Philip for a thrashing three weeks earlier.
Mr. Philip had shrieked at him, "Mr. Soogrim, come up
this very minute." The tamarind rod was in his hand. "You

like condensed milk, eh? That is why you does be licking
you nose all the time, not so? You getting a nice, creamy
dose every day?" His use of the dialect was usually a prelude
to a thrashing. "Put out your nasty little hand." Crack!
Crack! "And them holey pants, it does keep you cool and
breezy all the time?" Crack! "Tell you father that I, Cor-
nelius Titmus Patrick Philip, say that when he have time to
leave the rumshop to buy a good decent pair for you." After
class, Sorefoot Soogrim, crying, blubbering and licking,
had told us that his father was an obeah man who was going
to make Mr. Philip regret his error. "That black bitch, I go
do for him." I remember thinking that Sorefoot Soogrim
would surely grow up into the kind of criminal I'd read
about in the papers, men who flew from the rumshops with
their cutlasses, chasing after their tormentors.

"It name the Rougeleau estate, uncle."

"Yes, I know. Red Water."

Madhoo seemed impressed. "I didn't expect you to remember that, uncle. So you must be know the story 'bout
how they was to hang them slave and them by the river and
ever since the water turn red. Never change back. The story
is that all them slave ghost still waiting 'round the river cause
they can't find peace. Some people say that in the night you
could hear them crying and bawling and wailing like if the
world coming to a end. I think maybe they just waiting."

"For what?"

"I never ask them. Maybe for something. Or somebody."

All at once a crippling exhaustion swept over me. I missed
the suffocating stability of Canada, sitting silently with
Vanita, even the blistering arguments with my wife.

"Look over they. You see it?"

On the hill was an old estate house, smothered by a beetling samaan tree. A huge concrete wall blocked my view of everything but the vines slithering from the samaan and coiling over the shingled roof and around the wooden windows.

FOUR

The property was enclosed by a concrete wall spiked with upright teak logs, strung with taut, dangerous-looking tiger wire, creating a fearsome barricade about twelve feet high. The house itself, with its cracked concrete walls, the shingled roof patched with tar, the wrought iron balcony, the aluminium waterspouting running along the eaves, the worn cantilevered stairway with its rusted arches and twirls—a reminder of its French origin—seemed far too modest for such elaborate defences. I felt the two-storey house belonged in a postcard; a photograph taken in fading light, a sprinkle of yellow flowers in the foreground, a few grey clouds curling lazily overhead, a postcard that might have been titled simply "Retreat," with the suggestion of a man or a woman peeping from a partially open window, and dreaming of better days.

I could see that the place had once been well kept and the yard tastefully landscaped. There were fruit trees at the sides of the house, and stumps where others had been removed; two terra cotta jars placed on either side of an arched doorway on the lower floor and a potted asparagus fern clamped over the arch, the thick roots trailing down. There was a fountain, dry and useless, beneath a sprawling almond tree, and beside it stood a statue of a naked woman, her breasts covered with moss and vines climbing over her legs. Beyond the almond were huge samaan, balata and sandbox trees.

When I entered, Mr. Rampartap was fresh from his bath and water was dripping from his head onto his shoulders. He greeted me cheerfully and at once launched into an unbroken stream of talk. "When I was a boy growing up in Charlieville, I used to swim one mile every morning in the Caroni River. The other boys used to jump in and jump out after a few minutes but I would swim against the current until every muscle in my body was bursting. And after my swim, I would pull in my line from below the bridge, take out the cascadura from the hook, string them on a piece of cutlass wire and wait for a car to stop. Five cents a string. On some mornings I would stand at the side of the road for hours, then I would take my string and walk home. Sometimes I might just give it away free to some neighbour. A little boy breaking his back to make a living giving away his catch free. But that was a long time ago, when Trinidad was a different place. Before all this." He gestured to the drab wooden wall of the elongated living room, which was enlivened with framed letters and testimonials. There were five doors, one leading to the balcony and another to the outside stairway; and the other three were closed. The kitchen at the back was obscured by plastic screen.

My recollection of Mr. Rampartap was of a thickset figure, pacing the editor's office and continually glancing at his watch; he had seemed in a hurry and I felt that my ques-

tions were annoying him. The man I saw now had the proportions of an aging bodybuilder: thick forearms, wide
shoulders and a barrel chest, but his muscles were coated
with fat and his feet were absurdly thin in comparison with
his powerful upper body. Some quality in his face—not isolated in a particular feature but hidden in the set of his lips,
the broad nose, the eyes, alert and wary like a boxer on his
way down—hinted at extreme cruelty.

"So how was the trip? Did Madhoo give you a tour of
the city?" He didn't wait for a reply. "He is a good boy, very
obedient but a little empty up here." He tapped his head.
"And sometimes he like to talk too much for his own
good." At last he paused, and for the first time seemed to be
waiting for a response, but just then there was a knock on
the door. "Yes?"

Madhoo opened the door and pushed in his head.
"Somebody to see you, Mr. Ram. Is Mr. Haggers. He waiting outside."

"Tell him to come up. And go get a bag of grapefruit for
him." Mr. Haggers, very black and very tall, came in, wiping
the back of his neck with an old rag, and Mr. Rampartap's
tone changed. "What happen, Roy, I thought you forget
me?" Mr. Rampartap turned to me. "Roy is a very important man in the island. Have a finger in every pie." I was
about to be impressed but then he said to Mr. Haggers,
"And this is the writer I import from Canada. Highly respected and talented. He just arrive." Mr. Haggers, who had
the famished, harangued look of a smoker trying unsuccessfully to kick the habit, displayed no interest in me. He
pushed his hand deep into his trouser pocket and jangled
keys or coins. "Madhoo, show the writer downstairs. And
get Dulcie to make sure that he have everything." As we

were leaving, he added, "If anybody come during the next hour or so tell them that I asleep."

Madhoo led me down the stairs, to the lower doorway, where he fished a bunch of keys out of his pocket and fiddled with an enormous steel padlock. "Watch them long root coming out from that pot on top they. A scorpion could drop on you and crawl straight down to you gorgon."

I stepped back hastily. "My what?"

"You re-pro-duc-tive gorgon. What happen, they don't teach them thing in Canada?" Was he joking? His face was perfectly serious. He kicked open the door with his bad leg and almost toppled over. "Oops." The room was bigger than I expected. At the end was a four-poster bed, and next to it a solid wooden chest and a wobbly-looking fan. On a shelf running the length of the room were a cracked earthenware plant pot and a bronze candle holder. "The honeymoon suite. I believe Dulcie fix it up for you. Let me open the window." He fiddled with a rusty latch and pushed open the window. The dry mustiness was replaced by the odour of rotting fruit. "I does stay with the watchman and them in the bungalow 'cross they. The cemetree right in the back of it. You can't see the bungalow too good on account of the cashew and tonko bean tree. When last you eat one of them thing?"

"A very long time ago."

"I does carry up a bucket every morning. Good for jam. And wine too. One drink and you *tootoolbay* for a month. I going to get you suitcase."

"What cemetery?"

"For them slave people and them. Mostly li'l children from what I hear. Half of them must be *douen* by now, fooling up people in believing them is small children. I does keep me distance from they. It have a mad-ass fella from England or someplace, living on a hill not too far from the cemetree."

"Is that where the river is?"

"Which river, uncle? Oho, you mean the Red Water. Nah, that is way in the back, running through all kinda rocks and boulders. This estate is part of the Central Range, you know. Must be in a valley or something 'cause the land always sloping this way and that. It not design for one-foot people like me."

"So, have you seen it?"

"Well, it buss out lower down in the estate, way the village people does live. Them does call it Curse River and Dead River. People 'round here like to fish and thing but nobody don't mess with that river."

"The water might be poisonous. Coppery."

"Coppery-hoppery-bobbery. Is blood, not copper. Slave blood. But me grandfather, me *aja* had a different story. He say the old labourer and them use to do sacrifice they, so they wouldn't get punish for leaving India. And this *macco* wheel in the water just swallowing up all the goat and sheep and fowl they pitch in. You know what a wheel is?"

"Yes. A *huille*. A water boa." He was looking at me disbelievingly so I added, "An anaconda—a snake."

He shook his head. "Was a *prate*."

"A what?"

"A prate. A spirit. I hear it had this fella who rape somebody daughter and they tie him up and pitch him straight in the water. The river just start to bubble up and he disappear. The prate take him." He giggled nervously. "Anyway, I gone."

Prates, douens, huilles, slave cemeteries: it was hard to believe that just three days ago I was in the living room at

Ellesmere, flicking through the television channels and watching Martha Stewart prattling about the elegance of pastel picture frames and a well-fed man advertising a dual cyclonic vacuum cleaner. The room was about the size of the living room at Ellesmere but here it smelled of old paper and woodlice rather than pine freshener and unlit tobacco. There were small perforations on the wooden walls, which seemed at first to be the work of termites, but I saw that nails had been pried out. Perhaps pictures had been hanging from the nails.

A dragging scraping sound and Madhoo returned with my suitcase. "Where to put it?"

"You can leave it there. That's fine."

"Okay then. I going to pick some grapefruit for Mr. Haggers."

"Is he a politician?"

"Mr. Haggers a politician?" The idea amused him. "He real name is Haggernathy or something. He is a police in-specterer. One of the few that Mr. Ram does trust."

"What's wrong with the others?"

I had meant the question as a joke but Madhoo became serious. "I better go and start picking them grapefruit now." He tapped his bad leg. "This foot didn't design for climbing tree. More of a weather clock. And this morning it tell me that rain going to fall."

His leg was right; about half an hour after he had left, while I was arranging my clothes on top of a huge wooden box in the corner of the room, the rain began, first a gentle patter sprinkling from the cashew tree, then a raging downpour.

I had forgotten the intensity of tropical rainstorms. The darkening of the sky, the wind howling through the trees, the sudden explosion on the roof like a tumble of broken bottles, the bursts of thunder and lightning. Through the window, I saw the cashew tree straining against the wind and I heard the thump of fruits hitting the ground. As I was about to close the window, there was a faint knock. Something blown against the side of the house, I thought, but then I heard the knock again on the other side of the room. I opened the door. "Hello."

"I come to put up the mosquito netting."

"Are you . . . ?" I tried to remember her name.

"Dulcie? Yes. I had to patch a few holes. It okay now." She glanced at the white, lumpy bundle in her hands and I moved from the doorway. At the bed, she stepped out of her rubber slippers and wiped her feet on the mat. "I have to use the bed," she said apologetically. "To hook up the net."

Her shyness was touching. I smiled. "It's all right. Do you need any help?"

She glanced at me, puzzled, then she said, "You should close the window or the whole room will get soak."

"Yes. I was about to." I pulled in the window and when I turned around, she was standing on the bed, the net unfurled, one end in her hand. She reached up to connect it to the ceiling and her yellow cotton dress rose against her thighs. She looked down at me and smiled. "It fix now."

"Here, let me help you." Her smile faded but she held my hand and climbed off the bed, brushing against me. There was a faint aroma of fruit, ripe and syrupy, in her breath. Perhaps she had been eating cashews while she was mending the net. She moved away, to the door. "You shirt get wet up closing the window." Then standing by the door, she asked me, "You going to write a book about Mr. Ram?"

"I believe so."

"What kind of book it will be?"

"That's a good question. We haven't discussed it yet. I should ask Mr. Rampartap that question." She was looking puzzled so I added, "About his life, I suppose."

"Everything in his life?"

As I was about to answer, she walked away.

The rain fell for the entire afternoon and with the window closed the room soon became boiling hot. I took off my shirt and changed into a sleeveless jersey. I would have liked a shower and I thought of going upstairs, but I would have had to use the outside stairs; there was no interior stairway. The rain fell in a steady rhythm and when I peeked through the window, I saw sheets of water cascading down from the roof. It was five forty-five. Vanita would be in her room drawing pictures or writing stories of rabbits escaping from traps and princesses freed from evil spells. Or maybe her mother was out shopping and she was alone at home, looking anxiously at the telephone, praying for a call from either parent. I remembered reports of children locked in elevators, trapped in fires, falling from balconies. I closed my eyes; I had come too far.

I heard a little click, opened my eyes and saw a bushy head peeping through the door. "Mr. Ram say to come upstairs to eat. Use the ambrella. It look like is the same inginair fella who build the bridge what design this house." Outside, by the landing, he opened the umbrella with a flourish, gave it to me and went off whistling in the rain.

Mr. Rampartap was sitting in a rocking chair, his legs crossed, reading a newspaper. "Put the umbrella in the corner and come and have something to eat. Breadfruit, cassava and crab. Go ahead and eat." He did not look up from his newspaper. The woman I believed to be his wife was at the table, her face over a plate, spitting out pieces of crab. "Country food. How does it taste?"

I bit into the crab and a tooth shivered. "It's okay."

"People down here don't eat hamburgers and pizza and hot dogs, you know. Everything come from their own backyard. That is why they so healthy. Not like the town people who only looking for American and Canadian food. You probably craving for some of that, eh?"

"Not really."

"Dulcie make it. I dropped her home early because of the rain." The woman spat a sliver of crab in her plate. I pushed aside the crab and tested the cassava. Warm and buttery. "Tomorrow we will make a trip to the village. It will be good start for the book. Get to know the person himself."

"Which person?"

He looked up angrily. "The person you will be writing about."

The woman, her head bent, chewing and spitting, looked like a hungry wounded animal. Years ago she might have been an attractive woman, but her beauty had darkened and her rigid features now suggested spite and pettiness.

Some women leave traces of themselves in a room—the arrangement of the furniture, the colour combinations, plants, decorative pieces, lamps, paintings, the highlighting of some things, the concealing of others—but there was nothing of her here. The towering long-case clock in one corner, the marble-topped sideboard in another, both antiques, must have come with the house. In the centre of the dining room was a rectangular table, sturdy but clumsy, constructed of wooden planks; in the spaces between the boards, the nail-dents, the rough edges, it was possible to see the carpenter, building without specification, without style. An old, battered sofa and settee were placed on either side of a door that also opened onto the balcony. The testimonials and photographs were all of Mr. Rampartap. Perhaps she had bought the chair on which he rocked, his slippers scraping the floor. I felt sorry for her; Mr. Rampartap's indifference was so complete she could have been in another room. But she was attentive to all his movements and I saw her pupils moving up and down as he rocked.

"There is a bathroom at the back of the house. It's a separate unit." He flicked his newspaper. "This is a very old building. Some of the facilities are not up to the mark but no one has complained so far."

"Is there a light?"

"Of course. We are not heathens, you know."

Heathens. The word annoyed me. "Perhaps I should have stayed in a hotel."

"You are free to stay wherever you choose." He folded his newspaper and placed it on the floor. "But you are welcome here for as long as you want."

"I took it for granted—"

"In this island you take nothing for granted." His teeth flashed and I saw that he was beginning to enjoy the exchange. "You get soft living all these years in nice Canada, Mr. Writer."

I got up. Opposite, a crab leg cracked. "I trust there are no snakes."

He rocked and laughed. But in the bathroom I saw that a snake could easily hide among the vines climbing through the aperture at the top. I had to twist the faucet three turns before the water came rushing out, surprising me with its coldness. I showered hurriedly, draped a towel across my waist, and stepped into the rain.

"You see any snake, Mr. Writer?" Mr. Rampartap leaned out of the window and chuckled.

Not downstairs, you old bitch. The thought, so uncharacteristic, thrilled me.

Cocooned inside the mosquito net, I wondered about the woman upstairs, chewing and spitting. When had she been transformed into a cornered animal? And how? I thought: in a turbulent marriage, it's the amoral who triumphs, not the accommodating.

The girl I had married never showed her face again—or at least, she displayed with greater clarity what I had chosen to ignore. Instead I was confronted daily by a woman who found my jokes stupid, who sat on the toilet while I shaved and read magazine articles about office romances, who sneered at my attempts to write. Secretly I blamed her for my stillborn novel, my unfinished stories, my weak articles for *The Caribbean Crossroad*. She believed writing was a glorified form of laziness because it provided an excuse to mope around the house all day, to avoid looking for real jobs, to clutter the table with books and paper and to engage in regular naps under the guise of contemplation. Once, when she had just started working for the dentist, she asked me, "So when are you going to produce this fabulous story, mistah? The one you're spending so much time on."

Encouraged, I showed her the outline of a story that dealt with a successful, wealthy man who had inexplicably left everything in Canada and returned to a village in India because of a promise made forty years earlier to his parents. She read the outline carefully once, and then a second time.

I was nervous because I had never shown anyone my attempts at fiction before. When she had finished she handed
the three stapled pages back to me without a word. In the
evening, while we were watching television, I asked her
about the story. She said it was morbid. I asked her to explain. She thought for a minute then said it was gangrenous.
I removed my hand from her knee and got up. During the
following months, whenever I began a story, I always had
the notion it would turn out to be gangrenous and I could
never move beyond the first few paragraphs. She bought her
own books, historical romances set in European duchies,
and opera CDs that drowned out the sounds of my calypsos
(something I had never believed possible) so that after a
while, whenever I heard the wailing of her Valkyries, I
would bolt from the apartment. When Vanita was five years
old, I had already developed the habit of taking long walks
and on my return she would ask me, "Where have you been,
Daddy?" Enjoying my parole, I would think.

Separated by such a distance, I missed my daughter desperately. She, too, must have felt trapped at times, but unlike her parents, she was never allowed escape from her
prison. Except for school, maybe.

One night, we were watching a segment of *Trials of Life*
on television. A newborn moose, its fur soft and damp,
stood for the first time, teetered awkwardly and fell. It tried
again and tumbled to the ground. Vanita pressed her fingers against her cheek and chuckled. The camera panned
the hill and a great, fluffy bear lumbered into view. The
mother moose raised her snout and sniffed the air. The bear
came ploughing down the hill. The mother, alert to the
danger, made for some bristly shrubs with her calf, then
re-emerged, trying to draw the bear's attention. The bear

was not fooled. The scene cut to a close-up of the calf squirming under the bear's paw. The bear tore into its neck. The mother, from a distance, looked on helplessly. The narrator, in a cheerfully resigned voice, spoke about nature striking a balance between predator and prey.

"I hate bears. Why did the baby die?" Nature striking a balance. How could she understand? I tried unsuccessfully to explain, then her mother picked her up out of her little rocking chair and hugged her, and she was comforted.

The rain had slowed to a drizzle, so I opened the window, and with the soothing sound of the wind whistling through the trees, the raindrops sprinkling from the leaves and the water gurgling down the drain, I was soon asleep.

In the middle of the night I awoke from a horrible dream. I was at home, smothered by a blanket of flies streaming in from the window. I struggled to close the window but I was overpowered and driven into Vanita's room, where she lay sleeping. I lashed out in a frenzy at the flies but my feet were off the ground and I could no longer breathe. I heard Vanita screaming.

I rolled out of bed, switched on the lights, scanned the wall for a mirror—an instinctive reaction to my distress—and for the second time that night, I was infuriated with Mr. Rampartap. *This is the writer that I import from Canada. There is a bathroom outside. We are not heathens, you know. You see any snake, Mr. Writer?* But I was equally annoyed with my own attitude towards him. He had all the qualities of a bully—he was pushy, overbearing and self-important, and with his big head, his stocky frame and loud voice he even looked the part. I had known politicians like him before I left for Canada and in the Trinidadian manner

I had made fun of their pomposity. They were buffoons who were regarded with amusement rather than respect. Yet here I was, timid in Mr. Rampartap's presence. Perhaps I had been away too long, become too Canadian, too measured and obliging. I felt that I was acting like a guest in the country where I was born.

There were red spots on my arms. I went to the bed and searched for holes in the net. I saw three mosquitoes, their bodies bloated with my blood, seeking escape from the net. I clapped my hands savagely over them. "Allyou bloodsucking bitches. Haul allyou ass upstairs and suck." The dialect was so satisfying that I smiled. I found the hole, stuffed it with tissue paper from my suitcase and went back to bed, watching the mosquitoes buzzing outside, searching for an opening. Above me, I heard a faint creaking on the wooden floor, as if someone was padding quietly from room to room.

FIVE

"You look like a true-true Canadian tourist," Mr. Rampartap chortled, glancing at my sleeveless jersey, Blue Jays cap and white Bermuda trousers, even though he himself was dressed in khaki shirt and pants like an out-of-sorts expatriate civil servant in a bad movie about the tropics. But in the car, he was silent and seemed preoccupied. Nor was Madhoo his usual chatty self. He drove without asking directions, as if the route had been planned beforehand.

"My orange and grapefruit." Mr. Rampartap gestured to the fruit trees. "Four acres in all. Three hundred acres of citrus right there, and in the back by that side road another hundred acre of this and that." Madhoo swerved the car into the side road. There was a faint fragrance of chocolate simmering in the sun. "My tonko bean. Take a deep breath and smell it," he commanded. The trees were taller, spaced farther apart, the leaves darker than the citrus. Madhoo drove along slowly and carefully while Mr. Rampartap pointed to his cherries, his Julie mangoes, his bananas. Then there were no more fruit trees, just bamboo criss-crossing each other into a massive gauze wall.

The road was dangerous, often curving suddenly or forking into identical tributaries. We might have been going in circles. I could not see Madhoo's face. Next to me Mr. Rampartap bounced up and down like a huge frog, his jowls and cheeks trembling every time we landed in a pot-hole. At each fork, I scrutinized the trees, trying to establish a landmark, but they were all the same: clumps of bamboo and immortelle and mahogany with scabbed trunks and twisted branches grabbing the sky.

Finally, we emerged into a small village. The road was paved with pitch and there were small patches of tar that seemed to be melting in the sun. "My workers." Mr. Rampartap pointed to the small wooden houses, old but well kept, with tidy lawns bordered by crotons and hibiscus. A few men were walking unhurriedly along the road; they waved when they saw the car. Mr. Rampartap knew each by name. Alfonso, Theo, Portillo, Manswell, Sanchez. "Spanish. Very loyal and obedient. Like little children. You could trust them with your life. They will never betray you."

I had always admired these people, inaccurately referred to as Spanish but really African with traces of Carib, European and occasionally Indian blood. The mix gave them a beguiling impassiveness; they could be living as they had hundreds of years ago, obeying their own laws, operating according to their own standards. They reminded me of the Caribs, also a mixed-race people who lived in the outskirts of Agostini, in the Guanapo forest, where they would leave once a fortnight for the Rio Claro market to purchase cartridges, torchlights, and foodstuff. They bothered no one and were hospitable to strangers, but sometimes an outsider would mistake their impassiveness for subservience and weeks later, a mutilated body would be found in the forest.

In my parents' shop, late at night, pretending I had come for a tin of orange juice, I would hear the older villagers whispering these stories under a kerosene lamp, shadows jumping over their faces. I was intrigued with the bloodsucking soucouyants, serpent-headed *mama diglous* and shape-shifting lagahoos living all around us, pretending to be innocent neighbours. But by the morning, the stories would have lost their flavour and Trinidad became what it was: a land where secrets were frivolous, not mysterious and romantic—the local word, *mauvais-langue*, meaning gossipy and meddling. But now, watching the men and women carrying in their walk and the set of their faces a ponderous silence that was part fear, part pride and part pretence, I felt that the stories were not entirely contrived, and I understood why our parents and grandparents, their lives almost over, needed to believe in a world where nothing was real, where memories could be blurred to accommodate romance and resistance. And then, a strange, unconnected thought: I imagined that real writers must be desperately lonely people.

Mr. Rampartap was staring at me. "Are you thinking of your safe Canada, Mr. Writer?"

"No, actually I was thinking of Agostini, where I grew up."

"I have been there a few times," he said, not interested.

But a few minutes later, I *was* reminded of Canada. At the side of the road a woman and her little daughter, a child of six or seven, were filling their buckets from a standpipe. "Are there phones here?" I asked.

"Pull up across there," Mr. Rampartap said, as if he had not heard. "Before Mr. Writer dehydrate in the hot tropical sun. Get a cold sweet-drink for him." Madhoo swung into the yard of an old rumshop and revved the engine. Almost as if by signal, a boy rushed out of the rumshop. He stopped suddenly by the car.

"Mr. Ram!"

"Yes, Ramon?"

"You better come quick. Hurry up."

Mr. Rampartap opened the door and walked into the rumshop. He was very calm. I followed him. The rumshop was dimly lit but I could see a group of men standing around a tall, shirtless man clutching an upraised beer bottle. The circle parted, allowing Mr. Rampartap's entrance. "What is the problem here, Ashton?"

"Lopez call me a thief, Mr. Ram. He call me a lowdown thief."

At the other end of the rumshop, near the counter, someone drawled, "Every single day he inside here, drinking and having a good time. Always promising to pay me by month-end. Three month-end pass and I didn't see any money yet. Well, today he not leaving in one piece." The speaker walked forward and I saw a cutlass in his hand.

"You see, Mr. Ram? You see? Treating me like a lowdown thief." He made a motion as if he were going to throw the bottle. "Well, all that done now. I is a big blasted man with big blasted children. What they go say if they hear that any and everybody calling they father a lowdown thief. Well, all that done now." He brought the bottle down savagely on the table and pieces flew across the room. Holding the jagged end, he said, "If I is a thief, I is a murderer too." Blood was dripping from his fingers.

"He not leaving in one piece."

"Who going to stop me?"

"Me, you thief."

"Oh, God, Mr. Ram, you hear it? You hear it for yourself? Somebody hold me back."

"Thief!"

He turned to Mr. Rampartap. "Mr. Ram, I working by you for over ten years now. I ever thief anything?"

"Not to my knowledge."

I was astonished at how composed he sounded.

"Thank you, Mr. Ram. Thank you. *You* know that I is not a lowdown thief. Now tell *him* that." He pointed with the piece of bottle to the bartender. "Tell him so he wouldn't go round telling any and everybody that Ashton is a lowdown thief." Unexpectedly, he began to sob. "Tell him so nobody could tell me children that they father is a thief. Tell him now in front of me." He wiped his eyes and blood smudged across his forehead.

Mr. Rampartap stepped forward and took the broken bottle from Ashton's hand. He turned. "How much is the bill, Lopez?"

"Two hundred dollars, Mr. Ram. He promise and promise that he will . . ."

Mr. Rampartap withdrew a wad of bills from his pocket. "Okay, okay. Take this and count it."

The bartender placed his cutlass on the floor, took the money and began counting slowly, note by note. "Two hundred dollars in all, Mr. Ram. Exactly two hundred."

"So the bill square off now?"

"Yes, Mr. Ram. I will cross out the name from the book." He returned to the counter and the men drifted back to their tables.

"Is God and God alone who send you here today. Is God and God alone who know what would have happen if you didn't come." Ashton looked at me. "And if ever I hear anybody say anything bad about you, that is the last thing they go ever say. Thank God for you, Mr. Ram." I thought he was going to cry once more but instead he shouted, "Open one for me, Lopie."

"Coming right up," a voice replied from behind the counter.

Back in the car, I saw Madhoo gazing at Mr. Rampartap in the rear-view mirror. "Is a good place to start the book, Mr. Ram. All that excitement."

Mr. Rampartap waved his hand airily. "These writers know their job. We can't tell them what to do." His lips drooped into a smile. "The whole thing is like a art to them. Some might say that they are just malicious people who like to gossip. Minding everybody business and telling everything they think they know, but I personally have a lot of respect for them." He was looking straight ahead. "That is why I import Mr. Writer here." Now he turned to me. "There was a time when I was a top-class reader, you know. I was young and I had time to waste. One time, I read this book by a writer from the States. Good straightforward book. Especially the part about a man telling his best friend how he rape and murder this woman. The writer give all the details too, how he cut up the body in small parts and put the pieces in garbage bags that he left in the garage and driveway of all the people that he know. So in the story they all come accomplices. Now, after I read the book, I send the writer a letter saying the book was enjoyable and entertaining and all that nonsense. But I didn't stop there." He was looking at me carefully, his eyes shining. "I pretend I was . . . now I can't remember what . . . a victimized tenant or something. Anyways, I was a desperate man willing to try anything. You know the rest."

I had no idea but I didn't want to commit myself in any way.

Madhoo was shaking his head as if he knew what was going to follow.

"I thank this writer for showing me the way and I tell him by the time he get this letter I would already be dismantling this landlord. I even put my name and return address. Gulla Thomsingh. The name of a first-class dismantler. Anybody with a little sense could have figure out that it wasn't a real name. But this great writer reply back in no time, begging me to forget this crazy idea. The letter was nearly three page long and every line you read you could see how frighten he was. He couldn't even inform the police because it was his idea. Or maybe he inform them and this being Trinidad, they throw away the letter because it didn't mention anything about bribe. So what you think?"

My first reaction was to tell him that I knew that the story was as fake as the incident in the bar, but I held back. The argument appeared to have been staged to impress me, to show how important and influential he was, but I had no idea why he had concocted the story.

"This writer thought he was smart but he was no different from anybody else. Just as weak and when I use that weakness he was only a frighten little boy. Weak, weak little fella."

The story dismayed me; Mr. Rampartap was treating me the way he treated Madhoo, Ashton and undoubtedly everyone in his employ. To him I was just another employee, one he had *imported* from Canada. I had been annoyed by the accommodation he had arranged for me, as if it were an afterthought. I had not anticipated overly generous treatment but I felt it was foolhardy to offend someone about to write your biography. And for the first time, I wondered whether there was another reason for the invitation; whether he, too, had another agenda. "Pull inside here. It have somebody I want you to meet."

"Me?"

"Yes. You might find him interesting."

Madhoo drove into a secondary road just before the estate and stopped by an old wooden building. Two iron cartwheels covered with grass lay on either side of an overturned copper. Beyond the building, beyond the rubble of rotting scantlings, cows grazed under the orange tree. "The watchmen sleep in that bungalow. At another time, a different set of people used to live in it. Slaves, then the bonded labourers from India. You know about that time?"

"History lessons from primary school."

"You was bright in school?"

"I passed my exams."

"Then you went to Canada."

"I worked for a year in the warden's office in Rio Claro."

"Rich little boy, eh? Never had to sell fish at the side of the road."

"No, actually—"

"You see that tree over there?" He pointed to a tree with epiphytes clinging to the scarified trunk and hanging like mummified birds from the branches. "Inside all these nest, you will find manicou and squirrel living. They safe there. Nobody will disturb them." We walked to the tree. "The old people used to say that blood would flow from the trunk if you make a cut. But I put a stop to that. That branch hanging there is where they used to hang the troublemakers. Instant justice. The best cure. You tired in all this heat?"

"No, I'm okay." I was beginning to sweat but the breeze was cool and invigorating. "Which troublemakers?"

"There was a different set of laws then. And this was a different place." He slapped a mosquito on his arm. "When I bought the estate, it was abandoned. Derelict. The trees— it was mostly cocoa then, all the cane had been converted— was covered with vines and the building was useless. Nearly all the village people, these mixed-breed Spanish or *coco panyol* as we call them had already left for the towns. Chaguanas. Couva. San Fernando. Tabaquite. As far away as Port of Spain. There was nothing for them here. The older ones who used to work in the estate, they remained. Maybe because they was too old or maybe because they still remembered when the old owner, Mendes, was running the place. He was a rich man, powerful even though he never had political office. But in those days he was who he was and he didn't need that. And then things started to happen. Prices fall. Witch broom disease. The Black Power riots in the sixties. He pack up his bags and went straightaway to France. This powerful man who owned nearly the whole village. But that was how this place was. You come here, you spend a generation, you establish a little kingdom and then you leave.

"The estate was in the hands of an agent. Nobody else was interested because it was cocoa. It was just after the elections. But bit by bit, I put it back the way it was supposed to be. I clear out the bush, the *lathro*, I switch over to fruits and flowers, I repair the buildings, I fix the roads, I dig well and install pumps, I carve out drains and clear out the ravines, I put up dry walls, I give people work. I save the village." He laughed, as if all he had said meant nothing, as if it were some trivial accomplishment he had just remembered.

"One by one, they come back. Not everybody, eh. Not the troublemakers who in some jail or the other, rotting away now. And that was the way I wanted it. I didn't want any *peongs* running around loose here. The few that come back didn't stay for too long. I make sure of that." Perspiration was running down his face, and his khaki shirt, so inconvenient in this climate, was wet with sweat. He unclasped a button and blew on his chest. He picked a mandarin, pushed his thumb in the core and deftly removed the skin. "Here, try this. One of the sweeter trees. I know every single tree in the estate. Every one." He popped a peg of orange in his mouth and turned to me. Chewing, he told me, "I never expected you to come, you know. To leave your safe Canada to write about a man you knew nothing about. You didn't know my story yet." His teeth clicked as if they were loose. "You didn't know about a penniless little boy selling fish at the side of the road becoming one of the richest men in the island. Outsmarting all those who thought they were so powerful." A trickle of juice rolled down his chin and onto his shirt. "Magistrate. Lawyer. Police inspector. All of them, every single one had a weakness they thought nobody could

see, but they couldn't fool me. You see, I judge people by the
things they trying to hide not what they interested in showing me." He turned to me. "Isn't that the sort of book that
will sell millions in Canada and the States?" He spat out the
pulp and wiped his mouth with the back of his palm. "Rag
to riches. Everybody underestimating him but he always
finding that little crack to slip through. Always waiting for
the right time."

"There mightn't be that market there."

"Market? You let me down. You think is for myself I
doing this." The way he said it—the twist of his mouth, the
forced confidence—made me think of a beaten old man.
"You know, Mr. Writer, that first time that we meet in
Canada just for a few minutes and then when I read your
article, I thought that you was the right man for the job but
I not so sure again." He pointed to a tree, taller and healthier-
looking than the others. "The sourest tree in the plot. Several times I thought of cutting it down but watch how it
shading the other trees. Useless but I find a use for it." He
walked in the direction of the tree. "I saved this estate but
I can't save the island." This statement—the raw egotism—
surprised me but he had said it casually, as an afterthought.
"That is why I send away my daughter to Canada. She's
studying biotechnology now. Is that how you pronounce
the word?" He grew silent and I felt that he wanted me to
ask about his daughter but at that moment I thought of the
woman upstairs, perhaps the mother of the girl. "You all in
your nice, safe countries have no idea of what is taking place
in these little islands. You have no idea of the lawlessness.
One day a hurricane or a earthquake or a innocent-looking
mud volcano will wipe out the whole place. And it going to
happen soon."

"Why do you say that?"

"I am not a religious man but this nonsense can't continue indefinitely. This was a blessed place at one time. Protected from all the trouble that knocking the other islands year after year. We had everything. Oil. Natural gas. Asphalt. A paradise. But you know what happen to these places."

"In that case, what's the point of a biography?"

The question disturbed him. He walked in silence, then he said, "The only thing that will remain is the records." It was too simple; I knew he was lying. He glanced quickly at me. "But you are a man with your own views. You lived for too long in Canada. You lost touch. Like these people who come back for a two-week vacation and expect everything to be the way it was."

"You invited . . ."

"But I don't blame you. Even people who live their whole life here can't see what is happening. Let me fill you in. A few years aback, money was dropping from the sky and people who never dream of having so much money, who never work for it so they couldn't know the value, these people didn't know what to do with it. But the thinking was that since God give it to them then he probably wanted them to spend it. And that was what happen, on a scale you wouldn't believe. Overnight millionaires. Weekends in Florida. Gold-plated kennels. Champagne flowing like water. This is the kind of freedom that these people really want. Then all of a sudden the boom ended. But it was too late. They had already changed. One morning the prime minister at the time, a jackass name Makitoe, wake up and say, 'Okay, fête over. Now back to work.' And they listen to him because they went back to work thiefing, murdering and raping." He was walking slower, his feet dragging. "That was why I was glad I send away my daughter. I could stay and fight because that is my nature, but I didn't want to impose that on anybody else.

"Come, let me show you what this island could do to people who not prepared. The men are working on the other side of that slope. Watch your step." I followed him, walking carefully over a log bridging a ravine. We came to a clearing where the burnt stubs of bamboo protruded dangerously from the ground. At the top of a small hill was a derelict windmill with windows fashioned from the straightened ends of steel drums and a door that might once have been a car's bonnet. The hill itself was encircled, moat-like, by a drain, perhaps to keep away the bush fires.

"Mr. Choo." Mr. Rampartap cupped his palms around his mouth and shouted. There was a scraping metallic sound inside the windmill. "Hold the dogs." This time the sound of pots and pans crashing, the creak of a door on the other side of the windmill, some more scraping, then silence. Mr. Rampartap placed the tip of his boot on the drain idly, waiting.

"You can come now." The voice itself was scraping and metallic.

We walked up the steps constructed of broken bricks. Mr. Rampartap pushed open the bonnet. As we entered, I was jolted by the powerful odour of asafetida, automobile grease and an indistinguishable smell, acrid and foul.

"I've brought a visitor." Mr. Rampartap's tone suggested that Mr. Choo wasn't one of his workers.

Mr. Choo, pale and scrawny, his brown hair braided rasta-style with beads, did not look up. He adjusted his goggles and brought down a chisel on a cylindrical piece of cast iron. He said, "It is very quay."

"What is queer, Mr. Choo?" Mr. Rampartap asked, grinning.

Mr. Choo pushed up his goggles and acted surprised to see us before him. "There is a ball bearing inside here." He held up the cast iron by an attached electrical wire as if he were swinging an animal by its tail. "But how to get it? It is very quay."

The room was like a miniature junkyard cluttered with disassembled fans, lawn mowers, small engines and pieces of aluminium and steel. Against a wall, there was a couch that was really the rear seat of a car and, on a barrel, a battery with wires connected to its terminal. The wires snaked along the floor, disappeared beneath a pile of junk and reemerged with other pieces of wire spliced onto it.

"Mr. Choo is an inventor. First class." The compliment embarrassed him. He fiddled with a ball of copper filaments. The ball was hopelessly entangled. He struggled with it—parting his lips and exposing a line of brown teeth—then threw it into a clay oven. Two boxes were attached to the rafter with rusty chains and hung over the oven. I heard something bumping inside the oven and a soft, shrill cry, like a child suffocating. Mr. Rampartap was looking at me, grinning. "Bats. For guano."

"Fertilizer," Mr. Choo said. "Best starter for curcubicaes."

"Doesn't the heat bother them?"

He looked up at the boxes and pulled his chin. "It is very quay. I think it encourages the guano."

"He is also an ecologist. Would you like to show us your pond, Mr. Choo?"

Mr. Choo vaulted over a radiator and pushed open the back door. Two pothounds tied to a tree wagged their tails and jumped up and down. We followed him down the hill, which was difficult because he was almost running, skipping on the brick steps. I was sure he would run straight into the pond but he braked just in time, his toes pinching the soft mud. A steel cage braced with wooden posts hung unsteadily over the pond. There were screeching chickens in the cage and beneath them, swimming lazily, about twenty or thirty ducks, their feathers stained with droppings from the cage.

"The pond is filled with tilapia," Mr. Rampartap said. "The chickenshit feed them and they feed the duck and chicken. Mr. Choo is a vegetarian, you know."

A nice circle but one that excluded Mr. Choo. "In that case, they might be better off uncaged." I regretted the statement because Mr. Choo was pinching the mud with his toes and looking injured.

"Ecology," Mr. Rampartap said.

That seemed to cheer Mr. Choo a bit, because he uttered a half-hearted, "It is very quay."

Smirking, Mr. Rampartap pointed to a calabash bowl dangling from a knotted rope into the water. "He is developing a water clock."

"Ancient Egypt," Mr. Choo said in a rather startled voice, as if the connection had just occurred to him.

On the way back, Mr. Rampartap said, "His name is Chew." He spelled it. "But he thinks Choo sounds more local. Like a Carib name. He was a graduate student in the university at St. Augustine, doing research on local plants. Neem. Marijuana. Datur. When he came to the estate about five years ago, he said that he had discovered forty-nine new uses for the neem plant. Under normal circumstances,

I would chase away somebody like that straightaway but he had listed all these discoveries. All forty-nine of them, typed out neatly and carefully. But there was another reason too. You hearing the men on the other side. They picking the orange to send to the Chaguanas market."

"What was the other reason?"

"This young man, well dressed, with a shining brief-case, born in England but trying his best to help out the locals, visiting week after week. Finally, I tell him that he could stay in the estate to conduct his research. The only empty building at that time was the old windmill on the hill, break-up and useless. But he was grateful and whenever I went to his shack, he would talk about his research. I thought he was going in the right direction. He wanted to develop pesticide from organic material and fungicide from ashes. He talk about grafting mango with cashew and cherry with plum. Hybrid, that was his favourite word at the time. Hybrid to withstand drought, hybrid to withstand flood, hybrid that bigger, better and sweeter than anything around. He believe that everything could be improved. But as time pass, his research start getting . . . how to put it, it start going in a unsuitable direction. One day he say that he going to develop a straight banana. Then Madhoo and the boys tell me that his research on marijuana and datur was getting personal."

The long walk and the climbing had tired him. He was breathing heavily. "You see what this place could do to you if you not careful? Now I feel sorry for him, this man who five years ago had all these big plans to change this, to change that. He become just like everybody else, all these people with small head and big dream. A brilliant man like that." I remembered Mr. Rampartap smirking and talking to him as to a child. "I am a generous man. I leave him there to do his research. Sometimes people from the village bring things for him to fix. Half of them he fix and half he spoil. People not supposed to live in a place they not design for." I wondered whether he was rebuking Mr. Choo or myself.

In the car, he said, "Everybody have they own use. I support this whole village. Without me, they wouldn't last two months. This little boy who used to stand by the side of the road for five hours every morning, waiting for somebody to feel sorry for him and stop. You would think they would be grateful."

"The villagers?"

"The villagers are mine." He hesitated, then he said, "The outsiders."

While Madhoo was driving back to the estate, I reflected on what Mr. Rampartap had revealed. His link with men like Mendes went beyond the common piece of property, the estate: in his mind he was creating order from chaos rather than simply providing a livelihood for the villagers. He was relying on his idea of the obligations and the power of the old owners, and attempting to locate for himself an equivalent role, but it didn't make sense: the plantation owners had been proprietors and traders; they used their power for commerce, and only for themselves. When there was no more money to be made, they departed and the plantations crumbled.

Mr. Rampartap's concept of power—the punishment, the floggings—was backward and primitive. I remembered his reference to his boyhood and I felt that he wanted me here to chart his rise from that humble beginning to become a man of substance and authority. But there was something more: in his rejection by these enigmatic outsiders and his dissatisfaction with the scope of his influence, I also saw a slighted man preparing some sort of onslaught on his enemies. Perhaps my true purpose was to assist him in that assault.

"Lost in your thoughts, Mr. Writer? I know that you all are reputed to be deep thinkers but I never trust anybody who is quiet all the time."

"Maybe you should develop some more trust."

I saw anger creeping into his face. I was supposed to be impressed by his estate, his handling of Ashton and Lopez, his story about the writer, his generosity with Mr. Choo, his salvaging of the village, but I had said nothing, had offered no compliments. The entire trip, so carefully arranged, had been a waste of time. "In this country," he said, choosing his words carefully, "you have to be certain of your friends because everyone else is an enemy."

"Rampartap, you is a evil son of a bitch!" An old man with long furrowing beard and torn clothes bolted out of the bushes. He shook his fist as the car passed.

"Like that useless jackass there," he said, not missing a beat. "Time to get back home now, Madhoo. Mr. Writer here is not accustomed to the hot weather." Madhoo increased his speed, but slowed again by a small house built at the top of an incline. A oldish, pleasant-looking woman, picking something from a vine, stared at the car. "You have to get out in the sun more often, Mr. Writer. Get rid of that pale skin of yours." I smiled, just to disarm him. But he was staring at the woman and in the rear-view mirror I saw Madhoo glancing at him.

Back at the estate house, Mr. Rampartap remained in the car. "You go inside and take some shade, Mr. Writer. I have some business to attend." The car reversed and sped away.

SIX

That evening, while the woman gnawed at her bread, Mr. Rampartap rocked and flicked his newspaper impatiently. He was uncharacteristically quiet and when I asked him whether he had any ideas about the book, he told me that he was thinking about it and we would "discuss the matter tomorrow." But the next day when I asked Madhoo where his boss was, he said that Mr. Rampartap had some urgent business to settle in the village.

"Is it okay if I walk around the estate until he returns?"

"Not unless you want a good dose of chemicals." He chuckled. "Now is crop time and they have to spray the fruits 'gainst all them biting ants and weevil and spider and mealy bug." He stroked his beard. "I is a master chemist, you know. Mr. Ram teach me how to mix all them chemicals in the right dose for them miserable pests and them. I could tell a chemical just from the smell and the colour and the taste."

"Really? The taste too?" I smiled.

"Just a li'l drop. Anyways, is nearly time to go. You safe as long as you in you room. The breeze does blow to the other side."

In the evening, when I went upstairs for dinner, Mr. Rampartap was on the balcony talking to Mr. Haggers.

The next morning Dulcie brought me a brown envelope with my breakfast. "Mr. Ram leave this for you."

"What is it?"

"He just say to give it to you."

I opened the envelope and withdrew a newspaper clipping detailing Mr. Rampartap's donation to a Presbyterian church in Tabaquite. The article mentioned his "humble beginnings" and "his meteoric rise to power." At the top was a faded photograph of Mr. Rampartap, younger and thinner, shaking the hand of a man wearing a suit. Dulcie was looking at the photograph.

"Do you know how long ago this was?" I asked.

"Is that Mr. Ram?"

"It seems so. A long time ago though."

"That is how he use to look?"

I was a bit surprised by her interest. "He seems to be very influential."

"Influential?" She sounded scornful and impatient.

For the rest of the week, she brought down old newspaper articles about Mr. Rampartap. Sometimes she lingered while I ate—mostly homemade bread, soft and oily, and cheese or eggs with slices of boiled breadfruit and finger yam. She would ask if the mosquitoes had bothered me during the night, or if I wanted the room dusted. I suppose she wanted to talk but our conversations never graduated from her simple questions and my precise responses. I was unnerved by her shyness, a quality new to me (or one I had forgotten). She was attractive in an untrained, rudimentary way, like a woman who did not daily plan her beauty, who perhaps did not even know it existed.

After breakfast, I would gather soap and towel for my bath. The bathroom, at the back of the house, built with

sturdy concrete bricks, was partially encircled by clumps of
Hawaiian torch, the stalks almost as thick as tree trunks,
weaving into each other. When I returned to my room the
bed would be made and the dishes removed. I would sit
down and reread the articles Dulcie had brought down.
Most were more than twenty years old, and in the dusty
yellow paper with advertisements for Carib beer and
Bermudez biscuits, I read of Mr. Rampartap's wrestling
prowess and the fear that he inspired in his political rivals.
One story had him striding into an opponent's camp with a
revolver stuck in his belt. There was a gap of about fifteen
years before the articles resumed with his appearances at
meetings of the Kiwanis, the Lions and the Rotary clubs
and speeches at ceremonies opening bridges, access roads
and community centres. I suspected that during those fifteen years, power had been wrested from him.

Each night after dinner I saw him on the balcony talking
to Mr. Haggers. Once there were two other men, but in the
shadows I could not see their faces.

Forced into my room, and aware I was wasting time, I
improvised, from the articles, the beginning of the book:
"Mr. Rampartap, former wrestler and gunslinger, now spends
his time opening bridges, roads and community centres,
and in his leisure moments, attending meetings of the
Kiwanis, Lions and Rotary clubs." I recalled our first meeting and conceived another opening: "Mr. Rampartap swam
vigorously in the Caroni River every morning much like
Mao Tse-tung in the Yangtze River. As he later confided to
me, it was entirely possible that he had broken numerous
records, but at the time his only intention was to develop
his muscular upper body. And impressing his friends (who
jumped in and out after a few minutes)."

I was being unfair, but the routine I had fallen into bothered me. I wished the rain did not fall so often or that Madhoo was not constantly hovering outside as if he were waiting for me. Perhaps he just wanted to talk but I felt that he was steering me back into the house. He answered none of my questions, but he was full of his own. He asked about winter, the lakes, the Mafia, cowboys. Canada was indistinguishable from America to him. He thought that all writers were people with yellow teeth and hairy nostrils. He asked whether I had published any books and I told him that I didn't want to get yellow teeth and hairy nostrils. He laughed and said approvingly, "Nice one, uncle. Is the first joke I ever hear you make. What about the newspaper business that you say you in? The one that only like to print nice-nice thing." I told him that I was fed up with interviewing people from the West Indies and listening to how hard they had worked and how difficult it had been for them.

"It wasn't true then?"

No, it was all true, I told him, but people get tired of reading the same story time after time. He reflected on that. "You mean people does change so much when they go up in the cold? Over here, they beating they chest all the time and up that side they only low-rating theyself."

Laughing, I told him about the owner of a West Indian shop who had been furious when I inquired about the sanitary precautions for the meat products. The article could not be published because he had threatened to withdraw all advertising with the newspaper.

"So that leave you out in the cold." He cackled at his joke. "Friend with nobody." He asked about my wife's job. "You mean she does be digging up in people mouth whole day? That is not a nice thing for a woman to do." When he inquired about the school my daughter attended, I asked him whether there was a phone in the village and he said that ten years ago, a phone booth installed outside Lopez's bar had created a long line of customers who believed that it was a fancy urinal.

He liked making jokes and I never knew whether he was serious or not. He called me "uncle" even though, at thirty-six, I was just five years or so older than him. Later, I discovered he called almost everybody uncle.

One midday, I was writing a letter to Vanita when he popped into my room. "Hot off the press, eh?"

I didn't understand.

He whistled. "But you is a hellufa man, you know, uncle. You chook up in the room writing hands down all the time and you never tell nobody."

Not wanting him to pry, I did not correct him. He moved closer and I folded the letter. "So you does take notes and thing?"

I told him yes, without thinking, which was a big mistake, because he returned about half an hour later with a thick, shiny leaf. "Wonder of the world. For er-ic and *tay-tay* worm. Could grow for itself if you push it inside a book. Sprout out li'l root and branch right inside the book. Mark it down." He came again as I was about to go upstairs for dinner. In his hand were some black and red beads. "Jumbie bead. Best thing for keeping away jumbie. Good for cough too. Write it down." He gave me the beads. The next day he brought a lantana, a shrub with minute flowers good for dysentery, a cactus he called rachette, good for sores, and a tiny wriggling lizard, which he dropped on the bed. "*Zandolie.* Move faster than anything. Done someway below the pillow. Mark it down."

Later, I removed the sheets and pillows, but the zandolie had either scurried away or, more troublingly, was under the mattress. But there was a bright side to Madhoo's badgering. He was confused by the bareness of my room. Writers, he imagined, were surrounded by books, with paper strewn all around. I seized the opportunity and the next day, together with his specimens, he brought down an old radio and copies of *The Guardian* and *The Express*.

I could only use the radio at night when it was reasonably cool, because the fan was plugged into the single electrical outlet, but from Madhoo's gifts I was able to develop a routine. I read the newspaper for an hour or so, until he returned to take it upstairs. I'd wait for another hour or so, when I knew he would be out in the fruit field, at which point I'd head in the opposite direction, to the right of the house where the guava and cherry trees were shadowed by towering hog-plum, mora, samaan and savonette. There were rarely any workers there—unlike the citrus, the guava and cherries didn't seem to need constant attention—and the clumps of cockroach grass and paragrass and the vines braiding the branches made the area seem almost abandoned. But it was shadowy and beautiful. Most of the taller trees were covered with moss and lichens and giant bromeliads and because the leaves had been allowed to rot on the floor there were insects crawling all over: skinny spiders floating in their invisible webs, caterpillars waving at the edge of the leaves, and leaf cutters scurrying along the branches. On the floor there were rust-coloured armoured beetles, and stiff-looking lizards darting beneath the rotting vegetation. Once I saw a fearsome-looking black centipede and from then on I watched my steps carefully in case there were scorpions or tarantulas, or worse, coral snakes camouflaged in the compost.

After my aborted trip to the Guanapo forest, my mother had tried to instil in me a dread of snakes. For months she had frightened me with stories: of the mapapires hiding in the balisier, the tigros that could stiffen themselves upright and stare you in the face, the macajuels that could swallow you alive and the coral snakes, for whose poison there was no antidote. I was sure there were snakes hidden all through this field of putrefying fruits and rotting wood. The place itself smelled of decay, an odour that was sweet and damp and musty. There were small salmon-coloured mushrooms at the roots of the trees, and whenever I stooped to pick one, I wondered what Vanita would have made of it, how she might have sluiced these fairy umbrellas in her stories. But they were all poisonous. I dusted my fingers and a few minutes later, in preparation for lunch, washed my hands carefully by the garden tap at the side of the house.

The afternoons were more difficult. I read and reread all the clippings brought by Dulcie and sometimes tried to think of a beginning for the biography. I usually gave this up after a few minutes, blaming the heat and the humidity and the clanking of the old fan. Around five, I hurried upstairs for dinner, which I tried to prolong without being impolite. I ate slowly, waiting for Mr. Rampartap to say something that would miraculously provide a structure for his story. Once, when he had left for one of his regular discussions with Mr. Haggers, I asked his wife, "So how long have you been living in this estate?" She glanced at me in confusion, then swiftly left with the dishes. The next day I said, "It's really hot downstairs," and the following day, "I worry sometimes that a snake might crawl through one of the cracks." Not once did she offer a response, not even when, determined to provoke a reaction, I told her, "Mr. Rampartap and Madhoo remind me of Dr. Frankenstein and Igor."

The nights were the most enjoyable because I had discovered a two-hour radio program called "From Ecclesiastes to Elizabeth." This oddly named program had nothing to do with religion or royalty but was rather a call-in show, with a host who every few minutes would scream at the caller, "How much time I must tell allyou blasted ignorant people to turn down the radio when allyou calling me? How much time?" I was surprised that anyone bothered—or dared—to call, because he was driven to a frenzy by the slightest thing. Nevertheless, it was the funniest radio program I'd ever heard. Once he screamed at a woman who was complaining that the government was not providing enough assistance for her eight children, "Tell me, madam, was the government who was on top of you when you was opening you leg all over the place? Was the government who was pumping you for them eight children you spawn out? So how the ass you blaming the government now? Allyou people don't learn until it too late. If you had followed the precepts of the Gita or the Bible or the Koran ten years ago, instead of having eight little vagabonds running all over the place you would have had one or two educated little boys and girls quoting Byron for you. 'A lovely being, scarcely form'd or moulded. A rose with all its sweetest leaves yet unfolded.'" The woman thanked him profusely and departed, but he continued alternately berating her and quoting Shakespeare, Keats and Tennyson.

Most of his fury was vented at people complaining about the government, but he was equally enraged by the state's defenders. One night, a man called in to express his view that there was nothing wrong with the government favouring Indians because the last two regimes had granted the same privileges to blacks. "Listen, jackass," the host began ominously, "is people like you who causing all this confusion in Bosnia and Serbia and Africa and countless places around the world. Miserable cretinous people like you self. If I had the power I would march every single one of you to some erupting volcano and push allyou inside. And turn down that kissmeass radio, you donkey you." Another night, he called a man who was suggesting that there was nothing wrong with the aspiration of Tobago, the sister isle, to secede "a malodorous malkin," and I wished I'd brought my dictionary. Perhaps I had become too used to the tame, polite call-in programs in Canada, but I couldn't believe that he had not been hauled off the air or sued after his first broadcast.

Still, I looked forward to the two hours, and from this program and from the newspapers that Madhoo brought down every morning I glimpsed an island that was both familiar and strange. I learned about government employees falsifying documents and stealing teak from state lands, politicians shifting their allegiance to other parties because anticipated perks did not materialize, landslips cutting off coastal villages, others without water for months, government ministers promising imminent action while at the same time voicing suspicion that the villagers were manipulated into protest by opposition parties, businessmen taking unconventional actions to complain about erratic electricity, taxi drivers charged with assault, teachers and police with rape.

This was the Trinidad I remembered: where protest and excuses were rituals so meaningless that no one paid any attention to them, where sleaziness was a forgivable vice simply because it was so widespread, where comedy and tragedy could reside in the same story. The official charged with falsifying documents got off because he was a part-time preacher; the politician was quoted as saying, "I is me own boss. The people interest come fust. Fust and foremost." The teacher charged with rape was acquitted because he got the best common-entrance passes in the district; the businessman was advised by his psychiatrist to "haul his ass and jump fast" because he was a hopeless case and "was wasting everybody time."

But there was another island, unrecognizable and baffling. An island where there were references in the newspapers to Colombian cartels and the Russian mafia, where local drug barons routinely ordered hits on each other, where gruesome murders were committed every day, where the wealthy were barricaded behind steel gates and elaborate security systems, where the police were either accessories to the crimes or weighed down into ineffectiveness by the sheer number of offences committed.

There was, too, a kind of racial insecurity that I could not remember having existed before. The island had been governed for two decades by black-dominated parties, first by Henry Thaddeus Bodsworth, the mathematician-philosopher, who had been burdened with the sobriquet "Father of the Nation," and who had died one year after my arrival in Canada, replaced by Melvin Makitoe, booted out after one term in office, and then by Curtley "Cutlass" Cuthbert, so named because of his razor-sharp debating skills. But Cuthbert's eloquence was ineffectual against B.J. Jaggernath, the Indian leader, commonly referred to as "Baps" because of his resemblance to Gandhi. Baps, who smiled sagely at all of Cuthbert's accusations, managed to unify the Indians as a political force and, to everyone's surprise, won the general elections, though by the narrowest of margins.

But the files sent by our Trinidadian correspondent at *The Caribbean Crossroad* may have been misleading, because I now saw that the newspapers were stuffed with charges of bigotry against the government, which was endlessly scrutinized for racist policies. The composition of state-controlled companies and government boards, the disbursement of contracts, appointments and promotions in the public service were painstakingly examined for signs of racism. There were also lengthy debates reported in the newspapers about whether civilization really began in Mohendajaro or in the Sahara, and claims and counter-claims concerning the ethnicity of Moses, Buddha, Cleopatra, and more surprisingly, the first prime minister of the island. Tobago, by contrast, was held up as an almost sacred place. The word *purity* was invoked several times. I learned, surprisingly, that Tobago possessed a separate culture and dialect. As proof of its distinct nature, one letter-writer to the newspaper noted that Tobago was usually referred to as "Crusoe's Isle" in travel brochures. The writer then fashioned a tenuous history of Tobago featuring Robinson Crusoe, Man Friday and vicious cannibals. All of this could have been amusing, but I found the public airing of distress, the aggressive solicitation of sympathy, unnerving.

It was as if Trinidad were not one but two islands, existing side by side: one instantly recognizable, with its tarnished, presumptuous innocence, and the other a place sliding into hysteria and destruction. And in Tobago, the sister isle, the collision of history and romance had created an island that was part reality, part romance.

In the meantime, the host of the radio program recommended drawing and quartering, stretching on the rack

and death by volcanic eruption for those who were trying
to sully his paradise.

SEVEN

One evening there was a visitor who I assumed was important because Mr. Rampartap was at the table instead of in
his customary rocking chair or out on the balcony with Mr.
Haggers. The woman was absent. "This is the fella from
Canada I was telling you about," Mr. Rampartap said as I
went to the table. The visitor, a cadaverous man in his late
fifties dressed in a dark grey jacket, gazed at me with amusement. His lips twisted and I felt he was on the verge of saying
something gravely funny, but he had the look of a man who
enjoyed laughing at private jokes or saying witty things that
he alone could understand. "Mr. Pillooki is also a Canadian.
Or rather, an international man. But he was born here."

Mr. Pillooki buttered a piece of bread and snapped his
jaw over it.

I understood none of this. "Are you here for a visit?"
I asked.

He buttered another piece of bread. I noticed he was
still chewing the first bite.

"Are you here for a visit?" Mr. Rampartap repeated, provokingly.

Mr. Pillooki opened his mouth wide as if he were yawn-
ing, and swallowed. I saw the bread ruffling down his throat.
"It is a question to which I have often engaged my mind
during intervals of sobriety." Mr. Rampartap laughed.

I foresaw an uncomfortable dinner and decided to eat quickly and leave. "It all boils down to what your definition of a visitor is. Is it a person who visits other places or is it a state of the mind?" He fixed me with a horrible skeletal stare. I saw that his eyes were quite red. Then I smelled the alcohol. "We," he said, pointing to himself, "are the new nomads of the world. Swept from port to port, clutching the memories rushing past us like relics waiting to be restored. We are dispossessed of everything but our anxiety at being outcasts and our fear of being accepted. We are reckless and irresponsible. We pack our caravans with bricks torn from the houses we spent our lives building. But we are dreamers. Brick by brick we rebuild. We are the whores of the world. We are the future."

We are quite drunk, I thought. Or mad. Or both.

"Mr. Pillooki is a lawyer and politician," Mr. Rampartap said. "Known for his eloquence."

"Culled from one of my speeches," he confessed unabashedly. "The savages cheered wildly although they didn't understand a single thing." I decided then and there to hate him.

"Are you a practising politician?"

"It all boils down to what your definition of a practising politician is." I prepared myself for another of his rehashed political speeches, but then he said, "I confine myself to my legal practice these days. I prefer the company of thieves to that of scoundrels."

Mr. Rampartap guffawed appreciatively. "My sentiments exactly."

"There was a time when you could trust your wife, your children, your estate to a man of politics because they were creatures of honour. Beasts of a higher calling."

"That was then," Mr. Rampartap said.

Mr. Pillooki, with a very dramatic gesture, pointed straight at Mr. Rampartap. "Then was *that*." I was a bit unnerved but Mr. Rampartap was smiling. "That beast you see there is in danger of becoming extinct. And to be replaced by what, you may ask?"

He sat. I waited for an answer, but he pulled a carelessly folded sheet of paper from his jacket and waved it at me. "You are a writer, I understand. Have you written any novels?"

"No."

"Stories?"

"Not really."

"Essays? Critical treatises?"

"No but—"

"But you are a writer, *as I understand.*"

"I have written columns for a newspaper in Canada. *The Caribbean Crossroads.*"

"Ah, a columnist. Men with heads too big for their shrivelled bodies. Here"—he waved the paper dismissively—"they are nothing more than nuisances. Pests of the highest order. Idlers and troublemakers. Yet they have the temerity to call themselves writers."

"It all boils down to what your definition of a writer is," I said.

"Ah." He clacked his tongue. "Well said. I can see that you are a different breed altogether. Here, peruse this when you have the time." He gave me the paper.

I read the letter downstairs. It was typed hurriedly in a manual typewriter, with irregular margins and word spacing. "Those of us who are privileged to consider him a friend know that Mr. Rampartap is a man of unwavering dedication to the principles enunciated when he was yet a

fledgling lad growing up in Charlieville. These same principles were to surface time and again during the field into
which destiny hoisted him. As a politician he was feared,
admired, sometimes disliked, but always respected."

It sounded like a letter of reference and I suspected that
Mr. Rampartap had requested this testimonial. There was
nothing wrong with that: biographies are often littered with
well-meaning but fallacious characterizations by friends
and associates. Then I came to the final paragraph: "In less
than a month, I have formed what is, in my view, an accurate impression of Mr. Rampartap. If I were forced to sum-
marize this impression in one sentence, I would say this:
Mr. Rampartap is a man of honour among thieves."

At the bottom, my name had been pencilled in.

I should have been offended by this bit of presumptu-
ousness—did Mr. Rampartap really believe I would splice
this into the biography?—but Mr. Pillooki's testimonial
had laid to rest a bother. I had been puzzled both by Mr.
Rampartap's desire to have his biography written and by his
reluctance to provide the necessary information.

In Canada, the biographies I had read were polite,
bloodless and extremely boring, but my recollection of
those I had seen in Trinidad, usually self-published, suggested rich, idle men who wanted to impress their business
associates; they were really elaborate advertisements. Rarely
more than fifty pages, they were so badly written that they
were amusing to read. One of them—as it exists in my
memory—had this to say: "Jonah Thomas will swim seven
oceans, climb seven mountains, battle seven cannibals in
his quest for customer satisfaction." Jonah Thomas, it
turned out, was the local distributor for Seven Seas cod
liver oil. The biographies routinely sank a few weeks after

publication. (Although Jonah Thomas was rescued from oblivion about a year later by a magistrate, who with typical Trinidadian humour sentenced him to seven years for insurance fraud.)

I had assumed that Mr. Rampartap's motivation was similar to that of men like Thomas, but Mr. Pillooki's bogus testimonial revealed it was not simply the idle impulse of a wealthy, self-important, once-powerful man, but something I should have seen before: Mr. Rampartap wanted a book to rekindle his political career. His focus was on the future, not the past.

I had been annoyed by his carelessness about the book, thinking it was a reflection of his attitude towards me, an imported underling on the same scale as Madhoo, Ashton, Lopez and his estate workers. I had seen him recoil in petulance when his mockery, the theatrics in the bar, the contrived correspondence with the American writer had failed to seduce me into admiration; and he had concluded that I was silent not because I was intimidated but because I was detached. I was inaccessible. This, more than anything, jarred him.

He brought back Mr. Pillooki, he sent down letters he had received from aldermen, county councillors, teachers, preachers and journalists. One night after dinner he took me into a small room and opened a cabinet with glass doors that were milky with dust. He took out a book. I smelled the mildewed paper and the decaying jacket. "Albert Gomes. A former premier of Trinidad. A prolific poet and story writer." He replaced the book and removed another. "C.L.R. James. *Black Jacobins*. A study of the Haitian revolution." But he was reading from the back cover and I felt that these books had been received as gifts; that he knew nothing of them.

"Henry Thaddeus Bodsworth. *The Mathematics of Hunger.*
Destiny conspired with talent to make him the prime minister. You know of him. All of them"—he gestured with the
book—"are dead. Leaving just these." He tapped the book.
"The men who created this island. The only record of their
existence. I don't lend my books but you are free to look
at them."

There were books on politics and philosophy, dust-
covered copies of the Gita, the Bible and the Koran, and a
shelf of local biographies. *Perils and Power, Mission and
Motive, Truth and Tribulation*—they could all have been written by the same person, though there were different names
on the covers; perhaps one of these biographers had sparked
a trend. "Shallow men with shallow dreams. They boast of
their women and their cars and their mansions. Their
crookedness." He walked out of the room. "They think all
that nonsense will buy them respect." I felt he was telling
me that he was different, and in his uneasiness, his nervous
confidence, I glimpsed a man dwindling into desperation.

I couldn't understand it.

Nor could I understand his conversation the next
evening. I had just finished dinner when he opened his
newspaper and asked me to read an article I had scanned in
my room earlier in the day. The article was written by
someone named Alto Jackson and in the photograph at the
top he was open-mouthed and his eyes were slightly unfo-
cused as if he had run a great distance to the photographer's
studio.

"Take your time," Mr. Rampartap said. The woman,
chewing slowly, looked from him to me.

In the article, Alto Jackson was bemoaning the introduction of new criteria for admittance into the civil service,

which he believed would discriminate against "the little black boys from the hill, fatherless children who were too busy surviving to worry about school." He was also angry about a proposal by the state-owned water and electricity commissions to use academic qualifications rather than seniority as a basis for promotion. This "would undoubtedly discriminate against those who don't have the wherewithal to sign up for courses every two-three months." The affected ones, he pointed out, were once more the "hill people." And finally, he was incensed that the government had hired American and Canadian consultants who knew nothing about the culture of the hills.

Hill people. I was unfamiliar with the concept. But when Mr. Rampartap asked what I thought I told him that perhaps Mr. Jackson sincerely believed the hill people were getting a raw deal. The look on his face told me it was a stupid assessment.

"Culture of the hills! What they really interested in is corruption and slackness but they can't say that so they hide it in all this nonsense about race and discrimination. You know how people measure progress here? When they invent some new scheme to get money from the government. Like if is a God-given right." He was rocking evenly, his feet scraping the floor. "Day by day this place sinking in the gutter but they don't have time for that. The money run out but they still smelling the sweetness. *That* is the legacy of Bodsworth, Cuthbert, Makitoe and now Jaggernath."

The woman had stopped chewing and was staring at him. He got up from his rocking chair and clasped his hands behind him like Napoleon. "I was denied political success because I refused to be a part of this nonsense. Among thieves and scoundrels, I was a misfit." It was meant to be a dramatic moment, but I was caught by the woman's expression. Her eyes, bright and shining, seemed to be polished with malice and withheld knowledge. She had never spoken a word in my presence, and at that instant, I was more interested in what she was thinking than in Mr. Rampartap's grievances. She must have noticed my glance, because she tore into a duck's leg and her face went blank. I felt that her expression could reveal more about Mr. Rampartap than all his boasting, but when next I went up for dinner, she was absent from the table.

I grabbed the opportunity. "I have been reading some of the articles you sent down with Dulcie, but they are not enough."

"Are they that badly written?"

"They are, actually, but I meant they really don't tell me anything about—"

"I believe I already mentioned my youthful days. Not playing cricket or wasting time in the cinema but selling fish at the side of the road. Poor little boy rising to the top but pulled down by those who didn't like the idea of a humble man with any power."

"Well, maybe we could talk about that."

"I am a man of few words. I prefer to let my deeds speak for themself."

"It's going to be a very short biography then."

"But there are"—he waved his hand—"countless people willing to speak for me." I sensed the evasion but I was curious about what these unnamed people might have to say. "I will get Madhoo to bring over a few. To satisfy your curiosity."

"This curiosity is part of my job."

"Very well." He grinned. "Very well, Mr. Writer."

For the rest of the week Madhoo deposited a stream of old, ailing and sleepy-looking men who boasted of their families, their diseases and their livestock, but who after a few complimentary utterances revealed nothing substantial about Mr. Rampartap. One of them, Mr. Paul, a lanky man with long, wiry arms, spoke about the money he made diving for oysters thirty years ago when the Americans had a base in Chaguaramas. He had a lazy, rheumy eye and when I asked him about Mr. Rampartap, he revealed that they were classmates until Mr. Rampartap's parents took him out of school because they couldn't afford the expense. I tried to pump him for more information but he only blinked with one eyelid and said that turtle meat had almost cured his gout. He tapped his foot on the floor to demonstrate his recovery.

Another, Mr. Baldeo, well dressed but for his mismatched rubber sandals—one green, the other yellow—seemed intrigued by the idea that I was a writer. He assured me he was a budding poet and recited several nursery rhymes I had learned as a child. He closed his eyes. "Peter, Peter, pumpkin eater, had a wife and couldn't *feed* her. You understand what the poet really mean?" He opened his eyes. "Eating him out little by little. Cutting into the small savings he keeping for hard times." He fell into a sudden deep depression and I steered him out of the room. Just before he got into the car, he said, "But Mr. Ram not like that. He more like Jack. Nimble and quick and jumping over candlestick and thing."

Then finally, a fat black man with muddy nails and hairy forearms. He told me his name was Tookieram and that he sold sweetmeats, *kurma, ladoo, pamoose,* but business was bad nowadays because everyone wanted pizza and fried chicken. "Takeout!" He spat on the ground close to my feet and I drew back my chair. "With all the hormoons in it. Hormoons what they does feed the cattle and the fowls with. I hope nobody start blaming Tookieram when all these little boys start getting nipply and big-big breasts from the hormoons. Tot-tots." He screwed his lips and I thought he was going to spit once more but he said, "People like Rambo . . . that is how I does call Ram . . . people like him going outta style now. Anytime he say he going to do something don't doubt him 'cause by the hook or the crook he go do it."

I was growing frustrated with these old men and their grievances so I asked him, "What do you mean by the hook or crook?"

"Is just a expression. It mean to find a way somehow. A real Rambo. Not like these nipply boys nowadays with they big tot-tots."

"How long ago did you know him?"

"'Bout thirty years now. Give or take ten."

"But that could be either twenty or forty."

He tugged at the hair on his forearm. "Yes, yes. Around that."

I tried another line. "How were you two acquainted?"

"Yes, very. Very well acquainted."

I felt like pushing him off his chair onto his gob of spit. "I understand he had a few enemies who didn't like the idea of a poor man getting too much power."

"Yes, very and you know why? His diet."

"Whose?"

"Rambo. Good old-fashioned food. Cassava, yam, dasheen, eddoes, tannia . . ." He went on for a few minutes. I got up. "I hope I was helpful," he said.

"Yes, very."

At the end of the week, when Mr. Rampartap asked whether the information had been useful, I told him that the men were more interested in speaking of themselves.

He looked at me sternly. "These are simple people, you know. Not educated or eloquent like you."

"That's not the issue—"

"But they are honest, God-fearing people."

"Maybe I should speak with more up-to-date individuals. Like Mr. Pillooki or Mr. Haggers."

"They are both busy men. But I will see what can be arranged," he said, not convincingly.

Mr. Rampartap made one last attempt. Madhoo came into my room with what looked like a cream-coloured gauze rope. He told me it was the skin shed by the *macajuel,* a constrictor-like snake. He explained in detail the sloughing and revealed that every morning he saw a couple of discarded skins in the citrus trees. He made it sound as though there were hundreds of snakes hiding and crawling around and in the night jettisoning their skins. Then he said, "You have to suck plenty orange before you get the real taste of the tree." I thought he was still talking of snakes but he added, "Everybody have they own feeling about this and that. Is only when you talk to plenty people you will get the real flavour."

"Of what?"

He threw up a bunch of keys, caught it and tossed it from hand to hand. "I feel we should make a little spin in the village."

He drove recklessly, glancing at me and puffing smoke in my direction as he negotiated the dangerous turns and bends. I worried about whether he was using his bad foot for the brake or the accelerator.

The first time in the village, when I was driving with Madhoo, the trees and bushes had looked gloomy and deserted to me. Now I saw the order I had missed: the furrows between the trees; the drains that separated the different types of fruits; the clumps of bamboo on the slopes holding the land together; the retaining walls covered with weeds; the small tidy houses on the hills; the vines on the wooden fences streaked with fruits. Madhoo noticed my appreciation. "Not too bad, eh? This must be the onliest estate in the whole of Trinidad what don't have any thiefing."

"Why is that?"

He removed his hand from the steering wheel and shaped his fingers like a revolver. "Tock tock bam boodoops and somebody land on the ground."

"Mr. Rampartap?"

"Who else, uncle?"

"Has he ever shot anyone?"

"Not recently. You just have to pick off two-three"—he squinted an eye like a cowboy taking aim—"and the rest does get the message. That is the way you have to operate over here otherwise is real *bacchanal*. When people realize that you don't put up with no nonsense they does keep they stupidness to theyself. Look! You make out the place." He pointed to Lopez's broken-down bar.

As we entered the bar, I got a whiff of the antiseptic rising from the floor. Then the tobacco and the faint odour of old molasses. Five or six men, cigarettes dangling from their lips, stared from their tables. "A beer for me and a sweet-drink for uncle here." Madhoo spoke to no one in particular but a shadow stirred from the gloom and walked lazily to the counter. Lopez brought two bottles and returned to his table. There were casks of rum with faded labels and greenish bottles of wine on the shelves behind the counter. I smelled the dust falling from the cobwebbed rafter. My throat tickled. Madhoo shook his bottle and sipped at the foam. He was quiet for once. A chair scraped the floor at the far end of the bar and a tall black man walked towards us. "Everything under control?" It was Ashton.

"As usual, uncle. I think you meet the writer fella already."

"I notice him the other day with you and Mr. Ram." He placed his hands on the back of a chair and leaned towards us. "The problem straighten out now, thanks to Mr. Ram." His fingers tapped the wooden bar. "But he is a man like that." He spoke softly and I felt he was apologizing for his stunt with Lopez. He tapped the bar again, turned and disappeared in the darkness.

Less than a minute later, another chair scraped the floor and a stumpy man with boots to his thigh lumbered towards us. His boots sloshed with every step and as he came closer, I saw his tongue, thick and limp, resting on his lip. "Mis-saram hissagooman." I could not understand the rest of the sentence. His tongue settled back on his lip and he sloshed away to his table. At another table, a gaunt figure shifted, preparing his benediction. Behind me a sliver of light from a crack on the wall sliced through the darkness and I saw that the bar was thick with smoke and dust. I smelled the molasses, old and stale, once more. I told Madhoo, "I think we should leave."

I expected some resistance but he got up. "We have to leave now. The writer fella want to get back to he book. Finish ten-twelve chapter already." The men stared at us.

At the door he said, "Put it on the bill, uncle. Mr. Ram go straighten it out."

On the way back, he decelerated by a small house on a hill where a woman was hanging out clothes on a line strung between two trees. I remembered her staring at the car on our previous trip to Lopez's bar and I asked him, "Do you know her?"

He laughed roguishly. "Nothing could hide from allyou writers, eh. Allyou like real *corbeau*."

"So do you know her?"

Wagging his head, he said, "Know she? I think so. Outside craft."

"Whose?"

"The bossman. Nothing serious. Just target practice, is all."

The revelation was surprising. He was normally evasive, but I felt that he saw the boast as part of his mission to impress me.

"The woman upstairs. Is she his wife?"

"You could say that."

"She never talks."

"Some people like that."

"It's very strange."

"Mebbe she is a strange woman. Or mebbe she have nothing to say. Some people like that."

I wanted to ask him other questions but he suddenly jerked the car to the left and I was flung against the door, my head hitting the window. He opened the door, dashed out and wormed beneath the car. He emerged holding a small rodent by its long tail. The head was flattened by the tire and blood was dripping from its open mouth. "Manicou." He swung it by the tail and pitched it in the car, beneath a seat. "That is the law of this estate. Anything that not useful we does eat." He saw my shocked expression, threw back his head and cackled happily. "Is the sweetest meat on the face of this earth." He said *oath*. "You know why? 'Cause is a scaravenger. Nothing on this oath does taste better than a scaravenger. Mark that down."

"So who was the outside craft?" I asked him.

He pinched a strand of hair, clicked his nails and dusted his fingers. "That was a long-long time now, Mr. Writer. You talking about years aback now. When the bossman was young and he had plenty fire in he belly. He was a man and a half, you know. Walk half a mile with a hundred-pound bag of cocoa on he two shoulder." He removed his hands from the steering wheel and made a clasping gesture. "Muscles big like this. A real Dara Singh. Nobody was to interfere with him in them days."

"Otherwise?"

"Otherwise is fire in the *couteyah*." He cackled. "What about you?"

"What about me?"

"A man like you. Living up in that cold-cold place with all them blues movies people."

"That's America."

"Canada, America. Same difference. So you never had no outside thing? No deputy?"

I laughed. "No."

"You lie!"

"What?"

"You damn lie." He collapsed with a mischievous glee, banging his head against the steering wheel.

"Careful with the road."

But he paid me no attention. "Don't hand me that. Don't hand me that *at all*. Allyou quiet people too sly." He glanced at me, struggling with laughter. "So what was she name?"

"Watch the road, please."

"Oh God, oh God, oh God, *oy*."

Anastasia, beautiful and ravenous, bringing out her child from the bedroom, introducing me to her mother at school, unable to understand why I was avoiding her. I was so wrapped in this memory that I didn't notice, at first, the roguish glint in Madhoo's eyes.

"One of these day, when you have time, uncle, you must tell me what you was just thinking about."

"When you tell me about the woman upstairs."

My quick response surprised him. "What you want to know?"

"I haven't seen her for the last few days."

"She have a little problem. They does have to hide she away sometimes."

"What problem? Hide away where?"

"The full moon does have a bad effect on she. Sometime she does get real-real quiet like the statue outside, not saying nothing and sometimes she does go crazy, pulling out she hair and thing. *Bazoodee*."

I was astonished. "It sounds as if she needs help."

"Mad blood. It does come and go."

"Did a doctor—?"

"Mad blood," he repeated firmly. "When it pass she good as new."

"Where is she hidden away?"

He hesitated for a moment, then he said, "This is just between me and you." He lowered his voice to a whisper. "In the house by the cemetree."

"Is that why you told me about spirits there? To prevent me from going?"

He put on an offended expression. "No, not at all, uncle. The part about spirit is true. But one thing about them jumbie is that they never ever interfere with crazy people. Spirit and mad people like first cousin. So she safe they."

"How long have they been married?"

"I can't help you they. All I know is that it was a long time ago."

"Was she always like this?"

"Not in the beginning, from what I hear. According to the talk, she was first-class in the looks department."

"She must have had a hard life. I wonder what happened to her. Could you take me there?"

His mouth opened, his straggly beard scattering across his chin. "By the cemetree? Like you and all gone crazy."

"Just for a minute."

He slowed the car and in a worried voice said, "Listen, you better forget this whole thing. Forget all that I tell you. Forget this crazy woman. Is for you own good. People down here don't like anybody digging up in they business." He laughed suddenly, as if to alleviate the threat. "Trouble make monkey eat pepper."

EIGHT

At first, I had objected to Mr. Rampartap's characterization of Rougeleau as a little fortress in a clamorous island because I assumed he was taking the credit for it, but I soon began to understand its haphazard order. In the evening, he narrated stories of the corruption and indolence that had gripped the island, and as proof he invited me to read selected articles and columns from the newspapers. While I read, he bragged about his estate and revealed he had "eliminated" all the troublemakers and slackers. It had not been easy: there were detractors who spread rumours and enemies just waiting for him to fail. He had been stigmatized as a tyrant, a despot, a racist and a capitalist. "Capitalist! These people hear a word, the word sounding nice and suddenly they using it in every sentence. Like little children learning a nursery rhyme."

He spoke in the manner of an old principal, grave, authoritative and rambling, not inviting questions and ignoring those that arose. Sometimes I felt that he was no longer interested in his biography and that he really wanted an attentive and respectful audience. At other times, I thought that he was revealing himself bit by bit, sloughing off the layers like Madhoo's snakes. I regarded this as another trap—this waiting, this suspense. A few times I was on the verge of asking him about his wife but then I remembered Madhoo's warning.

One night there was a slight drizzle. Mr. Rampartap was in the gallery with Pillooki. I had just eaten and was about to go downstairs. As I passed, Mr. Rampartap asked, "You know what is the main difference between places like your civilized Canada and islands like this?"

I thought: We treat clinically depressed people differently, but I told him, "The climate." I was in no mood for conversation with the two men.

He remained serious. "Power. The way people get it, the way they use it and the way they lose it. Over here, they get frighten of a man with too much ambition and they start tearing him down whenever they get a chance. These uni-

versity people like to say that is because of the white man.
The massa. They like to say that we still suffering from the
barrack mentality and that is why we avoid work and mistrust people in authority. That is what they *like* to say."

"The past that redeem can also return to haunt you,"
Pillooki intoned gravely.

The drizzle had thickened, and in the distance thunder
rumbled. "More than a hundred years after all that finish.
You walk through the length and breadth of Trinidad and
see if you could find any slave or bound coolie." Mr. Rampartap thrust out his hand in the rain, turning his palms
like a dancer. "But visit a government office and watch how
the public servants operate. Walk through the streets in
Port of Spain and notice all the material wasting at the side
of the road. Stop and chat with one o' two people and hear
how the government evil and selfish because it refuse to
support they fourteen children scatter all across the island.
And the government, these leaders we have now, fall for
that every time because the biggest fear they have, the worst
shame, is being compared to a massa. Not inefficiency or
corruption, eh. All that is passable."

Mr. Rampartap stroked his wet forearm, smoothing
down the hairs, tensing the muscle. "And the handouts continue, the reparations, the little bribes. That is why people
here glorify in they weakness, because it point to a kind of
equality. If you move away from this weakness, is not a sign
of ambition or determination but a betrayal. You become a
traitor. Bound to people who dead and gone so long now.
Ghosts. That is all they interested in. Little children superstition. They see it everywhere. In the shape of a building,
the design on some government minister tie, the floral
arrangement in a office. Things like that get them frighten

and worried and excited. And because they afraid they get respectful. You know why? Because that government minister who wearing that tie might look stupid but he powerful in another way."

"Obeah. Obeah and politics. A dangerous blend." The darkness emphasized Pillooki's gauntness, the boniness of his face, the hollow eye sockets.

"So after all these years nothing really change. Nothing." Mr. Rampartap was not looking at me but staring in the distance, at the rain swallowed up by the night, distinguishable only by the breeze plunging through the trees and water battering the roof.

I thought of his wife, alone in the storm. Was there someone staying with her or was she locked away like an animal? And listening to Mr. Rampartap boast about his politics, watching his face contorted by the flashes of lightning, I thought: The purest form of corruption is instinctive; it is not hampered by calculation and consequence but enacted without forethought, without apology. This notion of Mr. Rampartap as being corrupt jolted me. There was a quality to him that usually made me uneasy, but I had attributed that to his hypocrisy and his casual arrogance. He laughed and said, "Force-ripe children. Playing man, but bawling when they don't get food."

The statement angered me. "Maybe they believe they deserve something better."

At that moment, the trees, the gate, the water pouring from the shingled roof were frozen by a bolt of lightning. "Good, better, best. They don't apply here. It all boil down to your purpose in life." I could not understand Pillooki's acquiescence to Mr. Rampartap. In spite of my early assessment of him as a man wrecked by alcohol, he was obviously well educated. Was there some mockery involved or did Mr. Rampartap have some special hold on him? Or was it the other way around?

"Production, tolerance and discipline. The national creed. You hear it over and over like children reciting a nursery rhyme. A chant with special powers that will protect them. Another superstition." Lightning flashed again and Mr. Rampartap's eyes gleamed. "The only thing some of these people missing is tails."

I was sure that the Trinidad of my memory could not have been so completely swept away, but I also knew— from the panic and the skittish outrage of local journalists and the silly racial wrangling—that his version of the island was not an invention. In the harshness of his criticisms, the bitterness, I saw disappointment, not with the condition of Trinidad but with his own failures. I suspected he had been treated badly or betrayed by someone he trusted.

So Rougeleau became another kind of trap; not the decadent prison I had imagined but a jail where I was daily fed doses of disillusionment and anger. I tried to hurry my dinner, made excuses to escape his speeches, hastened downstairs. The rain fell every day, sometimes in a persistent drizzle, sometimes in a raging downpour with sheets of water pounding the galvanized roof and exploding on the concrete landing. I was no longer able to go on my midmorning walks. I felt caged and cranky. When the thunderstorms eased, the sun came out and the heat and humidity were unrelenting. The heat also brought sand flies, mosquitoes and swarms of winged ants.

The old fan jumped all over the room, restrained only by its electrical cord. I wrote letters to Vanita. I told her of the storms but not the insects; I described the old estate house, the fruit trees, the little houses on the hills ("Like gingerbread houses") and I mentioned Madhoo, who delivered strange animals to my room.

When Madhoo came around midday to take the newspapers upstairs, I gave him the letters to post. He brought a cardboard box to put his shells, skins, bones, roots and berries. When the box was full, he brought another. Once, I asked him, "When will Mr. Rampartap's wife return?"

"Any time now."

"Who takes her food and stuff?"

"Dulcie mostly. Sometimes me, sometimes Mr. Ram."

"Mr. Rampartap?" I was surprised. "I wonder what they do, both of them alone in that old house?"

"Uncle!" He chuckled. "I think maybe they get too old for that."

"No, no. I mean what they talk about. Just the two of them there." I wanted to know more. "Describe the house for me."

"Is not too bad a place when you think of it." He scratched his head. "I believe it was build by the white fella who own the estate before. A kinda cottage set-up for when he wanted a break. Lemme see. It have a bed, a cot, a library with some old book and a generator for the lights and the fridge."

"So is she locked up there? From the outside?"

"Listen, uncle, she does just be taking a li'l break they. Just like the old white people and them." He changed the topic. "Make sure you don't throw away that box, eh. Carry it up to Canada and if anybody ask, tell them a half-crack fella name Madhoo give it to you."

One evening around six-thirty, I was on my bed observing a bloated lizard chasing a scrawnier version and wondering whether it was a blossoming courtship or a predatory ritual, when they both disappeared between two boards in the wall. I would have thought the crack too tiny for the larger lizard to wriggle through. How did it manage? Perhaps it was stuck. I stood up on the bed and peeped through the crack. The lizards were gone but I was overwhelmed by the violent beauty of the flowers scattered within the stalks of the Hawaiian crown in the backyard. The crown-shaped flowers, big as a closed fist, were normally pink but the setting sun had transformed them into a deep red, as if they were rinsed in blood. I decided I would pick some for my room the next morning. They would at least remove some of the drabness. As I was about to step away, I saw someone coming out of the bathroom at the back of the house. It was Dulcie. Her skin was wet and glistening and droplets of water, tinged in red, trickled down her body. She began wiping herself slowly, gracefully, almost languorously. She was symmetrical rather than curvaceous but her breasts were full and when she bent her head to towel her hair, they bounced up and down.

I should have felt guilty, like a peeping Tom, but she looked so much a part of her surroundings, towelling herself, gazing at the flowers, that I stretched to get a better view. I had never seen anything like it: this woman, surrounded by flowers drenched in crimson, taking her time, staring around, as if she belonged there.

Intruder! The word turned in my mind but before I could step away, she raised her head and looked straight at the crack. I was alarmed. But it was too small, she could not possibly have seen me peering from inside. Nevertheless, I stepped back hurriedly, almost falling on the bed. A few minutes later, I heard a dull scraping upstairs, the sound a chair makes when it is dragged across a floor.

She had already left when I went for dinner. The next morning when she brought my breakfast, I pretended I was gazing through the window. "What you looking at?" she asked.

"At the cashew tree." I didn't want to face her.

"You could see it from here?"

"Yes. I have a good view actually."

She said, "Oh," and I was sure she knew.

"But it's always raining so I keep the window shut most of the time."

"That will make the room hot and sticky." She came by the window and looked out. "What you does do whole day?"

You mean recently? Just peeping, nothing else. I felt she was reading my mind. "I read the papers. I write letters."

"To Canada?"

"Yes."

She leaned forward, her hands on the sill. "It must be a nice place."

"It is. For some people."

Now she leaned further out, bending over until her chin was resting on her knuckles. And standing like that, she turned slightly and looked up at me. "You don't talk plenty." She smiled to show no rudeness was intended. "I never see you laughing or anything."

I didn't know how to reply to that but I told her, "It's a habit I developed."

"In Canada?" She looked away and added as a clarification, "People not like that over here."

After a while, I told her, "I wasn't always like that."

The statement emboldened her. "You always look so worried and frowning all the time. You didn't have any friends in Canada?"

"I used to. A long time ago."

"And what happen?"

"We drifted apart."

"You don't have any"—she hesitated—"any special friend?"

"A wife?"

After she got the job with the dentist, I was happy for her, and relieved. I knew she was frustrated staying at home and being dependent on me. When Vanita started school, she had nothing to do and was irritated by the slightest thing. If, before I left for work, I paid her a compliment, she remarked that she was forced to be feminine, or if, while watching television, I whispered something tender, she stiffened and said that I was mistaken if I believed she was soft. For a while, she used that word all the time and I grew more cautious with my compliments.

I knew the job would release her from what she considered a life of drudgery. I awaited the results. On the dentist's office there was a sign: C. Foote. I pretended his name was Crab Foot because he was thin and spidery-looking.

During her third week at work, I asked her jokingly, "Does Mr. Crab Foot have any children patients?"

I was thinking of little boys and girls taking one look at this spidery man who was going to interfere with their mouths and screaming in terror.

"How dare you? His name is Clyde. Dr. Clyde Foote."

"Clyde, Crab. What's the difference? Just one letter? And he looks like a crab to me."

"He looks the way he is supposed to. Like a dentist."

I had never thought of dentists having a special look. "All of them? Like crabs?"

"If you have nothing good to say about other people, it

is better if you say nothing." For a while, that became her favourite maxim. As our marriage deteriorated, she uncovered others and her personality shifted accordingly. If I wrote a book about our marriage, I could title each chapter with one of her maxims: Dogs that accustomed sucking eggs never stop. Empty vessels make the most noise. Animals never see their own tails. Still minds are filled with mischief. Primitive people always look backwards.

Primitive. A word used over and over. A casual visitor to our apartment on Ellesmere, glimpsing my paleness and her darkness, would have been confused by her condemnation of the dusky races and at the defences into which I was pushed.

In the end, I pretended it no longer bothered me.

Dulcie was respectful of my silence. Bent over the sill, her chin on the crook of her arm, her face turned slightly, looking up at me, her eyes tinged with a quiet curiosity, her lips crinkled at one side as if in contemplation, I noticed what I had missed before: a dissimilarity between us not only of blood and history but in a way of thinking I could never understand. I saw in her face the trickle of several races blending and merging, and in that moment of separation I felt closer to her than any time before.

"I have a daughter in Canada. Seven years old."

"Oh." After a while, she said, "You going to carry all that for she?" She motioned to Madhoo's box.

"Not everything."

She peered into the box. "It wouldn't make she frighten? The snake skin and the dead insects?"

"She used to collect dead beetles whenever we went for a walk. Once she found a dead bird."

"What she use to do with them?"

"Bury them. In little graves decorated with flowers. She thought that all the beetles and the bird were babies and that their mothers and fathers would not want them just lying on the ground."

"That sound so sad. Is she . . ." She did not complete the question. I glanced at her face.

"Yes. I think she's lonely but I'm not sure. Maybe she isn't, maybe it's just me." She was about to say something, when I added, "I believe the most cruel thing you can do to a child is to steal her innocence. I don't want her to become a stranger like me . . . a stranger to everyone." Talking about Vanita choked me with despair. "I shouldn't have left her in Canada. I really wanted to . . ."

I felt Dulcie's fingers on my shoulder. "Is okay."

"I don't want her to think I am abandoning her."

"But you going to return. And she *know* that." The simple advice, so unexpected, filled me with gratitude. Then she said, "Abandoning is when your father don't want to—" she hesitated—"acknowledge you. But sometimes children stronger than you think."

Afterwards, I was less concerned that someone in the field could have seen us through the open window, could have misunderstood the ensuing embrace, than I was with violating her privacy the previous evening.

NINE

I went to bed thinking of Vanita, of Dulcie, of Mr. Rampartap's caustic opinions of the island, of his wife locked away. But I dreamed of Vanita, tucked in her bed, listening to my stories. In the middle of the dream, I was awakened by angry, shouting voices, muffled by the breeze but distinct from the metallic chirping of the insects. I opened the window, and beyond the cashew tree, I saw a light jumping and dancing. I stepped into my shoes and went out of the house, half expecting to see Madhoo lurking around. I walked along the drain to the front and then to the other side.

Someone said, "Be careful. She kicking."

At the base of the cashew tree, the broad leaves of the anthuriums nudged each other like the wings of a giant bat. I smelled the rotting coconut used as manure for the anthuriums and I remembered stories of soucouyants and douens lurking in the shadow of the plants, waiting.

The grass was dew-covered and slippery so I moved carefully, feeling my way with one foot, then the other. Someone was clutching a flambeau unsteadily, and the light shimmered in eddying circles that left a flourish of sparks scattering to the ground like plummeting candle flies. Faces, exaggerated into masks by the flickering light, appeared and vanished in a second. It was impossible to tell how many men there were. Some distance away, water gurgled in a ravine.

I moved closer.

The flambeau arched and fluttered in the blackness. I now saw upraised hands and men striking or tugging at something.

"Throw she on the ground."

"She kicking."

"Hold she other side."

A soft cry, almost tender, of pain.

An object brushed my shoulder and I yelped. The dark shape of a fruit bat flitted into the branches of the cashew tree.

"Who is that?"

"Show me the light."

The flambeau was held aloft. "Take you blade, Sankie."

"Shine the light for me."

"Joe, you circle on the other side. Don't let him get away."

Someone cursed.

I was frightened and excited. The house was less than fifty yards away. I could make it. The bush to my right rustled. Sankie uttered a murderous threat.

"Wait, wait. Is the writer fella."

"Who?"

"The writer fella that Mr. Ram emport." I recognized Madhoo's voice. "Show him the light."

Sankie was at my side. Another man stepped out of the bush. I had no idea they were so close. "Watch you step," Sankie said. "The ground slippery."

"But you is a hellufa man, uncle. You nearly give all of we a hat attack."

And another voice, more urgent. "Bring the light. It coming out."

"Pull. Pull harder."

"The light."

"Oh, God. It dead!"

"Make sure. Check it again."

"It not moving."

"Is what I did expect. The mother was too weak."

I saw the dead calf lying on its side. The mother, her neck stretched, was panting in strangulated gasps. "The mother was sick for the whole day," Madhoo said. "She too go dead before the morning clear. It look like she swallow a grapefruit."

"Could be poison."

"Grapefruit. I see this before."

"We should bury the baby one time. In the gutter." They grasped the calf by its legs.

"It don't make sense you too come, uncle. You go just get nasty up in the mud. You done have chapter twelve in the bag. Make sure you mark down everything."

"Get a spade from the shed. Sankie, you stay by the mother. Bawl out if she dead and we go dig a bigger hole."

Sitting on the bed, I looked at my muddy shoes, the laces not even tied, and considered this act of madness from a man who on any given day could chart out all that would follow in the next twenty-four hours. I had been frightened, but the fear had receded into a sharp, throbbing excitement. I remembered how when I was nine years old, on a dare from a schoolmate, Sam, I had unhitched a neighbour's gate, crept through a garden of dasheen and cassava, climbed onto the lowest branch of a hog-mango tree and released a *pawi* from its cage. The pawi was a wild bird found in the Guanapo forest. Every evening, on my way from school, I would pass the bird, its plumage dulled, fluttering around the overturned food bowl.

The next day at school, Sam gave me two *kay-kays*, the rainbow-coloured marbles that we cherished. In the afternoon, some of the other boys couldn't believe I had freed the bird, because it was widely known that the owner was an ill-tempered man who regularly threatened his wife and eight children with his double-barrelled shotgun. For days the class buzzed with crazy variations of this reckless act; for a while I was a hero but the truth was that I had been almost paralysed by the image of the neighbour training his gun on me, cocking the trigger and blowing a saucer-sized hole through my head or chest. Then something totally unexpected had happened. I felt as though someone else was carrying out this stupid act; another boy climbing the tree, loosening the wire, lowering the cage to the ground, jumping and landing on all fours, untangling the twine that fastened the latch. The same boy who had set out for the Guanapo forest. A thin, pale boy with long, straight hair falling over eyes that always betrayed his feelings. He was familiar, I knew him; but he was not me.

The next morning, I heard three loud knocks on the window. I thought it was Madhoo but when I opened the window, I saw Mr. Rampartap with a felt hat pulled low over his forehead. "Ten o'clock and you still sleeping, Mr. Writer. In this estate, we accustom getting up as soon as the first cock crow, eh. You ever hear the old saying that if the sun catch you in bed then you whole day spoil?"

"I went to bed a bit late."

"Yes, yes. I hear about. The workers tell me." His lips curved in amusement and I saw that he was talking to me in the old manner. "You was real lucky, you know. Is a good thing Madhoo recognized you. Over here we don't like the idea of strangers walking about in the night and sneaking around." He smiled sternly. "This is not your safe Canada, eh. We play by different rules." He was enjoying himself.

"Thanks, but I remember."

"You don't remember nothing. Come with me."

He walked with heavy plodding footsteps that left deep imprints in the mud. "You see these anthurium plants under that tree? I import them from Holland. They don't flower very often but watch the shape and the colour. Like a heart. Some say is the most beautiful flower in the world." He snipped off a flower by its stalk. "In the back across there, I have my ginger lilies and heliconia. Every variety of heliconia you could think of. Sassy. Golden torch. Nickerensis. Andromeda. Rostrata. Lady Di."

It was beautiful: a sea of colour in this gloomy plantation, the flowers nodding and waving and swaying. It reminded me of the colourful Carnival bands I had seen as a boy. "Walk down this slope with me." He supported himself by clutching the hardened stalk of the ginger lilies. "I had boulders placed on the track but every time the rain fall, it get covered over. This island changing every day." He turned around to see my reaction to his joke. I smiled. "You notice the local balisier I plant between the other heliconia? Is the same species, you know, but nobody paying attention to them because they growing wild all over the place. Let's go through that track." He pushed away the elongated, veined leaves webbing the path and pointed to a small plant with stalks and leaves that were thinner and wispier than the others. The flowers, smaller too than the local balisier towering above, were yellow-gold with red splashes and with orange-tipped florets curving from the bracts. "The issue of the union. It not fully grown yet." He traced a finger along a bract and collected a film of powder. "Some people say that the hybrids more resilient than either parent. You married?"

"Yes."

"Cross-pollination?" He saw the puzzlement on my face and laughed. "Mention that to a Indian from Felicity and he will take off your hand. Over here they calling it *douglar-ization*. Mixing up the races. The talk was that this was Bodsworth secret project. You ever experience any racism in Canada?"

"Only in an apartment in Ellesmere."

"Ellesmere? That is a Spanish horse?" He waited for my laughter, but I turned away. "You know, from my experi-ence these hybrids develop diseases faster than the original stock. They look nice and pretty but they lose something."

This was an intriguing statement, coming from Mr. Rampartap. "You mean like purity?"

"Purity is one of these words that have no meaning. One man purity is another man poison. But I am an old-fashioned man as you see. Old-fashioned values, old-fashioned thinking."

"An eye for an eye." I laughed to lessen the offence he might have taken.

"No, I don't agree with that. Is a stupid way to deal with a problem because you will both end up with one eye in the end. Two eyes." It took me a while to catch his meaning. "Before you say that is . . . what is the word . . . barbaric, consider this: that fella wouldn't be bothering anybody again because you put him out of commission. But you are a modern man. Educated in Canada. Refined. You don't know about these things."

"I grew up here, you know."

"Look over here. The workers swear you could call snake with this." He reached up to one of the pendulous flowers from the local balisier and broke off a bract. "Listen to the sound it make when you open and close it." He moved his hands as if he were playing an accordion but the sound that emerged was wet, shrill and sucking. "Maybe they believe this because the balisier is a common place for snakes. *Zanana mapapire.* They like to coil up and hide between these big leaves and before you know what happening, zap." He flicked his hand at me so swiftly that I jumped back, startled. His laughter bellowed through the field. "What happen, Mr. Writer? Canada make you soft or what?" He tweaked the skin on my wrist and I pulled away my hand. He howled with amusement. "Like pap. Soft-soft flour pap. Okay—" He stopped to catch his breath. "Let's cut across to the other side."

As we walked through a freshly dug field with drains and furrows prepared for the flowers, he spoke about the racism that was gripping the country, implying that not only was he above all that but that he was somehow the solution. I found his boorish derision tiresome. He said, "The world is divided into two groups." I thought he was going to say good and evil or rich and poor or smart and stupid. "Between those who are prepared to sacrifice everything for progress and those who are prepared to stop it at all cost." His face was set in a smile, the look of an honest man, the eyes suggesting sincerity and age. Then a sliver of seriousness intruded and was gone. But it had left its trail and I saw the deceit uncovered. I remembered his wife locked away in some old house and felt a sudden contempt for him.

"Is that why you want this biography?"

"You think is because I want to get back in politics, not so?" There was a forced mirth to his voice. "But is more than that. Much more." He stopped suddenly and turned to me. "This government need a sacrificial lamb."

Because he was blocking my path, I felt I should ask him, "And they chose you?"

"Let me give you a lesson in politics, Trinidad style. A few years ago, when you was in safe Canada, drinking maple syrup or whatever people there drink, a new government come to power in Trinidad. The natural question that come into your mind is, So what so strange about that? Well, the difference was that in the twenty-odd years of self-government, this was the first time that an Indian party or a party presided over by an Indian win the election and everybody who wanted to get in the news start predicting that was trouble in the *calaboose*. Forty percent Indian and forty percent black. A nice civil war in the making. Both sides even. But the transition was so smooth that these same people start talking about Trinidadian tolerance and all that nonsense. They get lull into a false sense of security as the educated people say. But I know my people and I could see what was happening underneath. This thing swelling below the ground had to be controlled. I decide to volunteer my service to the new government. Speaker of the House. President of the Senate. Even ombudsman. But they had no time for me because they was too busy celebrating. And dismantling. Senior civil servants fired. Permanent secretaries removed. Boards reorganized. The thinking was that these millstones had to go because they was hired by the previous government and still owed an allegiance to them, but when people start to watch carefully they notice that all the faces was black. And what was underground, all the suspicion, come out on top. Letters to the editor. Articles in the papers. You read all of them. The pot come to a boil."

He laughed, flashing his teeth, but the mirth was gone. "This new government realize finally that race is something that living in this country. Breathing and multiplying. Like a bacteria. You mightn't get the disease but it inside you all the time. Waiting for some weakness. They realize this too late, but they wasn't about to give up power because they had waited too long. Desperate men seeking desperate measures. They couldn't give in to the black people because they would lose all the Indian support and in any case, three-quarter of the complaints was just mischief. The problem is that they couldn't continue in the direction they was going either, because people start whispering about insurrection and revolution and all that nonsense. But desperation is a forerunner to brilliance and the solution they finally arrive at was nothing short of brilliant." He was walking quickly but every now and again he would stop as if to emphasize a point. "What about"—and here he stopped—"slaughtering one of their own. Not a member of the government, eh, not even a member of the party, but an Indian who is a national figure. An ex-politician still respected and feared."

"Like Mr. Rampartap?"

He smiled as if we were talking about a distant acquaintance. "You think about it, Mr. Writer. Is not for me to make assumptions."

I was about to tell him that he had done just that but changed my mind and asked instead, "How are they going to slaughter this innocent Indian?"

"There are many ways to destroy a man. Lies and rumours if you prefer the indirect method."

"What is the direct method?"

"You are the writer. I leave that to your imagination."

We walked in silence for about five minutes but I was thinking of what he had revealed and becoming worried, because in a crazy way it made sense. I reflected on the question in my mind. "Am I correct in assuming that the biography is a safeguard? A preemptive strike against these lies and rumours or whatever else these people have in mind?"

"Preemptive strike. You writers have a way with words. Look up the hill." He pointed to smoke curling from a thatched carat-palm hut. "The boys up there preparing a special meal. You know what?"

"Manicou?"

He gazed at me in feigned astonishment. "I didn't think you would remember that after so long. But I don't eat rodents. Tattoo. Or armadillo as you know it."

"They feed on worms."

He laughed aloud. "You know, you really beginning to surprise me."

Two men were bent over a huge pot, stirring and throwing in ingredients. I recognized one of them as Sankie. Another man, scrawny, with thick veins running along his hands, was washing a basin of either yam or dasheen by a barrel at the back of the hut. They both stood up as we approached. Just then Ashton and a slim Indian boy came through a thicket of wild cane.

"Morning, Mr. Ram," Ashton said. "We didn't expect you so early."

The Indian boy added, "We went to check out Mr. Choo. He can't make it today on account of a little accident." Ashton rolled his eyes as if Mr. Choo's accidents were routine. As they came closer, I smelled the marijuana. I glanced at Mr. Rampartap but he was smiling tolerantly.

"I bring the writer fella to get a real taste of country food. I believe allyou meet him already."

Sankie grinned. "Yes, boss. I believe so. I believe we meet him already." He nudged the man who had been dipping the basin into the barrel. "Was nice of you to bring him."

"And was nice of you to join we, Mr. Ram," Ashton said. "You not here as regular as we like. But we know how busy you is. Is okay if I crack one?" He took out a flask of rum from his pocket. Mr. Rampartap waved his hand. As Ashton was about to take his drink, there was a stirring in the bush. Sankie stood up and glanced at his companion.

An old, scruffy-looking man emerged from a tangle of balisier, walking unsteadily. "Allyou making big cook and nobody invite me self." It was the man who, during our journey from Portillo's bar, had shouted at Mr. Rampartap. He seemed quite drunk.

"Look, haul you old ass from here, you hear."

He ignored Sankie. "Don't mind nobody invite me, I not vex. I use to that by now. Just remember it had a time when—" He spotted Mr. Rampartap and froze. "You!"

"Don't come one step further if you know what is good for you." Mr. Rampartap spoke slowly but his entire face and his neck were swollen.

"Why? Why I shouldn't come one step further? When you had me burning down all these people property, I was you pally-wally, not so? When I make jail for you, I was the best of friend, not so?"

"Look, I warning you. Shut you ass and leave now."

"You shut you own ass, Sankie. Nobody talking to you." He turned to Mr. Rampartap. "When I nearly kill Ramirez, I was the best of—" He didn't get a chance to complete the statement because Mr. Rampartap lunged at him, grasped his shirt collar and lifted him straight off the ground. I had never seen a big man move so swiftly, nor was I prepared for his brute strength, raising him effortlessly, propelling him to the barrel, pushing him backward over the rim until his head was in the water. Then he pulled him out and flung him to the ground, where he remained on all fours, shaking his head like a dog. The Indian boy who had come with Ashton stepped forward and kicked him. He moved away to gather force and kicked him again and again. When he collapsed, the boy placed his boot on the back of the old man's neck and ground his face in the dirt.

"Leave him alone!" The voice was loud and nervous, panicky yet threatening. I didn't realize I had shouted at the Indian boy until I saw everyone staring at me.

"Yes." Mr. Rampartap was still staring at me. "Leave him alone. We are not beasts." His voice, sharp and ringing, cut across the hut. The Indian boy removed his boot. "Ashton, carry him home."

"Come, mister man. You cause enough trouble for one night."

The old man struggled up, falling on his face, then clutching Ashton's pant leg and pulling himself up. Particles of dried mud were embedded in his face and blood was streaking from his mouth. Ashton grasped his arm firmly. "Drunk people shouldn't leave the rumshop." He spoke softly, as to a child. I was surprised, given the violence of the last few minutes, at his almost gentle tone.

"Yes, Ashton, you is a brother. You don't forget. But you"—he glared at Mr. Rampartap—"you will roast in hell. God don't forget."

Mr. Rampartap waved a hand. "Carry him away. And make sure he reach home safe." At that the Indian boy began to laugh, a nervous, uncoordinated rasp. But Mr. Rampartap was serious and I was struck once more by his swollen face. He turned to me. "You staying?"

I shook my head.

On the way back from the camp, he held the stalks of the ginger lilies to steady himself. He was breathing heavily like a diseased man. "I should have deal with that jackass a long time now. But I am too soft. I get too modern. Like you. All that will change."

He was not going straight back towards the house but had turned aside into a narrow trail bordered with razor grass and stinging nettles. The interlocking branches of the cajuca and jiggerwood trees darkened the trail, and I could see from the overgrown grass that no one had come this way for a while. I wondered how I would fare in hand-to-hand combat with Mr. Rampartap. He was an ex-wrestler and, as I had just seen, still remarkably strong. But he was about twenty years older than I and he seemed tired. "So where are we going?" I asked him.

"The River of Blood."

"That's the name of the estate, isn't it?" I slowed my steps so that I was behind him. He noticed.

"Nothing to be afraid of."

"I'm not afraid, you know."

"You sure?" He stopped and turned, facing me. His mouth was open and his cheeks ballooned with each exhalation. His brown, deeply sunburnt face seemed darker than usual. A drop of sweat trickled down from his forehead over an eyelid but he did not blink. His hands were loose at his sides and I noticed the veins running down his forearms and the size of his fingers, calloused and lumpy like a labourer's. I had never been less intimidated by him. Finally, he said, "Yes, I see that. But only since you come down here. I didn't see it in Canada. My mistake." I expected him to smile, because he was speaking with an exaggerated Trinidadian accent, but he continued seriously. "Most of the time, you had these two-word reply to everything I say. Cussing your-self for coming to this backward place. This primitive, su-perstitious, backward place." How many times had those words been thrown mockingly at me? I must have smiled, because I saw his eyelids narrowing. "A fella with his own little secrets. Come. I want to show you one of mine."

"Why?"

He walked off. "Why?" After a minute or so, he added, "To satisfy your curiosity. To make you happy." He had misread me and I wondered now whether he, too, had been nervous in my presence.

I trailed after him, avoiding the nettles. We came to a small hill almost impenetrable with wild balisier. He cleared a path by flattening the stalks with his boots. The sap was slippery and I almost lost my footing a few times. We emerged from the balisier into a gorge bereft of plants. There were rocks and shale instead of clay loam. I heard the sound of a gurgling stream and smelled fresh water. Mr. Rampartap braced his hands against a rock and began to lower himself down an incline with small sharp pebbles and greyish gravel. The way down was precipitous and I fol-lowed him cautiously, clutching the large stones for support. At the foot of the hill I saw water, clear and pure, gushing from the ground and trickling over the pebbles and shale.

"River of Blood." He bent down, scooped a palmful of water and splashed it over his face. "You could drink it, you know. The cleanest water you could find."

I slapped the water over my arms and neck. It was cool and but for the faint odour of grit, clean and fresh. "It doesn't appear to be red."

He laughed and exhaled briskly, snorting out a drop of water. "Follow me."

What now? I wondered. I trudged behind him, watching the water flow over the pebbles and stones and then over smooth ropy rocks like clay suddenly hardening. There were saucer-sized holes in the ground and small mounds that looked like molten statues of chubby babies.

"Watch your steps with these vents." He placed a foot on a mound and folded his arms across his chest as if posing for a photograph. "You like the scenery? All of this used to be mud volcanoes." He tapped the mouth of the mound with his foot. "Is not real volcanoes, you know. Just natural gas pushing up. This entire estate is rich in natural gas. Build on a reserve, in fact. The outsiders try trick after trick to get the rights to drill but they wasn't dealing with some peasant from Debe or Penal here."

These elusive outsiders. Who was he referring to now? The oil companies? The government? "It could make you very rich," I told him.

He moved away in the direction of a wild banana grove. "I am already rich." The stalks of the bananas were thick and grew close together so we had to squeeze to get through. My legs were itching from the nettles and the tiny thorns that overlay the razor grass and my shoes were clumpy with mud and soggy from the water flowing between the suckers. I imagined Mr. Rampartap smirking at my discomfort. "Over there." He pointed to a cluster of shrubby trees decorated with red berries. He glanced at the scratches on my legs and my soaked shoes. "It's called—"

"Roucou. Used to colour food. A harmless dye." I had seen it shaded by the bamboo in Agostini.

He walked quietly to the cluster. I heard the deep echo of water falling from a distance. "Take your time here."

Then I saw it. A basin about twenty feet in diameter,

into which water plummeted from the overhanging rocks jutting out like splintered planks. The water was dark red, the colour of congealed blood. Mr. Rampartap clasped his hands behind his back and stared down. From the rise and fall of his chest I saw that he was breathing erratically but I could hear nothing beyond the sound of falling water. Berries floating downstream left a trail of red, like piranhas regurgitating what they had fed on.

"Rougeleau. The red water."

"How come no one knows of this? None of the villagers—"

"People believe what they want to believe." He squatted and picked out a berry from the ground. "The only choice that we have in this life is whether to believe or not." He squashed the berry and threw it in the water. "From the time we small everybody telling we what to do, pushing we in this and that direction." There was a reflective tone to his Trinidadian accent and when I observed his face I felt that he was speaking to himself, that he was no longer interested in impressing or intimidating me. "Is the only freedom we have and yet we give it up so easy."

He got up. "You ask why people never come to this spot. Two-three years ago, another set of mud volcano erupt in Piparo, just six or seven miles from here. Everybody from the village, even the educated people, say that is because it had a drug lord living there. That was the reason. You see, people here have a explanation for everything. If they get sick, somebody put a *mal yeux*, the evil eye, on them. If they acting different, something possess them. A old man living by himself is a lagahoo, a old lady, a soucouyant. Big educated people running to the obeah man to get back they husband or they wife. A baby born deform and everybody frighten of it. So you see, Mr. Writer, you right when you say that this is a primitive backward place."

"I never said that."

"You don't have to say it."

"Actually, there are people like that all over. Even in Canada. Psychic networks and—"

"Yes. I know that. No need to lecture me. The difference is that over here is a way of life. We have everything in this country but we will never progress. As it was so shall it be."

The statement surprised me. Twenty-five years ago I'd heard it regularly in Mr. Philip's class. Mr. Philip, grinding his teeth in rage, had spoken of the indigenous Indians falling easy prey to the Spanish conquistadors. "They thought these conquerors were nice, sweet people." He was discussing the Americans who had been granted permission to establish a base in Chaguaramas. The Americans, loaded with cash and spending freely in the brothels and nightclubs in Port of Spain, had been celebrated in calypsos and in carnival bands. "As it was so shall it be," he had thundered.

It was impossible to believe that in twenty-five years nothing had changed.

"Thinking about the river?" Mr. Rampartap asked. "Everybody have they own story for it. Black, brown and white. The white people had this story about a massacre. Rebellious slaves taking this whole family, man, woman and child, fresh from France and slaughtering them by the river." He got up. "That is what this place do to you."

"Well, I was thinking of Agostini."

We continued in silence on our way back, then he said, "I believe I keep you back too long in this place. This backward place behind God's back." He smiled as if he believed none of it.

I realized then the true purpose of the trip: he had calculated that I would be of no use to him; he was releasing
me from my obligation.

The next morning, Madhoo displayed no surprise when I
informed him I was leaving. He told me that Mr. Rampartap would be away for some business and he inquired about
any friends or relatives I planned to visit. I explained that
I needed an hour or so to pack.

Two hours later, he knocked on the door. "You ready,
uncle? The ship ready to sail." While he was carrying the
box into which I had stuffed his specimens, I glanced upstairs. "Where's Dulcie?"

"She went to the market to get some provision."

"And Mrs. Ram?"

"She went with Dulcie."

According to Madhoo no one was at home, but when the
car pulled off I saw a face peeping from the front window.

In the car, he hummed calypsos and Indian film songs.
Then he began chatting about his father and a younger
sister attending some college.

"Who is Ramirez?" I asked him.

"Ramirez?" He gazed in the rear-view mirror. "Dulcie
father. He cripple now."

I wondered whether he had been informed about the
night's events. "Did Mr. Rampartap know him?"

"I believe so, but all that is water below the bridge now.
Just like you deputy in the cold."

"What happened to him?" Now I regretted not waiting
until Dulcie returned.

"Nothing much. A little accident." And because I remained silent, he added, "The past is the past, uncle. No

need to dig up old grave. Sometimes you don't like what you find."

We emerged from the estate into the Churchill Roosevelt Highway. New cars sped by, honking at Madhoo's slow driving, but he seemed unruffled and just maintained his steady pace. In the car ahead, four children, three girls and a boy, their faces pressed against the back pane, were making faces at us. The girls stuck out their tongues and the boy tugged down his lower lip with his finger. I expected Madhoo to overtake the car because of the children's teasing but when I glanced at him, his eyes were crossed and his tongue out. "Be careful," I told him.

When he did overtake the car, he shouted at the driver, "Which zoo you pick up them children from, uncle?"

In the distance, I saw the San Fernando hill. It looked diminished: huge chunks had been removed so that it appeared like an unfinished jigsaw puzzle. In San Fernando, traffic slowed to a crawl. Crowds of people dressed in the latest fashions were walking on the pavements and under the shops and stores. They all looked bright and contented. "Okay, uncle. I have to drop you out here. I coulda drop you in Rio Claro but I have to go back for Mr. Ram."

"It's okay. I can get a taxi or a bus here to Rio Claro."

"You know the way?"

"I took this route for seven years. Drop me off by the library corner."

"I think the library get move out. They put up some cinema or the other. All right, this is the place. Take it easy, eh, uncle. And keep the box with the insects safe."

In San Fernando, waiting for a bus to Rio Claro, I reflected on my time at the estate. Mr. Rampartap's lectures and his cunning intrigues had made me forget Canada for a while, but not the way I wanted. It was time to revisit the island, the villages, the people I had known. I realized that the island I was about to see wouldn't be the idyllic Trinidad I had constructed for Vanita; that in this windswept land of laughter and lightness there were crevices of sullen rage and ignorance and wounds never allowed to heal. But it was the place where I had grown up and with which I associated the happiest time of my life. Repudiating Madhoo's advice, I was about to reclaim my past.

Two

TEN

On my way to Rio Claro, I sat at the window and stared at the signposts—St. Julien, Torrib Trace, Tableland, Poole, Libertville—and whenever the bus slowed, I searched stupidly for familiar faces. Perhaps some of the old men shuffling along the side paths had visited the warden's office during the year I had worked there. They would have been younger, stronger, more jauntily attired, their lips curling arrogantly from the beers they had drunk earlier. I thought of my standard five history lessons, dismal lectures on treaties and distant colonial arrangements, enlivened occasionally by local topics like Charles Kingsley's visit to Princes Town and the naming of a street after him, the expansion of Tableland into an important rural centre, the resettling in New Grant of black Loyalist soldiers from America following the war of 1812, and the Spanish influence in Rio Claro. Each village had a special history with stories flavoured by the ethnicity of the early settlers.

The bus bumped and groaned into the villages and through land once planted with sugar cane. A cocoa estate I had passed every morning on my journey to Presentation College was now populated with bison strolling on fissured hills and wallowing in the slushy ravines. There were more concrete houses, many of them protected by gates and wrought iron burglar-proofing. The vegetable stalls at the sides of the road were more elaborate than I remembered, with separate sections for the produce, the prices written on wooden boards. Ochro, bodi, plantain, breadfruit, cassava, avocado, pineapple and a range of fruits, mango, pommecythere, pommerac, star apple, plum, five fingers.

Across the aisle, a hefty man with short, prickly hair was asleep, his head sliding down the back of the seat and then jerking upright just before it hit the lap of a boy of about twelve. The boy, who had a gloomy, sneering, oval face, like a turtle, was staring at two girls in the row ahead, who were clapping their hands and reciting a nursery rhyme.

I had often imagined Vanita making this trip with me, her face pressed against the window while I pointed out the *gayelle* in New Grant where stick-fighters held their tournaments each Carnival; Princes Town where I changed buses; the little snackette, where each afternoon I would buy, for five cents, a bottle of orange juice, the taste of the fruit barely distinguishable in the watery concoction, and a tough pancake we called biscuit cake. My mother would be plying her with the syrupy sweets she made on birthdays and special occasions. (The sweets caused my father to chide her gently about the excessive oil and the high cholesterol, but when she was not looking he would pop a few in his mouth and pretend he was suffocating.)

The most distinct memory I had of that time was of my parents sitting on wooden stools about eight feet apart and chatting with the men and women, mostly older villagers who knew them well, and others who could not get credit from the new supermarket owned by Aleong, an immigrant from Hong Kong. As far as I could recall, the shop was not well stocked—the shelves were usually half empty—and because they did not have a liquor licence, they never really prospered. The decision against the liquor licence was my father's. He believed it would attract the wrong kind of clientele, and my mother, who had initially argued in its favour, eventually gave up.

My parents were well respected, not only because they offered credit (as I had believed as a boy) but also because my father was well educated by the village standards (his five subjects in the Cambridge exams could have guaranteed him a good job if he had opted for the town) and because my mother was a sympathetic woman who listened with genuine concern to the problems of the customers.

My father was unusual in another respect: he was a liberal at a time when most other parents were unflinching in the demands placed on their children. In spite of my mother's gentle protests, he offered credit to villagers he knew would never be able to settle their accounts by the end of the month as they promised. My mother's obligatory objections melted after a few minutes and sometimes these villagers brought, in lieu of cash, gifts of fruits or vegetables. Once a man came into the shop with a cardboard box stuffed with old copies of *The Reader's Digest* which my father placed in his bookcase next to his religious texts and his books by Charles Dickens, Marie Corelli, Victor Hugo, R.K. Narayan and Tagore. While my father and I never had any long conversations, he mentioned several times that poverty was not usually the result of laziness and that most of these people could not do any better. He was thin and slightly stoop-shouldered, and whenever he was speaking with someone he would focus his gaze not on the person, but on some object above or beyond. Ordinarily, he just listened and nodded in agreement. His fingers were long and frail, and thinking of him in Canada, I sometimes felt that they would have been better suited to a paintbrush or piano keys than to the tins of sugar and rice and flour that he packed and arranged in the shop. When I expressed my desire to leave Trinidad, he said that we should always pursue our dreams because we would otherwise spend the rest of our lives wondering: What if? What if?

My mother was more conversational and some of the younger women called her *didi*, elder sister. I suspected that she, too, wanted something other than a life in the shop but she was always smiling or chatting with some customer. I believe she saw how much my father needed her. She was more practical in financial matters and oversaw all the credit.

Although they hardly spoke with each other, I felt they were happy to be together in the mostly quiet shop, sitting on their stools a few feet apart. Once, when I was in standard four, a young woman had come into the shop, sniffling, her head bowed. My mother spoke to her softly and my father moved from his stool but I remained, listening. Afterwards, when the woman had left and my father had returned, I heard my mother saying that the woman, recently married, hardly saw her husband because he drove a taxi in Port of Spain and came home after midnight. When it was too late, he stayed at his sister's house in San Juan. Shaking her head, my mother had said that there was no replacement for a family. A number of women confided their problems to my mother and although my father would be silent during these conversations, later he would utter some statement which would leave my mother nodding in agreement. They were like all the other couples from the village, rarely speaking to each other—at least not in the presence of their children—but once I heard my father teasing my mother by reciting a line from a poem. "Barefooted came the beggar maid in front of King Cophetua."

Our house was adjacent to the shop, and at night I would bring along Varun on the pretext that I needed my father's assistance with my homework. While Varun fooled around with the lower shelves, arranging and rearranging the brightly coloured tins of clarified butter and evaporated milk and Ovaltine, I would sit on the floor and listen to customers talking about some neighbour who had inexplicably gone mad, neglecting family and walking the streets muttering to himself. The consensus was usually that it was retribution for an ancestral misdeed committed years ago. On weekends, I would play snakes and ladders and ludo with Varun, until a friend from school came along with a bamboo fishing rod.

When I passed my common entrance for Presentation College in San Fernando, I took the bus at five in the morning and returned home at six, but on the weekends I was allowed to go fishing and to the recreation ground opposite the Ecclesville school. I was never very athletic but I was left-handed and could make the ball cut and curve, so I was picked for both the village and the school cricket teams. And I was popular with the village boys, partly because I was going to a school in San Fernando, but more significantly because I made fun of the town boys, who, as I reported, were all awkward and nervous and knew nothing about hunting with slingshots and bailing the river for guabeen and cascadura. (I was not immune, though, to the hypocrisy that affected all the country-bookies at school: for the first two or three years, I also made fun of the shirtless village boys returning from the rivers, their bodies stained a different kind of brown.)

I enjoyed my seven years at Presentation. I was fascinated by the gowned brothers who taught us and whose authority was slyly subverted by weekly "revelations" of their perversions: bestiality, obsessive masturbation and necrophilia.

In Canada, I often thought of the other students in my advanced level class. I knew that most of them had migrated to America and England. Canada was not yet the port of choice. I also imagined what their reactions would be if they knew I was teaching foreign students from places we glimpsed only in geography classes and what they would say about my writing ambitions. In our literature class, we had neatly categorized all writers: fiction writers were madmen and poets drunkards. This line of thinking had been encouraged by our literature teacher, Mr. Oswald, a frustrated poet and short-story writer and also an alcoholic veering towards madness.

The year that I worked at the warden's office in Rio Claro was one of my happiest, but many of the memories are truncated, like stories without beginnings or endings. I can recall now only fragments of the river limes, the nights in the bars singing calypsos and songs from Indian movies, the girls whose fathers had warned them to be home at six and, in particular, the steady stream of eccentrics who filtered in and out of the office.

In Rio Claro at that time, eccentricity was more a clarification of character than a handicap. Minor quirks were exaggerated, their owners made special by the gift of being different. In Canada, I remembered these characters with a degree of fondness. Even Titmus, the old frazzled-looking custodian who cleaned the Ecclesville Government School every morning recess and at nights. He had one marble eye with which he would terrify the girls playing hopscotch

and hoop, removing it from the socket, licking it and polishing it with his dirty shirttail. Because of his marble eye
and his long beard plaited into two pigtails, we suspected
Titmus of being an obeah man but we had no proof even
though Sorefoot Soogrim swore he saw him push a frog
into his dusty khaki knapsack, which hung on a nail in the
stockroom.

His secret, we knew, was in the knapsack. For almost a
week, five of us—Jattan, a slim boy who sold river conch
after school, Ken, whose father was a police officer, Sam,
Sorefoot Soogrim and I—planned our move. The knapsack
itself was accessible but Titmus usually hung around the
school, sharpening a cutlass outside by the taps or watering
the straggly plants at the back. By Friday we could wait no
longer and when the dismissal bell rang we posted Soogrim
to watch out for Titmus and opened the stockroom door. At
first no one wanted to touch the knapsack, but then Jattan
took it down from the nail and Sam and I pushed our hands
inside, nervously feeling around. Sam brought out a mouldy
half-eaten mango, and I retrieved a dog-eared copybook
smeared with illegible numbers and letters. No frogs, no
toads. We replaced everything and slung his knapsack once
more on the nail. On Monday morning I had already forgotten about Titmus but when I opened my desk, on a sheet of
paper I saw the words in the same garbled scrawl from the
copybook, "Youngboy, crapaud smoke your pipe," and beneath, written more carefully, "You have exactly ten days."
None of the other boys had received a threatening note. I
worried about this all day. Was it a collective threat? Why not
Jattan who had taken the knapsack from the nail? Or Sam
who had also felt around inside it? How had he spotted us?
That night I ate quickly and went to bed earlier than usual.

The following day at recess, Titmus walked by the cricket pitch spitting and polishing his marble eye. Then he stopped and wagged a finger at me. I froze. That weekend I stayed at home and pretended I was doing my homework. My mother clucked appreciatively. On Monday he passed the class carrying a pail. He glanced at me and his finger rose and wagged. On Tuesday I tried to avoid him but as I was leaving school he emerged from the stockroom and wagged. This wag lasted a full minute. I fled home and jumped into bed. My mother asked if I was tired and brought a glass of orange juice. That night I calculated my chances of survival. I had lasted nine days. Tomorrow was the critical day. How would disaster strike? Snake? Scorpion? I jumped out of bed and checked beneath the sheets. But it might be something completely beyond my control like an earthquake or a tidal wave from Mayaro, about twelve miles away.

The next day in class, I kept my eyes on the clock on the wall. Mr. Philip screamed at me, "You little ears clog up with wax? Come, let me unclog it." He loosened his belt. Death by thrashing! But I survived. The day passed. After school, when Titmus wagged I wagged back at him and he erupted into a wheezy, congested cackle.

There were other, less threatening eccentrics. Haridas Sadhu was a short, slightly built man who owned a bull that was contemptuous of Haridas's urgings, and chose its own route (a common spectacle was Haridas screaming obscenities while the bull dragged him along the gravel road). Bhoendrilal Patanjalidal was named for his severe stutter, more tragically because he was a pharmacist who was continually asked to explain the properties of antihistamines and vitamins and cortisone. Dagdag—a nickname, I believe—the best herbalist in the village, had run afoul of the law when he began issuing prescriptions with "Dr. Dagdag" signed at the bottom. Nobby, the one-armed mechanic and plumber executed all his repairs by blowing into tubes and pipes and cylinders.

The warden's office itself, lodged between two rumshops, was quiet most of the day, but by three in the afternoon, when the other government offices had long been closed and the workers had already benefited from a drink or two, the wooden benches were packed.

Harrylal, an art teacher at the Rio Claro government school, was one of the most frequent visitors, but his business there was never established. He was at the time compiling a dossier on *whe whe*, an illegal form of gambling in which the numbers from one to thirty-six each corresponded with a particular object and in which bets were placed on the basis of dreams. Someone who dreamed of a *jamette*, a prostitute, would place a bet on sixteen, while a snake would suggest thirty-five, its numerical equivalent. During these visits, Harrylal routinely revealed that after his retirement, in five or six years, he would be free to pursue his true vocation, that of a priest. Then he would dip into his battered briefcase and withdraw copies of *Watchtower* and *Awake* and other religious tracts. But I was sceptical of his impending priesthood, because scattered between his magazines were photographs of nude teenagers. Surprisingly, he never bothered to explain this anomaly.

But his real business was with Lalchan, a soft, ascetic middle-aged man whose dreams seemed out of character: the wives of important men copulating with animals, men and women blessed, or cursed, with extra appendages and orifices, secret orgies, late-night trysts. I was certain that Harrylal's visits had nothing to do with *whe whe*.

Once, I had gone to Lalchan's house with Keith.
Lalchan was celebrating the birth of his third child and first
son with a *barahi* and during the festivities, while the guests
were singing and dancing, he had stood under an almond
tree, hands clasped over his white kurta, looking more like
a pundit than a warden's officer. I felt that he was contemplating one of his dreams but perhaps his thoughts had to
do with other matters: he was the first person I knew who
wanted to emigrate to Canada. One Monday morning, he
announced that this was his last week in the warden's office,
because he was leaving for Canada on the weekend. On Friday, we threw a party in one of the adjacent bars. Congratulations were offered, speeches delivered. Even Lalchan
himself, normally so shy, was encouraged to say a few
words. The following Monday he turned up for work as
usual. Two months later, he notified us once more of his
proposed emigration. Another party was arranged. The day
he was supposed to leave he turned up for work. In time,
we grew accustomed to his impending departures and
didn't bother to arrange any more parties.

But Lalchan must have persisted, because eight years
after I left Trinidad I met him in Toronto at the intersection
of Markham and Sheppard, waiting for a bus. At first I did
not recognize him. He expressed no surprise at our chance
encounter and in his quiet manner invited me to his two-
bedroom apartment in a high-rise. When we arrived, his
children, whom I remembered as shy and well-behaved,
were screaming at each other. He offered me a cup of warm
milk. The children shouted obscenities. He sipped solemnly.
I was shocked by the range of profanities. He finished his
milk, walked me to the door and said, "One of these days I
going to grab on to one of them little bitches and pitch they

ass straight over the balcony." His voice was soft, almost gentle; he could have been boasting of their accomplishments. Before I left, he wrung his hands and asked dejectedly about Keith and the other workers.

Keith was one of the smartest people I knew in Trinidad. Like Lalchan he was withdrawn, but his diffidence was rooted not in shyness but in an unobtrusive cynicism. He professed to be both a devout Hindu and an atheist, and for most of the time I knew him, he was trying to reconcile this contradiction. He believed that Hinduism, stripped of its intrusive mythology—the gods and goddesses were incidental in his version of the religion—was essentially a theology of cycles: birth, death and rebirth. We were about the same age and I was the only person in the warden's office he confided in. Most of the other workers thought he was aloof, but he accompanied us to all our Friday-night binges in the rumshops scattered through Rio Claro, and while we pounded the tables and sang the latest calypsos and Indian movie songs, he chain-smoked and tapped his knuckles. He lived in Navet, about twenty-five minutes from Agostini, and since I did not have a car he usually dropped me home. On the way, his reticence would melt and he would speak passionately about his theological insights. One evening he told me that the soul was really a catalogue of all the experiences that we carried into successive lives. All that we dreamed of and imagined—"the furniture of the spirit"—sprang from this repository. We had been trained to think in finite terms, but there was no beginning or end; everything was interconnected.

On Fridays, he gave me a lift to the Palm Village Hotel. He never spoke. I would see him glancing in the rear-view mirror at the girl seated next to me. Later that night, if I peeped out of the hotel window, I would see his cigarette glowing beneath a coconut tree. Although he disapproved of these brief liaisons, he never conveyed his reservations directly. One night, he told me that we are made to account for all our transgressions not because of some sacred ordinance but because the guilt stored in our data bank carries its own need for expiation. Our karma, he explained, is not orchestrated by a distant divine entity, but directed by the simple law of cause and effect.

I was nineteen years old at the time and guilt was the furthest thing from my mind. My life was predictable and uncomplicated and I was happy. One morning our supervisor, Banfield, showed up for work in a white shirt buttoned at the cuffs and a bow tie that kept slipping down. He normally dressed in loose flowery shirts and rubber slippers, and would spend the morning in his office reading the newspapers before disappearing into a rumshop in the afternoon. He explained the transformation: we were to be visited by some American researcher who was compiling statistics on the stress levels of government workers in Third World countries. The researcher had already visited places like Singapore, Malaysia and the Philippines. When Banfield clumsily adjusted his bow tie, we all applauded.

The researcher, who was surprisingly young, drew charts, displayed slides and lectured earnestly about the work ethic and job motivation. Then he turned on his tape recorder and read questions from sheets arranged in an elegant binder. He gazed expectantly at us. Banfield was reading his newspapers, Sankar had fallen asleep, Hackshaw, who regularly stole stationery from the stockroom, was staring greedily at the binder, and everyone else was either bored or bemused. The only response came from Lalchan who extrapolated a tenuous connection between stress and dreams. The researcher was crestfallen; after his study of workers in the Far East we were clearly a disappointment.

That evening in the rumshop we made fun of his earnestness, his alien concepts and his accent. Hackshaw said that he had been just waiting for him to put down his binder. Later, on our way home, Keith told me that the American was a CIA trainee. I laughed because it sounded like something from a movie.

When I was leaving for Canada, Keith was the only person from work who showed up at the airport. I remember that his clothes were rumpled and he looked exhausted. Because my parents were busily offering advice, we barely spoke but just before I entered the immigration lounge, he shook my hand and said, "The cycle continues in another country."

I thought he was joking. "What about you?" I asked.

He tugged at an ear as if the question pained him. Then he pushed an old dog-eared book in the pocket of my jacket.

Varun was also at the airport, bursting with wonder and disbelief. Fifteen at the time, he was at the awkward stage where any display of emotion was viewed as foolish but on the day of my departure he could not hide his excitement. I suppose he was imagining his own departure.

He had passed his common entrance for Presentation College, professed a love for the subjects I had taken in advanced level classes, and played with the younger brothers of my friends; through me he was able to envision his future.

In Canada, before the death of my parents, I often thought of him and wondered whether the boy trailing

after me to the recreation ground, travelling to and from
school, insisting that I take him fishing, would be replaced
by a lonely man who could not account for his losses. But
when he left Trinidad, it was for England, not Canada.
And his letters were crammed with his accomplishments—almost as if he wanted my approval—captain of
the university cricket team, the dean's list, his marriage to
Rita (whom I mistakenly believed to be from the West Indies or the Subcontinent) during his final year, the birth of
twins a year later. I wanted to warn him but there was no
need. He sent me postcards from Ireland and Scotland,
photographs from Paris and Milan. I saw him posing before cathedrals and fountains and statues of intertwined
men and women. He and his wife, clasping each other just
as tightly. Then our parents died in quick succession and
the letters stopped.

The little I have achieved in my life I owe to my parents'
kindness and their gentle admonitions. I always believed I
would return to Trinidad after my degree and discover that
nothing had changed: the crowded rumshops, Banfield and
Lalchan and Sankar in the warden's office, the trip to Palm
Village in Keith's car, and my parents sitting on their stools
listening patiently to the customers, my mother clucking
her tongue and sympathizing with them, my father dis-
pensing advice and encouragement. I had been misled
by my early years in Canada and—more than I cared
to admit—by Keith's belief in an unbroken cycle. I took
it for granted that when I returned from work, Varun
would push open the door, sit on the bed with his legs
crossed and ask me to read his essays, that he would glow
with pride when I complimented him on his thoroughness,

and chat about how he had learned to make the ball twist and curve.

Sometimes, when Vanita insisted on my attention, or beamed when I praised her tidiness, she reminded me of Varun, but as she grew older, I felt as though she had drawn a translucent curtain around herself, occasionally peeping out, then withdrawing when it became necessary.

I knew that this aversion was her defence against a world in which she was constantly forced to take sides, and I occasionally felt a guilty pride at her defiance but mostly I just felt sad at the life into which she had been pushed. I wanted her to share my satisfaction when I told her stories of Trinidad, of climbing trees and throwing the fruits to my friends beneath, of the picnics we organized, of my parents sitting on their two stools in the shop, their faces lighting up when my brother and I returned from school. I wanted her to sit with her chin propped against her fist when I related the stories.

Maybe I wanted her to be more like Varun.

As the bus passed the Rio Claro junction with the market on one side and the stores on the other, it occurred to me that we are constantly searching for change because we do not expect it; we savour the anticipation of untested experiences in a world that is immutable, where we imagine that journeys can always be retraced, where mistakes count for nothing, where memory is an invitation to innocence and innocence a reinvention of lies. For the nineteen years that I lived in Trinidad, little had changed: my parents, my friends and the wooden house, resurrected, I was told, from a crumbling old building and built slowly and painstakingly according to my parents' specifications.

I had flirted with the idea that my visit to Trinidad was to test the validity of my wife's revulsion, her horror of the confusion and the blackness—they were, in her mind, inseparable—but as the bus approached Agostini Village, I felt the trickling nervousness and the excitement of meeting an old acquaintance; a young man, nineteen years old, who always assumed he would be young and the pleasures of the world perpetually within his grasp. I wanted to understand his friendships, his laughter, his ambition, and to understand why all of this had fallen away and left instead a man hovering uneasily between detachment and desperation.

ELEVEN

I was concerned that the house might have been converted into an unrecognizable building, the louvres replaced with stylish windows and the solid wooden doors leading into the shop with tinted sliding doors. Or perhaps the house was no longer there, just an empty lot with rubble and rotting wood, but as the bus approached, I saw that little of the external structure had changed.

Standing before the house, I thought of my daily journeys from Presentation College in San Fernando, my impatience to get home to a hot meal, invariably rice, lentils, chicken and some vegetable plucked from the backyard garden.

"Yes?" The vines smothering the wooden fence rustled and a head appeared over the top. He was oldish, perhaps in his early sixties, balding and with worry lines raked across his forehead. He glanced nervously at my suitcase. Now a woman joined him and she, too, stared worriedly at my suitcase as if it were packed with useless gadgets soon to be foisted on them.

I explained that I had once lived in the house and wanted one last look. The man cleared his throat with a prolonged trill and looked at the woman. She fiddled with a ball of brown twine and gazed, once more, at my suitcase.

"Just five minutes," I promised.

The man walked slowly to the gate as if he were still undecided. He said that he was tying cucumber vines on the fence. I repeated my promise. The woman tightened the twine and began sawing the middle with her teeth. They were both staring at me uneasily, so I explained that my parents, now dead, had lived most of their lives here. The woman stopped sawing and with the twine between her teeth, looked at her husband. He asked me my name and when I told him, he released a rasping sigh, pointed to the end of the fence and asked if I wanted some passion fruit. I shook my head. A drink then, made from the fruit? I didn't want to disappoint him so I said yes. The woman placed the ball of twine somewhere behind her apron and walked slowly to the yellow fruits.

The man said that he spent most of the time gardening. He disliked plants and was allergic to pollen. When he had purchased the property from a Mr. Sumair and moved from Arima, he imagined a prosperous grocery teeming with contented customers. Mr. Sumair had even projected his monthly profits and had assured him that he would recover the principal in a year and a half. He pointed to the padlocked door. The first week he had twelve customers. Each wanted credit. He patiently explained his financial situation to them. They never returned. The next week there were five customers and the following week, one. After six weeks, he closed the shop.

The woman returned with a glass of juice. The man, staring at the vines, asked in a tired voice the amount my parents had sold for. Fifty-three thousand, I said. He rubbed his palms together as if dislodging dust and the woman uttered a stifled sigh. They had paid twice that amount. Was the juice good, he asked sadly?

It was, I assured him.

He smiled a little and stared at the lines on his palm and asked if I wanted to look around. I agreed so quickly that he seemed taken aback and for a minute I was afraid he would withdraw the offer.

They followed me to the back of the house, to the concrete stand where my mother had stood over a ribbed tub and washed the clothes. The tub was no longer there and the stand was green with moss. When I kneeled by the stand, pulled away the grass and clawed at the dirt the woman emitted a muffled groan. The man kneeled too and pushed his face over the hole.

"Money?" he asked hoarsely.

I shook my head. About a foot down, I hit the lid of the Ovaltine tin. I clutched both sides and pried it loose. The man was so close I could feel his breath on my neck. I held the tin against my ear, shook it and listened to the clatter. The woman made a suffocating sound.

"What it have inside? Some kind of treasure?" His hands were now clasped across his chest.

I struggled with the rusted lid, twisting and turning it until it was loose. I stepped back because they were so close to me, put my hand inside and grabbed a fistful of marbles.

His eyes opened wide. "Marbles? Just marbles?"

I shook the marbles in my hand and they caught the sunlight and glinted. The colours seemed to be scattering from my hand. I remembered a story I had, more than two thousand miles away, told a spellbound little girl. "Fairy eggs."

The woman slapped her hand against her mouth and stepped back.

"Is marbles, Deokie. Just marbles." He uttered a nibbling little laugh. "Kay-kay marbles, not so? You bury them here?"

"A long time ago. I won them in a bet. From a friend named Sam. I didn't expect to find them."

"Do you want them?"

The question surprised me; I hadn't thought of ownership. "For my daughter."

"Okay, take them. Is yours. Tell she is a gift from a uncle. You want to look inside the house?"

"It's okay."

"You sure? What happen?"

"Nothing, nothing," I replied quickly and walked on.

While we were walking to the front gate, he asked if I was going to visit my friend and I told him that Sam had moved with his family to Port of Spain after he wrote his common entrance exams. He said, "Oh," as if he were not fully convinced. I asked him about my friends from primary school. Jattan had left the village about ten years ago, Ken was a soldier at the barracks in Chaguaramas and Soogrim had been hauled off to St. Ann's for psychiatric treatment.

I walked silently to the front of the house. He asked where I was going and I said to the Palm Village Hotel in

Mayaro. He offered me a lift in his Kingswood parked at the side of the road.

He drove nervously, his hands clamped over the steering wheel, frequently braking and looking back, as if he had hit someone. He spoke about his old job as a bursar and about Mr. Sumair who he hoped would die painfully in an accident. But he was friendly with me and I felt it was because he viewed me as another of Mr. Sumair's victims. He occasionally asked for directions and was curious about why I was not staying with a relative. I had no close relatives, I told him. But would it not be expensive in a hotel, he asked.

Up to the morning when Madhoo had chauffeured me to Couva, I had no idea where I would stay and I was surprised when, in San Fernando, I checked a directory for guest houses in Mayaro and saw the advertisement for Palm Village Hotel in Ramose Trace. When I telephoned the number, the voice at the other end sounded startled as if he couldn't believe that someone was actually interested in a reservation.

Ramose Trace was exactly how I remembered it: crumbling boulders with skirts of para grass trailing off into drains, where they flourished, climbing above the knotty shrubs. Beyond the drains were stunted cherry trees and a breadfruit tree, the broad leaves like oriental fans. From a distance, the scrubbed-away grey hotel looked like a condemned building awaiting demolition, but as we drew closer I noticed the wild flowers, red and salmon, and the camponella vines wreathing the edge of the concrete driveway. The hotel was about seventy feet from the ocean and I could hear the surge and tumble of the waves. The man was saying something about money and exchange rate and

because he seemed to be heading straight for the water, I
pointed to the building. While I was removing my suitcase
from the trunk, he told me, "If you ever decide to come
back to Trinidad to stay, give me a call. Is not a totally bad
place for a grocery when you think of it." I offered to pay
for the ride. He waved his hand. "Is just the credit part.
How you could give credit to people who too busy sleeping
to find a work." As I walked towards the hotel, he added
solemnly, "Have a nice time in Mayaro. It have some nice
beaches." He reversed and drove off.

I checked into the hotel, got a room facing the ocean,
opened the window and immediately felt the rush of the
cool sea breeze. The odour of the water, faintly fishy, the
seaweeds swept on the sand and the coconut trees, at once
distant and familiar, summoned a memory, a scene cap-
tured in the blink of an eye and stored away for seventeen
years, as unalterable as a photograph. The setting sun, the
blood-red water, driftwood twisted and pounded into the
orange-coloured sand, Keith standing beneath a coconut
tree, a palm flat against the trunk, a pile of corals at his feet.
And closer, the sound of running water, a young woman
emerging from the bathroom brushing her straight long
hair, looking out of the window with me, asking what my
friend intended to do with his shells. Telling her he was
going to build a boat with them. Her confusion and my
awkward explanation that I had been joking.

The next morning, I walked along the beach. Gulls
were dipping in and out of the water. And because of the
lazy calm, the trade winds drifting in from the ocean and
ruffling the trees, the absence of crowd and chatter, I was
able to distance myself from Mr. Rampartap's bitterness,
his clumsy ambitions, his locked-away wife, his unexpected

brutality on the hill. But instead the desolation reminded me of my life in Canada.

Our arguments obeyed their own rituals. They began and ended in the same fashion. Like visiting a dentist: the initial prying for defects, the violation of an exposed nerve, the dull anaesthetized pain and the raw ache that lasted for hours after the event. It's not easy to accept the naïveté of the early years. I thought that all unions were like ours and that one day—perhaps a day in the middle of fall when the sky appeared close to the earth and the leaves spun a silent melody as they whirled to the ground—we would uncover our appreciation of each other and the memory of the latest argument would be erased. But fall came and went, the sky kept its distance and we drifted further apart.

Those memories, as always, disturbed me. I pushed the distress aside and walked along the beach. Two hours later, sitting on a barnacle-covered log, I wrote in my diary: *I walked for a mile on either side of the hotel but the only people I saw were a stocky black man staring at the water, a couple basking like walruses in the sand and a boy chasing after his dog. The beach is decorated with shells of all sizes and shapes. Chip-chips like pink baby slippers, oysters like open palms. Grey and babyish. It reminds me of a poem we learned in primary school about an Indian collecting shells on a lonely beach while Columbus's caravel bore down on him. The sailors would have spotted the forested mountains, then the trees lining the beach. Later, other conquistadores would have ventured into the coastal villages and seen the mayo plant from which Mayaro derived its name.*

If Vanita had grown up here, she too would have known the poem and the stories of the royalists who, following the French Revolution, were given tracts of land in far-off Mayaro to separate them from the republicans living elsewhere in the island. I would have brought her here on weekends to wade in the warm water and to collect her special "Trindadan" shells. Or to the Buccoo reef in Tobago, to look at the fishes from the glass-bottomed boats.

When she was six years old, she had pestered me into buying an assortment of coral pieces at a garage sale. She pretended they were from Trinidad and placed them in a glass jar next to her stuffed toys. During a show-and-tell presentation in grade two, she had carried the jar to school. At her monthly conference, her teacher at the time, Mrs. Stewart, mentioned the presentation. Vanita had spoken about a beautiful island with magical waterfalls and playful creatures no outsiders had ever seen. Students whose parents had immigrated from other countries—Sri Lanka, Bosnia and Somalia—had displayed accurate portrayals of these countries. They spoke of the wars and the suffering and the beggars and the small, crowded houses. I told Mrs. Stewart that Vanita was simply repeating the stories I had told her. She was startled and expressed concern that Vanita would not know truth from fiction. I had a quick urge to strangle her and left quickly, a bit alarmed at my anger.

On my second day at Palm Village, I chatted with the bartender, who told me that the hotel had been deserted since a family had drowned about half a mile away. He spoke dispassionately; the tragedy, as related by him, possessed no drama, no consequences. In his version of Trinidad, unforeseen death was a normal occurrence; men and women got up, ate their breakfast and went out into a dangerous,

uncertain world. I remembered Mr. Rampartap's talk of
rape and murder, but the bartender's accounts were more
detailed: he knew the names, the motives, the weapons
used, the wounds inflicted. He spoke with an insider's
knowledge.

The only other employee of the hotel was a woman,
who brought a bucket every morning, which she exchanged
for a broom and mop. Food was served from the bucket:
breakfast and dinner, hops bread and a pasty mixture of sardine and onion, and lunch, a soup with vegetables and indistinguishable chunks of meat. The bartender referred to
the mixture as a "three-in-one soup." A European couple,
their skin a bruised red, ate with exaggerated relish, crunch-
ing and slurping noisily. They were full of questions about
Trinidad, but their curiosity was not directed at the spate of
criminal activity as related by the bartender, or their own
safety or even the kind of trivia I imagined most tourists
would be interested in—festivals, historical sites, special
landmarks—but towards bizarre statistics. They wanted
to know the number of men and women mauled by
wild beasts in the last year. The incidence of cannibalism.
Female circumcision and genital mutilation. Children prepared for a life of begging by having their limbs lopped off.
And what about doomsday cults, the woman asked one
evening, passing her tongue over her lip and collecting a
dribble of beer.

I glanced at the bartender. With his unblinking eyes, his
wide nostrils and the toothpick protruding like the fork of
a tongue, he was the picture of saurian repose. He answered
all their questions patiently: the laconic barkeep brimming
with eclectic knowledge. Perhaps he too, encouraged by
their questions, had been deceived into posing. When the

couple, their curiosity satisfied, held on to the railing and hoisted themselves up the stairs, I expected him to make some cynical comment, but he only went to the sink and began wiping the glasses.

The other occupant of the hotel, the stocky black man who had spent most of the previous day with his hands clasped against his back, staring at the ocean, sipped at his rum and soda. He asked for a dash of Angostura bitters to enliven his drink and while the bartender was searching for the bitters, he walked across to my table. When the bartender brought the vial, the black man threw a few drops into his glass and stirred it with his thumb. He was completely bald at the front, but the hair at the back was very thick, so that he looked as if he were wearing a cap pushed backward. He glanced up at me and I saw that his eyes were small and set close to the bridge of his nose. "These people fleeing their ordered lives for some idealized version of the tropics have no idea what they are up against. Even danger, reduced to an ephemeral thrill, is made exotic." He could have been speaking to himself, but his voice was soft and he spoke slowly as if he had put a great deal of thought into the observation. He looked at the stairs and I realized he was speaking of the couple. "You see," he continued with a slight British accent, "we are mostly tourist-brochure people, but sometimes we get an unexpected promotion that recasts us into worthy anthropological subjects." His small eyes twinkled as if he saw some humour in the statement. His thumb was still in the glass, stirring. "Are you a visitor?"

He was obviously an educated man and I almost told him about Mr. Rampartap and the biography but instead I said, "Yes. For a few weeks."

He cocked his head slightly, then put the end of his thumb in his mouth and licked it. "Whereabouts?"

"I grew up in Agostini but I moved to Canada."

"I see." He sipped the mixture. "Yes, very good. Now—" he took another sip "—tell me why you moved?"

The question was intrusive, but he had spoken in a friendly manner. I reflected on an appropriate response. He noticed my hesitation and said, "We never really know, do we?" And in his precise, cultured voice he told me that he too had spent some years abroad. In England. Now he was working at the University of the West Indies. He was on a three-week vacation and came here because the Savoy Hotel had been booked until the weekend. His wife and children preferred to stay at the family home in Maryville in the interim. He counted waves. He also counted dead fishes, crab holes, corbeaux and the number of coconuts on the trees. He drank from his glass and revealed that he usually finished it in thirty sips. Except in conversation, which lengthened his drinking time and added another five sips. He peered at his watch, the face cracked and misty. Ten-thirty. Time for his sleep.

The bartender was still wiping his glasses and placing them on a glass shelf. On the wall behind him was a dust-covered painting, framed with varnished bamboo, of a boy riding his bicycle up a hill. The artist was not good at figures and the boy had the proportions of a grown man, but reduced. If the face were blocked off, he might have been a midget. But the artist was more skilful with colours: the shadow of a solitary tree hanging over an old cottage, the jaded blue of the sky (although the fading of the colours could have caused this effect), and the vagueness of the clothing. I felt that the shadowy drabness of the painting expressed a time that existed only in the cobwebbed minds of men and women whose memories had gradually grown unreliable.

The bartender saw me staring at the picture. He motioned with his rag. "It hanging there for over thirty-five years. Since they build the hotel."

Yes, I thought. I know that. But the picture I had seen then was different. I had missed the shadows, the drabness, the boy's disfigurement. I must have seen a young boy, happy and excited, pedalling to his house, eager to meet his family, secure in the comfort of his home. I must have thought of my own parents, my brother and our house in the village of Agostini.

TWELVE

The stocky black man's name was Angus Bartholomew Seamore. He told me to call him Angie, which was difficult, because I had known another Angie long before, and she was pretty with pampered eyebrows, a sleek, provocative smile and long shapely legs.

He was going to Rio Claro and had offered to give me a lift. At first, I thought it was another instance of Trinidadian generosity, but after about fifteen minutes I began to suspect that what Angus really wanted was an audience. He spoke in a cultured voice, but he grimaced after each sentence so that although his observations were generally amiable, there was a bite to everything he said. I thought of a man who was trying to keep his true excitable nature under wraps. Every now and again, he would pause and stare at the odometer or the fuel gauge or the tachometer. He also slowed and gazed at the pedestrians waiting on the pavement as if he expected them to cross to the other side. At the Mayaro junction, two blond young women strolled out of a grocery. One held a white plastic bag and the other a crate of bottled water.

"Tourists. They are so careful." He slowed, waiting for them to cross, but they continued on the pavement, striding athletically. "Tetanus shots, malaria shots, yellow fever shots. They leave nothing to chance. Sunscreen, bottled water, insect repellent. You wonder why they take all the trouble to come down here." He glanced at the oil gauge. "For a black stud." He bit on the word *stud*, lisping slightly. "Then they get drunk and have unprotected sex. You can see them all over the place in Tobago now."

The women must have reminded him of England, because he began speaking about his undergraduate days. He had won a scholarship and both his teachers and his parents expected him to study in England. When he mentioned his desire to enroll in an African university, they were horrified and warned him about the famines and the riots and the ramshackle little universities.

While Angus droned on about his foiled ambitions, I looked out, still imagining I would see a familiar face. During the trip from Agostini in the old Kingswood, I had had little opportunity to observe the scenery, but now I saw much that was familiar, much that I remembered from the journeys in Keith's car. I saw the concrete houses with paved yards and the smaller wooden houses behind orderly lawns and gardens, the stretch of Crown land inhabited by buffaloes soaking in the pools of warm mud, the water barrels lining the road, the wooden stalls arrayed with ochro, cooking fig and dasheen, the young men dangling strings of crab at passing vehicles, the cars parked dangerously on the road, the bridges with their accompanying piles of gravel, perennially awaiting repair, men and women walking lazily to their neighbours' houses.

I could have been nineteen, in Keith's car, some woman from a department store or a bank next to me, reminding me of her curfew. So little had changed. Banfield (who had never left Trinidad) once remarked that if someone returned to Rio Claro after ten or so years, he would see the same people, seated on the same stools, carrying on the same conversations.

Angus was still talking about England. He regretted not following his instincts. "As time passed, I found that I was losing my perspective. It happens, you know, when you are in a foreign country, confronted with a new culture. You must have experienced this too—do not deny it." I was about to agree when he added, "People began to appear shorter than they actually were. Or taller. Or blacker or whiter. Or thinner or fatter. As time passed, it grew worse. I discovered I had lost completely the ability to gauge. The six-footer in the rugby team could be really a midget. The fat woman in the store, a model. The blue-eyed professor a Watusi. You understand the sort of problems I had? My social life suffered because I might proposition the ugliest woman in the room. Or worse, the ugliest man."

Because he seemed so serious I stifled my chuckle. A car sliced past us and Angus squinted at the licence plate. I half expected him to pull out a notepad and scribble down the numbers but he grimaced at the speedometer and continued, "Now tell me, are you married?"

I told him yes.

"Yes? But your family is not here with you. Is there any particular reason for that?" Once more, the Trinidadian nosiness; the assumption that reciprocal disclosures were entirely natural. Angus must have noticed my hesitation. "I can see that you have spent too much time abroad. Do you know what I once recorded in my diary? The coldness of the concrete seeps into my bones. What do you think of it?"

The kind of line that should not be allowed to escape from a diary, I thought, but I told him what I felt he wanted to hear. "It's an inspiring line."

"Inspiring?" He puzzled over the word. "It's complete rubbish. The things that bad writers say. Yet you found it inspiring." It sounded like a challenge. He stopped the car and pulled across to the side of the road. I thought I had offended him and that he was about to ask me to step out but he opened the glove compartment, withdrew a pipe, stuffed it with tobacco and applied a match. He took deep puffs and I could hear his teeth playing with and biting the stem. "You say *inspiring* and I think of inhaling iron filings. Tell me another word." His teeth were clamped over the pipe but his lip, twisted up for the smoke to escape, gave him a snarling expression.

"Maniac."

"An edible root. Another, please."

"Charlatan."

"An old woman grilled on a spit." He snorted out a string of smoke.

"Oddball."

"A deformity. He walked as though he was afflicted with oddballs." His lip straightened in a smile. I looked away just to discourage him from his game. He knocked his pipe against the door, replaced it in the glove compartment and drove off. "A little diversion I developed in England. During the difficult period."

I changed the topic. "What do you lecture in at the university?"

"I am not a lecturer. I work with the department of social sciences conducting surveys and polls."

"I thought you were a professor." I shouldn't have said that because he glared at me with his tiny eyes.

"Professor? I am hired by the university to gather data on racial attitudes and racial preferences. Officially, I am the chairman of Datacom. Haven't you heard of it?" He must have anticipated my reply because he added quickly, "I am also contracted by the government to conduct surveys."

"It sounds interesting."

He switched off the radio, clicked on the scanning function, stared at the flashing green light, then switched it off. "All the polls I am commissioned to conduct are about race. I spend weeks up in Laventille and Morvant and more weeks in Caroni and Tabaquite and I come up with results any fool could anticipate. Black people don't trust Indians and Indians are afraid of black people. And they are all suspicious of white people, who couldn't care less about them. How interesting is that?"

"You make it sound very simple," I said defensively, but the statement pleased him. He snapped out a laugh.

"I am offered every manner of bribe. I doubt there is anyone who know these politicians as well as I do. You mention a name, I will fill in the rest." I suspected it was a variation of his word game so I said nothing. "Do you want to hear another line from my diary? We exiles from between two worlds emerge protean, choosing any shape we desire."

"Do you by any chance happen to know Mr. Pillooki?"

I had asked the question with a touch of sarcasm but he answered immediately. "Oh yes. We studied together in England. We were in the debating clubs taking on all the heavyweights from Britain." He dropped some unfamiliar names. "Two local boys. I think he went to Canada afterwards and then stayed for a while in the States."

"He ended up with Mr. Rampartap."

"Mr. Rampartap the politician?" His habit of repeating my questions was becoming annoying. "A man of letters."

"I heard about the letters," I said, encouraging him.

A boy, about eight or so, was pushing a boxcart loaded with pitch oil tins across the road. "He was the MP for Tabaquite, you know. It was generally accepted that he had a bright future. The local crowd admired his recklessness. He spoke like a badjohn. He went to parliament with his gun. One Friday, while the house was in session, he grabbed the Speaker's mace and threatened to mash up the attorney general's skull. He spent a night in jail. The public admired all that. All the gun talk. He boasted about his wrestling skills. During a press briefing he had called to protest the standardization of textbooks, he clinched a reporter and applied his hammerlock."

I laughed and Angus frowned, his cap of hair slipping forward. "The reporter spent two weeks in hospital. The rumour was that even the prime minister was afraid of him. Then he wrote his letter."

"To whom?"

He slowed down a bit. "To the Queen. Requesting she send down a battleship or two and retrieve the island. I think he may have been affected by the Falklands war but his timing was terrible and the contents of the letter even more so."

"Why was that?"

"Well, he praised the previous colonial administration and stressed that black people did not have the capacity to govern because they were short-sighted and possessed no administrative skills. This, mind you, just after the Black Power riots. They began to view his recklessness in a different light. He lost his deposit in the next election and became something of a crackpot, engaging in a series of spurious lawsuits. Seven to be exact." He laughed suddenly, as if he remembered something amusing. "He and Pillooki were a perfect pair. A reporter from a weekly rag referred to them as the 'Madcaps,' the name of a local wrestling tag team."

I wanted to know more but we were in Rio Claro. He drove past the Rio Claro composite school, the government quarters, the recreation ground, past video stores and restaurants I didn't recognize, past the roundabout and to the maxi-taxi stand, where he pulled up. "My wife is here," he said glumly. A huge woman, her hands folded against her chest, glared at the car. At her side sat two boys, chins propped on their hands, on a pair of large canvas bags. Angus glanced furtively at the clock on the dashboard and at his watch. The woman, sweating and with a frightful sunburn, now ignored him as he rushed out of the car for the suitcases. I thanked him for the lift but his attention was elsewhere, as his wife heaved her bulk into the passenger seat. His two sons loped to the car and looked at me but without curiosity.

The buildings in the heart of Rio Claro had improved: there were concrete attachments, burglar-proofed windows and glass showcases displaying shoes and clothing. I walked to Khan's gas station. Keith had often stopped there for gas and Khan's wife, Zobaida, an attractive, flirtatious woman of about forty or so, would look up from the batch of bills on her desk and ask us about our girlfriends and make suggestive remarks about these inexperienced younger women. Her husband, a benign-looking man, would occasionally enter with a wad of notes and laugh at her comparisons. They seemed a happy couple and I felt that her flirtations were harmless.

Would she recognize me? I opened the door. She was at her desk peering solemnly down at her papers, fingertips pressing her cheeks. Her lipstick had been applied carelessly and the powder daubed on her face was irrigated by streaks of perspiration that ran into her neck, caking into little waves like hardening lava. "Yes?" She looked up; her voice was edgy and unfriendly.

I didn't know what to say. "Is Mr. Khan here?"

She stared at me suspiciously. "Whatever business you have with"—she hesitated—"with Amin, you could tell me."

"I was just passing by . . ."

"You is a creditor?"

"No, no. I was just passing by."

"And?"

"And I thought I would drop in."

"Well, he not here now." As I opened the door to leave, she said, "He dead nearly ten years now."

After meeting Zobaida and hearing about Khan, I almost returned to Palm Village Hotel without visiting the warden's office. But I was comforted by the three old wooden steps that led to the front door; from outside, the building was unchanged. Inside, I saw steel cabinets and glass-topped tables, with young men and women tapping away at their computers. They were wearing ties and starched white shirts and looked bad-tempered gazing and frowning at their monitors. As I turned to leave, an old, paunchy man got up from behind a computerless desk. A Canadian Tire penholder in his shirt pocket was stuffed with pens and pencils. He stared at me shyly.

"Lalchan?"

"You better believe it, men." I had been worried about my accent but Lalchan's was ridiculously exaggerated. "Here for a little vakashun to catch up on your old buddies." He glanced at the young men and women tapping away. "Let's head down to the pub to swallow some ale. Ruthven, you take over until I am back." Ruthven glared at Lalchan's empty desk. "Catch up on the Blue Jays and the Maple Leafs. And Doug Ghilmoor," he said, making it sound like an Indian name. The effervescence didn't suit him, this paunchy man with a quiet face and grey hair neatly parted and slicked down, and once we were outside, it was gone.

"So how are things going, men," he said with an untidy desperation. "Last time we saw each other was . . . how long . . . twenty years ago?" Had he forgotten our chance meeting at Sheppard and Markham and my visit to his apartment where he had calmly assured me that he would fling one of his raucous children over the balcony?

We walked across the street to Ziggy's rumshop. A tout hanging from the door of a slowly moving maxi-taxi shouted something and Lalchan muttered, "Faggin' savages, men." His voice was amiable. We sat on stools and he ordered two beers. The bar was crowded; men walked in, ordered their drinks, pitched them down their throats and walked out. But a few remained, squeezing through the packed seats. I looked around, searching for familiar faces.

"Faggin' alcoholics," Lalchan said sadly. "So how are things up in the cold, men? What's the latest? Did Koobeck move away yet?"

"Not yet," I said vaguely, scanning the bar. Some of the customers were in their twenties and early thirties, maybe students at the Rio Claro composite school when I worked at the warden's office. Perhaps I had seen them loafing beneath the bank, surreptitiously reading comics in a store, climbing into the bus.

Lalchan was still talking. "It's a good place to live, men. Medicare, subsidized housing, UI. Wife and kids still there, you know. Eldest son in college. Seneca." I wondered whether that was the one he had wanted to fling over the balcony. "Family doing well. Best place to live, according to some report or the other. It's a pity I had to return. Static." I waited for him to elaborate but he went silent.

A young man, holding a string of crabs, their gundees clawing the air, entered the bar, moving from customer to customer. Lalchan observed his approach apprehensively. "Want something for the wifey?" He dangled the string before Lalchan. A gundee snapped and Lalchan shrank back.

"Not today, men. Some other time."

"Twenty dollars for the bunch. Cost you forty in the market."

"Some other time," Lalchan pleaded, staring at the gundee.

"Fifteen dollars then. Fifteen and is yours."

"Look, I don't eat crab. Try somebody else. Those guys in the other side."

"So why the fuck you didn't tell me that all the time then? You!" He thrust the string before me.

I shook my head and he went off, grumbling, to another customer.

"Faggin' savages, men. Poosies. They eat everything. Crab, river conch, manicou. Drop like flies too. Salmonella. Would have remained if it wasn't for the static."

"Is that why you left?"

"Sure, men. Damn static everywhere. Getting shock whole day long. Couldn't touch anything. Cold weather you know. Was bad for the heart."

"The cold weather?"

He giggled softly. "The static. Could have suffered a serious heart attack one day just opening a door or closing a drawer. Had to wait half an hour sometimes for somebody to come and press the elevator button."

"What about gloves?"

"Gloves?" He repeated the word slowly as if the idea was new to him. Then he said, "Would have looked damn funny sweating in gloves all through summer." I was about to ask him if the static affected him throughout the year when a bulky black man squeezed into the stool next to him and tapped him on the shoulder.

"I know you from someway."

"I doubt it, buddy." Lalchan did not look at him.

"You sure? I think we meet before." He turned to me. "I sure I see you someway before. About a month aback. You remember? Right in this bar in this very said stool. You promise me a drink. Remember good." The threat was unmistakable.

"I haven't been here for twenty years."

"Then it was twenty years. On this very said stool." It was worth the price of a beer.

He poured the beer down his throat in a few swift gulps. "That just full up the hole in me teeth." I felt he deserved another beer. He sipped this one slowly, as if suspecting it would be the last he would inveigle from me. He became conversational. He said the government was evil and spiteful. They were firing all the black people and replacing them with Indians. They were building new roads in all the Indian districts and ignoring the towns populated by the blacks. If he had the money, he would have escaped to Tobago. In a little while there would be a revolution. Indians would be rioting too because they too were offended by the racism. He spoke with excruciating slowness and paused at the end of each sentence. His nostrils flared each time he opened his mouth and settled down when he paused. "The revolution coming soon. Any day now." He closed his eyes, his nostrils stabilized and his head slipped to the counter.

Lalchan had been looking at the man distastefully. Now he glanced at his watch, an old Timex with a faded leather band, but I was unwilling to leave. I ordered two more beers. I wanted to know about Banfield and Sankar and Hacksaw and the other workers. I wanted to arrange a meeting with Keith. I was sure Lalchan had a car. "I couldn't recognize anyone in the warden's office," I told him.

"Only little children there now showing off with their computers. Did a few courses at Seneca, you know. Four-eighty-sixes. CD-ROMs. Lightning-fast modems, advanced systems. Can't figure out these toys they have across here—too primitive." He laughed guiltily. "Just waiting for the system here to break down. Guess who they will come running to?"

"Lalchan?"

He cheered up a bit. "Could have been a supervisor by now but I preferred to give these young guys a break."

"They look efficient."

"Efficient? Half of them must be in Aloes bar by now. They need a air-conditioned place for the jacket and tie. But I still prefer the old watering holes." And I suspected that they had never invited Lalchan to their drinking sessions. "The old hawk-and-spit rumshops. The places we went to in the old days."

"What happened to the other workers?"

He glanced at his watch again as if the question had reminded him of an appointment. "Banfield went back to Barbados."

"Went back?"

"He was born there. Didn't you know that?"

I shook my head.

"Trinidadian by boat, not birth." The man next to Lalchan, his head on the counter, snorted.

"What about the others?"

"Hacksaw had some trouble with the police, then he turned to preaching. Sankar passed away. Diabetes. Ramlal too but nobody sure what it was." He gazed at the bottle in his hand. "Most of them are dead, as far as I know."

"But they would have been just fifty or so. Even younger."

"People die young here," he said with genuine sadness. "Don't you remember that?"

When I had left Trinidad, I had always imagined that I would return flushed with some unspecified success; returning and building a house next to my parents who would contentedly watch their grandchildren growing up. I imagined returning and telling all my old friends that they too were responsible for my success and that I had never forgotten them; I imagined that my wife and I would grow into a quiet affection, sitting close to each other, chatting with neighbours, happy and secure.

"What about Keith?"
  Even before he answered, I knew.

On the way back, I looked through the window at the houses, the trees, the people, the landscape I had seen so many times before. It could have been just yesterday and I in the back seat of Keith's car, wrapped in anticipation of a brief pleasure. But the familiarity was misleading: the island had changed, men and women had grown old, had become unrecognizable, had died. Even my own past was uncertain.

THIRTEEN

Morning is announced with a flourish at the seaside; the sun rises from the ocean, briefly igniting the waves and the sand and peeling away the duskiness from the trees, so that for a moment the world seems new, charged with energy, and all our problems inconsequential. But then the eyes adjust to the light, and details intrude: rotting seaweed, the spines of decomposing fish, vultures poised on the trees. And on that morning, the day after I had met Lalchan, I thought, We train ourselves to see what is convenient; the land is just a reflection of our mood.

  The news of the other workers had both comforted and frightened me. I had glimpsed the naturalness of deterioration and realized that by comparison, I had not suffered so badly, but I also saw what might have happened to me, what could still happen. I thought of Keith and little incidents I had forgotten came back to me. My first day at the warden's office, his tentative handshake. Months later, his quick glances at me and some girl in the back seat of his car. Meeting his father in their old house in Navet, Keith hurrying me as if he were ashamed. The night in a secluded bar in Cushe Village, when, bursting with excitement, I informed him I was leaving for Canada. The look of surprise and confusion on his face. My final day in Trinidad. His gift of a book that I never really read.

Walking on the beach close to the waves, the cool water swirling around my feet, feeling the squishy tufts of seaweed washed ashore, I recalled shreds of conversation with Keith, who was speaking as he always did when he was explaining one of his theological convictions, with a slight stutter. During each trip to Mayaro, he would collect a rock or a coral and place it in the rear seat of his car. Sometimes when I was leaving the hotel, I would notice the wet folds of his pant cuffs and I would know that he had been walking along the beach, collecting his rocks and corals. Once, after he had dropped off my companion, he told me that every molecule of water in the ocean had existed since the formation of the earth. Nothing changes, he had said, it just moves into another cycle. Birth and death were just part of a journey without end.

Continuity. It was comforting to think of him this way.

When I had revealed my plans to emigrate, he offered his congratulations, but I knew he was sad, because I was the only friend he had. That night, in a bar hidden in Cushe Village, without electricity or pipe-borne water, the gas lamp spluttering and gasping, he told me that he wanted to

improve villages like Cushe. He had been thinking of entering politics. He revealed ambitions I had never previously
glimpsed. When I told him that I would return and build a
library or open a school in some impoverished village, he
rapped his knuckles on the table and stared at the gas lamp.

He had wanted to "enter politics." I must have been surprised. He was introverted, sensitive, occasionally brusque
with people who annoyed him, intelligent and idealistic:
not the qualities I associated with politicians. When I left
Trinidad, the only politicians I knew were imperfectly educated county councillors, who cut deals and disparaged
anyone not useful to them, who ordered whisky for their
sidekicks in dark restaurants, becoming drunk and boastful, then waddled unsteadily to some other restaurant,
some other deal. They usually died in their mid-fifties of
diabetes or some heart ailment, and their funerals were grand
affairs where their former co-drinkers congregated anxiously around their potential successors.

Caught in these memories, I didn't realize how far I had
wandered down the beach. I must have walked for a mile or
more, past a solitary shack on the bank of a tributary, past
the patches of broken coral, past a shallow basin that looked
like the imprint of a huge shell, past the dead stingrays
washed ashore and the small black nuts—beach balls we
called them—until I approached a small village and two
fishermen pulling their seine into a boat. I bent down to the
bundle of rope and corks and helped them heave the seine
net into the boat.

"Cigarette," one of them said and I shook my head, not
sure whether he was asking or offering.

"Come back about tennish," the other one told me.
"We will bring in the net then."

As I was about to walk away, the fisherman who had mentioned the cigarette said, "The fish drying up on this side." He pointed to an oil rig barely noticeable in the ocean. "Amoco. Smell you hand." I brought my hand to my nose. Oil.

The other fisherman snapped shut a switchblade and pushed it in the pocket of his bleached khaki trousers. "Maybe we should do like them other fellas and use we boat for something else." He scrunched his lips and spat on the sand. "You see that piece of land pushing out across they"—he pointed to a narrow peninsula—"that is way the boat and them does come in. Direct from Venezuela."

"Fish?"

He laughed and fiddled with the switchblade in his pocket. "Yeah. The Colombian variety. One trip and you make the amounta money it will take we a year to make."

"Leave the man alone," the other fisherman cautioned. "He don't want to hear that kinda talk." Now he turned to me. "We not in that, brother. I doing this since I seven years. Never went one day to school. Was the onliest thing me father ever teach me. Visitor?"

The rig, beyond a natural stairway of rocks cutting into the sea, shimmered hazily in the distance.

I shook my head.

On the way back to the hotel, I saw a truck parked on a track between the coconut trees and four men with spades, digging and filling buckets with sand. They seemed surprised to see me walking along this deserted stretch so early in the morning.

A little distance away, the European couple, spilling out of their swimsuits, were examining something on the sand. When I walked closer, I saw it was a spiny seashell. The

woman's fingers were wrapped around one of the larger
spines and the man was peering into the pink cavity. They
looked up at me briefly, and resumed their examination.

My wife had frequently accused me of being unfaithful but
the first time I returned the accusation, she misunderstood
the breadth of my condemnation. Trinidad to her was a
hole, an island peopled with illiterate vandals, a place from
which one escaped. At first, I had no serious problem with
that—I had heard the same thing from many Trinidadian
immigrants—but after a while her criticisms of me and of
Trinidad became indistinguishable. I knew that the sullen
backwardness she saw in other Trinidadians and in the
island itself also applied to me. I responded by mocking her
aspirations toward whiteness, the irrationality of distancing
herself from her roots (a clumsy word, a clumsy argument:
I could never think of it without imagining eddoes, cassava
and yam). I told her she was unfaithful.

She took Vanita to Marineland, museums, the lakes, her
friends' cottages and in the evening, when they came back,
I would sit on the couch with her and tell her of the scarlet
ibises and flamingos colouring the sky, about cascadura and
cascarob and guabeen leaping from streams, of agouti and
lappe and tattoo scurrying through the bushes, of creatures
like the pawi and the waterfowl living deep in the forests.
I told her of children climbing cashew and tamarind trees
and throwing the fruit to their friends below. I told her of
mysterious animals that came out at night and disappeared
at the first sliver of light. I told her of another enchanted
island, unspoilt, uncorrupted, existing just as it had thousands of years before, an island where a shipwrecked sailor
named Robinson Crusoe lived as in a paradise, domesticat-

ing wild animals, fishing in the warm water, fashioning clothes from leaves, finding everything he needed around him. I told her stories my own father had told me, stories I had embellished for Varun, until I noticed, looking at her eyes, that she was exhausted from her day's outing and struggling to keep awake.

After my walk on the beach, I told the bartender I wanted to make a call to Canada. Vanita answered, coughing, speaking softly. She had the flu. "I didn't go to school yesterday, Daddy, but I'm going today," she said.

Her mother was getting dressed and Vanita was on the couch, waiting for her. When I told her that I was staying at a beach house and that the sand was covered with shells she said nothing, but coughed in a muffled way as if the back of her palm was pressed against her mouth. And in that pause I wanted to tell her how much I missed her and that I wanted to return to Canada immediately. She told me that she got my letters and had put them in her toy box. In the background I heard her mother telling her it was time to leave. The bartender was clicking his ballpoint pen impatiently.

I paid for the call—the cost arrived at with much adding, subtracting and scratching by the bartender—and went up to my room. She'd been at home yesterday. No, she had said that she wasn't at school. Did her mother take the day off? Did some friend babysit? I felt panicky thinking of her being ill when I was so far away. For the next three days, I awoke from troubling dreams in which Vanita was in the hospital, struck with horrible diseases and badly in need of blood.

In the early mornings, when the only other people about were the two fishermen, I would walk down the beach and feel the sand shifting under my feet. A few small dead fishes, their bodies soft and tender, had been washed ashore, and nimble spidery crabs darted into tiny holes. Seagulls dipped into the foam and flapped away, sailing and careening in the breeze. Sometimes I saw frigate birds and once, a man-o'-war. Tiny fishes like silver lizards were swept onto the sand, wriggling and leaping until the next wave rescued them. Every day by exactly eight-fifteen, when I knew Vanita would be on the couch waiting, I returned to the hotel to phone. I listened carefully to her voice—it was difficult, with the continuous clicking of the bartender's pen—for signs of congestion, and when I was assured of her recovery, for traces of either sadness or nonchalance. Later, when the woman brought her bucket, I would look away from the soup, afraid that I might see weevils or the eggs of some insect floating on the surface. The European couple slurped noisily and the bartender gazed impassively over the counter.

After I ate, I would sit at the table watching the couple drinking their beer and attempting to engage the bartender in conversation. Towards midday, I would walk past them to the shallow water where the waves were less billowy and the ocean calmer. I liked the smell of the warm salty water and the absence of human noise. Floating on my back on the gently rocking waves, I put aside all my concerns; I gazed at the clouds through the spray and fell into a restful state of tranquillity. During these two hours or so, I did not think of my life in Canada, Keith's death or Mr. Rampartap. Or rather, my recollections settled on the less troubling aspects of each.

This solitude was different from my isolation in Canada. When I had arrived in my new country, I had no grand hopes, no expectations of favours or privileges, and initially

I was amused by the way perfect strangers would speak to me, with a kind of wary friendliness, as if they were safe-guarding themselves against my loneliness with superfluous courtesy. I couldn't tell them that their politeness was un-necessary, that I preferred to be alone, but as time passed the set of my face must have marked my distance, and gradually my wish was granted. I was left alone. I walked the streets apart, I sat by myself in the bus, I only spoke when it was absolutely necessary and I developed the habit of instinc-tively stepping back if someone drew too close and intruded into my space.

I should have been happy and grateful, but in time I re-gretted this silence. In spite of our best intentions we allow the unintended reactions of others to define us. Perhaps it had happened too fast, perhaps I was unprepared, but I felt lost, like a man who had no face, or who was daily losing something he could not identify. I had read of people who valued this invisibility, portraying it as a subtle strength, but I felt that such people were just lying and that they were really lonely, insecure old men, retreating into the only option left for them: mockery, cynicism and the fan-tasy of being able to manoeuvre like ethereal beings. They had made themselves invisible because their weaknesses would be less glaring. But in the beginning, I too saw it as strength.

One morning, after I had helped the two fishermen load their net into the boat, one of them said, "Every morn-ing you here, brother, helping we out and yet we never see you around picking up any fish when the boat come in. What going on?"

"Leave the man alone, nah man. He like the early morn-ing exercise. You can't see that?"

He laughed awkwardly. "I don't mean nothing by it."
But I saw he was waiting for me to say something.

The other fisherman asked where I was staying and as if
apologizing for his friend invited me to a "fish broff lime"
that evening.

After my morning walk, I arranged the shells I had collected for Vanita and wrote her a long letter. In the evening,
when I arrived for the lime, the little *fête*, the two fishermen
were joined by a fattish, middle-aged man who, with his
open mouth and fleshy cheeks, looked prickly and crabby.
"That is Doggie," one of them said, pointing to the
paunchy man who was arranging kindling, driftwood and
dried coconut leaves, in a triangle of rocks. "And this here
is . . . what is you name again?"

"Sagar."

"Like a saga-boy, eh?" They all laughed. "By the way, I is
Marvin, you could call me Marve if you want, and this ugly
fella here is TJ. Short for Toe Jam."

"Terence," the other fisherman said, howling. "Terence
James."

"Grab on to them coconut leaf and stick it across they
to block the breeze," Marvin said. "Otherwise Doggie go
never get that fire going."

Doggie scratched a match, and leapt backward as the
dried leaves and twigs crackled and blazed. "Shit."

I staked the coconut leaves into the ground. Marvin
went into a small wooden hut and returned with a basin in
one hand and a bucket in the other. He pulled out a silvery-
grey fish from the bucket. "Carite. The real thing for a
broff." He began slicing the fish deftly against a flat rock.
He flung the head and tail into the water about twenty feet
away and threw the slices in the basin. He did the same with

another fish. "And now for a piece of *gran takai*. Feel this."
He pushed a slab of meat towards me. "More like meat than
fish." He looked at me. "So you from around here?"

"Agostini."

"But that is not so far from here. How come I never see
you before?"

"I was away for a while."

"In the cold, eh. I thought so. You down here for a holiday?"

"More or less."

"Meaning?"

TJ answered for me. "Business and pleasure, not so?"

"More or less."

They laughed and Doggie said, "Why allyou don't leave
the shitting man alone? Is any of allyou shitting business?"

"You does have this kinda lime up in the cold?" Marvin
did not wait for a response. "Every Friday evening as a rule,
we under this same coconut tree."

"And everything free," TJ added. "Doggie does thief the
lemon from he horner man next door."

"Watch you shitting mouth."

"Or sometimes he does send the madam to collect
them. You bring it?" Doggie stood up and pulled out four
lemons from his pocket and threw them into the bucket.
Marvin, still bent over the bucket, cut each in half and
squeezed the juice into the basin. "When I add some shadow
benny and thyme, I could guarantee it go be the sweetest
thing you ever smell." He raised the basin to his nose and
inhaled. "Yes, bro-ther. I want you to remember this when
you head back to the cold and snow mashing down the
place. According to Doggie, it does cover up people and car
and thing. Is true?"

I laughed. "Not all the time."

"Well, partner, one time is enough for me. You does take any of the hard stuff?"

"I used to."

"Well, it look like you have no choice because I does season the fish with it." He produced a flask from a canvas bag and sprinkled a few drops over the fish. Then he raised his head and took a deep swig. "*Brabash*. Bush rum. I prefer it to the rumshop variety. And nobody could make it better than Doggie."

"You shitting mouth go land you in jail one of these days."

TJ disappeared in the house and emerged clutching against his chest a bottle of Old Oak, a jug and some Styrofoam cups. He placed the jug on the sand and passed the cups to Doggie and me and poured himself a drink. "It have coconut water in the jug as chaser if you want."

Doggie filled his cup to the brim and took it all in one huge gulp. "Right. Now pass me the pot. Time to get this shitting broff on the road." I stirred my drink and sipped slowly. Doggie hefted the pot on the rocks, poured himself another drink and squatted, squinting at the fire.

We sat on the sand, the four of us, drinking, watching the sun disappear into the ocean. The fire flickered as the shadows of the trees merged with the night's darkness, and listening to the pot bubbling and the waves lapping the shore, I felt I could live out my life this way. A simple, uncomplicated life, free from pretence and rivalry and blame. I would awaken each morning and push my boat in the water and in the afternoon, I would tend my little garden. Sometimes Vanita on her way from school would stop by the garden and we would walk along to our small wooden house.

Marvin, as if sensing my thoughts, said, "You understand why we not in that other stupidness, brother? The money small but the life good."

TJ uncorked the bottle and passed it to me. "Up in the town side, every day is murder and thiefing and skullduggery. Everybody worshipping this new trend."

"Drugs?"

He corked the bottle and rested it against a piece of twisted wood. "Money. By any means possible. Things changing too fast, brother. Sometimes I does worry . . ."

"Is the people on top. Them shithead and them. And them other high-class people what encouraging this slackness 'bout independence for Tobago. Not too long ago, a brother tell me that he had half a mind to go to Tobago because that is way he belong. You believe that?"

"Is only a matter of time before the stupidness reach down here. Progress. It must be different up in the cold, eh? Doggie too went but he land back after one week."

"And he spend that one week following some woman bottom." Doggie scowled at TJ, who was bent over laughing. "Tell him the story, Doggie."

He poked into the fire with a smouldering piece of driftwood. "Was me first day in Canada. In the underground train they does have. This woman was standing up, holding on to the post on the train and I was sitting below she and all the time that the train stopping and starting back again and people filing in and out, I watching that bottom. And I can't tell you all the thing that spinning round in me mind."

"Tell we, brother."

"Was the most perfectest bottom I ever see in me life. Round and juicy and push out and friendly."

"You hearing that? A friendly bottom."

"Shit, man. I telling you. If it coulda talk it woulda say, 'Follow me, Doggie, follow me.' And that was exactly what I do. The train stop, the woman get off and I start following the bottom. I must be walk for nearly a hour, behind it every step of the way. In the store when she went to buy cigarette, in the bookstore when she watching through this and that book and I pretending that I reading too, in the bus right behind she, straight until she drop off and walk up the step of she house. And all the time the bottom telling me, 'Follow me, Doggie, follow me.' But you know what is the strangest part?" Marvin and TJ were laughing so loudly that if there were houses nearby, their neighbours would have been startled. "The strangest part is that I never see she face. Not even a single glimpse. I don't know if she black or white, young or old—"

"Man or woman," TJ spluttered.

"Woman. I shitting sure of that one. Was the same story for the next few days. I following bottom all over the town. Big bottom, small bottom, soft bottom, hard bottom, flat bottom, pointed bottom, young bottom, old bottom. Even when I start applying for job I just waiting for these lady manager and them to turn round or get up and open some drawer or something. I could tell you that me mind wasn't on any question they asking me. But sometimes—" he tossed in the driftwood and took a deep drink "—sometimes I was force to look up at the face." Marvin stopped laughing and a sombre look crossed his face. "Anyways, enough talk. Time to eat." He passed the bottle. "It have one last drink."

"Bottoms up," TJ said, draining his glass, and I saw Doggie's scowl relaxing into a smile.

While we were eating, I thought: this is why I have returned; this is the night I imagined a thousand miles away encircled by an icy dryness that slapped down my naïve assumptions about myself, that corroded the laughter and made me, in so many ways, into a disagreeable stranger. Afterwards, TJ brought out a cuatro from the hut and Doggie strumming the instrument, sang calypsos and parang tunes I associated with Christmas. Surprisingly, he had a pleasant, relaxed singing voice and we listened appreciatively, sometimes joining in the chorus.

They encouraged me when I remembered a snatch of verse. Between songs, Marvin poured drinks for everyone. "Yes, brother. This is exactly what you need. To drive away the cold from you system."

Late in the night, TJ told me, "You want we should reach you halfway, brother? Is a longish walk."

I got up a bit unsteadily from the rum. "No, it's okay. It will clear up my head."

"All right brother, take care. If you around next week you know way to find we."

"And don't follow no bottom on the beach, eh."

"Don't worry with shitting TJ." He hesitated. "Was nice having you in the lime."

While I was walking back, I remembered an article in *The Toronto Star* about an irresponsible father who had kidnapped his son and returned to his native land in some Mediterranean country. I had found myself sympathetic to the father and I wondered what this bearded, fittingly vacant-eyed man, whose blurry photograph appeared under the headline *Father kidnaps son*, would have revealed if he had given his side of the story. I thought of the son, too, wavering between enmity and a dull trust, forced to take sides in a fight he could not understand, and as he grew older, transferring his hatred from one parent to the other.

And now, remembering the article, I thought, We are shaped by our tragedies more than by anything else. We savour the brief pleasures, we laugh and feel good with the world, but when they are gone they are gone. It's the tragedies that mark us.

In the lobby, the couple, their beer bottles on the table and on the floor, had fallen asleep on the couch, the woman's head on the man's shoulder. I should have been repelled by the casual vulgarity of this clumsy couple in their drunken sleep, their bottles spread around them, the man with his face tilted upwards, snoring loudly, the woman with her lips against the man's shoulder, pressed into a snout. That was what I thought when I walked up the stairs into my empty room: I should have been repelled.

FOURTEEN

I saw her in the bank. I had left Mayaro thinking I would visit Lalchan, but when I remembered his strained enthusiasm and the attempts to impress the young workers, I felt it would be better to wait until the warden's office had closed and he was on his way out. In the meantime, I needed to convert some Canadian funds into local currency. While the cashier was changing the money, I noticed the woman, attractive in a relaxed, contemplative way, working at a computer. She glanced up at me, and I saw her fingers stiffen at the edge of the desk; I thought she was preparing to get up and walk towards me, but the hand went limp and returned to the keyboard.

The cashier, a young woman, clicked her tongue after each hundred dollars. It was almost closing time and she seemed a bit impatient. Finally, she got to three thousand dollars. She pushed the seven hundred Canadian dollars in a drawer and put her thumb over a dotted line. "Sign on this line here." When I looked up, the woman by the desk was gone.

She was in a car, a new Honda civic with the engine running, just outside the bank. Because she was staring at me so pointedly, I walked over. The lock lever on the passenger's side clicked up. When I opened the door, I saw her green skirt, the bank's uniform, falling back into the seat's declivity. She had soft, shoulder-length hair, a few strands drifting around the purplish blush on her cheekbones. She looked very attractive sitting in her car, her skirt peeled back.

"What you doing here?"

It was the kind of simple direct question with which I always had difficulty. "Nothing really," I said, as I seated myself beside her.

We drove off and I wondered where we were heading. She obviously knew me. I wished she would give me some clue about herself. I decided to wait.

"So where you living now? America?"

"Canada."

"You here for a holiday?"

"More or less." Then I added, "And to look up some old friends."

She smiled and pressed down a stem of hair behind an ear. "I didn't think I would meet you again, you know. Not after so long."

"Well, life is like that," I said vaguely, hoping to draw her out, but she just smiled. "So where do you live?"

"Cedar Grove. One of those big houses built by the ex-
pats during the oil boom. They sold them for next to nothing before they left. It's one of the advantages of working in
the bank. I'm the accountant now. Did you come alone?"

"Yes."

It must have been the two beers I had drunk earlier, or
perhaps the peacefulness of the secluded country road, almost hidden by bamboo and the arch of teak and cedar
trees, but I felt that she carried something of the evening
with her, the slowly sinking sun and the languor of the
breeze barely ruffling the trees. She swung into the driveway.

"It's a big house."

"My daughter is away for common entrance lessons
until seven. My husband works offshore at Amoco. He
comes home every fortnight." I felt a small ripple of excitement. Alone with this beautiful woman in her isolated
house for the next two hours. She switched off the engine
and a man holding a watering can emerged from the garage.

"My husband." She turned to me, I saw the tiny mole
on her chin and remembered.

Shakira.

For the next twenty minutes, I felt as though she had
enticed me into her house just to exact revenge against her
husband, an older man with neatly barbered greying hair,
a crinkly smile and the relaxed fitness that many wealthy
people develop from jogging or swimming. Her flirting was
not tentative or playful either, but demanding and brazen
and desperate. She sat carelessly, squeezed my finger when I
took a glass of mauby, made surprisingly lewd remarks and
fingered a necklace of tiny seashells. Like a holy man
counting his beads she passed the shells one by one against
her lips, pressed down on a conical shell against her blouse,

and circled a nipple. I was embarrassed and a bit afraid that her husband, in spite of his amiability, would suddenly become violent in the manner of insulted Trinidadian men, and produce a cutlass or revolver, but he seemed not to notice or care, straightening the vases on a space-saver, blowing away the dust, standing back to appraise his adjustments, and turning around to smile at his wife's comments. I felt she was enjoying my confusion and nervousness, but when on our way back to Rio Claro she suggested that we meet again the following day, I accepted.

The next evening, she drove beyond her house in Cedar Grove, past a rice lagoon in which two men were wading for cascadura with a cast-net. At the junction of two roads she turned into the smaller, an agricultural extension road. We crossed a shaky bridge of wooden planks, then sped around an unexpected and dangerous curve, which led to a stretch of teak. The asphalt had flaked away from the road and tufts of knot grass sprouted from between the exposed boulders. There were shallow furrows at one side of the road where a bison had dragged away a teak log. A little farther on there were a few wooden houses perched on gently sloping hills and in the valleys, rows of dasheen, the leaves like green berets. The place looked familiar and I was certain I had passed here before.

She swerved away from the furrows and potholes and around the bigger boulders, spinning the steering wheel carelessly through her fingers. I was disturbed by her silence and by the suspicion that she was trying to intimidate me with her reckless driving. She turned up the volume on her radio and again increased her speed. I thought of a headline, *Couple meets end in teak plantation.* No, "couple" was misleading. *Adulterous couple dies in accident.* There was a sheen of perspiration on her lip and a faint aroma of cherry blossom that I had not noticed the previous day. An air freshener beneath the seat, I imagined.

At the crest of a hill she braked suddenly, leaned over to turn off the radio and in the same motion placed her hand on my shoulder and pulled me towards her. "You remember." Her voice, so sharp and sudden, sounded like the wail of an inflamed woman. But before I had a chance to reply, she clutched my head and kissed me with an abruptness for which I was unprepared. When I groped for the key to turn off the engine, she grasped my hand and directed it down. She was naked and damp under her skirt and with her breath hot and uneven against my face, I wondered when she had taken off her underwear. I smelled the cherry blossom, stronger now. Her nails were digging into my wrist and unexpectedly, she pushed away my hand, climbed on top of the seat until she was astride me and leaned back with her elbows on the dashboard. It was an uncomfortable position and when I looked at her face, I saw beads of perspiration like tiny translucent scales on her face. I closed my eyes.

And opened them almost immediately. The car was easing down the incline. I grabbed the hand brake and jammed it up. The car shuddered to a halt and I was flung forward. At that moment I saw her looking down at me, her eyes half closed and hooded and I felt her nails on my back. "Are you crazy!" I sounded shrill but I was already laughing.

She fumbled across to her seat, rearranged her skirt and said seriously, "We wasn't in any danger, you know. Is a small hill and there aren't any trees around." She repeated her earlier question. "You remember?"

"Now I do. But you could have just reminded . . ."

"You used to work in the warden's office and I had just joined the bank." She pulled down and smoothed her skirt around her legs, a strange show of modesty, I thought. "One of your friends was having a birthday party and you asked me to go for a drive with you."

"Guerra. But it was his wedding anniversary . . ."

"You borrowed somebody car and said that you could only go in these back roads because you didn't have your licence."

"That was true."

"Really," she said, as if after all these years she didn't believe me. "And right on top of the hill, in the middle of the night, the car started rolling down."

"The hand brakes were not working. I didn't know it at the time."

"I used to believe everything you say." A small ripple of anxiety crossed her face. "You remember you used to tell me that my mole was sexy. Like Marilyn Monroe. A few times I thought of removing it but I changed my mind." She passed a finger lightly over the mole, as if smoothing make-up. "Sometimes I came here after work." I was touched, but then I realized that she might not have been alone. I imagined the shock and fright of her companions if she had pulled the stunt with them too, and I smiled.

Then she said, "Alone," and I didn't know what to say.

On the way back, she drove more carefully.

I thought she would drop me off at Rio Claro, but she swung into Cedar Grove. "We still have an hour or so before I pick up Reshma." I remembered my previous encounter with her husband and asked her whether he would be there. At first she acted as if she hadn't heard, then she said, "Boysie is with his friends in some bar or the other. He usually spends his weekends there."

The previous day, I had not noticed the glamour of the house, the expensive furnishing, the statues and oil paintings, the computer work station with fresh flowers in a ceramic vase, the encyclopaedia set on a scrolling wall shelf next to a mantelpiece pendulum clock with a built-in music box, the bevelled mirrors on every wall. The walls themselves and most of the furniture, wheat-coloured and homely, contrasted sharply with the tinges of lilac in the paintings and some of her ornaments. They were, by Trinidadian standards, very wealthy. She was conscious of my appraisal. "Boysie is an engineer at Amoco," she said, unbuttoning her blouse.

Not knowing what to say, I murmured, "Hmm."

"He makes close to twelve thousand a month. Double my salary." She folded her blouse and placed it on the sofa. "So you could say that we are a rich, comfortable couple." She hesitated and I asked her what I thought she wanted to hear. She turned, flashing me the arrogant look of a wealthy, attractive woman. "There are no *buts*. Why should there be?"

"I didn't mean . . ."

"You must make a lot of money too?"

She took off her skirt and smoothed it against an arm-rest. But I knew she was waiting. "I try to make ends meet." I imagined I saw her face tightening, either in scorn or to suppress a smile.

Earlier, I had been unprepared for her fervour, but now there was a tidiness to her undressing, and in her deliberate, careful manner I saw a nurse preparing to minister to an ailing patient. She removed a bowclip, tossed her head and her hair unravelled around her shoulders. A vaccination mark on her upper arm was the only blemish on her body. "Did you know I was still working in the bank?"

How could I reveal that I had completely forgotten her? A goldfish was swimming around in a small bowl on one of the corner shelves. In the centre of the bowl there was a small neon castle.

"Well?"

Feeling stupid I said, "To survive in another country, you have to forget everything that once made you happy."

She laughed. "You haven't really changed, you know." She turned around and reached up for the ceiling fan's cord. Then, she looked over her shoulder, gauging my reaction. "What are you smiling at?"

I had remembered Doggie's first day in Toronto. She stood before me angrily and I saw a woman, about thirty-four or thirty-five, with the flashing, sullen beauty few younger women could pull off. "You haven't changed much either," I said. She walked away, slowly and provokingly. I heard the hissing sound of water and I thought: Was that all she wanted me to say?

She returned about twenty minutes later, dressed in jeans and a loose cotton jersey.

In the car she turned on the radio, discouraging conversation. Just before we arrived at Rio Claro Junction, she asked me where I was staying.

"Palm Village Hotel."

She laughed exhaustedly, as if at a feeble joke.

That night I called Canada, and after three rings I heard my wife's voice on the answering machine. She had erased my message and her voice, either from the distance or because it

was recorded into a machine, sounded strange and thread-
bare, like the sound of someone I had never met. And because of that I felt that in my encounter with Shakira, I had
taken a step to a place from which I might never return.

FIFTEEN

I saw her at Palm Village two days later, sitting at a table, a
glass of some greenish liquid in her hand. The bartender,
bent over the counter, was pretending he was reading from
his dog-eared copybook. I had just returned from my afternoon swim and my feet were sandy. I was conscious of her
eyes sweeping over me as I walked to the table. "Hi. What
are you doing here?"

She drank carefully, keeping the rim of the glass from
her lipstick. "I dropped Boysie at Amoco and felt like coming here for a swim. But you didn't wait for me."

"I had no idea you were coming," I protested, but
laughed when I saw she was joking.

"I see you have stopped exercising."

"It's difficult . . ."

"But at least you still have your hair. That's a good sign.
Here, try this." She offered me her glass and I tasted the
minty, faintly alcoholic liqueur. "How does it taste?"

"Minty."

"It's a dangerous drink. You could get quite drunk
without knowing it. I think I'm going for a swim. You can
finish it."

"How many have you had?" I asked jokingly.

"Just one." She flashed me a look of defiance. "I hope there aren't any peepers around."

"You can change in my room." But she was already in her car, parked at the side of the hotel, beneath a coconut tree. In the rear seat, she took off her bank blouse and raised her hips to slide out of her skirt. I looked away because I felt awkward standing at the door while she undressed but also to see if anyone was strolling down the beach. I was surprised by her daring, this thirty-four- or thirty-five-year-old woman who had just dropped off her husband.

"How do I look?"

She was wearing a green bikini cut high on the legs and a red-lined top. She raised her hands over her head and arched her back, like a model posing.

"Beautiful." But she did not hear me because she was already running along the sand, past the eddying waves, into the breakers. She looked over her shoulder and hearing an incoming wave, dived under its curl. She came up about fifteen yards further in, bubbling and waving me on. I swam towards her but she was already beyond the breakers, her hands slapping the water. "Careful of the undercurrent," I shouted although I realized she could not hear me. Tangled fingers of seaweed floated past me as I tried to catch up with her. I had never been so far out before.

The billows curved and swelled. A huge wave rolled towards us, one of those waves that rise deep in the ocean, scraping the floor and churning the seaweed as, gathering strength, they plough towards the beach. Perhaps she had seen me waving frantically, or maybe she had felt the sudden pull as the water rose around her. I saw her feet clipping the crest as she dived, then it was upon me, twisting and tossing. I tried to swim beneath but I was shot into an unending loop. Then it was over, dissipated into foam and idle ripples. I stood up shakily, kneading my eyes and searching for her.

"Here." She was behind me, bent over, her hands stiff on her thighs. Her shoulders were shaking and I thought she was sick, but when she straightened, she was laughing. Still off balance, she held on to my arm to steady herself. "Ride the breakers," she said breathlessly, turning her face up to me. "A popular calypso a few years aback. Let's go to your room now." She went to get her clothes from the car.

In my room, I took off my trunks to shower but she pushed me to the bed. I was about to ask if this was her favourite position when she leaned down and sank her teeth into my shoulder. I yelped, expecting her to laugh, but she bit down on her lip and grasped the hair at the side of my head. We were both dirty with sand and I imagined that she was as uncomfortable as I was, or worse, raw, abraded and in pain. Her eyes, still red from the salt, were looking not at me but at the bedhead, as if she were offended by its shape or colour. Only at the end did she look down, shuddering, her hair on my face.

While we were walking to the car, she said, "I lied."

"About what?"

"I had more than one." She squeezed my arm like a mischievous teenager and got into her car.

"Old craft, eh?" The bartender was leering and grinning. I expected him to wink at any minute. It was the first time he'd been friendly with me.

He did not seem surprised when she showed up the next day. He grinned at her as if she were a regular guest, pushed his pencil over his ear and scrutinized his copybook.

"Did you drop off your husband again?"

"No, I came to meet you. Let's walk along the beach." She took off her shoes, shook away the sand and tossed them in the car. During our previous encounters, she had been closed by a simmering edginess, but now, holding my hand and walking along the beach, she was calm and pensive, like a runner unwinding after a sudden burst of energy. She looked towards the sea. "What would you have done yesterday if I was in trouble?" I framed my reply, but she went on before I could speak, "I wasn't in any danger, you know. I usually go down to the pool at Amoco. I swim for hours, then order my grasshoppers and leave." She was trying to impress me but I felt she was revealing something very sad. "You taught me to do both."

"Both what?"

"To swim and to enjoy grasshoppers. You tricked me into getting drunk because I could not taste the rum." I was about to protest when she said, "You told me that yourself. And one night, when we were both drunk, we went into the sea and you put your hand around me and showed me how to stay afloat. I was cold and trembling and I thought it was the most enjoyable thing I ever did. I was sick for the entire week but I felt I was shivering from happiness. I didn't see you that week. You were out with somebody else." I knew she was correct but after all these years, it seemed silly to either deny or confirm it. She seemed to be evaluating my silence. "We used to come here with your friend from the warden's office. You were so cruel to him." There was an edge to her voice. "And he was so quiet."

"That's not true. I mean, he was quiet but I was not cruel to him."

Her fingers tightened on my arm. "We remember what we choose to. Let's go back." She seemed upset and I thought she would leave but she walked into the hotel with me. She hesitated by the door when she saw the couple seated at a table and steered me instead to the balcony. She released my hand and stood with her hands on the iron railing. "The other day I asked you if you recognized me in the bank."

"You asked if I knew you were *still* at the bank."

"But did you recognize me? And please don't tell me any nonsense about people abroad forced to forget all their happy times to survive."

"No, I didn't recognize you. It's been almost sixteen years, you know. And what I told you was not nonsense."

"I knew the minute I spotted you." Her voice was firm and composed. "Then I thought I had made a mistake."

"Everyone gets older, Shakira."

She raised her head. "Of course we all age," she said, holding the expression to show she was exempt. "But it was your eyes."

"Like a dead fish?" I asked jokingly, because I was afraid of what she was going to say.

She looked at me, at all my features, one by one. "A dog. A dog that had just been kicked."

The sound I heard coming from me was not quite laughter but something forced and fake.

"Everything is still a big joke to you. You could never see other people's concerns because you was so"—she looked away as if she were trying to distance herself from what she was about to say—"so selfish." Through the aluminium shutters swinging and swaying in the breeze, I saw the bartender wiping a table and glancing at us. For no reason,

I was enraged by the clanging of the shutters. I wanted to scream that she was talking about a man she had known only for a short while, sixteen years ago. I almost asked her to leave. "You couldn't care less about the people closest to you."

"Which people?"

She looked at her watch. "It's late."

"Which *people*?" The couple looked up.

She brushed her lips on my cheek and smiled the way some women do when they have discovered a secret.

My impatience the next day was worsened by the unexpected friendliness of the couple. In their heavy accent, they revealed they were enjoying themselves tremendously and that they now planned to take all their vacations here. Their friendliness caused me to doubt Angus's harsh judgments about foreigners but my mind was far away from their grandchildren or their retirement plans or even their discovery of some new breed of dog running along the beach. As a means of discouraging conversation, I concentrated on my drink, focusing on the greenness and creamy mintiness. I'd had four when she arrived.

"I see you have been enjoying yourself."

I carried my drink to another table. "Why is that so important to you?" It came out wrong, like a taunt.

She took my drink, finished it and looked at me levelly. "Because I'm trying to decide if I still hate you."

"Well, I'm glad it's only that." I pulled at my lips with my fingers, the annoying gesture of a drunk man.

She looked at me coldly. "Maybe it was a mistake coming today."

"Nobody forced you to." I tried to match her glare but I was too tipsy.

"Do you remember *anything*?" I noticed how perfect her teeth were. The couple was staring at us with undisguised fascination. "You are so foolish."

People whose emotions are aroused by drunkenness veer smoothly from bravado to jollity to melancholy. I felt fatigued with sadness because of what she had just said and because the couple had heard and because they believed every word. I got up and walked away. She followed me outside and when I heard her screaming about running away as usual, I walked faster. I stumbled against a root rippling across the sand and fell. I spat out the sand and felt a lancing pain in one of my toes. When she put her hand on my shoulder, I thought I would push her away roughly but she bent over and I saw her face, warm and gentle, glowing against the evening sun.

I sat on the sand, pulled my foot up and inspected the toe. She flattened the sand and sat beside me. Her shoes, some distance away, were like two dead fish washed ashore.

"I'm sorry."

"It will heal."

"No, I mean what I said was stupid."

I wanted to tell her that there was no need to go on.

Then I didn't want her to stop.

Her marriage was unhappy from the start. Her husband was disappointed that she was not a virgin and every evening he came home in a drunken rage with some alleged episode from her past that he had extracted from his drinking buddies. He called her a *jamette*, a *jagabat*, a whore, a shameless woman. At first, she tried to reason with him but he made threatening calls to her co-workers in the bank and accused her of screwing every one of them. Sometimes he beat her and left bruises that, out of shame, she tried to cover. He began spending more time in the rumshops and she braced herself for his return.

"Why didn't you leave?"

"Leave him? A husband? In Trinidad? Fifteen years ago?" She had believed that things would change, though.

Did they? I wanted to ask because she had grown silent. But I had seen her husband and I already knew the answer.

Perhaps it was some inner strength that she summoned in the face of this constant abuse or perhaps it was simply despair, but she stopped responding to his accusations, stopped defending herself. She became friendly with the other women in the bank, something she had previously been afraid of doing, she involved herself more with her daughter's school, she joined the parent-teacher association, she bought books and subscribed to magazines and in the evening, when she was alone at home, she listened to music and read. She signed up for yoga and aerobics classes. She joined various charitable organizations and donated her time and money to these groups. She invented a separate life.

"Were you happy?" I asked her.

"I survived."

"But were you happy?" I was thinking of my own life.

"I don't know. Compared to who?" She drew a spiralling circle in the sand with her forefinger. "If I was happy, I wouldn't be here with you. But I was stronger. He no longer affected me and when he started drinking so much he didn't have the energy to quarrel, I didn't care. When he got his job offshore, I didn't care. When he had his affairs, I didn't care. When he spent all his weekends away from home, avoiding me, I didn't care." She was reciting all this in a weary, dismissive tone which caused me to disbelieve her but when I looked at her face, I couldn't see the tension I associated with untruthfulness.

"Is it possible to be happy in an unhappy relationship?"

She flicked away the sand from her finger and considered the question. "It is possible not to be unhappy if in your mind you have ended the relationship." She got up. "I'm glad you came back."

"Yes," I said quietly.

While we were walking, she said, "The strange thing is that I felt guilty of everything he accused me of. I acted as if what he said was true. But then I realized there was no need to defend myself. Because apart from you, there was no one else. No one. That is why"—her eyes narrowed and I thought she was going to say, I hate you—"I remember everything. Every time he accused me of being a whore and a second-hand woman, I remembered you. And you know what else? When he slapped me and pushed my head against the wall, I thought of you in your foreign country with your pretty little wife and your happy marriage. In some ways, that was the more difficult pain. I thought of you two laughing together and chatting at breakfast and listening to music and going to the cinema and . . . But I knew that we would meet again."

SIXTEEN

She came every evening, as soon as she had dropped off her daughter for lessons, and from her hair, curled into ragged waves, and her skin, dried by the sun, I knew she had been speeding. And in my hotel room, the first thing she did was comb her hair and wash her face. She enjoyed my waiting and staring. When she was finished and had wiped and creamed her face, she would ask me seriously, "How do I look?" Questions like that puzzled me but I always gave the expected responses. Soon she would unpack her Styrofoam containers with noodles and small nuggets of chicken she'd bought in a Chinese restaurant and we would eat in bed. Sometimes she bought mangoes and pommecythere and pommerac and other fruits I barely remembered—*caimite*, balata, soursop, star-apple and sapodilla.

I loved the warm, syrupy taste that these fruits left in her mouth. Occasionally, she would pull away and with her palm flat against my chest, gently keeping us apart, and her head bent slightly, like a macaw, she would look at me solemnly, studying my eyes. Then she would giggle, her fingers pressed against her lips.

That was disconcerting and when I told her she was behaving like a teenager, she tossed her hair, bounced on the bed and patted the pillow with flirtatious winks. The beach seemed to improve her appearance. In the evenings, her cheeks were slightly flushed and there was usually a fine sprinkle of perspiration on her neck. I thought of her as blooming in the sun, the warm water, the cool trade winds. Each day I found her more attractive. One evening I told her, "I can't believe your husband gave you up."

Her response was sharp. "Do you believe I'm like this with him?"

I had never thought of the intimate aspect of their relationship, and I asked her, "How *are* you with him?"

We were in bed and she placed her palm flat against my chest and looked up at me. "Are you jealous, Stephen?"

The question was asked with a smile but I reflected cautiously on my answer. Finally I told her, "No, I'm not." After a while, I added, "I have no right to be."

An indecipherable look crossed her face. "Really?"

I had never been so content. Every morning, I ran along the beach until I was exhausted, then sprinted into the water and, invigorated by the waves splashing against me, swam for another hour. After that, I ran again in the opposite direction. I did push-ups on the hot sand until my chest and arms ached.

When I went to my room to shower, my body burning from the sun, the salt and the sand, I felt hard and fit. I imagined water trickling over muscles that had not been there before. One evening, she bought me a sleeveless jersey with a scarlet ibis flapping over a tree. While I was putting it on, I tensed and flexed my muscles and she laughed and said, "So who is behaving like a teenager now?"

She brought other gifts—a box of chocolates, handkerchiefs, a leather-bound copy of *Orlando*, a leather wallet (into which she had slipped a condom) a Parker pen, a sport watch with a sea-blue face and a doll's house made with shells. I felt awkward accepting these gifts, because I could not offer her anything in return. But if I protested, she became sulky and said, "I'm not trying to buy your affection, you know." I never mentioned it again.

In the night, after she had left, I would open the book and smell the perfume she had worn earlier in the day and which she had also sprinkled on the handkerchief and over the dollhouse. I felt that she was constantly reminding me of her presence. One night, I got the pen out of its box to write my weekly letter to Vanita and I saw her initials carved in gold, on the barrel.

Before I fell asleep, I imagined what it would be like if we lived together. I saw a secluded country house with fruit trees scattered on each side. I saw her getting dressed in the morning and leaving for work, dropping off her daughter and Vanita (I imagined them as alike) at some quiet school. I saw myself wandering through the fruit trees and reflecting on stories that, later in the day, I would sit before my cedar desk and write down in thick notebooks. Or perhaps I would have a job at the warden's office, which even though it paid very little would allow us to have lunch together at some small restaurant with a friendly, nosy proprietor. We would take our children to the cinema and the library and on weekends to the beaches. We would plan excursions to the old forts in Maracas, the mud volcanoes in Devil's Woodyard, and to Valencia and Caura where hidden springs trickled from the mountain into shallow basins of crystal-clear water.

One evening, while I was reflecting on this imagined life, she asked what I was thinking of. I told her and moments later I noticed her crying into the pillow. I placed my hand on her shoulder but felt she would be offended if I expressed sympathy. Then the shaking stopped, she raised her head and I saw that although her cheeks were damp with tears, her face was hard and remote. "We shouldn't fool ourselves. We can't turn back the clock." But in the night, she clung to me and I worried she would be late for her daughter. When she said she would not see me the next day I thought she was still angry but then she mentioned there was a parent-teacher meeting at her daughter's school.

The next morning, I sat listlessly at a table, drinking a beer while the bartender leaned expectantly over the counter, as if he expected a titillating review of my week. After my second beer, the taste bitter in my mouth, I got up and walked down the beach. Doggie and Marvin and TJ acted as if they were expecting me. They had missed me during the last lime and made jokes about my quietness. "Yes, brother. Like the *tootoolbay* take you good and proper," Marvin said when he saw me staring in the direction of the ocean.

"Leave the shitting man alone, nah. You think it easy in the nighttime when all you family up in the cold."

I was thinking of *her*. While we ate, while Doggie strummed his cuatro, while we sipped the rum and coconut water, while I was walking to my hotel afterwards.

But in the night I dreamed of my wife. In a secluded country house with fruit trees on both sides.

I awoke late the next morning with a nasty hangover. My head ached, my lips and tongue were swollen and I felt as though I had swallowed a bucket of iron filings. I went to the sink, plugged my finger down my throat and tasted the rum flowing out, stale and bitter. I splashed water on my face and hair and when I looked in the mirror at my swollen eyelids, I saw another person, another race entirely.

The doorknob twisted; she entered, took one look at me and said chirpily, "I see you have been enjoying yourself," which made me feel worse. "I know exactly what you need," she added.

In the car, I asked her, "How do you know of all these remedies?"

"Oh, every Saturday morning, I was awakened from my bed and ordered to fetch hot, peppery doubles and a few sodas." Perhaps it was my headache but she sounded as if she were boasting. I rubbed my head and groaned while we drove through Mayaro looking for a doubles vendor. Finally, at a desolate junction, we spotted a man resting against his bicycle equipped with a wooden box at the front.

She stopped and I leaned over. "Two doubles. Spicy please."

"All out, boss. I just sell the last one not even two minutes now to some people from Amoco. If only you did come a little before." He looked humiliated.

"It's okay. Where can I get some?"

He pushed aside the canvas covering his box and peeped inside. "I thought it mighta have one or two hide away inside here. Now which part I could find a next doubles man?" His voice, coming from the box, was muffled and whispery. He pulled up his head and kicked away the bicycle stand. "In fact, a idea just take me. You have some time on you hand?"

"I believe so."

"Okay, follow the train." He wobbled onto the road and we followed him onto a bumpy, narrow road. He was pedalling furiously, his buttocks off the seat, and I expected him to topple over but eventually we came to a wooden house on posts of uneven length. He wheeled his bicycle against one of the posts. "In fact, it look like you go have to park in the road because the garage just get full up." He whistled and a boy with a thin, acne-covered face came down a creaky stairway. "Hurry up and tell you sister that it have two people here waiting for doubles. Quick shop." The boy fled upstairs. He dragged out a bench from behind a sooty cardboard partition. "Sit down, nah. Allyou must be tired from the drive." Shakira sat with her legs crossed and her hands on her purse. A girl of about five or six, with plaited hair, came down the stairs with a bucket, went to a barrel at the side of the house, rose on her tiptoes and dangled the bucket inside. She heaved the bucket out and I thought her father would help, but he scratched an arm and watched her struggling up the stairs. "So allyou leave the children in the beach house?" He glanced at her ring, then at her necklace with sudden interest. "I have five in all. Four girl-children and one boy-child. The boy who allyou see just now is the biggest and the little girl what carry up the water is the last one. All of them does get up four in the morning to help make doubles and in the evening, Bhola, that is the boy, does go with me in the garden. No school for them. I can't afford it." He stared at his nails. "The mother dead and gone nearly three years now. She was making child."

Just then, another of his daughters came down, clutching a brown paper bag. She stood before us and although her cheeks were streaked with ashes and she was wearing an oversized frock with hems dirty from dragging on the ground, her strong, pretty face radiated purpose. The father told her, "Give it to Tantie." The girl pushed her hand out.

"How old are you?" I asked.

"Ten." She had a surprisingly sharp voice.

"Have some respect, Sumati," the father chided. "Say ten, *mister*. Now give it to Tantie." The girl looked up at us. I watched her eyes and worried for her.

Shakira took the bag from Sumati and fumbled with her purse. She had been silent throughout and now I saw that her face was gaunt and lifeless, like a woman cradling a dying child. She gave the girl two twenty-dollar bills and whispered, "Keep the change," and to me, "It's time to go."

The father seemed relieved. "I put in a few extras for the children and them."

"Thanks," I told him. I saw her hurrying to the car.

"In fact, is no problem. Drop in when next you and the madam in this side."

She reversed in the gap and drove off. "What's wrong?" I asked.

"Nothing. How's your headache?"

"Passing."

She had been affected by the poverty and the abrasive beauty of the little girl. In spite of what she had revealed about her marriage, I knew nothing of her. And I remembered so little. She slowed by a roadside stall and bought two coconuts. She tipped back her head and drank the water from the nut. Some men in the bed of a pick-up truck whistled; I thought she would be offended, but she cheered up. "How's the doubles?" she asked me, wiping her mouth.

"Hot."

She turned to the vendor, a middle-aged man with nervous, flashing eyes. "Could you cut a spoon for me?"

He took the nut from which she had just drunk, spun it in his hand, cut out a spatula from the base, spun it again and with a short chop, sliced it in two. She scooped out the jelly with the spatula and slurped greedily. Then she licked the underside clean. The seller's tiny eyes were on her. She circled her lips with her tongue, collecting a glistening drop of jelly.

The throbbing came again and I was afraid the headache would return. "Would you like to go to the hotel now?"

"I want to get you something." She drove past the shops and the little parlours and the flat concrete houses until we were out of Mayaro and into a coconut plantation, with cattle grazing on the vines beneath the trees. A shirtless boy raised a string of conch as we passed, and a few minutes later another man, hunched and miserable over his oyster stand, stared gloomily at us. Then there were just coconut trees and in the distance, the ocean rumbling. She pulled in to a sandy trace at the brink of a concrete bridge. The water was clear and shimmering and there were broken shells all along the beach. "Nobody comes here, because of the current. Isn't it beautiful?" She grasped my hand. "Keep your shoes on."

"What are you looking for?" I asked because she was kicking the shells.

"A surprise."

"I hate surprises."

She glanced at me fiercely. "Me too." She bent down and picked up a broken coral, twisted like a deformed bird. "Your friend used to collect these."

"Yes, I know."

"You do?" She raised an eyebrow, more in style than surprise. "I'm going for a swim."

"What about the current?"

"Don't worry about it." She pulled off her jersey and unzipped her jeans. She was wearing a satiny swimsuit under her clothes. "Hold these for me." I took her clothes. She scampered into the water, ducked and came out, shaking her head. She pressed an oyster shell into my hand. "Your surprise. Don't throw it away."

She sounded so insistent that I muttered, "I won't. I will take it with me to Canada."

"Will you give it to someone else?" It was exactly what I was thinking. "Never mind. I don't want to know."

In the days that followed, she stayed longer than previously, gathering her clothes, dressing hurriedly and rushing out. But we made love in a slow and relaxed way and because

I always had a beer or two while I was waiting for her, I was usually in a state of dazed contentment. She too seemed to be happy but I began to understand her moods and the uncertainty that could flare into resentment. I knew that our relationship was temporary and I tried to preserve it from bickering on one hand, and stale acceptance on the other— not an easy task, and I was surprised at my patience. Sometimes I felt that she was on the verge of saying something that would affect us both in some irretrievable way, but at the last minute her shoulders would slump and she would remain silent. I learned to wait out these moments until her mood softened and her hand, hot and sweating, fell upon me. She was proud of her position in the bank and was flattered when I expressed an interest. Occasionally, she would become very quiet, and ask me questions about Canada, but when I responded vaguely about the weather, the people, the prosperity, she would lose interest and change the subject. Once she asked about my girlfriends at university, and I told her, quite truthfully, that she was more attractive than any of them. My own questions about that dim period in my past, so important to her, were rebuffed with some cynical statement, a warning I should go no further. We spent more time driving through Mayaro and Manzanilla and walking through the crowded beach on Church Street. I had always assumed that women were secretive and cautious about their affairs but I began to suspect that she wanted us to be noticed, wanted us to draw knowing glances from people who recognized her. This absence of guilt, which should have been so convenient, frightened me, and when we were at the beach crammed with teenagers playing football and cricket and middle-aged couples eating from paper plates while their children scampered around, I felt separate.

Whenever she stopped to chat with someone, I would continue walking and wait some distance away but I would catch the furtive, awkward glances and wonder about these brief conversations. Once we came upon Angus examining the barnacle on a piece of driftwood. He got up when he saw me. "The most resilient creatures on the face of this earth are parasites." He looked to the water and I saw his wife rising from the sea like a mythical sea creature. A sharp tremor jerked his body and I felt that he was hearing his wife's massive pink legs stomping towards him. "But in their own way they are undoubtedly useful."

She was smiling when we walked away. "I didn't realize you still had friends here."

"I met him a few days ago."

"What about your old friends from the warden's office? Sabu, your trusty *mahout*, and Abdul your faithful camel driver. Did you have nicknames for your girlfriends too?" She stopped, but did not face me. "You must have visited some of them?"

In the hotel room, she stood before the mirror and without any self-consciousness, stroked her hips and belly, cupped and hefted her breasts. "I take care of my body, you know. I do yoga and aerobics. I swim. I watch my diet."

"It shows."

The statement, as I expected, pleased her immensely but she did not come immediately to bed. Caressing and stroking, she said to her reflection, "But I have no one to notice these things."

Later, she spoke of noticing some new disfigurement every day, of witnessing her beauty dwindling each time she faced the mirror. She worried about aging into the kind of woman she had pitied: women whose attractiveness was overshadowed by permanent frowns, by weak, evasive eyes and jaws compressed with denial. Her vanity surprised me but I was touched by her honesty. "At least you don't look like a dog that has been kicked."

"Don't joke about these things, please."

"I rarely ever joke."

"That phrase, after all these years." I got up from the bed. "Don't bother walking me down." At the doorway, she turned her head, offering me her profile. "We should never reveal to people more than they are looking for. What do you think of that?"

"It sounds stingy."

"Does it? I wonder where I first heard it?"

The version of my past self that she was presenting me with was disturbing—a man who casually made and broke promises and dodged his way out of complicated situations—but what was even more disturbing was that I remembered so little. And I could not determine whether the person she was reconstructing was shaped by her own insecurity and need for revenge or whether she truly was exposing what I had chosen to forget. She had obviously once loved this man, this complete stranger, and I wanted to know the redeeming qualities he may have possessed.

The next morning, dark grey clouds hung over the water, inching slowly forward like vehicles caught in a snarl. It was colder too, like some spring mornings in Canada. So maybe it was the weather but when she sat in the bed, her feet crossed, eating noodles from a cardboard takeout box, I felt that something had ended. The thought drew a memory. An old man sitting on a chair, eating from an enamel plate while his wife stood either at his side or behind him. A boy, ten or so, was in a dirty yellow couch opposite the couple. He too had a plate of food but he wasn't eating; instead he stared at a hole in the old man's sock and a wriggling toe.

"What are you thinking about?" She was twirling the noodles around her fork.

"Something I remembered. A boy. Maybe it was from a movie." She said, "Oh," in a bored way, then I added, "He was leaving someone. Or maybe they were leaving, I'm not sure. But he was sad."

She replaced her fork in the cardboard box. "Are you returning to Canada?"

"Not immediately."

"I see." She leaned over and threw the box into the bin. "Why did you come?"

"I was contracted to write something. Didn't I mention that?"

She smiled sweetly, determined to punish me. "So why aren't you writing?"

"I came for another reason." Because it was a simpler explanation, I added, "To meet my friends."

"Have you met them?"

"Not the ones I knew. Some of them have moved to other places and some are dead. But I met you."

She stretched her legs and sat with her back against the wall. I got up from the chair and went to sit on the bed beside her.

She tapped a finger on her lip as if contemplating something. "The boy who brought us here, your friend, I met him about two months after you disappeared. He was always shy but that day he was totally ashamed and I knew that he was embarrassed to meet me. Afterwards I realized it was because he had driven other women with you. Do you know he is dead?"

"Yes."

"Were you here for the funeral?"

I shook my head. "I didn't know at the time."

"Would you have come?"

"I didn't come when my parents died."

"Why?" she asked, frowning.

"Fear. Guilt. Cowardice. All of them put together. I had reached a point in my life where all I had left was memories and I didn't want them to be tormented too. It was stupid of me and now I regret it."

She was staring at me, her eyes wide. "What *happened* to you in Canada?" She repeated the question. And on that grey overcast day, when I had planned to coax her into revealing what she had known of me years before, I found myself telling her my story instead.

SEVENTEEN

In the beginning, there was the university. I was young and full of energy and there was nothing I couldn't accomplish. I revelled in the strangeness of Canada—the clothes, the food, the climate, the people, the liberties granted and accepted. Everything that depressed other foreigners was exhilarating to me. I made friends easily, barely concerned about the quality or the durability of the friendship. I knew I would move on to other companions, other liberties. This casual and in many ways frivolous attitude drew more friends, more uncomplicated relationships. I suppose I was seen as a sort of happy savage, not yet burdened by self-knowledge, not yet torn by guilt and longing. My needs were simple: I was still a Trinidadian, but one freed from the pull of unrealizable yearnings.

In retrospect I can see that I must have created ripples of concern among the other foreigners who undoubtedly saw me as pushy, silly and perhaps treacherous. Racism, victimization, colonialism, oppression: I couldn't understand the anger and excitement these terms generated among shy, nervous men and women. During my first year I received a number of warnings, disguised as concern, about my friendship with Angie. But I was drawn to her humour, her playfulness and her fickleness. Her colour didn't matter, she could have been black or brown instead. When, at the end of her first year, she transferred to Ryerson for a journalism degree, Otis Hooblal, a Guyanese student, intoned, "Narrow escape." His stern eyes, magnified by his thick lenses, made his judgment appear more sombre and my escape luckier.

My first disappointment was the Indians from the Subcontinent. The Indians I had seen in movies in Trinidad were passionate and enthusiastic, running around trees and chasing villains and romantic partners, but at the university they seemed closed-minded, secretive and sly. They rarely spoke to me or the other West Indian students, although I recall Prashan frequently boasting of his family's wealth in India. Prashan, short and yellowish, though generally pleased with Canada, was annoyed with the welfare system and housing subsidies. He believed those who were dispossessed deserved their fate and should not be helped in any way. He was racist and intolerant and like many weak people who disguise their indecisiveness with bold but empty statements, seemed thrilled with his prejudices. Refugees, boat people, his family's servants in India, the lower castes, the *sudras*, single mothers, the homeless: all were lumped together and condemned as unworthy.

One evening I was sitting with Sarika, with whom I had gone out a few times, and two of her friends, also from the Subcontinent, when Prashan strolled out of the library with an armful of books. Sarika, a beautiful woman with long wavy hair, had been talking about Amitabh Bachchan, her favourite film actor, and about the songs he lip-synched. I mentioned that some of this film music had seeped into calypsos and *soca* and had led to a remarkably serious debate in Trinidad about the purity of the art form. That directed Sarika into a discussion of the similarities and differences between Indians from the Subcontinent and those else-where. At that point, Prashan mentioned the *Kala Paani*, which he translated as the black water. He added that Indi-ans who had left their homeland had lost their caste and were consequently diminished. At first, I thought that this was a confession created from sadness and regret, but as he continued, I realized that he was excluding himself from this debasement. He was so serious and stuffy that I began to laugh and Sarika told him he was an idiot.

The women were much less stuffy than the men. They were talkative and intelligent and energetic but drew their lines and explained so articulately the reasons for these boundaries that I respected them for it.

Gregg, from my postcolonial literature class (how I hated that designation), had referred to Indians from the Subcontinent and Chinese as my "fellow Asiatics" but I felt no affinity with these groups. I was more at ease with the few black students from the West Indies.

I had grown up in a village where racial difference was a source of wonder rather than mistrust. I had marvelled at the freedom of my black friends and their knowledge of forbidden things, and they had listened with fascination when I spoke about the *pujas*, the rituals, the rules my brother and I were subjected to, but on the river banks and the cricket pitches, and in the roadside parlours where we took our first secret puffs of cigarettes, we were simply friends of the same age, daring each other on. The only references to race that I can recall hearing were those made by Mr. Philip.

At the beginning of my second year, Gregg told me, "You guys will never suffer from ulcers."

I was a bit groggy from the beer we had been drinking. "Why is that?"

"Because everything's a big joke," he said, sounding aggrieved. "Must be a Trinidadian thing. Calypso, *mahn*." He mimicked a Jamaican, not a Trinidadian, accent. His mistake was understandable: there were a number of Jamaican students at the university and only two other Trinidadians.

Myrna had the look that in Trinidad would have been described as "pleasantly plump." She was shy but had a loud, warbling laugh and could be startlingly cynical at times. That year she sat next to me in class, we shared books and studied and ate together in the cafeteria. I liked her because she was from Trinidad and because she was smart and made photocopies of every article cited by the lecturers. I felt we were a good pair: she was adept at collecting information and I helped her with her essays.

One evening, when the air was cold and crisp and the grass had already turned brittle, she mentioned that her sister in Trinidad was getting married. The sister, whom she described as very pretty, was just eighteen, two years younger than she was. Perhaps it was the mood into which she had slipped but her constant references to marriage made me nervous and jittery. I could understand neither her sadness nor her bitterness and I missed her warbling laugh and her sly jokes.

On Saturday, around noon, we were in the library poring over the poems of Blake (whom I admired) and Wordsworth (whom I hated). For reasons I could not understand, I was frustrated by their stylistic differences. I had just finished reading "The Sick Rose" when I told her that our friendship was becoming a burden to both of us. We spent too much time together and were missing out on most of the opportunities offered by the university. She snatched her books from the table.

I did not see her in class the following day but in the night while I was attempting to make sense of Arnold's "The Function of Criticism," she pushed open the door and flung two hard-cover books at me. She called me an amoeba, a jellyfish, and a slimy lizard. I told her I was happy I was evolving. Her eyes could have sliced me to ribbons but she took a deep breath and said she wouldn't be able to see me any longer because she had signed up for the yoga classes that were held in the gym every evening. That weekend, when Gregg mentioned her in a gentle, prying way, I said I had pointed her to the path of religious devotion. But I was sorry our friendship had broken and I tried to talk to her. This angered her even more and she spewed quotations from her religious texts like curses.

I married the other Trinidadian. Much later, I felt we got married really because my friends distrusted her and her two friends from Singapore hated me. I was frequently warned that she was proud and pretentious. In a way, she looked the part: she was tall and dark, with defined cheekbones that accentuated the thinness of her nose and lips and gave her a look of stylish importance. A few students thought she looked like the daughter of someone important, like a diplomat or a government minister. She was warned that I was frivolous, unambitious and generally shallow. I'm sure that I, too, must have looked the part. Later, we both publicly regretted not heeding our friends' advice, and their characterizations of us surfaced during every argument. At the time when I was not yet thinking of marriage, Gregg had remarked rather cautiously that she seemed to be a perfectionist and jokingly said, "Be careful she don't direct that against you."

I blame myself for much that happened afterwards. I should have seen the signs. During the end of my second year, about six or seven months after we had started seeing each other, she began to ask about the women she saw me chatting with in the library, the cafeteria, the hallways. If I leaned over a table, she would ask later, "How did she smell? Did you get a good whiff?" Or if, on my way to class, I stopped to speak to a female classmate about the topic we were covering, she probed, "So what were you two chatting about? Must have been very interesting. The way you stuck to each other. Like dogs in heat." She listened intently to my telephone conversations, studied the doodles I drew in class, followed my gaze in the café, made caustic comments about the summer clothes worn by other young women, their loud laughter, the way they sat in the library. Once she told me, "These Canadian women are so full of hangups. Always bitching about something." Her eyes brimming with fury, she added, "Only an idiot wouldn't see that." She hated all the white female students and would make assessments based on some feature or expression: snub noses and thick lips signified a sexuality verging on perversion; green eyes and gummy smiles slyness; pointed chins and flaring nostrils calculating envy.

She formed swift opinions of everyone she met and in these instant judgments I saw not pettiness, not insecurity, but strength and confidence. I had never met anyone like her; even when she was uttering some caustic opinion, I felt that she was different from the other gossipy students, with their sly insinuations about scandal. I saw her as haughty, decisive and assured. At that time, tired of the parties, the drinking, the little affairs, the instability, I believed I needed someone like her. She offered escape; a way to purpose and boldness. I was convinced she would bring stability to my life and I imagined that marriage would loosen her up. This heady, unrealistic optimism was typical of my confidence at that period in my life.

I graduated from university, got a job at a Bank of Montreal and we rented a small but comfortable flat on Ellesmere Road. She was in her final year at university and we were constantly strapped for cash but she organized our finances with precise lists that detailed every possible type of expenditure. She was usually annoyed if I came from work a few minutes late, but I saw her as childish and vulnerable, and imagined I loved her more because of it. We were two innocents exploring each other and fascinated with each discovery.

Two of my fellow workers at the Bank of Montreal, Clements and Sammy, were from the West Indies. They were around my age, and they, too, viewed their jobs as temporary. They were frank and talkative in the West Indian manner, slapping their knees and laughing boisterously but whenever I invited them to the apartment they became quiet, gloomy and apologetic. She never said anything un-pleasant to them or showed them any direct discourtesy, but they usually hurried away after a few minutes. I was amused to think they had been disconcerted by my wife's elegant, important look. The next day at work they carried on as usual.

I have often tried to locate a specific moment that ushered in some new knowledge, some incident that marked a break with everything that had happened before; some-thing I had accepted as a routine interruption in a normal marriage. Several incidents stay in my mind, and at various times I have seen one or the other as the dividing moment.

Once, as I was getting dressed for work and was comb-ing my hair in the bedroom mirror, she raised her head from the pillow and asked, "Am I supposed to admire you, then?" I had had no idea she was awake. About a month later, I returned from work and saw my diary from univer-sity, which I had kept at the bottom of my drawer, on the kitchen table. Green crosses were drawn across several of the entries. I lost my temper for the first time in our marriage. I went into the kitchen, broke a saucer against the table and cut my finger. But I said nothing. I bandaged my finger and left the apartment, first to a doughnut shop, then to the cin-ema. I returned contrite, regretting my display of temper and the broken saucer. She was sitting at the kitchen table with a worried smile. She said she had forgiven me.

Another time, Clements mentioned in her hearing that he had an appointment in the evening with an insurance company, because he had been involved in a car accident a few months earlier. Later that night she said to me, "Some people are not yet evolved properly to operate certain types of machinery." The statement, uttered so casually, shocked me and if I hadn't known her, I might have thought that some injury had been inflicted on her family in Trinidad, leaving her with a special resentment of blacks. At university, she also had a derisive attitude towards my white friends: they were cold, calculating and manipulative, they divulged all their private affairs to outsiders, they were slaves to silly fads, their children were crude and unmannerly, the wives adulterous, the husbands lecherous, the young women utterly shameless. At the time, I saw all of this as the defensive conceit of someone who had come from a less privileged society, a means of simplifying the complications of race and wealth. And I forgave it; she was not alone in having such feelings. I also realized that her resentment was connected with my casual attitude to everyone, regardless of race.

Her contempt for immigrants was more difficult to understand, and I suppose it was that, more than anything else, that marked the point at which a distance began to widen between us. At first I was amused by her criticism of people from whom, in every physical way, she was indistinguishable, but after a while I became deeply offended by her condemnation of Trinidad, which began to seem more and more like a criticism of myself. Trinidad was a hole, a deformed society lacking in taste and judgment. Most immigrants had not evolved enough to appreciate finer things like the ballet, the theatre, the opera. She once commented that she hated the Scarborough Town Centre because there were too many coloured people there.

After a while these statements, so blunt, so brutal, so direct, like the punch lines of jokes told too often, lost their ability to shock me; I began to give neutral responses like "Oh well" or "I see" or "Okay then." She complained that I was being dismissive, which was true, because by then I had realized that there was no rational basis for her prejudices. She had never been victimized, never subjected to insults or disparaging remarks hurled in the street or the subway. She suffered from no historical grievances, no overanxious lecturer unburdening his guilt. I saw her prejudices as fashion statements, like the sunglasses she took to wearing in the dim apartment, or the slim cigarettes, rarely lit, that she waved around in her hand.

I began to see her casually bundled condemnations as springing from an erratic tension, which could splinter off into any direction. I began spending more time at the Durham Adult Education Centre, where I had started working a year after my marriage. I marked papers in the evening and made myself available after work to students who needed assistance. I thought I was being a good teacher but I suppose I had begun, by then, to avoid her. Another teacher, Jones, also hung around after school but I felt it was because he needed to talk with someone.

It was easier to understand the precise indignation of Jones, a little man who wore lopsided ties and scruffy shoes with uneven heels, chain-smoked through every recess, and saw racial slights everywhere. All of which he confided to me. I asked him why he didn't return to Barbados and he said, "Those bloomin' idiots down there still worshipping these whitos." I had no idea where he had picked up the term *whitos*, but he uttered it with a kind of perverse relish, as if he were sucking a slightly rotten fruit. He suspected that the bus he took to work arrived a few minutes late every day just to spite him, and he disapproved of my friendliness with the other teachers and with the students: "Anytime you step out from your crease, you bloomin' well looking for trouble." The politeness of Canadians set his teeth on edge. "You ever noticed how they always talking about the weather and asking you questions about winter and how you making out?" Unusually for a thin man, he had puffy cheeks and whenever he was annoyed his cheeks seemed to swell. "You ever wondered what is the real purpose of all these questions? What they really thinking?" He mimicked a Canadian accent. "Gosh, I hope the black savage is freezing his ass off. I hope the winter finishes him off. I hope his ears and other portions freeze and drop off."

Jones had migrated to Canada soon after graduating from the Hugh Wooding Law School in the Caribbean. The idea was that he would set up a successful legal practice, make a lot of money while helping out the other immigrants, then return to Barbados famous and "primed for success." Instead he ended at the adult education centre, "saddled," he said, with five children who expected him to continue slaving until it was "time for the glue factory" and a wife who was perpetually visiting her sick mother in Barbados. "Ten years now that *morocoy* on her deathbed and she still hanging around. Land and property my ass." He was certain his mother-in-law would outlive him and all his children.

His bitterness gave the stories he told an unintentionally funny edge and, listening to him, I wondered whether the racial slights minorities complain of really stem from a more generalized kind of frustration: lack of money, family troubles, job insecurity, cultural discomfort, nostalgia for the homeland. "When these whitos look at my face they don't see Mr. Jones as such but one of my ancestors yoked like a mule. And when they look at you they see the heathen who mutinied and slaughtered their own kind."

I doubted that Canadians were so familiar with Indian history, but I enjoyed listening to Jones and I found his frenetic bitterness and his wriggling eyebrows amusing. "One day," he told me, "old Jonesy will lose his cool and run amok all over the place. And he will start *ramajaying* from a side. Then we will see what these whitos and that pretentious old *morocoy* in Barbados will do."

I could not take him seriously. I made little jokes to lighten his mood, but he only redoubled his warnings about my closeness with the other teachers. "Cockroach have no place in fowl party," he muttered to me one recess. He was a cartoon character, living off his distress, and I suspected he found a perverse comfort in recounting his misfortunes. He was driven to hysteria by his wife, his children, his mother-in-law, his job, the teachers, the students, the syllabus, whitos, Canada and Barbados.

But I valued Jones for another reason: he emphazised my difference. My problems were temporary; if I ignored them, they would go away. When he told me that he was being transferred to a school in Courtice, forty miles away, I was genuinely sorry and I said I would miss him.

On a Friday afternoon, almost four years after he left, I was standing behind another teacher, a young woman, waiting my turn at the coffee machine. The woman took her time, stretching out her movements, as if there were nobody else there. The bell rang. I flung my empty Styrofoam cup in the bin. I was only thirty-four, twenty years younger than

Jones, yet as I walked to class I knew that if there was a younger teacher at the school, someone from the Caribbean, I would sound just like Jones.

Four years. During a casual conversation, perhaps over a beer, a man my age might idly enumerate his accomplishments and then, not wanting to boast, move on to other things. But his friend would not be offended; he too would mention his job, his family, the impending vacation. They would order more beer and envision the ripening of their lives. But in four years, I had lost all the things I had once taken for granted. In school, I walked quietly to my classroom, taught my lessons and withdrew to my corner of the staffroom.

Selfishness is the least tiring transaction, the easiest response in a life without spirit and motive. It takes us unawares, in icy waves we never notice until we are frozen in a world of doubt and meanness. It is the only emotion we are unable to anticipate, but it is the one that marks us the most. The face accommodates the withering of joy with wrinkles, flattening, swelling, and with a harshness that cannot be disguised by smiles.

After four years, I had begun to hate the things that once thrilled me. I was infuriated by the change of seasons, children playing in the ice, footprints in the snow. I felt that I was being pushed backwards into a place I had departed many years ago.

I was surrounded by racial distress; everyone, it seemed, had an agenda or a grievance, everyone was fighting a shapeless battle. I began to shut myself off; for the first time I started to miss Trinidad and to re-create for myself, and later for Vanita, an island that a seventeenth-century traveller might have described, an island that was strange, primitive and exotic. I withdrew more and more into this imaginary island.

I had become the kind of person I always regarded with a mixture of amusement and pity. Jones would have been proud of me.

EIGHTEEN

I stopped, too exhausted to go on, but her eyes were bright with fascination. "What happened during those four years?"

"I changed. The way people change."

"But what happened?"

"I lost my freedom." Almost imperceptibly, her eyes flickered and I knew she didn't believe me. Or maybe she was drawing some parallel with her own dark period.

"All marriages are like that, you know," she said with a slight air of superiority. "In any case, it couldn't have been as bad as you make it out to be."

"It wasn't. Not all the time. Not in the beginning. And it wasn't just my marriage."

"What else?"

"Well, my parents died while I was in Canada. About five years ago."

"My parents are also dead. These things happen, you know."

The tinge of mockery in her voice almost stopped me. "You went to their funerals. You saw their last—"

"And who prevented you from doing the same?"

After a while, I told her, "No one."

"I thought you were going to say your wife."

"Maybe you should stop making these assumptions," I said icily.

She flashed me a look of surprise. "What about her parents? Are they alive?"

"Her mother is. Her father died when she was very young. She never spoke much about them."

"Did she ever?"

I shook my head.

"Maybe she felt they would be ashamed she didn't marry somebody rich."

"The thought crossed my mind," I told her.

"Good old-fashioned Trinidadian parents. Do you think she was afraid of being poor?"

"Well, most of the early arguments were about my job. Why do you ask?"

"Rich little children don't like to grow up and lose everything they accustomed with." I reflected on this observation. Shakira's condescending air was irritating but what she said was true. Pulling away slightly, she asked, "You said your marriage was okay in the beginning. Did you love her then?"

There were moments that spun from nowhere, had no connection with what had happened before and possessed no context other than their presence; glittering little gifts that could withstand neither analysis nor foolish expectations. For the briefest of moments we were husband and wife, grateful and passionate; they were heavenly interruptions but when they were gone they were gone.

Vanita was conceived during one of these interruptions. My first glimpse of her—soft and glistening with pouting baby lips—made me believe that everything that happened before was worth it. And our lives changed too. Vanita became the point of connection; the area where we met and felt a common delight in her twinkling smile, her gurgles, her fists clenched around our fingers, her attempts to roll over, her first tentative steps. I was part of a happy family and the days spun seamlessly into each other. When I told Shakira this she said, "Well, at least things improved." It was a sensible statement but I felt she was defending my wife.

"I think I mentioned," I said, with a note of impatience, "that this didn't last too long."

Now, I realized that I was guilty of several assumptions: that this connection would last forever, that she too was happy. Caught in my own peace, I believed we were a happy little family. We should have spoken to each other, discussed our concerns, but the routine into which we had settled seemed straightforward and natural. I interpreted her silence as a sign of contentment. I made silly little jokes, whistled in the kitchen, sang in the bathroom, patted her stomach and told her she would soon lose her puffiness, crept with Vanita on the floor, threw her in the air and caught her, matched her shrieks with my own laughter.

Was that when I became the enemy?

One evening, while she was in the kitchen, I was in the balcony watching a young woman pulling a baby in a blue cart. The baby, a hand resting on either side of the cart, looked quite grave and businesslike, like an aged Chinese being towed in a rickshaw to a place of meditation. There was a tired joylessness about the woman's manner; perhaps she was a babysitter wooed into supervising this smarmy baby only because she desperately needed the money.

At that moment, I suddenly felt my wife's resentment. Her distaste was amplified in every splintered sound: the hiss of water, the tinkle of cups and saucers, the banging of the saucepan. And in the pause between sounds, I could sense her wordless, choking contempt.

As our marriage faltered, I mentioned other couples, happy and secure, imagining she would see how much we were drifting apart, but she was outraged by this and would say that I wanted to sleep with all these contented wives.

Shakira was looking at me intently, trying to interpret my silence, waiting for me to continue. As I said nothing, she asked, "What about her job? Did she enjoy it?"

"Yes. She returned with stories of her co-workers and their cottages by the lakes and their European vacations. They all seemed very rich."

"Did that bother you?"

"Not at first." She seemed to be reflecting on something, so I asked, "What?"

"You told me once that you never wanted to be rich. Something your father had mentioned about wealthy people. Anyways, she sound happy."

"It was everything I wanted, but I felt miserable because her attitude towards me was the same. I felt she was saving all her coldness for me and that to people I did not know, she was warm and funny and friendly."

"That is how she must have felt when you were working and she was at home."

"We are speaking about my marriage here, not yours." She was stung and I apologized. "I'm sorry. I didn't mean that."

"It's okay. But you always seemed to be able to deal with these things. You ignored them . . . or you moved away."

She sounded satisfied, as if she had won an argument we were having—or at least gained a moral victory. But maybe it was just that she thought I deserved to be paid back for my youthful indiscretions.

I looked away, acknowledging her criticism. "I had another life, Shakira. In the beginning. One that was separate from hers. And I always believed that once this life was okay, no one could affect me. And for the first couple years, that was exactly how it was. Then this other life, the separate one, began to fall apart. As I said, my parents died. Within five months of each other. Not too long after, I discovered that my job at the DAEC was threatened by cost-cutting and worse, that friendships didn't count as much as I imagined."

"What did you do?"

"I dropped out. Not because of cowardice," I added quickly, "but because I didn't have the skills to engage in this contest."

"Was your wife displeased?"

I laughed. "Around that time she had developed a close friendship with two other workers at the dentist's office, who according to her had already diagnosed and disposed of me. They both owned cottages and their husbands, Bob and some other name I can't recall, were both wealthy. Bob had his own company."

"Were they whites? I thought she didn't like white people?"

"Yes. So did I. I used to find that funny. I began to call her two friends Mumbo and Jumbo or sometimes Molar and Wisdom. It infuriated her. Anyway, after I left the job she reported that Mumbo and Jumbo had not been surprised. In fact, they expected it all along. I sort of wondered what she had told these people about me. And whether they believed her."

She regularly compared me with people I did not know. I usually laughed at these insults or made some silly remark, which was not totally an act because it was only later, when I was alone in my room, that the things she said affected me—even the minor insults carried an unnatural weight. Then suddenly it was gone and I would be filled with a ridiculous lightness and imagine that the quarrel had not been as serious and I would want to do something that would improve her impression of me. Then a day or two later, she would return with some fresh assessment. At times, I felt it was unnatural to have such hatred and that she was seeking revenge for something I had done.

"Was there someone else?"

Shakira was looking at me so intently, with so much expectation, that I almost told her no, but after a while I said, "One afternoon, when she was at work, Vanita's school called for her health card number. I went through her drawer searching for the card and found the note creased inside a postcard. In the evening, when she returned, she was mad that I had gone through her things. I had replaced the note in the postcard which I slipped back in the bottom of the drawer but she must have known. The first time I saw them together, they were coming from a secluded Greek restaurant and I howled with laughter like one of these crazy, deranged men from an Italian movie because her dentist was so spidery-looking. I'm sure she was surprised to hear me laughing like a madman that week." The memory drew a smile from me but Shakira was staring at me doubtfully.

"You took it very well."

"Yeah? Well, that mood didn't last more than a week. When the shock wore off, I was sick and miserable because she preferred this spidery man to me, and he was twenty years older. I wondered about this attraction. Was it colour? Money? Status?"

Because of that, because of my job, and especially because of my parents' death, I began to respond to her insults with a hatred I hadn't known I was capable of. It was as if another man, someone I knew only vaguely, had taken control. I was shocked by my own urge to inflict pain. Not a physical pain but the shattering of everything she knew about me, every piece of knowledge she possessed. And even when I had composed myself somewhat, when my voice was lower and I was pretending to be rational and calm, I still felt an urge to say something that would prove to her that she had never known me, that everything I had said and done before was lies; that I was a stranger.

This stranger surfaced during every argument and sometimes he remained. And from his perspective I began to observe her in a new way. Sometimes, when we passed each other in the kitchen or the living room, I would glance at her and just see raw, abraded flesh, the skin oily, as though recovering from a scalding.

The outsider's perspective, unhindered by attachment. I was ripe for an affair but I found it difficult to detach myself from this unpleasant mood. I carried it with me to the library and all I could see of the woman seated opposite was her body straining against her undergarments, the spilling flesh, the welts caused by the elastic seams, the tiny abrasions that I fantasized would lead to lesions. And in the coffee shop, an attractive woman fingered her cigarette, and I saw how the freckles scattered down her neck to her breasts, sprinkling around her nipples. I saw she exercised frequently and that she concentrated on her lower body, the thighs, the glutes. She had a slight softness in her abdomen, a gentle fold just beneath her navel—perhaps she had a child of about four or five—but her legs and buttocks were hard and tight, and when she arched and tensed her lower back and looked in the bedroom mirror she saw two parallel cords of rippling muscles.

I was ripe for revenge, for an affair, but my vision of these things dampened desire. The joy of discovery, the pleasant surprises, tracing my finger along some curvature, testing the suppleness of the flesh—all of that was gone. And because I had short-circuited foreplay, I felt I was only capable of union like an animal, mating without anticipation, without passion, without consequences.

When Shakira asked, rather impatiently this time, what I was thinking of, I told her and she pressed her palm over her neck. "That's so horrible." And after a while, "So?"

"So what?"

She was looking at me eagerly, her palm still on her neck. "So I am sure you didn't just accept it like that. There must have been other women." I shook my head, but I could see that she didn't believe me. As I was silent, she added, "You!"

"The person you knew maybe, but I've changed, you know. We all grow older."

She sighed in exasperation. "Goodness. Now I don't believe a single word. I'm sure . . ."

"No," I said quickly and before she could demand a clarification, I added, "The distance was necessary. I can't imagine how I would have survived otherwise. It gave me a kind of . . . troubled peace."

"Troubled peace?" A tendril of scepticism had crept into her voice. "I don't understand. You sound like two different people."

I laughed. "I was. I was this horrible man who stared at women and noticed the perforations and wrinkles and swollen pores concealed by make-up. This cruel man who saw how the spectacles hid the narrowness of the eyes, how the lipstick rounded the pinched lips, how the hairstyle softened long angular faces. This miserable man who drew dirty glances if he did not look away in time." I lowered my voice. "I was a stranger peeping out from the shadows."

"That's so evil."

I laughed when I saw her shocked, almost childlike expression. "It's from a comic book." I looked at her face and laughed again.

"What about the rest?"

"It's true." After a while I told her, more seriously, "It's how I felt. Ten years from now I might interpret it differently. The astonishing thing was that, after a while, her criticism of me began to matter less than her condemnation of Trinidad, of all that she assumed was close to me. I felt obliged to create another island for my daughter. An imaginary island that I sometimes believed in. A little Eden."

"Eden? Over here!" She chuckled. "You seem to have recovered very nicely." Perhaps my laughter had broken the mood; she sounded more cheerful.

"Recovered? I don't know. I was able to see all that was wrong with my life. I noted my growing silence, my lack of friends, the way I was beginning to look . . . like a dog that had just been kicked. I saw how desperately she was trying to blend in. The skin-lightening creams, the hair dyes, all the little gestures. At one time, I had seen that as vulnerable, and loved her more for it. Later I thought it was pretentious and hated her more. But in the end I just felt it was wrong and wished it was different. I felt sorry for Jones. Sorry I never understood his distress and made fun of him . . . I felt helpless. More than anything else, I felt a sadness at the way my daughter was growing up."

"Why didn't you separate?" she asked finally. "Isn't that common in Canada?"

During the months before my trip to Trinidad, I often visualized a solitary life, living alone in a one-bedroom apartment reeking of old socks and stale food. Clothes strewn across the floor and garbage forgotten in some corner. I imagined decay and neglect and a miserable interminable boredom. I saw myself sitting on an old couch watching some television show detailing routine ailments which, if left untreated, developed into debilitating diseases. At other times, my mood shifted and I imagined myself cleaning and polishing and rearranging with the keen, crazy enthusiasm of the obsessive. Wiping away tiny smudges from jars, searching for lint on the carpet, scraping cups and saucers.

I thought of telling Shakira about my parents sitting on their two stools sharing a quiet appreciation undetectable to a stranger, of my mother's statement that there is no replacement for a family, of my father's gentle lectures on duty, of my daughter wrapped in a world of sadness and apprehension; instead I repeated an incident of a few years ago.

One day, I had spotted an announcement in the *Scarborough Mirror* of a meeting for divorced men and women. The next evening, I went to the session held in a church. The meeting had already begun and a woman gestured grimly, gave me a tag and requested I write my name and

affix it onto my shirt. I chose a chair on the edge of the
semicircle and glanced around. Some of the women were in
tears and the men all looked shellshocked, as if they had
been violently mugged or involved in a train wreck. The
moderator—it may have been a priest—revealed that it took
five years, sometimes more, to recover from a divorce. The
women sobbed louder. The men, as if to confirm the moderator's ominous revelation, recalled their own miserable lives,
eight, ten, twelve years after their divorces. They hugged
each other and shouted a few inspirational quotes from the
Bible. I pretended I was going to fetch a pamphlet from the
table near the door and bolted out. I almost ran to my car.

Shakira looked at my face, placed a hand over her
mouth and bent her head, trying to stifle her laughter.

"Well, I'm glad you find it so funny." But I began to
laugh too.

She touched my leg, tracing little circles. After a while,
she said softly, "It is difficult to separate yourself from
something you planned for and dreamed about for half
your life." She paused, then added, "No matter how hard
it is."

About an hour later, I glanced at my watch. She had
half an hour to pick up her daughter. "Would you allow a
stranger to walk you to your car?"

"Don't say that." She kissed me lightly. "You didn't become a stranger. You just paid your dues." She said it with a
slight smile as if she were relieved I had suffered. Before she
got into her car, she said, "I wasn't sure I believed you in the
beginning because I couldn't imagine you without friends."
She pushed the key into the switch. "In Trinidad you was
so popular everybody wanted to be with you. But you
never cared about anybody else."

I was ashamed to tell her I had returned to recapture
precisely that freedom.

NINETEEN

In revealing the details of that period of my life, I felt as
though I had sloughed off a thick, calloused, warty layer of
skin. A leathery hide, blemished but tough. When my wife
had repeated the advice given her by Mumbo and Jumbo, I
had flinched, not only because she had embellished their
suggestions but also because I had no equivalent listener. It's
doubtful I would have said anything, but the presence of
that person—friend, relative, sympathetic listener—could
have been enough.

Unexpectedly, Shakira had seen consideration on my
part, not selfishness. She said that the difficult period was
not pointless because it had led to renewal.

This was surprising and I believed none of it.

She, too, acted as if she were relieved. The nibbling uncertainty, the dark moods, the harking back to our youth,
the insistent gifts—all of that disappeared. She became
pleasant, thoughtful and humorous, and seemed to have a
new, sympathetic appreciation of me. Three days later, she
said she wanted me to meet someone. We drove out of
Mayaro to a small, sparsely populated village with goats
strolling at the sides of the road and bareback boys, speckled
with mud, returning from the fields. At the Caruna junction, where a vendor was slicing a *carite* on a huge stone,
she turned into a narrow street and after about five minutes

pulled up by a concrete flat with tinted louvres, a garish red
roof and a sign planted on the overgrown lawn: Swami
Bhasker. Palm Reading. Birth. Death. Marriage. Repairs.
She honked and the front door opened immediately. A
frightfully fat man emerged and without looking at us
stomped, with a ponderous crouch as if he were pulling an
invisible weighty tail, to the side of the house.

"Should we follow him?"

"Yes. His office is at the back."

He was seated in his office, a small circular shed with
long varnished benches that looked as if they had been
bought or stolen from a school. He had already adopted a
lotus position, precarious on the narrow bench.

"*Awo beti*. The dog tie." As clarification he added, "I does
keep him tie ever since he nearly bite out a lady foot." He
shook his head, distressed with the memory. "But is a good
dog otherwise. Don't touch meat." He pinched off a leaf from
a tulsi plant, kneaded it and popped the ball in his mouth.
"Now, what is the problem this time? Child*buth*? Or just a
simple palm *deeveneshan*?" He made it into a Hindi word.

"Palm reading, swami."

He seemed disappointed. "Okay, come sit down on this
bench here." His big eyes, hooded at the top and exposed
by slack skin at the bottom, combined well with his flaring
nostrils and made him appear sinister and philosophical.
He spat out the tulsi leaf, closed his eyes and traced his fingers along the lines of her palm. He had small fingers, surprising in such a big man, but the nails were coated with
grime. He parted his lips, and uttered a sound that could
have been a chuckle, a belch, a mystic syllable or perhaps a
gathering premonition. "I see you had plenty problems in
you life, *beti*. Plenty nastiness and grease."

Did he say *grease?* I wanted to ask but his eyelids were fluttering and I suspected he was peeping at us. "But you is a courageous girl. You was able to jump-start you life with nobody to help out." He circled an area in her palm and opened his eyes. "The road might have one or two bump but you will drive through with no problem at all." He may have felt that his prediction was insubstantial because he added, "Stay away from the colour mauve and don't leave the house if anybody sneeze." He pulled away his hand gently and crossed them on his belly, signalling he was finished with her. He looked up at me and I pushed out my hand. "Is you a right-hander or is you a left-hander?"

"Left-hander."

"Hmm. Just as I thought." He frowned. "Something get clog up right here." He tapped a line. "You have any children?" He glanced swiftly at her.

"One," I told him.

"You sure?"

He pulled my palm closer to his face and twisted it. "I seeing two children here. One boy, one girl. Two in all." He released my hand. "The clogging up will stop but careful of the fumes."

"What fumes?"

"The fumes what cause the clogging up." He pinched off another tulsi leaf, kneaded it and closed his eyes. She took out a twenty-dollar bill and placed it between his kneading fingers. He opened his eyes. "And adjust the timing belt." As we were leaving, he glanced at Shakira, his hooded eyelids drooping spectacularly. "What is to is must is, *beti*."

"What was all that about?" I asked as we got into the car.

"He is a well-known palm reader. People from all over come to get a reading."

"Seriously?"

"Yes. He's been doing this for nearly fifteen years now. Ever since he left his job as a mechanic with the bus company."

"No wonder we got an engine job instead of a palm reading."

Previously, she would have been offended but she giggled. "You always used to say silly things like that."

"I used to?" I asked, but gently.

"You made fun of everyone."

But innocent fun, I wanted to say, *because I can't even remember any of it.*

"I saw him once before. About eight years ago. I went to other psychic people too. A *sadhwine* from Barrackpore, and pundits who read from their *patras.*"

"I didn't know you were so religious."

"If I was religious, I wouldn't be here with you," she said with such directness I was astonished. "But I believe we pay for all the things we do."

"Then in our other lives we might be reborn as . . ."

"In this life. We pay in this life. I see it happen over and over again."

"Anyways, I don't believe one word the mechanic said. He speculated that I will have two children."

She went silent.

And I realized why she had forgiven me.

I began to see this other side of her. She maintained she was not religious but she interspersed her observations with words like *passages* and *renewal*, concepts I associated with glossy best-sellers whose authors routinely appeared on talk shows to promote their miracles. Once, she told me, "We must not live for the moment but in the moment." I felt that she was relieved that I had not escaped the torment that characterized her own marriage. I began to understand, too, her belief in a kind of equivalent punishment: I was absolved because I had suffered; the slate was wiped clean.

I was grateful for this change. One evening an American, quite drunk, was chatting with the bartender. The American, whose huge nose and small, slender body made him look portable, was commenting on a story related to him by a fellow worker at Amoco. The worker had told him about the *papa bois*, a creature that he said protected the forests of Biche and Guanapo. It was the scourge of hunters; sometimes the *papa bois* assumed the form of a quenk or an agouti and led hunters deep into the forests. They would never be seen again, but there were stories of half-eaten bodies and gnawed bones. The American slapped the table and laughed uproariously. Another worker had sworn he had spotted a mermaid swimming merrily around a rig. But this worker had also seen a *mama diglou* enticing him into the water. He had not taken the bait because he knew that beneath the brown water was not a voluptuous woman's figure but a scaly serpent ready to coil around him.

I was looking at the sly smile on the bartender's face when Shakira nudged me and pointed to the American's knapsack bundled beneath his chair. Jutting out of his pouch was a folded copy of *News of the World*, and its headline, "World War Two Bomber Discovered On Moon."

She was shaking. I took one look at her face and I too began to laugh. The American, misunderstanding, started another story about obeah and satanic rituals. The European couple, if they were still around, would have been fascinated.

We took long, leisurely walks along the beach; sometimes she came into my room just to wash her face and comb her hair before she left. Our relationship changed; I felt peaceful and relaxed. I told her that and she asked for my definition of happiness.

"Forgetting," I told her.

She walked on, biting her lips. "No, remembering," she said.

Two seagulls were flapping above a gently rocking boat moored to a coconut tree. In the setting sun they seemed cast in fire. Then perhaps realizing the boat held nothing for them, they flew off, diving into the ocean again and again, flying farther away until they were just flaming specks. I felt like taking her hand and wading into the water. "Anticipation."

"What?"

"Anticipation," I repeated. "My definition of happiness."

She glanced at me as if she were going to say something then relaxed her clasp and walked on silently. "When I was a little girl, my mother used to tell me a story."

I waited.

"About this oyster that lived deep beneath the sea. Waiting for this special moment when it would rise to the surface and collect one precious drop of rainwater. Its entire life just for this one second but years later a pearl would be formed."

It was a beautiful story but I felt, to a little girl, rather sad. I tried to imagine the circumstances under which her mother related the story.

"What do you think?" she asked.

"I don't know. I feel sorry for the oyster."

She smiled. "Come. I want to show you something."

"Where are we going?" We drove past Mafeking and the other little villages.

"By a friend."

"Whose?"

"Wait and see."

We approached the house in Agostini and I saw the Kingswood parked outside the wooden gates. "I used to live there."

She slowed. "Do you want to stop?"

I shook my head.

"Does a relative live there now?"

"No. The property was put up for sale by my brother. Someone from Arouca bought it. He said he was out-smarted by a man named Sumair."

"Where is your brother now?"

"He lives in England."

"Is he married?"

"Happily."

"Maybe he deserved it."

"In what way?"

"You should have paid more attention to your friend. Would you be annoyed if I told you something? It was a long time now." I said nothing so she continued. "You were talking about this man from Rio Claro who won the first prize in the lottery and left his wife and seven or eight children for some pretty young girl."

"You remember *that*?"

"You thought this man was so lucky. But your friend said that he didn't deserve it and that his happiness wouldn't last. And throughout that conversation, while you were laughing and defending this man, I was thinking, What am

I doing going out with you when your friend is so much . . . more thoughtful."

"You remember all that?" I repeated stupidly.

"Oh yes. I remember when your friend used to say that we have to account for every little thing that we do. Do you recognize this place?"

The windows, nailed shut now, had always been open then and the small yard carefully maintained. Now it was overgrown with knot grass, and the branches of the chenette tree, once neatly pruned, were hanging over the front door. The brown paint flaking into rusted patterns had covered the entire house. "Why are we here?"

"I want to show you something. Aren't you coming?"

A young woman, perhaps hearing the car, opened the front door. She was very dark and her oiled hair was tied in a bun. She stared at us suspiciously.

"Is Uncle home?"

"Where else you expect him to be? On top of a tree?"

"Can we see him?" I asked.

"Anybody holding you back?"

She stepped back, to the side of the door, and we entered. An old man, his face blurred in the darkness, was sitting on a rattan settee.

"Uncle?"

"Yes, *beti.*" It sounded like a question.

"I bring somebody to meet you. From Canada."

"Ka-nay-da?"

"Yes, but he was to live here longtime." He raised his head and I saw he was blind.

"Uncle Mahadeo?" I said. Shakira glanced sharply at me.

"Yes, *beta.* Who son you be?"

"Sagar. Sagar from Agostini. He dead now."

"Don't know him, *beta*." His fingers were clasping and unclasping the settee. "You here for a visit?"

"I use to come here. Long-long time now."

Even though he was blind, he turned his head to me. "Come. Give me you hand." His fingers were long and bony and I felt their pressure as he gripped my wrist. "You know?"

"I find out after, Uncle."

He released my hand. "He was a bright-bright boy, *beta*." He rubbed the skin on his neck as if testing for bristles. "Never talk much. Children like that does know they time short. They quiet-quiet because they hearing God whispering to them. Talking to them all the time." He leaned back. "They didn't find the body until two days later. Just quarter mile from here. The same spot way we was to go for swimming when he was so high." He raised a hand to indicate height. "Just a little *bacha* that time but he was a good-good swimmer. I self what teach him." He dropped his hand. "Some people say was the current, 'cause of all the rain. Other people say he get hook up in the bamboo below the water. What you say you name was again?"

"Stephen."

"You and he was good friend, *beta*?" His body stiffened and his hand, trembling, reached for his walking stick propped against the settee.

"He was my best friend."

"He didn't have much friend," he said as if he didn't believe me. "Especially these politic-sing people what was to come in this same room"—he tapped his stick on the floor—"asking him to do this and do that. If he did take all the bribe they bring, he would of be a rich-rich man. But he was never interested in that. When he was going up for

the county council, he was to say that he go help the poor
people fust. To get water and 'lectricity. Build school and
thing for them." We followed him out of the room. When I
touched his shoulder because the yard was rocky and uneven, he said, "Is okay. I know this spot good. Now me one
does come here in the evening." His stick clicked between
the stones. "And these people bringing they bribe was to get
vex sometime and leave the house cussing too bad. All the
rich people who 'custom getting government contract.
They was to come all hour of the night with they bribe. But
you know what he prefer to do more than anything? When
the pressure start getting too much?" He raised his stick.
"Building that wheel."

She drove slowly, glancing at me. After about five minutes, she asked, "Do you know what that was? What's the
matter?"

A few months before I left for Canada, I had visited Keith's
father. Keith was reluctant but I insisted. In Canada, whenever I thought of that visit, I wondered whether Keith's hesitation and embarrassment stemmed from the fact that
they were, by Trinidadian standards, not a normal family.
His mother had died when Keith was four and his father
never remarried. Although his father was not blind then, he
seemed tired and worn. Keith had hurried me away from
the small house, away from his father sitting on his chair, to
the backyard, where he had already bent and twisted the
steel rods to form a circle with a diameter as wide as the
span of my arms. Littered at the base were his rocks and
corals. He must have worked painstakingly in the years that
followed because the concrete base upon which the wheel

stood was studded with sea conchs. On the spokes that converged at the centre were pieces of coral, polished driftwood, the spiny bones of fishes and hundreds of shells, each shaped differently.

But perhaps his wheel was unfinished because pieces of steel and angle-iron jutted from the lower section. From a distance, it looked like the crude outline of a dancing figure. I wondered how long ago he had stopped his construction.

"What's the matter?" Shakira asked again.

I tried to change the subject. "How did you know about the wheel?"

"I came to the funeral because I had met him again some time after you left. And because he was your friend I came back and the old man showed me the wheel. He wasn't blind then."

"Who was the girl?"

"Some relative who take care of him, I suppose."

"She doesn't look too happy with that. I wonder who pays her?"

"That's none of our business," she said quickly, then asked, "What does it mean? This wheel. What was he trying to do?"

"The dance of time."

"What?"

I tried to remember a conversation but I could recall only Keith's reluctance to elaborate. "He was trying to rework an ancient Indian motif. The dancing Shiva."

"I don't understand, Stephen."

"I'm not too sure I do either." I wished I had paid more attention to Keith's faltering explanations. "I think he was trying to prove the unity of all things. That's the phrase he used. He used to say that all these incarnations, Brahma, Vishnu

and Shiva and so on, were one. Different forms—different
shapes—were chosen according to the circumstances."

"I didn't know he was religious."

"He wasn't. It was just part of his belief. Out of chaos
comes order. It's a Hindu theological idea."

"Well, it didn't work for him." I agreed, and wondered
whether she knew more of him than she cared to admit.
She drove in silence then she said, "The old man doesn't
believe his death was an accident. He said Keith was a good
swimmer."

The same suspicion had crossed my mind when Lalchan
had disclosed the nature of Keith's death; but Lalchan had
also mentioned that it was a time of continuous rain and
that the rivers were bursting. "I don't believe it was an accident either." I was surprised at how soft my voice sounded.

"Was he murdered?"

After a long while I told her, "No."

TWENTY

The next day, I walked past Marvin and TJ's boat rocking
in the water, past little clusters of huts built on the brink of
a ravine flowing muddily into the ocean, past the red
flags planted on the shore to indicate that bathing here was
prohibited. I walked until the sand gave way to shale, and
the coconut trees to mangrove, the aerial roots like the
gnarled remnants of some primitive massacre. In this unlikely spot, I saw a house built on long logs, and on the
veranda a man, maybe in his fifties, his body hardened by

the sun and the sea, scraping the flesh from a sea conch. He glanced up at me, tapped the conch on the railing and continued scraping.

He was unfazed by my sudden appearance; I could detect no interest or apprehension in his brief glance. But I was curious. Did he have a wife and children playing somewhere in the house? His methodical scraping suggested a man unaccustomed to disturbances. Had he left his family in some noisy, crowded flat for this secluded house in the swamp?

The following day, the front door and window were shut and the house looked uninhabited. I wondered whether I had imagined him bent over the railing and scraping his conch or whether he had hurriedly fled because his privacy had been uncovered. For the next three days I walked to the mangrove, thinking I would ask him to explain the pleasures of his reclusion, but he was not to be seen.

That Friday, when Shakira asked where I had vanished to all week, I told her I had been walking. She had thought at first that I had returned to Canada, but the bartender had explained that all my things were still in my room. She watched me closely as I told her about the mysterious man in the mangrove swamp. She was not wearing make-up and small beads of perspiration glistened on her neck.

"Would you like to go to Tobago?"

"Why?" She still had her guarded expression.

"I'm trying to keep my promise."

"Typical. Seventeen years later." She relaxed a bit. "Then you didn't hear."

I shook my head.

"While you were wandering around in the bush, searching for the crazy man, the big talk was about independence in Tobago."

"The same old story . . ."

"No, this is serious. The people in the Assembly refused to stand up when they were playing the national anthem and some of the flags on the government building were destroyed."

I laughed, then she added, "They also stoned the prime minister car when he went to investigate and some businessman or the other from Trinidad was pulled from a guest house and beaten."

"Seriously? Maybe they'll send down the regiment to maintain peace."

"I doubt that. They have a bit of support in Trinidad too. The opposition party and some group from the university. Some back-to-Tobago movement."

I remembered the man from Ziggy's bar who had inveigled two beers from me. "I'm sure these people never lived there. What's the population of Tobago now?"

"I dunno. Maybe fifty or sixty thousand."

"Interesting."

"You sound like that big-ears man from TV. What you thinking about?"

"Something Mr. Rampartap mentioned. Well, that's that. I guess Tobago's out."

"I want you to go to a fête with me. At the Amoco sports complex." She said this quickly, as if it had been in her mind all along, but it was only after she had left that I remembered her husband worked at Amoco.

I grumbled about the dark green suit she had bought although it was the only thing I could have worn to the fête, because my clothes were all rumpled from the hotel's rickety washer.

"You look very spiffy. Here, let me straighten your tie."
I moved away and she giggled. "Be a good boy now." My
face reddened and she laughed, throwing back her head.

"Are you enjoying this?"

"I want you to look as handsome as you used to."

"Thanks."

She laughed again, but in the car her mood changed
and she grew silent, contemplative. I saw her tapping her
fingers on the steering wheel.

"Will your husband be at this fête?"

"Most likely. Why?"

"I would like to return to Canada in one piece."

She patted my leg. "You don't have to bother about
that. We're here. Come." She got out of the car, took my
hand and steered me past a huge auditorium from which
calypso music was blasting, to the dimly lit pool area.
There were small groups seated around plastic tables rim-
ming the pool.

"It's crowded in here." She fanned her neck with her
palm and I caught the aroma of her perfume, hot and cloy-
ing. At the edge of the pool, a couple got up and headed for
the auditorium. "There."

"Do you know them?" I asked, glancing at the men at
the table.

"No. Quickly, before it's taken." The three men looked
at us and, slouched over their beers, resumed their conversation. "Wait here. I'm going to get something to drink."
She drifted off, beautiful in her black dress.

One of the men glanced at her, winked at no one in particular and said, "These fellows don't know what they getting in. The latest I hear is that they designing they own
flag and they own national anthem and—"

"I don't want to cut you across but they know damn well what they getting in. Bacchanal and confusion. Just another fête. A big lime. They like that."

The third man, clamping his cigarette holder like a small tube, pushed it into his mouth and sucked. Between puffs, he said, "They only good at destroying . . . they leave the building for others to do."

"These fellows in Uganda do the same sort of nonsense and they end up with only run-down business and equipment nobody could—"

"I don't want to cut you across but is they partners in Trinidad who giving me the headache. Nobody saying this, but it turning out to be a big race thing. Black against Indian. I don't understand all this grievance talk they talking about."

"Race have nothing to do with it. What they interested in . . . is glamour. Like these little boys running around with they earring and they bad music. Is just . . . the glamour."

"I wonder if these fellows ever think of the consequences?"

"Glamour . . . have no consequences."

Shakira returned with two glasses of wine, sat and gazed around.

"Are you looking for someone?" I asked.

"Not really."

The three men, seemingly oblivious to our presence, continued their conversation. Shakira waved away the smoke drifting around her face. "Goodness." She sounded exasperated.

"Where are you going?" I asked as she got up.

"To the tennis court. Take your drink." I saw her scanning the crowd as we made our way between the tables and the couples coming from the auditorium.

The pathway to the tennis court was overlaid with cobblestones and bordered with bougainvillaea, the petals a pale pink in the dim light. Beyond the bougainvillaea, a silvery shrub glittered with leaves like tiny coins. The tennis court was covered, tent-like, with tarpaulin. At the entrance, the doorman nodded as if he knew her and allowed us entry. "It's only for members," she said.

The atmosphere was pleasanter here, more relaxed. Men and women moved around, chatting, drinks in their hands. They all seemed familiar with each other.

"Hell-ow." A woman stalked towards us. "So glad you could come." Shakira's nails dug into my arm. The woman turned to me. "Have we met?"

As I was about to answer, Shakira said, "He's a Canadian here for a vacation."

The woman pushed her face to me, wrinkling her forehead and grimacing. "How's it been so far? Enjoying yourself?"

Shakira's nails dug deeper. "It's been great," I told her.

"Have you checked up on all your friends and relatives?" she demanded.

"I've spent the entire time with Shakira actually."

The woman's lips, still holding the grimace, twisted into a smile. She glanced at a dancing couple. The man, his belly bulging through his suit, was kicking his heels wildly and the woman in a sari was spinning around and pawing the air. "There's nothing as ridiculous as an Indian in full flight on the dance floor." She turned to Shakira. "Well, have fun. Bring him across some time, Shakira." She turned around abruptly and walked away.

"What do you think?" Shakira asked me. I was awestruck by the woman's ugliness, which I had at first mistaken for the kind of grim, calculating expression that some people develop as a warning to interlopers, but as I watched her elongating her body until her face was almost smashed against a wincing young man, I saw that the look was etched deeply on her face. Shakira seemed mesmerized and I thought that it was because of the woman's striking ugliness. "What's the name of the kind of animals that look like rats?" I didn't know what she was talking about. "Like manicou. They live in Australia."

"Bandicoots?"

"Yes. That woman remind me of a bandicoot. A hungry one." I was shocked by her malicious expression.

Then it hit me.

"Where's your husband?"

"He must be nearby. The bitch is in heat." I had to smile at the look in her eyes, the shape of her mouth and her poisonous anger as she spat out the words. But later, in the auditorium, while she was dancing to a calypso with utter abandon, grinding against me and pulling away, so that a few couples stopped dancing and cleared that portion of the floor to gawk, I wanted to say: I thought you were over all that.

In the middle of a calypso, she shouted into my ear over the loud music, "Let's leave."

She reversed recklessly, the tires screeching. At the Baileys bridge in Manzanilla, I saw the glare of an approaching vehicle, but she accelerated, almost knocking the car into the river. The driver shouted a curse.

"I should drive."

"I'm all right."

The front bumper grazed a barrel at the side of the road. "You wouldn't be allowed to drive in this condition in Canada."

"Well, this is Trinidad, thank goodness. Didn't you notice?" Mercifully, it was after midnight and there weren't many vehicles on the road. I crouched on my seat gripping the dashboard until we arrived at the hotel. "It's closed." She sounded the horn.

"It's late."

"I want something to drink."

"You've had enough. What about your daughter?"

"Are you trying to get rid of me? She's with a babysitter. I can afford it, you know. Put your hand here."

"Let's go to my room then."

"Did you see how ugly she was? Like a manicou." She began to cry in short, snappy inhalations. I removed my hand hurriedly.

"Are you okay?"

"I'm tired." She got out of the car and I turned off the headlights.

While she was showering and I was hearing the slap of water on her body, then the slushy, soapy sounds, I was weighing whether I should ask her the question that had been on my mind the entire night. She emerged, wiping her hair. "Was this entire thing just for revenge?" I asked.

"What entire thing?" Her eyes were red.

"You know what I mean."

Straightening, she rolled the towel like a scroll. "I'm grateful we met." She went over to the mirror and seemed to be speaking to her reflection. "I enjoyed the time we spent together. It was the best . . ." She hesitated and I saw her eyes blinking quickly. She turned around, facing me. "I'm also grateful if Boysie was hurt. Does that mean that I used you?" She returned her gaze to the mirror. "There is no coincidence in this life, Stephen. You were the source of my distress. The reason why I was called a *jamette* and a used woman." She passed a finger lightly across her lower lip. "You were also the source of my final freedom. You remember what your friend used to say? That everything is connected and we could never escape from that?"

All that she was saying—even her expression in the mirror—seemed so contrived yet I knew that she was sincere in this belief. "You sound like a bad soap opera. Or an Indian movie." She glared at my reflection as she slipped into her dress. "Well, now that the circle is complete, I suppose . . ."

"Don't say that," she said, rather melodramatically. But we both knew it was over.

TWENTY-ONE

Shakira and I had spent only two months or so together. It seemed so much longer. If it had happened to someone else and I had heard the story I would have thought it was all a complicated game of the woman's revenge, against the lover for his youthful fling with her, which had made her damaged goods in the eyes of her husband, and against the husband for his abuse and then his complete indifference. But it was more than that: there was also her faith that we are made to pay for all our transgressions and that the punishment always matches the injustice. It seemed a brutal belief, because in spite of our earlier conversations about forgiveness and redemption, there was a grim calculation—almost as if these things could be hefted, weighed and categorized—of equivalence. But I admired her pride, her persistence and her patience.

She had shown me that our obligations to the past had more to do with repair than with romance. In that, she had shamed me and Mr. Rampartap both. I knew that with the slate wiped clean, and our affair in a sense cleansed and purified, she would perhaps want our relationship to continue at some other level, but we had reached the end.

She had asked about other relationships and was sceptical of my awkward disavowal. I almost told her about Anastasia, but was afraid that she would read too much into it and grow sulky and gloomy and accusatory.

Anastasia was a student at the adult education centre, about a year or two older than I was. One day at the end of class she asked me in her eager but confusing English for a lift to her basement apartment.

In the car she was mostly quiet and worried, glancing nervously at her watch and attempting to explain that her cousin or friend or aunt—I was not sure—who babysat her child had to leave at three-thirty that afternoon. She said what sounded like, "Oh, good grief," when she saw a fat scowling woman waiting by the open door. The woman glared at me, disdainfully snorted something in Spanish, and left. Anastasia went into the bedroom and returned almost immediately with a wide smile. Her teeth reminded me somehow of a horseshoe and made her dangerous-looking and maniacal. She could chomp off a pound of flesh if she were roused. She began to chatter in her hybrid English, talking faster and faster. It was difficult to keep up, so I said yes after each pause. Then she started to undress. My gaze shifted away from her teeth. Her olive skin was flawless, exactly the same colour from head to toe. While I was removing my clothes, she leaned back on a huge brown couch, opened her legs and giggled. She was wild and rapacious, her teeth clipping my ears and neck. When, concerned about my safety, I asked her to turn around, she grinned as if it were a joke. Afterwards, she went into the room and brought out her baby. I was horrified. I made an excuse and left. A few months later, during the parent-interview day, she was accompanied by her mother who had recently arrived from Venezuela. Like the baby, Anastasia's mother was dark and stocky with kinky hair. In the months that followed, I felt guilty about both my reaction to Anastasia's baby and my infidelity.

When I returned home that evening, my wife looked at me suspiciously and asked where I had been. We had grown apart then and hardly spoke to each other. I was frequently late, staying in after school to mark papers and plan the next day's lesson. Sniffing the air around her, she asked about my day at school, the lessons I had taught, the other teachers, the students. I was certain she knew. That was the beginning of my theory that a woman's infidelity, clothed in love and passion and sincerity, is easier to disguise than a man's, who stands before his wife, as naked as he was a few hours previously with the other woman.

For the month or so that I remained at the centre afterwards, I avoided Anastasia, and even though my marriage was already on its downward spiral, there were times when I felt that this single episode had marked me for punishment. Shakira would have agreed.

Walking on the beach a few weeks earlier, I had imagined that the land was just a reflection of our mood: when I examined the thought later it seemed silly but now the idea

returned and I clung to it; I pretended that in the crash of
the waves at night the rocks were scraped clean, and little animals, released from the sand's camouflage, scurried around,
darting and streaking off into the sea. Later in the night, I
listened to the breeze bustling through the trees and I pictured the epiphytes and the smothering moss loosened and
blown away.

From this, rather than from any conscious sense of
lightness, I believed I was better. I imagined Shakira's reaction to all this and smiled; it was the sort of thing that ap-
pealed to her.

I was glad we had met. I had underestimated her faith
in herself and could not see how this faith was rooted in a
canny expectation of revenge. "Time takes care of everything," she had said, and another time, "Nothing ever happen before its time." If anyone else had said this I would
have scoffed at the vision of a life simplified and reduced to
interminable waiting and delaying in anticipation of that
special moment. But I could no longer pass judgment:
everything had worked out the way she had expected.

I had, over the last few years, become the kind of person
I always disliked and feared, and I was able to see this with a
vivid clarity: distancing myself from this bitter man was
both a blessing and a curse. Because I saw him each day,
like a perfect stranger whose routine I knew perfectly, I
glimpsed all his minute blemishes. I saw him hurrying to
his car, looking away swiftly if glances were returned, afraid
of what his eyes would reveal. I saw him searching for wisdom in senseless songs written by women of barely twenty.
I saw him with pen dangling over paper, afraid to reveal his
thoughts, and I saw him during moments when his mask
would slide and he would be moved almost to tears by

some insignificant action: a woman reaching into a purse to buy ice cream for her daughter, a father restraining his young son as they crossed the street, an arm placed gently but assuredly around a shoulder, a simple exchange of glances; and I saw how afterwards he would harden himself once more against this pain and repeat to himself, Never again, never again.

One night, a few minutes before twelve, I was awakened by the harsh cry of a night bird. Over and over it screamed, as if it were being wrenched apart by a predator. I got up and looked through the window, but saw only the leaves of a coconut tree like huge black combs clawing the air. In the distance, I heard the waves rippling along the shore and in the dull moonlight, I saw long flecks of foam. I concentrated on the sound of the sea and imagined that the bird's hoot came from deep inside the ocean. I must have listened for close to half an hour before I opened the door and walked down the stairs.

The water was chilly, but as my body adjusted to the cold, I waded out and dived into the crest of a wave. It was too shallow and my chest and knees grazed the sand. I swam a little farther out and then back to the shore. A sprinkle of shell, like a broken bouquet, glittered faintly on the sand. I sat on the beach with my knees against my chest and listened once more to the bird. As my teeth began to chatter, I thought about my decision to return to Canada, and I was sure I was right.

During the week that remained, I visited Marvin and TJ and Doggie, and when I told them that I was leaving for Canada soon, they brought out a bottle of rum, even though it was midday and they had planned on one more fishing trip for the day. They provoked Doggie with their "bottom" jokes and in his glum manner, he offered this advice: "Nothing wrong with following something that looking good. But you have to know when to stop." That led to more laughter and jokes and other bits of energetic advice from Doggie. By the afternoon we were all drunk and I had already promised several times to visit them whenever I returned to Trinidad. I was touched by the simplicity of their friendship, offered without conditions or expectations.

I also visited Lalchan.

He seemed almost startled when he looked up from his desk and saw me standing at the warden's office door. Outside, in the sunlight, I noticed the dark circles under his eyes, and in Ziggy's bar, he glanced continually over his shoulder.

"I'm leaving in a little while."

"Leaving?" He gulped down his beer and repeated the question.

I nodded.

"But we didn't make the lime yet. I hardly ever see you at all. I was planning a nice little fête by the river bank. Take a little swim while the pot bubbling. Throw in a line or two for catfish. Curry duck and dasheen. Just like old times." I was astonished by his distress. His eyes were red and he had reverted completely to a Trinidadian accent. I felt guilty about leaving. "Everybody else gone. I alone in the boat now." He sniffled and wiped his nose. Then abruptly he got up. "Come."

I finished my beer and followed him out of Ziggy's. "Where are we going?" He was so upset I didn't want to ask again but when I realized we were heading for the bank, I touched his shoulder. "I will wait here."

He turned around. "Here? Underneath Bata store? You going to get some shoes?"

"Go ahead. I will be here."

He seemed undecided but finally he left. While I was waiting for him, an old man with striking black hair and grey stubble on his chin emerged from Bata, clutching a battered briefcase. As he was about to cross the street, I called out, "Harrylal?" He hesitated and looked around.

"I know you?" He walked towards me.

"I used to work in the warden's office. With Lalchan and Banfield and Hacksaw and Keith."

"That was a long time now. What you doing here?"

"I came for a holiday."

"And what is you name again?"

"Stephen."

He squinted. "Stephen? Stephen what?"

"Sagar. You used to work at the school then."

"I still working there." He smiled, uncovering a row of crooked teeth.

Perhaps he had misunderstood. "At the Rio Claro composite school." I was sure he was about seventy years old now.

He dipped into his briefcase and brought up a crumpled brown envelope. "Open it." He was grinning. I opened the envelope and withdrew a birth certificate. "Read it."

"Harrylal Samaroo. Born at Mudland Road on the sixth day of September, nineteen twenty-seven."

"Okay, now read this one."

He gave me another envelope. "Harrylal Samaroo. Born at Lengua Village on the eighth day of April, nineteen forty-five."

He exhaled a short, dry laugh, like a melodious wheeze.

"You have two birth certificates?"

He replaced the envelopes in his briefcase. "Four. Four in all. Come in real handy. I could teach until the year two thousand and five. Then I going to come a preacher." He reached into the briefcase once more and produced a stub with scrambled numbers. "I going down by Steve now. To bet a few numbers in *whe whe*. You want to come?"

"No, I'm waiting here for someone."

"For Ramrattan daughter?"

"Who?"

He grinned and rushed off.

I waited for about five minutes, watching the young men and women breezing by. Four workers, shirtless, stood around a gushing water main, chatting with each other and occasionally tapping the exposed mud with their spades and shovels.

Lalchan came out of the bank and a middle-aged woman of mixed ancestry, wearing an old, dirty-looking dress, trotted towards him. They were some distance away and I could not hear their voices but the woman seemed angry. She tapped a canvas bag slung from her shoulder, then removed the bag and threw it at Lalchan's feet. He bent down and retrieved the bag. She was still gesticulating. He reached into his pocket and withdrew what seemed to be money. She took her bag and the wad and left. While Lalchan was walking towards me, I decided to pretend I had not seen anything.

"That woman! She will suck me dry."

"Who?" I asked stupidly.

From his shirt pocket, he took out some red Canadian bills, held together with a rubber band. "Three hundred and fifty dollars." He gave me the money. "Give this to

Mahadaye. This is the address here." He pointed to a torn-off sheet stuck inside the wad. "Me boy still at Seneca. He could use the money. Tell she that loneliness does cause you to do all kind of stupidness. No, no, don't tell she that. Tell she that when a man hook up by himself in the forest . . ." He didn't complete the sentence because a mangy pothound came up to him, rubbed against his leg and sniffed his crotch. He pulled back in alarm, shouting at the dog, "What the hell you smelling they for? You expect to find food inside they? A nice hot meal? Eh?" He fired a useless kick at the pothound, which was already ambling away.

"Tell her what?" I asked him, struggling to remain serious.

"Kissmeass parasite. On every damn side." He gazed at the pothound. "All of them have only one ambition in life from the time they born. Find Lalchan. Find him and feast on him. Feast on him good and proper."

"I should leave now."

He shook my hand. His palms were hot and sweaty. "One more beer?"

He drank the beer silently, tearing off the label with his thumb and staring at the bottle. "I had everything I ever wanted right here, but I couldn't see it. Now is just the old Lalchan alone." He tilted back his head and drank, making sucking sounds. "Man overboard." I didn't know whether it was a joke or not.

In the taxi, reflecting on the conversation with Lalchan and my chance meeting with Harrylal, I remembered the man Harrylal had referred to. Ramrattan. I had escorted his daughter, Sitara, to a graduation dance at Rio Claro composite school and when we were leaving, Harrylal had complimented her on her outfit.

Just before boarding the taxi I had called Canada and got a recorded message saying, "Sorry, we are unable to take your calls at this time. The occupants of this house will be away at Disneyland for the next four weeks. Please leave a message. Ciao." The inclusion of Disneyland in the message made me smile. She sounded chirpy; perhaps the dentist was accompanying them. Surprisingly, this did not bother me, and more astonishingly, I felt a vague, inexplicable sense of relief. And gratitude. Vanita would be surrounded by gaiety and laughter and children her age playing and screaming.

Disneyland reminded me of another kind of enchantment; a story repeated over and over to Vanita, but for the conclusion. I was the only passenger in the taxi and as we passed the house in Agostini, I asked the driver to divert into Ermat Trace.

"You going to the Ecclesville school? I thought was Mayaro you say?"

"I just need to look at something." The house where I had released the *pawi* was now a concrete structure, with decorative balusters and a paved garage. Many of the other houses had been modernized with asphalt yards and wrought iron gates. "Okay, stop here."

"Here? By this old house? It don't have nobody living here." As I made my way to the house, jumping over the drain, he shouted, "Careful with the wild cane. The leaf sharper than razor."

The door had been knocked down and the walls were rotted, with perforations made by wood lice. The chair he had sat on, cradling his special clock, had been torn apart. There was a chillum on the floor, some empty green bottles and cigarette butts. A bat disengaged from the rafter, flapped through the room and disappeared somewhere in the ceiling. The driver honked his horn. As I turned to leave, I heard a tiny, metallic sound. I stooped and picked up the spring on which I had stepped. A mainspring from one of his clocks.

"That is where the coke addicts and them does hang out," the driver said when I returned. "What you have they? A spring?" He drove off. "It had a old fella what use to live they long time. Some people say that he gone back to Venezuela, some say he land up in some poor house in Morvant, and one or two say they spot him sleeping in some street in Port of Spain. But you know what I think? I hear that he was a lagahoo and one of these days, he go come back cool-cool and rumfle up them addicts what hanging out in he house." He drove in silence, then he said, "It have spirit all over the place, you know. Some living, some dead and some in-between."

"Do you know Titmus? He was a custodian at the school."

"Custodian? I don't know no custodian. Oho. You mean the caretaker fella with the marble eye. He dead donkey years now."

"And Mr. Philip?"

"Chief Iguana? I could see that you away for a long time now." He loosened up with this realization. "He living in the same spot for as long as I know him. But now he have he boy with him. And half-dozen iguana roaming 'bout the yard."

"Which boy?"

"The one what use to live in the forest with he Carib mother. But the best joke is that while Philip take up all them old Carib habit, minding all kinda bird and animal and thing, the boy more modern than town people self. It have a saying that most teacher does end up either in the madhouse or in the rumshop so Philip lucky in a way. He end up with iguana. So way you say you from again? States?"

"Canada."

"New Brunswick sardine. Is me favourite, you know. Sardine and rice." He clacked his tongue as if he was tasting the meal. "Plenty people from the Rio Claro area does go up to Canada to pick apple and when they come back they playing more white than the *Young and Restless* people. It had one of them who come back after just four-five years wearing short pants and tie and white socks and gloves and smoking one of them long tube like the Penguin from the TV show. I use to spot him a few time by the market ordering avocado pear and split peas sandwich. You understand what I saying? Not zaboca and doubles, eh, but avocado pear and split peas sandwich." He chortled happily. "You see that dog sleeping in the middle of the road like if is he owner property? Is years I trying to bounce it down." He accelerated and the dog, at the last minute, bounded to the side of the road. "If this car had a little more speed I woulda finish him off years now. So far this year I kill six dog and three cyat. This is a public road not no damn backyard."

He leaned over to the passenger's side and opened and shut the door. "The lock a little rusty. So how you know all them people? You use to live here or what? To tell the truth, I personally know nearly everybody in this area. Uncle Cyat and Tantie Dog. I driving taxi donkey years now. It look like people does just open up to me. Must be me face." He glanced around offering me a glimpse of his drowsy eyes, his pudgy nose deviated slightly to the left and his crooked smile. "Come to think of it, you *own* face looking a little bit familiar."

Because he seemed like a gossip, I told him, "I left here a long while ago."

"And I driving taxi *donkey* years now." He began to hum an old calypso. "So what you say you name was again?" He had posed the question in the calypso's bouncy rhythm and for a moment I thought he was extemporizing. He repeated the question, I told him my surname, he uttered a forced gasp and braked. "But ain't you dead?"

I was a bit startled by his flurry of dramatics. "Maybe you have me mixed up."

He pummelled the first gear into place and drove off roughly. "Sagar son. The people with the shop. He leave nearly twenty years now. But he get blow up in some plane crash." I thought of Varun and felt a rush of panic, then he added, "In the Gulf War. That is why he didn't come down for the funeral and them. People say Saddam blow up he backside." He emitted a short, snappy laugh, like the bray of a startled mule.

Could it have ended like this, I wondered? My entire life reduced to a cynical bray; remembered only for the manner of my death. Was it possible that nineteen years of my life was wiped out the day I left for Canada? I felt a dry emptiness in my stomach, like someone who, weakened by exhaustion, had not eaten for days.

The driver was still mumbling about my death. "To tell the truth, I never believe none o' that nonsense. I tell meself that you must be freezeup and dead with ganga-rene or something." He looked back as if expecting me to thank him for his faith. "You parents and them was nice people, you know. Although the talk running around was you father get a little strange in the end. From what I hear, he use to spend hours on end prop up on he stool doing these crossword puzzle. Hardly ever talking to anybody. And when you mother pass on, he just start giving away everything from the shop. Sometimes in the morning when I driving me taxi I use to see a long line o' people waiting to get inside the shop for the freeco. I and all went one evening, I not shame to say. And he was on he stool eating some sardine and hops bread. Taking he time and biting slow-slow. Opening the bread and picking out all the bone and feeding it to a old, rusty, half-dead cyat with a funny sorta name. Comforter or something."

"Cophetua?"

"Yes. That sound like it. To tell the truth, I don't think that is a proper name for no cyat. Anyways, on that said day you father was acting like he didn't have a worries in the world. Taking he time, as I say. Peaceful-peaceful but God alone know what was going through he mind. To me, it look like if he was someway else. Like if he wasn't in the shop with all them half-empty shelf. He was never suit to that line o' work and when the old lady pass on, well, it look like he just . . ." He peered at the rear-view mirror. "But you must be know all that."

Yes, I thought. I know.

He chuckled hoarsely. "I never believe none o' that talk 'bout how he lost something up here." He removed a hand from the steering wheel and tapped his head. "Maybe he was smarter than everybody else." Now he lowered his voice to a whisper. "He choose he time. You understand what I saying? He choose he time."

During my father's last year, his letters increasingly became incoherent. He was a quiet man not given to lengthy discussions. He selected his words carefully and occasionally he would refer to a conversation of a few days earlier as if he had been thinking of it all along. But he wrote long elaborate letters in his distinctive handwriting, a flourish at the end of each word. A stranger who stumbled across one of his early letters might have thought that my father was garrulous, smug and slightly boastful, but if it was one of the letters of his last year, my father would have seemed different: wise, paranoid, enigmatic, talkative, schizophrenic.

And that was how I read those last letters; like a stranger; not knowing what to make of them. I tried to locate traces of the slim, stoop-shouldered man who, with a faraway look in his eyes, had read me stories from *The Royal Reader*, about buccaneers and castaways and strange animals.

When my mother passed away, he called, advising me not to come to the funeral. Varun was there on vacation and would perform the rituals. It was the first time I'd heard his voice in over three years. At the end of the conversation—which lasted less than four minutes—he said that we should not be saddened by the inevitability of things and that we should consider our lives as a long train journey where passengers left at regular intervals. If someone else had said this, I might have seen it as silly, but my father sounded like the person I had known: thoughtful and contemplative. When he hung up, I went to my cabinet and took out a brown envelope stuffed with pictures taken in Trinidad and arranged them on my bed. Perhaps it was my mood but in these faded, grainy photographs my parents appeared sad and tired with shy, evasive eyes. My wife was in the living room with Vanita. I wanted her to come into the room and see the photographs on the bed. I wanted her to ask why I had arranged them there. I wanted someone to touch my shoulder and hold my hand.

The next morning at breakfast I broke the silence with news of my mother's death. Five months later, I didn't bother mentioning my father's passing away but I related to Vanita a story my father had often repeated to me, in changing versions, when I was a child. It always began with an old Chinaman who walked from village to village in Trinidad, asking questions in a language no one could understand. In one version he was searching for his family, who had been indentured from China years earlier; in another he was just asking for a job. The rendering I related to Vanita was this: the Chinaman, a scholar in his own land, was searching and searching for any kind of job, never giving up, never troubled by the indifference or the bewilderment that greeted him at every turn.

"Look at this assness." The driver swerved to avoid a truck winching teak logs piled at the side of the road, slamming me against the door. A worker on the truck's bed was levering the logs into place with a canhook. Egrets were poking into the furrows left by the logs. "For telephone pole," he explained, when he noticed me staring back as we drove along. "Good for post and furniture, but to tell the truth I prefer tapano and sip. Can't get mahogany and balata again. Too much thiefin' from state land, if you ask me. People cutting down tree like if the forest is they father backyard. So what sorta job you doing in the cold? Computering? It had a fella from here, Doodoon nephew who tell everybody that he doing computering in America, but the best joke is that somebody from the village who gone up for a holidays spot him janitoring some train station in New York."

"There's nothing wrong with that. Sometimes students do these jobs to pay their fees."

"Janitoring? A big county councillor nephew? You know when Doodoon lose the election he blame it on that talk. So what you doing up they?"

"Computering."

He drove in silence for a while, then abruptly he began humming a calypso. Midway through he stopped and said, "To tell the truth, I don't see nothing wrong with janitoring and them sorta job." He cleared his throat and spat out the window. "So when you heading back?"

"In a little while."

He overtook a pick-up packed with papaws and pineapples. "You know, you just like you old man. Talking like if you does have to pay for every single word. Take care you don't end up eating sardine and bread with a rusty, half-dead cyat name Comforter or something, eh." He forced a wheezing, raspy laugh. "The more thing change the more they does remain the same. I driving taxi donkey years now and I see it every single day. You have a son too?"

"Four."

"That good 'cause when you have boy children you only have to worry 'bout one tingaling but when you have girl children you have to worry 'bout all the tingaling in the village." He glanced back and chortled gleefully at his joke and I thought: that is the face of a rapist.

"And two girls."

"Eh? Girl children too? Six in all?" He shifted smoothly. "But boy children too harden if you ask me. Too duncy-head. I have eight children in all. Five inside and three outside. You see them two house facing side by side?" He pointed to two concrete buildings, identical but for the ornate balusters on one. "Ramjohn living in that one and Robinson living in the next one. Side by side for donkey years and every day they quarrelling 'cause Johnson say that Ramjohn curry fumes does affect he asthma and Ramjohn say that Johnson does wash out he pig meat and all the blood does flow in the drain in the back of he house. The latest I hear is that it reach up in the courthouse. What you think 'bout that?"

"The more things change the more they remain the same."

"Eh?" He looked back confused and for a moment I felt I was being unfair to him. He was just an ordinary taxi driver who happened to know my parents.

"That day . . . did he say anything?"

"Who? Ramlal or—?"

"No. My father."

"Is a good time now since that happen, you know. Lemme think." After a while, he said, "Nah. He was just eating sardine and feeding he cyat. The next boy was they doing visitation from England at the time. You brother. Two-three time I spot you father walking slow-slow and you brother holding he hand and helping him along."

"Really?"

"Yeah, man. And sometimes the rusty cyat use to be following them too." He glanced back and catching my smile, grinned broadly.

By the time the taxi driver had dropped me off at the Mayaro junction, I was no longer annoyed with him.

For the rest of that week, I sat up late every night and wrote a journal for Vanita. I mentioned Madhoo and Mr. Rampartap and Doggie and TJ and Marvin and Lalchan and even the taxi driver, but I wrote nothing of Shakira. I felt better after I wrote the journal, and less guilty about returning without having written—or even started—Mr. Rampartap's biography. I recorded the events I believed would interest Vanita, the people with whom she would be fascinated. And in doing this, I recalled a thought of two months earlier during a conversation with Mr. Rampartap. Autobiography is not clarification, not revelation, but the redefinition of a life; it is part justification, part pretence. It was the first time I had balked at the task he had imposed on me and I remember thinking then that writers need a sense of nobility, the idea of some sacred mission they alone can undertake, because they are constantly pushed into such abject hypocrisies. Perhaps the judgment was not without a tinge of envy, because as a newspaper reporter, I saw myself as a lesser breed.

In the mornings, I walked for about half an hour and purchased the day's newspapers at a little parlour that sold bitter concoctions made from fruits and peppers. Then I went back and sat under a coconut tree, where small crabs scuttled in the dry sand among the trails of the camponella, the lustrous vines found nowhere else in the island. In Rougeleau, reading those same newspapers, I had surrendered to Mr. Rampartap's torpid visions of racial insurrection, of constant plots and counterplots, and of men who thought of nothing but revenge.

Perhaps it was the remoteness of this resort on the periphery of the island but I was unable to sink into my earlier fretful discomfort. I now saw in these articles how much had been borrowed and awkwardly refurbished to suit local needs. I glimpsed the oblique references to Guyana and Fiji, the ethnic strife in Africa, the nationalist eruptions in Europe, the communal uprisings in India; I saw the distant romance that flavoured these stories; and in this lighter mood I saw all of this as being funny. I imagined Mr. Alto Jackson, the self-appointed saviour of the little black boys from the hill, in his air-conditioned office, his starched shirt collar smudged with sweat, pacing up and down, searching for a clever way to unload his racial distress, and a few streets away, a government minister stepping into the glare of a photographer's light like a trapped rodent, weakening into promises he knew could not be fulfilled, promises that would sink Mr. Jackson ever further into his racial ruffle.

Then one day, all this remoteness was laid to rest. On the front page of *The Express* I saw a photograph of Mr. Pillooki. The photograph was taken from a low angle that elongated Mr. Pillooki's face and made him appear starved and slightly deranged. But it was the right photograph for the article, which began with the lines: "Mr. Rampartap, former wrestler and politico has applied a stranglehold on the Prime Minister." I read with growing interest, a bit amused by the writer's irreverent tone. Mr. Pillooki was representing Mr. Rampartap in a lawsuit against the prime minister for blocking his appointment to the position of ombudsman, in spite of "Mr. Rampartap's impeccable credentials."

The prime minister, asked to comment on the lawsuit, replied that, "Crazy people have the right just like everybody else to make public nuisances of themselves." He may have been referring to Mr. Pillooki, who burbled on about "Rights enshrined in our hallowed constitution." Mr. Rampartap had refused to grant an interview to the writer.

The next morning I packed my suitcase, pushing into the pouch the shells I had collected for Vanita and the book given to me by Shakira. I took a few of the specimens Madhoo had forced on me, but I left most behind, imagining the bartender's shock on discovering the wrinkled snake skin and dried beetles in the cardboard box beneath the bed. Or maybe it would be unearthed by some foreign visitor. I laughed aloud.

I went downstairs to pay the bill. The bartender produced his copybook.

"Here. Please have this." I took out the initialled pen given to me by Shakira.

He seemed surprised. He twirled the pen, stared at her initials, scratched it against his wrist and finally resumed his calculations. Accustomed to his pencil, he moistened the nib with his tongue from time to time.

"Okay, this is what you owe me." He placed the book before me. While I was paying him, he asked, "So you heading back to the cold now?"

"In a day or two. I have some unfinished business to take care of."

"Yes. Yes. I understand." He laughed, exposing his blue tongue. "Tell she I say hello."

I didn't bother to explain and in the taxi to San Fernando, I wondered whether Mr. Rampartap would be annoyed by my sudden appearance. Maybe he would be relieved when I explained that I had come to notify him of my departure and to repay the majority of his advance. Or perhaps he would guess that I was curious about his lawsuit against the prime minister.

Two and a half hours later, the taxi I had taken from San Fernando dropped me off at Rougeleau. There were a few cars parked inside the compound, which I found strange, and three small groups chatting in the yard, which I found even more puzzling. Someone broke off from the smallest group and came towards me. It was Madhoo, scratching his head and flashing me a worried smile.

Three

TWENTY-TWO

"What you still doing here, uncle? I thought that all now you up in the cold writing them story about all them snake skin and boo boo that I give you. I hope you still have them." I was about to reply when I realized he was joking. "The bossman look all over the place for you."

"You sure I didn't come at a bad time?"

"Nah, man. As I say, the bossman was looking for you." He raked his fingers through his hair. "You know you beginning to sound like a real Trinidadian now. You remember the nurs-ree rhyme about those who eat the cascadura will always end up in Trinidad they days. Don't doubt it."

"So what's the party about?"

He flashed me his worried, insecure grin again. A tall Indian with a crew cut was telling a younger woman, "I in top of everything." He was speaking rather loudly, and when he opened his mouth, I noticed his teeth dyed with tobacco. The woman, who had a careworn, tight face, was trying to look thoughtful by alternately frowning and then relaxing in a vacant gaze.

"Is exactly what the bossman was searching for you all over the place." He hopped closer. "You remember it had this crazy-ass old man who could never hold he rum, harassing any and everybody."

I remembered the old man who had been hoisted off his feet and almost pushed into the barrel by Mr. Rampartap but I had assumed the gathering here was connected with the lawsuit. "With long grey beard?" I asked.

"The very said man. Well, it look like he run into a little trouble."

"What sort of trouble?"

"Somebody gone and poison him."

"Is he in the hospital?"

"You could say so. In the last floor. In the morgue."

"He's dead?"

"It not so easy to live when you drink all them chemicals, you know, uncle."

"Do they know who did it?"

He ran his fingers through his hair and stared at the ground. "Well, that is the interesting part. They find the body near the mud volcano and them. Not too far from the Red River. But it had a tub of chemical inside of Mr. Choo place. Gramazone and Roundup and a little bit of fungicide." He was attempting to scratch the ground with his bad leg, but his toes skated over the grass. "It look like he must be drink some of Mr. Choo experiment."

After a while I asked him, "Is Mr. Choo under suspicion?"

"Is not for me to judge, uncle, but the fact speak for themself as these lawyers like to say."

"What would be his motive?" I couldn't believe that the bumbling, absent-minded man who had almost run into his pond was responsible for a murder.

"Mad people don't need no motive, as far as I recall." He glanced at the men and women chatting in the yard. Three men, who might have been brothers, walked to the gate. They were all wearing striped shirts rolled to the elbows and they each moved with a slack, loping gait. "Anyways,

I should tell Mr. Ram that you land back." He reached for my suitcase.

"Don't worry. I will carry it." As we made our way up the stairs, I saw the tall Indian glancing at us. He was chatting with a small, oily, grey-haired man, whose hands were folded tightly against his chest. A maroon handkerchief dangled from his back trouser pocket. He, too, glanced at us and in his tiny eyes, I felt I saw confusion and apprehension and spite.

Upstairs was a complete surprise. A thick maroon carpet now covered the living room. The crude wooden table had been replaced by a hexagonal one of polished mahogany. A cabinet with glass doors showcased a variety of china plates and decorative mugs. Three pictures, placed at declining angles, displayed the sun sinking over a hill, a poui tree and a small cottage. There were potted plants in each corner of the room and a trailing vine dangled from the top shelf of a bookcase. Neither Mr. Rampartap nor his rocking chair was there but a living-room set, two couches and a sofa tastefully occupied that area. At each end of the larger couch stood a small cabinet with lion-face brass handles.

"Nice, eh? The bossman madam put them. Wait here." He knocked and entered a room at the front, adjoining the balcony. After a few minutes he emerged and pointed to the room. I entered and saw Mr. Rampartap, wearing spectacles and reading from a hardcover edition of the Bhagavad Gita. His hair was neatly barbered and slicked down and he seemed slightly thinner. The weight loss had created new lines around his eyes. He looked like a solicitor poring over his notes.

"The ego pushes us to the middle of events we have not initiated and at the centre of a world over which we have no control."

"Which ego?" I asked, contemplating this new incarnation.

He closed the book. Perhaps he had been quoting. "You look good, Stephen," he said, peering over his glasses. Had I ever told him my first name, I wondered? "The sun has done you much good."

What a complete fraud, I thought, but I said, "You look good too."

He got up and walked to the window. "These people outside"—he waved his hand as if pencilling a circle—"they have all come to help."

"To help with what?"

"Haven't you heard about Mr. Choo?"

"Yes. Madhoo told me."

He turned around and glanced sharply at me. "Well, Stephen, Mr. Choo is one of my own and I am not going to let him be sacrificed." He forced a smile. "Even though that is exactly what they are accusing him of." He returned to his desk but did not sit. "Foreigner living by himself in the bush. Not too right up here." He tapped his head. "People start talking. They jump to conclusions. You can't blame them." He sat and reopened his Gita. "Duty. Above everything else, that is what count. Mr. Choo came to *my* estate. *I* offered him hospitality." He turned a page. "How then could I forsake him?" He spoke slowly, using a pundit's intonation. "What sort of a man do they think I am?"

"Things are heating up in the estate."

"Things are heating up in the entire island."

"I was referring to the lawsuit."

He turned another page, traced a finger over a line and smiled sagely. "A man who live by principles is never afraid of consequences."

"So what about the lawsuit?"

"Shelved, as they say." He gazed down and blinked slowly. "There are things more important than . . ." He hesitated, searching for a word.

"Justice?" I almost said *glory*.

"Justice is for everyone. Even for people who can't fight on their own." He leaned back in a more relaxed posture. "Away from the public eye. That is how I've fought many of my battles, you know."

"The lawsuit isn't a private affair."

"Shelved, as I said." Unexpectedly, he smiled and I noticed that his teeth had either been recently whitened or capped or he had replaced his dentures.

I was surprised at how easily I made the decision to remain. Perhaps it was the reporter in me that insisted I follow up on this unexpected twist, or maybe it was just a morbid fascination with this new game Mr. Rampartap was playing. He made it easy, too: he waved away my repayment, insisted that I remain and offered once more the downstairs room. He was more amiable towards me and although this may have been an aspect of his new masquerade, I felt that my function had changed from that of a biographer.

After the two months at Mayaro, running along the beach and swimming each morning, I was determined not to be holed up, as before, in the downstairs room. In the evening, I wrote a long letter for Vanita and pushed it to the bottom of my suitcase. Then, exhausted by the long trip to Rougeleau, I fell asleep.

The next morning, showering in the bathroom, I thought of Dulcie whom I had seen bathing here, and of Mr. Rampartap's wife. I had seen neither the day before.

After I changed, I walked to the side of the house, the ripe cashew squishy beneath my feet. I reached for a fruit from one of the lower branches and tasted the slightly pungent flesh. *Cassa* we called it in Agostini. I walked past the anthuriums towards the plot planted with grapefruit, where Madhoo and some other workers had delivered a dead calf. Someone was coming from the opposite end of the field. It was Madhoo, hopping swiftly. I waited for him. When he spotted me, he stopped abruptly. "What you doing here so early in the morning, uncle?" he shouted.

"I came to get some fruits." I plucked off the external seed from the tip of the cashew. "People used to say that if this is roasted in a house with chicken around, the chicken would all die."

He laughed, confused. "Way you pick up that from?" I gave him the seed. "Just the smell alone could kill them?" he asked, sniffing. "I better mark that down." He grinned at his joke. I noticed that his fingers were muddy. He glanced at me and said, "I went to set some trap for dove. Way you off to this hour?"

"Grapefruit."

"I could get them for you."

"It's okay. Don't bother." When I walked away, I didn't hear his footsteps on the dried mud but when I looked back after a while, he was gone.

"How was your morning walk, Stephen? Were you searching for Mr. Choo? He is no longer there, you know." His palms were flat on the table.

I wasn't thinking of Mr. Choo but I asked, "So where is he now?"

"Caged."

"In jail?"

"Is where they usually put murderers."

"I thought he was innocent."

His fingers on the table were beating an erratic rhythm. "Guilty until proven innocent. In this island poor people have very little recourse to justice but I am doing what I can." He shook his head. "I am just one man."

"What about the people from yesterday?"

"We are doing what we can," he said, not answering the question. "I want you to meet one or two of them later. Good honest people. Poor but free. It is only when the mind is rid of guilt that we are free."

You insincere old bitch. The phrase rang through my mind and I had to turn away so he would not see me smiling.

"I hope you are comfortable in your room."

"Yes. Where's Dulcie?"

"She no longer work here." He paused, then added, "You seem bothered by that." He seemed to be awaiting a response. I gave none. He glanced over my shoulder. "Will you be joining us this morning, Radha?" I turned and saw his wife, dressed in green slacks. There were dark rings beneath her eyes but she seemed more composed than I had remembered her to be.

She poured a cup of tea. Mr. Rampartap was smiling but I could see that he was disturbed. "I am so glad you returned, Stephen," he said finally. "This is a difficult time but"—he glanced at his wife—"but everybody is pulling together. We are a people like that." His wife was ignoring him completely and in her poised defiance, I caught a glimpse of the beauty she once possessed. She buttered a slice of bread and took small bites, looking all the while at the window, the living room, the new furniture. She seemed to be silently appraising and I was struck once more by how different she was from the crab-chewing, spitting woman of two months ago. "The little people are rising up, you know, Stephen. In the little villages and back roads all over the place. Bush fire, but it could get out of control."

"I thought it was just in Tobago."

"Oh no, no," he said, startling me with a ringing burst of laughter. "It is all over the place. People are discussing it in all the rumshops and street corners. As an educated man yourself, wouldn't you say that this is how revolutions begin?"

I was about to ask him what the people were talking about when Radha said, "It will blow over." She was still looking at the window and could have been thinking aloud, but I was surprised because it was the first time she had spoken in my presence. Mr. Rampartap too seemed startled. His lips crumpled as if he had swallowed his dentures.

"Why do you say that?" I asked, but she had withdrawn once more into her role as a silent appraiser.

Mr. Rampartap was rocking his chair from side to side as if he were about to get up. "I have a meeting to attend to. Let Madhoo know if you need anything."

"Will Dulcie be back?" I asked him.

"Will she be back, Edwin?" his wife asked in a sweet, mocking voice.

Edwin?

He stood up abruptly. "Let Madhoo know if you need anything." As he walked away, I heard a low purring sound next to me, like a pleasant, ebbing laugh. She too got up and with a little smile on her face, went into the kitchen.

When I went downstairs, I didn't see Madhoo so I decided to stroll around the estate. The statue of the naked woman, once covered with moss, had been cleaned thoroughly and there were sprinklings of hyacinth and marigold around the base. A few small holes had been dug at the foot of the fence, the fresh dirt piled in little mounds. A sturdy electrical cord trailed from the house to the statue's pedestal.

"It doesn't work." I turned around and saw Radha in a broad-brimmed white hat with a silky bow at the front. She was still wearing her indoor slippers. "The pump itself work but not the fountain." She twisted a garden tap with an attached green hose and water trickled from the spout. She pointed to the pump placed between two boulders at the back of the statue. "It makes a humming noise but no water comes out." Because she was staring at me expectantly, I went to the pump and pretended to study it. "Could you fix it?" she asked.

Not likely, I thought, but I wanted to talk with her so I grasped a trowel lying on one of the mounds and awkwardly attempted to use it to loosen a screw.

"Maybe I should unplug it first."

"Yes, you should," I replied stupidly.

She went into the house and returned with a screwdriver. "I asked Madhoo to look at it but he is not too good at this sort of thing." I removed the plate at the top and stared at the copper filaments. "Do you know what is wrong with it?"

I remembered Nobby, the mechanic from Agostini who did all his repairs by blowing into pipes and tubes. "It might be clogged up."

"It's practically new."

"Hmm." I wanted to suggest that she return it for a replacement when I noticed that the plastic tube that led to the fountain had not been inserted far enough to catch the water settling in the bowl. I took hold of the pump and pushed the tube farther in.

"Was that the problem?"

"Could be." I replaced the plate and tightened the screws. "Could you plug it in?" She went once more into the house and a few seconds later the pump began to splutter and the water rose from the fountain, first in uneven spurts and then, as the pressure adjusted, into a full flow cascading over the statue.

"Well, finally." She sounded pleased.

"Did it ever work before?"

"No." She hesitated then added, "So you still planning to write your book? I thought you would be back in America by now."

"Canada. I had planned to return but I may stay a while longer."

"Because of Mr. Choo?"

"Yes. Yes, because of that." But I was thinking of her husband's lawsuit. I wanted to see how it would play out.

She was staring at the water sprinkling mistily over her flowers. "He was murdered, you know."

"You mean the old man? I heard that . . ."

"But not by Mr. Choo," she said emphatically.

"Do the police have other suspects?"

"The police usually suspect the people who could do them the least damage." She removed her hat and fanned her face. "You were asking about Dulcie earlier. You having trouble making up your bed?" She said it as a joke and I smiled.

"I just wanted to know why she is no longer here."

She stopped fanning and bent her head slightly. "Hired help is like that. They work for a while, then move on."

"She seemed like a part of the family."

"Really? Which family?"

"This family." She was looking at me closely. "I suppose people who cook and do all these things usually end up being accepted as a family member. You grow used to them."

"Is that how it is in Canada?" The notion seemed to interest her.

"I'm not sure about Canada. I was talking about here in Trinidad."

She walked to the other side of the statue, looking at the ground, at her flowers. After a while she said, "When I was growing up we had a maid named Geeta. She was murdered by her husband. He got off because his lawyer was able to prove undue provocation." She stooped and examined a ladybug on the leaf of a hyacinth. "It happened more than forty years ago but I still remember her sitting below a mango tree every evening and telling me that she wanted to go back to school." The ladybug opened its red wings and flew away. "She was about sixteen years at the time, just two years older than me. More than forty years ago and it is still all over the place."

"You must have been . . ." I wanted to say sad but it had happened so long ago.

She moved away, towards the small mounds of earth fringing the fence. "I was shocked and frightened but it passed quickly. We got another maid and my parents arranged for me to stay in the college dormitory. I was young and rich and popular and I forgot about her." She was gazing into one of the holes. "But the mind remember what the body forget. Everything is shaped by time." She laughed and as if speaking to herself, said, "The crazy shape of time."

"What do you mean?" I remembered Madhoo's talk of her insanity.

Then she said, "We see things we missed the first time. Because of our own experience, we feel sorry for people we never thought of before. Some people are never capable of sympathy because nothing in their life prepared them for it. Not because they are heartless." She was still staring into the hole as if its depth was undefined and I felt that she was remembering her own difficulties. I spoke some words of a reply, but I thought she was not listening.

"What are you mumbling about?" She was now looking at me with a vaguely amused expression.

"Nothing. I was just thinking of what you said."

"No. You were saying, 'Sometimes we are over-prepared.'" She said this in a comfortingly disbelieving manner, like a parent insisting that a child's wound was not serious enough to warrant the tears. While she was waiting, I thought: We are really interested in other people because of their secrets. Then she said, "I sent away Dulcie because of Edwin."

"Mr. Ram?"

"Yes." She walked slowly to the house. I followed her. "He was getting too attached to her. It was for her own good too."

She seemed a bit disturbed, so I said, "It happens a lot in Canada. Especially with rich powerful men with mistresses half their age."

"Mistresses?"

Perhaps the word had shocked her. "With younger partners."

"That is what you think Dulcie is?" There was a twinkle of amusement in her eyes but her voice was stern. She had stopped walking and was looking at me squirming in embarrassment. "Edwin is Dulcie's father." This news, so shocking to me, was delivered with just a tightening of the voice.

"Does she know?"

"Of course she knows. Her mother must have told her years ago."

"Then you . . . ?"

"No. Her mother lives in the village with a crippled husband." She was speaking rather loudly and I wondered whether Mr. Rampartap was somewhere in the house listening to her.

"It must be difficult for them."

"I'm sure Edwin visits from time to time."

"I mean financially. Especially with a crippled stepfather."

She tapped her slipper against a stone, dislodging a small pebble caught under the clasp. "I send a cheque every month to her mother."

"It's not Dulcie's fault . . ."

She cut me off. "Nobody said it was. My daughter is returning in a few days' time and it is best for both of them."

She was sounding a bit offended so I said, "You must be looking forward to it. You and your husband."

Her voice softened somewhat. "Yes, I haven't seen her for . . . for a very long time. She was taken away from me."

"By whom?"

"If you stick around in this estate long enough, you will get enough stories to fill up your book. But then that is not the kind of book you have been contracted to write." She smiled and walked into the house.

TWENTY-THREE

"Hurry up and bathe fast, uncle. The bossman say we going to meet some joenalists." I had just returned from Mr. Choo's now deserted hut and with my eyes closed and soapy water running over my face, I couldn't see Madhoo but I heard him chuckling somewhere above me. I opened an eye and almost fell backward. His head was pushed up over the top of the partition, his fingers gripping the edge; he looked like a puppet in a theatre. "You minding a small snake they, uncle?" He began to laugh and his hands released their grip. I heard a small plop as he landed, then a small howl of pain. Perhaps he had landed on his bad leg.

In the car, Mr. Rampartap said, "So how was the morning walk? Did you find anything in the windmill?"

On impulse, I told him, "A watch."

"Good, very good, Stephen. We will keep it for him when he is released, as he will be."

"He didn't wear a watch the day we visited."

"Well, you know, Stephen, sometimes we remove our watches when we are working on something or the other. Sometimes it is not waterproof or shock resistant."

"I don't think he ever wore one. His wrist was tanned evenly."

"You see the way these writers operate, Madhoo? They don't miss nothing." Mr. Rampartap was handling my little deception admirably, but Madhoo, sitting directly in front of me in the driver's seat, was disturbed. I could see his straggly beard moving up and down as he chewed his lip. "That is why I want Stephen to see what is going to happen tonight and then give me his assessment."

The car swung out of Rougeleau onto the highway. "So where are we going?"

"Port of Spain. A little meeting." He stretched the word *little*, leading me to believe it was just the opposite.

I had forgotten how beautiful central Trinidad could be in the night. The windows were rolled down and I smelled the aroma of the cane, the wild flowers growing in the ravines bordering the road, and farther away, the slightly musky aroma of Caroni Swamp where scarlet ibises, flamingoes and cocricoes nested; where years ago, I had made a trip with Varun in an old leaking boat and marvelled at the long-legged birds wading in the water and flapping among the rushes. We had seen an alligator, its snout above the water, and a morocoy plodding away on a bank. There had been delicate fern-like plants and old trees, the branches twisting over the water like ancient petrified ropes left over by some long-perished tribe. Pale, salmon-coloured flowers from the immortelle trees floated downstream and occasionally a cascarob leaped above the water.

I had never returned, in spite of the many promises made to Varun, who was four or five at the time. These promises were repeated years later in Canada.

"You want me to drive a little faster, Mr. Rampartap?"

"Take your time. Let Stephen enjoy the view."

The mountains in the distance were outlined by the lights twinkling along the little plateaux and foothills and slopes where settlers from Grenada and Antigua had built their neighbourhoods, protected by that northern range—so it was said—from the hurricanes that devastated the other islands.

To those of us who grew up in the southern part of Trinidad, most of the city of Port of Spain was strange and foreign—Laventville, Morvant, Belmont, the place known simply as "behind the hill"—it could have been another island. We knew of the steel bands and the men who left their families behind to practise on the drums night after night in preparation for the Carnival, men whose loyalty to their bands was so great that any slight could lead to violence; to us they seemed like the desperadoes of the Old West. We knew of the bustling, overcrowded nightclubs (so different from the sleepy village rumshops), the prostitutes, the bad-johns who emerged each Carnival to reestablish their claims, the men with their multitude of children, many of them "outside" children, raised by poor, proud women. Stories of these characters were told to us in the Trinidadian manner, with so much colourful distortion, so many dramatic twists, that they acquired the fanciful tone of fables and soon took their places in the island's folklore.

Sam, my seatmate, visited his cousins in Belmont every month end and returned with stories of their girlfriends, their hidden cigarettes, their sexual secrets. We were amazed that boys barely older than us were granted so many privileges and possessed so much clandestine knowledge. But when Sam expressed his wish to one day join his cousins, I assumed it was because of the gentler, more romantic aspect of the city: the horse races in the savannah, the beautiful churches and cathedrals built almost a century ago, the coconut vendors slicing their nuts by the dim light of a flambeau, the cinemas with huge posters of Sean Connery and Bruce Lee and Raquel Welch.

Sam was the only person I knew who wanted to leave for the city. The Indian customers at my parents' shop occasionally expressed a disbelief that any Indian would go to the city and the few blacks who lived in Agostini expressed a similarly harsh view of city life. Mr. Philip blamed all of this on the plantation owners, who, he explained, needed to divide and rule because they were a minority. The city dwellers, he told us, also viewed the villagers through a distorting lens: we were cutlass-wielding heathens who, in spite of our sedate appearance, could be roused to a savage rage and wipe out an entire family, sometimes our own. Later, despite Mr. Philip's assessment, I came to feel that it was the perfect arrangement: two races linked only by the brutality of the plantation system, existing side by side but knowing each other little, heightening isolated events into romantic legend so that it was sometimes impossible to tell where fiction ended and reality began; two groups professing bewilderment at each other, and each fashioning from the patchwork of these stories a shaky superiority.

Mr. Philip usually spoke in the language of a politician and one of his heroes was the then prime minister, Henry Thaddeus Bodsworth. Once he brought a radio to school and forced us to listen to a speech by Bodsworth. He sat at his table, his hand propping his chin, riveted, but the class was bored stiff. What I recall most clearly from the speech was Bodsworth's staccato manner of speaking, and his advice that we could only heal ourselves by examining our wounds and understanding the motives of those who had inflicted them. His analysis of mercantilism, the plantation system, the Haitian Revolution and finally, the island's taste for imported food put us all to sleep.

He had been the prime minister of the island for fifteen years and was given to pithy utterances, which Mr. Philip loved to quote to us: *When rain fall, goat and sheep have to mix. Time is longer than twine. Colour is a state of the mind. Massa day done.* Mr. Philip assiduously explained these adages and compared Bodsworth to the philosopher-kings of centuries past. Bodsworth may also have been a mathematician because he often described events in precise stages and enumerated the three or four steps necessary to effect some change. He carefully steered away from direct racial accusations and at various times had his ministers issue claims that he was infused with equal portions of African, Indian, Chinese, French, British and Portuguese blood. He was slim, bald and (but for his teeth, which jutted out menacingly in newspaper photographs) gentle looking. He was also very black.

A little over a year after my arrival in Canada, I had read a one-paragraph announcement in *The Toronto Star* of his demise from an epileptic seizure. He had been the prime minister for all of my adult life and I tried unsuccessfully to find out more about his death from the other West Indian students at the university. The woman I would later marry said that he was a monster, which surprised me, because even though I had just gotten to know her, I assumed that her animosity was directed only against white women. In the weeks that followed, I bought all the Trinidadian newspapers that were available in the West Indian shops. His death had created quite a ripple in the island; it seemed as if his long tenure as the leader had created the idea that he would be there forever. No real preparations had been made by the party for a successor. His son returned from New Zealand, where he had been living, and after consulting his father's lawyers announced that the prime minister had requested a Hindu cremation, and had also left orders that his close friend Melvin Makitoe was to lead the party until the next general election, due in a year and a half. Makitoe had studied with Bodsworth in London, but had left the university prematurely; he had eventually secured the position of prime ministerial chauffeur.

It was the former request that created the biggest stir. The blacks were clearly offended, the Hindus were ecstatic and the son, photographed with his glamorous wife, a white New Zealander, uttered confusing and contradictory comments about his father's genealogy when pestered by journalists.

Melvin Makitoe turned out to be a remarkably able administrator—there were plenty of witticisms about his being a "careful driver" and "steering the country in the right direction" and "using the gas prudently"—but after the election when he was booted out of power by a new party made up of former allies who had never quite adjusted to the idea of a chauffeur leading the party, it was rumoured that he had a sizeable amount of money stashed away in a Swiss bank. One newspaper wrote that "he had been overcharging his passengers."

"Did you know Bodsworth?" I asked Mr. Rampartap.

"I see the trip to the city is stirring old memories." He laughed moodily. "Yes, I knew him very well. We were in opposing camps so to speak but he was a honourable man. Died like a semp. With no friends. Some people say is from *mal yeux*."

"What about Makitoe?"

"A jackass of the highest order," said Mr. Rampartap, and Madhoo, without turning his head, erupted into laughter at his boss's pungently expressed opinion. "But I am being unfair. He do what he was capable of doing. I didn't realize you was so up to date on local affairs?"

"Newspapers in Canada. I can't recall reading anything about you though."

He made a soft grunt as if food were settling in his stomach. "That is not surprising. The things that I do don't make the news too often. As I said before, I conduct my affairs away from the limelight. Settling disputes. Panchayats. Giving advice. Little donations here and there."

"Weren't you a member of parliament?"

"That was a different time. Different people and different needs. People was simpler then." I wanted to say, *Easier to exploit?* but he added, "Tonight if you lucky you might see how much this place change. We nearly reach."

The meeting was a disappointment. A little over a hundred men scattered around the stage in Woodford Square chatted noisily with each other, occasionally breaking off to applaud a speaker. Some of the younger men drifted around, buying coconuts or boiled corn or pudding from the vendors who really had the most to cheer about. The speakers, arranged on wooden chairs on the stage, their arms crossed across their chests, were all wearing shirt-jacs, a variation of the Nehru jacket, which I thought had gone out of style but it gave them the correct look: phlegmatic, superior, exotic and irrelevant.

Perhaps the crowd was bored by it all, because speaker after speaker discoursed in the same chiding, humourless, slightly irritating manner of university lecturers. They each mentioned that the Tobagonian culture, nourished and preserved for so long, was in danger of being swamped by that of the larger island. One speaker, reading from copious piles of paper which he arranged and rearranged, the rustling sound magnified by the microphone, produced a list of Tobagonian words and phrases that, sadly, were rarely used now. Another speaker claimed to have proof of a letter written three generations ago by the colonial secretary in Britain to the governor general in Trinidad advising separation of the two islands. The crowd, drawn by this mystery, sensing mischief, quieted down. A few men at the front who were encouraging him to produce the letter lost interest when he revealed that it was probably destroyed. A short, bespectacled man with a beehive beard and shoes two sizes too large, speaking in an impeccable British accent, warned that Tobago was for Tobagonians and then rather irrelevantly branched off into a discourse about the nutritiousness of the average Tobagonian diet, especially when compared with that of Trinidad. He finished by counselling rather poetically that "the past is a flame which can be kept alight only through the oil of devotion and the wick of vigilance." He was followed by a thin, gangling young man, the only Indian in the group, who had nothing to say except that independence was not such a bad idea. He had an uneven, tilted stance, one foot bent at the knee as if he was standing on an incline, and unlike the other speakers, talked in a nervous, high-pitched whine.

But if the speakers were disappointing, if I had been led to expect a much larger crowd, I was impressed by the show of money. The stage did not consist of the crude wooden boxes I remembered from the political meetings in Rio Claro but was tastefully constructed with aluminum stairs and covered with a gazebo-style canopy. At the end of the meeting, the listeners who hung around were rewarded for their patience by the young Indian, who moved around shaking hands and passing out what seemed to be ten-dollar bills. The secession movement was certainly not lacking in funds.

Mr. Rampartap was chatting with a group of men who had formed a little circle around the thin Indian. I drifted off, looking for Madhoo.

"Nice little meeting, eh?" I turned to the man who had spoken, trying to place him. "Goonai. We met on the plane."

"Oh yes. Hello." I was about to extend my hand when I noticed he was holding a bag of groundnuts in one hand and broken shells in the other.

"You believe this nonsense? These bitches will never learn." For a minute I thought he was recalling some experience in Canada, then he added, "Everything is a pappy-show." He cracked open a groundnut, blew away the shell and popped the nut into his mouth. "That is why this kiss-meass place could never progress." He spat out a piece of shell. "You put up a stage, find some topic about oppression and you sure to get half-dozen jackass lining up to bray. They always complaining about some damn thing or the other. Is like a full-time hobby." He foraged his bag. "When last you ever went to a government office? They take a hour to read a little piece of paper and a next hour to sign it." He chewed and spat.

"What happened to your escort?"

"Escort?"

"The woman from the plane. The writer."

"Oh, she." He threw his bag beneath a bench and slowly dusted his palms. I felt he was thinking up a lie. "I couldn't keep up with she. Visiting all them old sugar factory and railway. God alone know what she was looking for."

"Time to leave, uncle."

Goonai glanced at Madhoo, then took out a pencil from his pocket and scribbled something on the back of a bill. "My number. Call me if you have the time."

Madhoo dipped a finger into a small Styrofoam bowl. "Souse. You want a bite?"

I shook my head.

"You sure?" He bent his head over the bowl and bit into a piece of meat. "Is a long time since I eat souse. They hardly have it in the village again." He licked a finger dry. "Pig meat with all the blood drain out and season up with some nice lemon and pepper and cucumber. Some people say it good for the back. Long time I use to make it meself. Get a nice, juicy pig and sling him up on a tree and bore a hole in he neck for all the blood to drain out. But I can't stand the noise them pig and them does make when they sling up. They too fussy." He spotted Mr. Rampartap waiting by the car and threw his bowl on the grass.

In the car Mr. Rampartap didn't say much, other than to ask if I enjoyed the speeches. I replied that I had found them amusing. He asked Madhoo to turn on the radio and for the rest of the journey he listened to Indian religious songs, *bhajans*.

So I was surprised when, the next morning, he showed me the daily paper, with the headline "Movement Gathering Steam." The article was written by Alto Jackson. It mentioned "the tension coursing through the massive crowd as the able rhetoricians lashed out against an insidious government." In the concluding paragraph, Jackson predicted that it was only a matter of time before Tobago was "delivered."

"The question we must now address seriously as a nation, nay, as two nations unnaturally linked, is whether the parting will be amicable or whether it will be accompanied by the sound of fury and the cries of the wounded."

While I was reading, Mr. Rampartap was tapping his teeth with the spoon's handle. "You still think it funny?"

"Is Mr. Alto a Tobagonian?"

"No. Not at all. He is a respected journalist from somewhere in Port of Spain."

"He must have gone to a different meeting."

"These fellas . . . these journalists covering the beat over here understand better than anybody what going on. The pulse of the place, as we like to say."

"They may just be trying to sell their papers."

"Or maybe they paid to write all these things." Mr. Rampartap looked up at his wife. "Money could buy anything in this place." She opened the door and walked out.

Mr. Rampartap became pensive. He pushed away his plate and knotted his fingers. He seemed set to talk about duty and destiny but he said nothing, although from time to time, he cleared his throat. I ate slowly, waiting.

"As a writer, this is a good opportunity for you. This independence movement."

"I really don't believe it is serious. In any case, I've been away for too long."

"Don't try that, Stephen. All that talk yesterday about Bodsworth and Makitoe. In addition, I am at your disposal." He said it in a light-hearted manner but his face was serious. "You could begin with this whole business about Mr. Choo."

"Mr. Choo? I thought you wanted me to write about Tobago?"

"Come on, Stephen. You are a sensible man. A writer. A man of the world."

I didn't like his tone, chiding and syrupy. "Maybe I'm not as smart as you believe." He was grinning, so I added, "I really can't see the connection between Mr. Choo and Tobago. Is he responsible for the secession movement?"

He erupted into laughter. "Good one, good one. I always knew that you writers are very sarcastic people. But let me explain." He got up and walked to the gallery, taking the newspaper. His wife was outside by the statue, patting the dirt around some freshly planted ixoras. "Look at her. Like a woman reborn. We are alike, you know." He placed a hand on the railing and stared at her like a husband fondly appraising his wife from afar. "We are both gardeners. She is happiest when she is in the garden tending her plants."

"She said the plants are benign."

"Really? Did she use that word?"

"Something like that."

He laughed pleasantly. "Women are so easy to please. Not just women, eh. Everybody."

"Except the people from Tobago."

"Not at all. Their demands are very simple. All they are asking for is a little respect. But when you push people like that in a corner, what you expect? This government don't have a clue how to deal with the common people." I was about to remind him of the view he had expressed just two months ago about the necessity of returning to the harsh discipline of the plantation system when he added, "And on top of that, they are so predictable. Trying to divert the attention of the population. Imagining that if they sacrifice one of their own, the people will suddenly decide they are honourable. Poor Mr. Choo."

I couldn't believe what he was saying. "One of them? But Mr. Choo is a foreigner?"

"Mr. Choo is inconsequential in the grand scheme of things. It's me they are after."

Did he really believe this? I saw his wife glancing at us. "That is why the story must begin with Mr. Choo. Innocent foreigner caught in a web of intrigue. How that sounding?"

"Unbelievable."

"Not in this place, Stephen. Things like that happen every day here." He removed his hand from the railing and flicked open the newspaper. "AIDS cure discovered by local evangelist." He turned to another page. "President of archaeological society claim that knife prove the existence of Africans down here long before Columbus make he li'l trip." He was speaking in an exaggerated Trinidadian accent, lilting and singsong, like a child reciting a nursery rhyme. He flipped the page again. "County councillor get in a accident. Family blame it on obeah. Man chop up wife. Say that she only talking 'bout some fella from the *Young and Restless* show. School close. Teachers say jumbie roaming about in the class." His wife, no longer tending the plants, was looking at us, or rather at her husband but I could not read her expression; she was too far away. "You want me to go on? Things like that happen every day here. Things that a outsider will never believe. I will pay for the book, you know. But it must be finished fast. Within three months."

"During our last conversation before I left here, I got the impression that you were no longer interested in this biography."

"Things have changed since, as you noticed. I not talking about any best-seller, you know. Fifty-sixty pages."

"It's impossible. I don't think I can do it."

"Why?" he asked, smiling.

"Maybe I'm thinking like an outsider, but I can't believe any of this. What about your journalist friends?"

"They wouldn't have the credibility. They work for too long in the job. They make too much enemies. Anyways, think about it." His wife stood up and walked to the back of the house. "Are you anxious to get back to your wife? I know I asking a lot from you. It have no replacement for a happy family, you know. I tell you that my daughter is arriving tomorrow? I didn't see her since she was fifteen. She's twenty-two now."

"About the same age as Dulcie?"

"A few months apart."

"Must have been a busy year for you?"

He looked at me, perhaps measuring my expression. His own was hard to read: a flash of anger quickly transformed into a pocket of uncertainty. He took a deep breath, like a diver poised on the bow of a boat; then a little smile at once bland and enigmatic appeared on his face. Once more, I was impressed. "Let me know when you have made up your mind," he said, walking away.

When I went downstairs, his wife was washing her gloves by the garden tap. Her face was red and flushed from the morning's exertion. "The planting is agreeing with you," I said, too casually, but she didn't seem offended.

"Everything happen for a time. We will see how long it will last. How long everything will last." And from the quiet sadness in her voice, I saw what I should have seen before: her rehabilitation had nothing to do with any affection or remorse on the part of her husband. It was really a part of this new image he was creating, of a man centred around duty and obligations. Maybe his daughter's return fell into this scheme too.

"You said your daughter was taken away from you?"

She shook off the water from her gloves. "She was sent away to Canada."

"But isn't that normal over here? People sending their children away to colleges or university?"

"I had no say in the decision. I didn't even know until a few days before she left." Perhaps it was the morning's activity but she seemed wearied, less self-assured than during our last conversation. "She was sent away so she wouldn't see what was happening."

"With her father?"

"He was"—she hesitated for the briefest of moments—"he was a cruel man but he never saw it that way."

"Cruel with you?"

She looked up at me. Perspiration from her face was running along the wrinkles on her neck. "With everybody, not just me alone. He bought this estate for next to nothing. The people who lived here used to work in the cocoa estate, but they had no deed for the land. He said they were squatters. They refuse to leave because they had nowhere else to go. They say that they not budging an inch because they father and grandfather build up the estate. But they didn't know who they was dealing with. Houses get burn down in the night. Little children running out screaming. Big-big men standing up next to the burn-down house and holding on to some black post and crying."

"Wasn't that illegal?"

Now, for the first time, a flash of anger. "What illegal in this place? He had police protection wherever he went. Pillooki and Haggers with him every step of the way. When

he was bulldozing the houses, when he was moving about
in the night, doing what God alone know, when he was
cutting deal with the villagers who realize that it was useless to fight him, when he went to court to get rid of
some troublemaker, as he put it. One by one, he get rid
of them."

"Is that why you think Mr. Choo is innocent?"

"Mr. Choo couldn't hurt a fly. You know who use to
bring some little toy . . . some little nonsense to distract me
when I was locked up in that old house by the cemetery?
Who use to come and talk with me?" She smiled bitterly.
"Two mad people talking mad people talk. But he wasn't
mad. Not mad at all. Just out of place."

"Like you?" I had no idea why I said that but she looked
at me with something like gratitude. And I seized the moment to ask, "Do you believe your husband had anything
to do with the murder? That he killed the old man?"

"These are two different questions." I was about to
rephrase the question when she added, "No. That is not his
style any more. He is very careful about everything these
days." She must have seen that I was puzzled. "He had
nothing to gain from the murder."

"Perhaps the old man knew something?"

A small tremor of uncertainty passed through her face.
But she shook her head and I wondered whether she was
afraid of divulging any further information. "Maybe Edwin
is protecting the killer," she said.

"Why would—?"

"You must understand how things work here. Edwin
have plenty people who would do anything to get on his
good side. This estate is his little kingdom. He like to believe that he is in control of everything."

"He said the whole thing is a set-up by the government to get rid of him."

She laughed with her lips pressed together, the sound hollow, like a clearing of the throat. "He could twist around anything to make it useful to him. Twist it and twist it until it suit his purpose. That is his real talent. Every single little thing."

"But murder is not a little thing."

"Really?" She pretended surprise. "In this place, with a little over a million people, ten-twelve people get killed every day. Who counting again? The police?"

"So it wasn't a plot hatched by the government?"

I spoke in a light, provoking manner, just to get her reaction. She laughed—loud, ringing laughter this time. "If you believe that, then you no better than Thackordeen and Bhogerattie and the rest of them. All his little *metcai.*" She laughed again and I glanced upstairs.

"What about the lawsuit? Maybe it was launched to divert attention from the murder."

She grew serious thinking of it, but then she shook her head. "No, I don't think so. That is not his style. He's more interested in all these crazy schemes cook up by that drunkard Pillooki. I don't know what hold he have over Edwin."

"Maybe they operate on the same wavelength."

"Or maybe Edwin like the idea of a big-shot lawyer hanging on to him."

"A formidable pair," I said. "The government must be scared."

"You believe the government have him to study? He lost all his power years ago and he still can't accept it. Always plotting and plotting and twisting and twisting and talking all that rubbish about how he so different from these new breed of politicians." She shook her head. "And people say I is the mad one. But he have a way with people. He know how to fool them up good and proper." A worried look crossed her face and I felt she was thinking of her daughter returning from Canada. "Always looking for some little weakness he could use."

I wanted to reassure her. "Your daughter may be smarter than you imagine."

She seemed surprised by the statement. Finally she said, "And you may be smarter than he imagine." She smiled faintly. "Two months ago I didn't know who side you was on. Or why exactly you wanted to talk to me. And about what. I tried to figure out how you fitted in with Edwin schemes. This pretentious writer from Canada." She looked at my face and smiled. "Oh no, I said something wrong."

"You make me sound like the kind of person I always hated. People like that—"

She said "Oh no" again but she seemed amused. After a while she said, "Well, you never talked much. And I used to see you watching around with a little smirk on your face. So I didn't talk to you." She pressed her fingers against her mouth. "But I'm glad you came here. Is the best thing that happened around here for a long while."

I wanted to ask her why but instead I said, "I am going to be out of here soon."

"You not going to write the book again?"

I shook my head. "Mmm-mmm."

"You told him that already?"

"A while ago."

She seemed set to say something then she changed her mind. I had expected a sense of relief but she seemed disappointed. And I couldn't help feeling that she saw in my presence in the estate some sort of guarantee that she would not, once more, be locked away and ignored.

TWENTY-FOUR

Men and women who try too hard to be enigmatic are the most difficult of acquaintances. Their studied behaviour is meant to convey that beneath the artful polish is some delicious riddle, some secret power that must be nurtured and kept from prying eyes lest it become diminished. The threat of exposure makes them dangerous. They weep at the least provocation—but they are complete frauds.

On the way to the airport for Mr. Rampartap's daughter, I thought of how much my father had influenced me. This was surprising because apart from his homilies, which he offered without explanation or elaboration, we never engaged in lengthy conversations. Yet I was like him in many ways. He was distrustful of the rich and powerful, cynical about the pretentious, and (I suspect) impatient with those whose fickleness confused him.

Seated next to Madhoo, I wondered what my father would have made of Mr. Rampartap's preparations to receive his daughter: the hiring of a limousine; the invitation to me to be part of the entourage, which was more like an order, despite its offhand phrasing—"I invite over a few fellas you might be interested in meeting"; the way he strode through the crowd at the arrival lounge, turning heads with his white suit and his imperious manner; the way his wife followed a dutiful distance behind him, impassive in her sunglasses.

He looked like a relic from some other era—a Mafia don or an aging gigolo—as he made his way forward to greet his daughter, kissing her on both cheeks, ignoring her companion, a blithe-looking young man in cutoff denim trousers, then stepping back and allowing his daughter to kiss her mother and gesturing to Madhoo to look after the suitcases. Poor Madhoo.

I wondered whether people were staring because they recognized Mr. Rampartap or because of the unembarrassed Trinidadian fascination with spectacle and display.

When, after twenty minutes or so, the limousine pulled into an open-air bar at the Churchill-Roosevelt highway, Madhoo followed, parking alongside. Mr. Rampartap got out and waited for his family and the young man. The chauffeur remained at the wheel.

I felt that some grand show was in the offing.

Hillview Bar, strangely named in the unending plains of Caroni, was really a number of carat sheds surrounding a boxy little building. As Mr. Rampartap and his party moved towards a hut at the far end, I saw Pillooki walking next to two men, one of whom, a small, oily man, I recognized from the gathering on the day I had returned to the estate.

"This is Mr. Pillooki, a respected legal luminary," Mr. Rampartap said, when we were all seated. Pillooki smiled crookedly. "The gentleman on the left is Mr. Bhogerattie and the other one is Thackordeen."

"Call me Tack," Mr. Thackordeen said in a steely voice. He narrowed his eyes and pressed his lips together. I felt he had seen too many Clint Eastwood movies.

"And this is my daughter from Canada here for a vacation. She is a student of—is it biotechnology, Cynthia?"

His daughter smiled in a preoccupied manner. She was looking at the group and I felt that she shuddered when her eyes met Pillooki's.

Without looking at me, he continued his introductions. "And this quiet gentleman is a writer from Canada." I objected to his use of the word *quiet*, because he had said it in a dismissing way, but I let it pass. "I believe you are familiar with Mr. Pillooki," he said to me.

"It all boils down to what you mean by familiar," I said.

Pillooki opened his mouth like a decrepit librarian who has received an impossible request but Mr. Rampartap laughed amiably and I saw his daughter transferring her attention to me. "Well, maybe not so quiet any more. He went away somewhere for two months and now he is behaving like a real Trinidadian."

"What do you write about?" asked Bhogerattie. His glass was raised to his mouth but he did not drink, his eyes above the rim tiny and unflinching, like a rat's. He was well dressed, with a maroon handkerchief carefully arranged in his shirt pocket.

"Nothing much. Mostly Canadian stuff." I was being evasive but as Bhogerattie downed his drink swiftly and slapped his glass on the table, I saw that he had interpreted it as a boast of some kind and that he was offended.

Radha leaned over and whispered in her daughter's ear. The daughter blushed and glanced at her companion, the cheery young man. A waitress with a bored, sour look strolled over to our table and stood scratching the ankle of one foot with the toe of the other. "What allyou people drinking?"

"Whisky. Black and White." Pillooki slurred the words and I realized he was quite drunk.

"A bottle for these gentlemen and a flask of rum for me. Old Oak. Wine, Cynthia?" He ignored her companion.

"I will have whatever Mummy is having."

"Are you sure . . . ?"

Radha cut him off. "Just a Coke, dear."

"Rum for me. A man drink." Tack raised his head and tensed his jaw muscles.

"Same here, boss," Madhoo said.

When the waitress brought the drinks, Mr. Rampartap stood up, glass in hand. "I will like to propose a toast to my daughter, Cynthia. I hope your stay here is long and enjoyable."

"Here, here," Pillooki recited in a lifeless manner.

"I hope that she returns to Canada safe and sound." Radha's voice was clear and steady and the statement seemed sensible, but Mr. Rampartap sat, frowning.

"Nothing could happen to she in this place." Tack uttered this as if he were her protector. "I could guarantee that." He tipped his head and tossed in the drink.

The young man touched the glass with his lips and grimaced. "Wow." He replaced the glass on the table and slid slightly down in the chair. Cynthia, seated between her companion and her mother, tugged at an ear as if an earring were creating discomfort. Mr. Rampartap was talking loudly about the secession movement with Bhogerattie, who every now and again glanced at me. Pillooki's eyes were shut; but for the occasional nod he could have been fast asleep.

A nice little gathering, I thought, just before a souped-up Escort screeched to a halt beside the limousine. A shirtless young man, nineteen or twenty, his chest shiny with sweat, rapped his knuckles on the car window, looked at us, then waved three other men out of the Escort. They could have been brothers but one of them was a shade less dark than the others. And it was this young man, his hair divided into corn-rows, who spoke first. "That car belong to you?" He scanned our group, his gaze resting momentarily on Pillooki.

"Any particular reason why that may interest you?" Mr. Rampartap, not looking at them, wedged a finger between two teeth.

"Is just a question. All I asking is who the car belong to?" His voice was smooth, almost polite.

"Allyou looking for trouble or what? Why allyou don't answer the man?" said one of the others: a short man with a flat, boxy face.

"Cool it. Cool it, Sledge," the man with corn-rows cut in.

Pillooki, his eyes still closed, said, "Trouble make the monkey eat pepper."

"What the fuck?" Sledge erupted, but Pillooki's gaunt, lifeless face seemed to have impressed him; his voice was tinged with uncertainty.

"What is your name, young man?" Mr. Rampartap, ignoring Sledge, directed his question to the first speaker, maybe gauging that he was the leader of the group.

"Calvin. Call me Calvin. Listen, boss, we was just passing through and spot this nice little hangout and decide to have a drink."

"Really? As simple as that?" Cynthia's companion said.

"Simple? Simple as what? You is some kinda smartman?" Sledge contorted his face into a menacing mask, but his expression was unconvincing, it was too smooth and practised.

Cynthia's companion looked at his watch. "The travel brochure was right. They usually crawl out around this time."

Now a third man, his lanky trunk twisted unnaturally as if afflicted with sclerosis, placed a clenched fist on the table and leaned over. "In this country, we keep all the comedian and them in the calypso tent." The smirk on the young man's face seemed to infuriate him. "So if I was you, I would watch me little ass."

Cynthia placed a hand on the young man's arm. "Rob, it's okay."

And Rob did something totally unexpected. He chuckled, loud and long. Then, looking skywards, he said, "Oh Lord, the guilt. The guilt, the guilt."

"Listen, Mr. Comedian, if I hear anything from you again, you go have to make a li'l trip to the hospital, you understand?"

Mr. Rampartap, a hand on his trouser pocket, was looking on speculatively. Pillooki still looked asleep but Tack was a complete surprise. Hunched up over the table, his shoulders pulled to his ears, he seemed positively petrified.

"Rob!" Cynthia's voice was charged with exasperation, and I thought—quite unfairly, because her concern was reasonable—that if they ever got married she would nag him to death.

Radha reached into her purse. "Youngboy. Take this and go on your way. Go!" She pushed a hundred-dollar bill across the table.

Mr. Rampartap, remarkably controlled before, snatched the bill angrily and creased and folded it. "Go tell the barman to give you a bottle of rum. Tell him to put it in my account."

With a slick flick of his wrist, Calvin relayed the order to Sledge. The lanky man stepped back and folded his arms. He was still glaring at Rob. When Sledge returned with the bottle, Mr. Rampartap said, "Let me crack the seal for you." Sledge looked at Calvin uncertainly but the lanky man began to grin. Calvin passed the bottle to Mr. Rampartap who twisted the cork and took a swift swig. Some of the liquid rolled down his chin. Still holding the bottle, he dusted his trouser with his free hand. "I have lost practice with this sort of thing. I think I wet my pants."

Madhoo was grinning mischievously. Tack erupted into a high-pitched whinny. I was looking at Tack's little transformation, his reversion to Clint Eastwood, so I didn't see when Mr. Rampartap pulled out his revolver and laid it on the table. He wiped the handle. "Can't afford to get this wet. It's licensed, you know. Not like the one you have in the dashboard." Sledge's mouth opened, his lower lip dangling. "Is the same one I carry to parliament every Friday as a rule." He passed the bottle to Calvin.

"You is a politician?" Calvin was staring at the revolver rather than at Mr. Rampartap.

"Not any more. I not in that stupidness again. I leave that for these new breed of fellas who don't even know it have people living behind the hill." He was speaking loudly. I glanced at Radha, but in her sunglasses she was unreadable.

"If it did have more people like you around here, boss, a lot of this stupidness that going around might never have start. Over here not suppose to get like them other place." Calvin was speaking slowly as if he had put a lot of thought into the observation.

Mr. Rampartap laughed and replaced the revolver in his pocket. "It all boil down to duty, as my esteemed legal colleague like to say." He glanced at Pillooki.

"It's the same thing wherever you go. Easy pickings," said Rob.

Easy pickings? I had been trying to place Rob but his accent was totally Canadian. The phrase, however, suggested a Caribbean connection. Perhaps he was born in Canada of West Indian parentage. His remark had a different effect on

Mr. Rampartap, who, from his expression, had taken it as a rebuke of some kind. He turned to his daughter. "I didn't have the pleasure of a proper introduction to this young man. Where did you pick him up from?"

"I didn't pick him up, Daddy. His name is Rob and he is from the university."

Rob stretched his legs, scratched a thigh and grinned. And with this little gesture, this indifference to the insult, my impression of him changed and I felt that years ago, we could have been close friends. Radha leaned over to her daughter and whispered, "Never mind, dear. He look like a nice boy."

Mr. Rampartap looked disgusted. He jerked his head towards Calvin. "Enjoy the drink."

Calvin understood the dismissal, but Sledge put in the last word. "You owe it to we bossman. All of allyou owe it to we. We wait long enough. The time up. Don't forget that. The time up."

"Contact me when you all land behind bars. I will give you a group discount." Surprisingly, they all grinned at Pillooki's offer, taking it as a joke of some kind.

"The nerve," Cynthia said when they strode off.

"Children. Little children." Mr. Rampartap was still smarting from Rob's casual reproof.

"Children! They lucky. They damn lucky tonight." Tack passed a hand over his hair, testing the bristles.

Pillooki snored and grunted. Rob looked at him and whispered to Cynthia. She pinched his arm and covered her mouth with her fingers. I felt that Radha, behind her sunglasses, was observing the young couple carefully.

"Speaking of bars," Mr. Pillooki said. "I visited Mr. Choo yesterday."

"Who is that, Daddy?"

Mr. Rampartap seemed unwilling to discuss his former employee and he appeared upset when Madhoo blurted, "A crazy fella who use to live inside the windmill on the hill."

"A real windmill?" Rob asked.

"Yeah. He use to spend most of he time spoiling thing." If Madhoo had noticed the expression on Mr. Rampartap's face he would not have gone on. "And inventing all kinda new plant. Hi-breed he use to call them."

"Hybrids? Really?" Cynthia seemed fascinated, and I remembered she was doing biotechnology at university. "What was he working on?"

"Trying to make a straight banana."

Rob, misunderstanding Mr. Rampartap's sarcasm, laughed, slapping his outstretched legs.

Cynthia seemed confused. "That's so interesting. Do you know that all these pharmaceutical companies are focusing their research on the rain forests? It's a treasure trove."

"Like the neem plant," Tack said. "It have one thousand and one use."

Bhogerattie coughed as if he were about to make a weighty contribution, but Mr. Rampartap cut in, "Suddenly all these big scientists discovering what the simple country people know years ago."

"I cure a big, nasty boil on me bottom with aloes alone. Three days and it gone completely. It only leave a li'l mark." Tack stood up and for a minute I thought he was going to display the mark but he sat down once more.

Now Bhogerattie got his chance. He blew on his hands as if they were cold. "These people shouldn't interfere with what God put down here. They playing with fire. Like putting bacteria in all these crops."

"Maybe that is what Mr. Choo—" Madhoo stopped suddenly.

"Can I meet him?" Cynthia asked.

Mr. Rampartap said abruptly, "He's in jail." Pillooki opened his eyes and snorted.

"In jail?"

"It look like he was playing with the wrong kinda bacteria and them," Madhoo said.

Mr. Rampartap stood up. "Well, is time to call it a day." His wife and daughter also stood up but Rob remained seated.

"Aren't you coming?" Cynthia inquired.

"I'll get a lift back with the driver."

Mr. Rampartap seemed glad to be rid of him, but his daughter looked a bit annoyed. She swiftly scanned the group and because her gaze rested on me, I said, "We should be back in the estate in an hour or so." She turned and walked with her mother to the car. The chauffeur started the engine and Pillooki peeped at his watch with one eye and lumbered towards the vehicle.

"This is no place for a woman in the nighttime. Any number could play. Better to be safe than sure."

Tack's statement was meant for Rob, but Bhogerattie said, "These people can't get used to the fact that they get boot out from power after all them years of mismanagement. They just not design for management."

The familiarity of the remark was shocking. "Which people?" I asked him.

"The niggies," Tack exclaimed, curling his tongue and giving to the slur the flavour of a disease. "Why you think they so interested in this Tobago nonsense? Eh? Well, lemme tell you." He squinted. "Because it give them a chance to have a little fun. Li'l tiefing here, li'l tiefing there. But the day they interfere with any of me family . . . well . . ." He laughed spectacularly.

"Is not their fault. Is how they design. To put it in a nutshell, they have no choice." Bhogerattie was trying to look reasonable and thoughtful and I suspected that they had both played this game several times.

"You guys are crazy." Rob seemed astounded. "Crazy, man."

Looking at me rather than at Rob, Bhogerattie said, "Over here things operate a little different from Canada. Is only when you living in a place that you understand what going on. Otherwise, to put it in a nutshell, is just idle talk."

"See, that's not true. There are people like that in Canada too. And people like you."

The observation was made in a casual manner and I was sure that Rob did not see how much he had offended Bhogerattie. I tried to change the topic. "So what do you think is going to happen in Tobago?"

"The faster these bacteria go the better for everybody. All this kissmeass talk about how they so different and all them blasted demand. To hell with them. Let them go and see how long they go survive. Bet you anything that two months later they start crying and begging to come back. Different my nasty ass. Demand my nastier ass."

Rob obviously found Tack's crude indignation highly amusing. I stifled my own laughter, watching Bhogerattie screwing up his face, preparing to say something reasonable. "You have to look at it this way, Tack. Ain't they getting all that they asking for? Ain't the government giving them everything?" He forced a smile. "Ain't they getting through with the game?"

"Game? They better call off this game because of bad light or rain or something, because I not playing. And if anybody get in me path . . . well . . ." He offered once more his dramatic laugh.

"So what *you* think, speaking as a journalist yourself?"

I began my usual response. "I haven't been here long enough." Then I saw Bhogerattie's little sneer and added, "I prefer to reserve my judgments to issues with which I am familiar."

"Good. Very good. That is a good answer," Bhogerattie said icily.

"So what part of Canada are you from?" Rob asked.

"Scarborough. And you?"

"Etobicoke."

"Etty-be-coor? What sort of name is that? French?" Tack asked.

"I never asked. It's spelled as Eto-bi-coke."

"Coke?" Tack nudged Bhogerattie and they both began to titter.

"Gentlemen, I propose a Berlin wall." Bhogerattie raised his glass unsteadily, some of the rum tipping over. "Right here in Trinidad between we and them."

"Spill it out, brother-man," Rob mocked.

"We"—he took a long drink, placed his glass on the table and wiped his lips—"we are a race of philosophers, descended from the people who wrote the Gita and the Upanishads, who invented the zero, who developed indoor plumbing long before . . ." He stopped in midsentence as if he had suddenly recalled some more magnificent invention. "I am working on something too. A little project. Little project, but it might make me famous. Is not my fault, is the genes." He laughed, rat-like, his lips trembling.

"So what is this little project?" I asked.

He shifted in his chair and tried to look modest.

"Tell him, Bhog. Tell him. He in the same field like you. He go understand. Not like these publishers' bitches it have down here. He might even help you get it publish up in the cold."

"Well, is just a theory. A little theory. Nothing much." His eyes were blinking rapidly.

"Is the same damn thing they say about Einstein before they lock him up in a lab and clone him. Tell the man."

I heard Rob choking. Bhogerattie cleared his throat and spat beneath the table. "Is a little theory as I like to say. The implications are big but the theory itself, I prefer to say that it little. For the time being."

"Go on, Bhog. Go on. These things too big to keep to youself. He might get it publish for you."

"All right, you force me." He stretched his hands before him, his fingers splayed as if clutching a globe. "Everybody like to say that these Eskimo and Red Indian and Aztec and Carib people come from the east. Some place near China. Through Siberia. That is what everybody like to say."

"They mad no ass." Tack was scrunched forward, peeping at the space between Bhogerattie's hands, as if he could see weary travellers struggling through frozen mountains and tundras and desolate plains.

"Now, what if it didn't actually happen that way. What if"—he clapped his hands suddenly and Tack jumped back—"what if it happen the other way around. What if these fellas leave from around here instead, move through America and Canada, went through the same Siberia and then land up in the east." He leaned back. "A little theory, as I say, but the implications, well, that is a different matter altogether. To put it in a nutshell, it could change the way we look at the past. At our own self. And time, in general."

"You have to get a title for it, Bhog. A good title with plenty of drawing inside. Or you could take out drawings from other history books and put below, 'Oops, sorry. Wrong direction.'"

Bhogerattie shook his head. "In my profession, you must never pull down other people. You have to help them out. In any case, this project too big for that."

"How about 'The Crazy Shape of Time'?" I suggested.

"'The Crazy Shape of Time'?" I saw, too late, that he was taking me seriously. "Is not a bad title. I like the shape of time but crazy . . . that might give people the wrong impression."

"Really?" Rob asked, and after a while, "How about, 'In a Nutshell'?"

"Nah, Bhog. That crazy part wouldn't work at all." He turned to me. "Is exactly what all them blasted publishers down here was saying. That the man gone mad. You believe that? A kissmeass genius like him. If he mad, then I mad too."

Rob was enjoying himself. He cracked up once more.

"I will think about it though. I might just have to change the word, crazy."

"Change it, Bhog, but not too much." Tack seemed to be reflecting on something. "It must have you mark on it. Show these kissmeass publishers and them. Especially Babwah, that ugly little monkey with he hand always black with ink."

Bhogerattie smiled graciously. "He doesn't exist."

"Eh? But I see him just this—"

Bhogerattie, still smiling, raised a hand. "Look at it this way, Tack. *You* believe Babwah is a ugly monkey. I *know* he is a envious, money-hungry *chamar*. He workers think he is a dictator and his mother, if he have one, poor woman, might think he is a good, nice—"

"Never happen! If she think so, then she worse than him."

"The point, Tack, is that everybody have a different impression of him. Now the question that running through everybody mind here"—he glanced around the table—"is which is the true one? The answer is all. And none."

Tack shook his head.

"So you see what I getting at," Bhogerattie continued. "People exist only in the mind of other people."

"You mean, 'cording to how we interpret them?"

"Exactly, exactly. You using you head. So nobody could tell who the real man is. Maybe"—he slipped into an unnaturally resonant voice—"maybe they don't exist."

"Eh? So you mean all the time Babwah didn't exist?"

"In a manner of speaking."

"That kissmeass, sly monkey." Tack laughed uproariously. "Giving people so much pressure and all the time he never even exist. He is a real lagahoo."

"That is a different issue altogether. It have two important things about lagahoos. Number one, they does live alone. And number two, they does change they form as they see fit. Changing in the shadow when nobody watching and coming out as something new. The old people used to call it the shadow act. That is why they always living by themself."

I saw that Madhoo looked worried, rubbing his hands nervously. "It look like we go have to leave this jumbie talk for a next time, uncle. The bossman must be reach home nearly a hour now."

In the car, I asked Rob, "Is this your first visit?"

"Yeah. How about you? You grew up here, didn't you?"

"Yes. I left about sixteen years ago."

"Must have changed a lot?"

"In some ways. It's more modern now but some of the old"—I searched for the word—"the old rivalries are still there. Maybe even more so."

"Yeah." He nodded as if he understood. "What's all this talk about secession?"

"A little island nearby. Tobago. Some people are pushing for independence."

"I know of Tobago. Germans buying up the land."

"Are your parents from over here?"

"My father. My mother is from England."

"So what do you think?"

He didn't get a chance to answer because Madhoo braked suddenly. A policeman was in the centre of the road. He walked to the driver's side. "You have a licence for this thing?"

"Yes, boss." Madhoo unwrapped a bundle fastened with a rubber band on the sun visor.

The policeman glanced at the licence. "So who is them two fellas in the back seat?"

"They from Canada, boss."

"And what they doing here?"

"Visiting," Rob said. "I hope it's not illegal."

"What he just say? Step out from the car for me, mister." Rob opened the door and got out. "You ask if it illegal? Well, let me tell you something, mister man. It illegal if I say it illegal. Stretch you hand." He patted Rob's sides. "I hope you don't have any stuff on you, eh, because the jail and them down here not air-conditioned. You laughing? You find that funny? You have any stuff hiding in you bottom? What the ass wrong with this man?" He looked to Madhoo. "Everything is a big joke for him. Like he on drugs or what? All right, mister man, drop you pants."

"He's had a bit too much to drink, officer." I opened the door.

"You stay right they." He pointed to me. "This boy here is you brother?"

"A friend."

"What allyou doing here? It too cold in Canada? What the ass. He start up again!"

"I'm a journalist," I said, distracting him from Rob.

"Journalist, eh? I hear allyou fellas does make a lot of money."

"Not really. Just small change." I reached into my pocket and withdrew a fifty-dollar bill.

"Let me see that." He stretched the bill taut, pretending he was inspecting it. "This looking like Trinidadian money to me, not Canadian." He pushed it into his pocket and turned once more to Rob. "What you still doing outside, boy?" He grabbed his shoulder and directed him into the car.

"Thanks, boss. Keep up the good work." There was no trace of sarcasm in Madhoo's compliment.

"So what do you think of the place?" I asked Rob.

He had been grinning throughout but now I saw that he was a bit shaken. "Typical Third-World country. Drunk politicians, loopy journalists and corrupt cops."

I felt obliged to correct him. "It's the same all over, you know."

"I'm sure you never bribed a cop in Toronto."

"True." After a while, I asked him, "So do you plan to stay for a while?"

"As long as it's cool. How about you?"

"A few weeks, maybe."

"Do you have family there?"

"A daughter."

"Who is she staying with?"

"Her mother."

"Oh."

I was surprised at how easy it was to talk with him. I felt as if we had known each other for a long time. The car swung into Rougeleau. "This is Cynthia's father's estate."

"A real asshole," he said, too low for Madhoo to hear. "Do you believe those two guys we met at the bar? And the creepy one who was sleeping. What is he? An undertaker?"

"A lawyer."

"I was thinking of one of those guys from the old Hammer films. From a film course I did at university. Narrative theory in film and literature. Shitty course." He gazed out of the window. "Hey, this is a perfect setting for one of these films. Peter Cushing could be living in an old cottage behind the bushes." Madhoo, his head pressed against the backrest, was attempting to listen to the conversation. "Or maybe a murderer. Christopher Lee or Donald Pleasence, hiding from the police pretending to be a farmer or something. Somebody well respected but with this secret life. What's the joke?"

"It's the kind of things tourists say." I remembered the woman from the plane. "Or travel writers."

"C'mon. Look at the trees and all the shadows. There could be anything inside there. And that house on the hill. Look at the wall and the vines hanging like snakes over the roof."

"That's where you will be staying," I told him.

"Oh really? Oooooh." He uttered a low wail.

Madhoo jerked forward and brought the car to a sudden stop. He took a deep breath, got out and opened the gate. There were two figures in the gallery and as Madhoo drove into the yard, I recognized Cynthia and Radha. Just before Madhoo switched off the headlights, I saw Cynthia walking down the steps with a worried, annoyed look.

"Oh-oh. Trouble's a-brewing," Rob said, not sounding the least concerned.

TWENTY-FIVE

I was glad that when Madhoo knocked on my door earlier, I had told him that I would have a few fruits instead of breakfast. Both Mr. Rampartap and his daughter had been in a sour mood the day before and I preferred to avoid any unpleasantness. Returning, I saw Rob up in an orange tree, throwing fruit down to Madhoo, or rather, at Madhoo, on the ground.

Madhoo caught an orange with both hands and another narrowly missed his head. "Oh God, uncle, you go buss me head or what? Take you time. The day young." When he spotted me, he said, "You better help me catch these thing and them because this fella up they throwing down orange like if he is a monkey." An orange bounced off his shoulder. "Oh God, man, uncle. I make outta flesh and blood, too, you know." He hopped backwards and looked up. "All right, you better scale down from that tree now. We have enough." Ripe fruits, about twenty or thirty, were strewn around him.

"Catch me," Rob yelled, making as if he were about to jump. Madhoo placed his hands over his head in a protective gesture and Rob jumped, about three feet from him.

"So how was your first night in Trinidad?"

"Scary."

"Really?" Then I saw he was joking.

"I've slept on harder floors."

"You better take this bag, Tarzan. It look like you have too much energy. Too much *jhoor*." Rob took the bag and sprinted towards the house. We followed him. "Is a good thing you coming too, yes, because I don't think I coulda deal with that wild man. That Tarzan."

"Coming where?"

"Maracas. The bossman daughter want to do a little touristing and it look like Tarzan too going for the ride." Rob, the bag slung on his shoulder, stumbled and got up swiftly, running even faster. "You see what I mean? I never-never know that they does grow up children so wild in Canada. Like Tarzans. I thought we was the wild one down here. Watch him. I bet you he fall down and mashup he head." Rob whooped and leaped over the drain. "Lord father."

"So we're going to Maracas?"

"Correct the first time. Me, you, the bossman daughter and Tarzan. It go get him away from trouble."

"Yeah?"

"Digging up by the windmill like if he is a Hardy Boys or something."

As we were about to leave, Radha came down the steps with a hamper basket. Because she was wearing a straw hat and her dark glasses, I thought she had decided to accompany us but she gave the basket to her daughter and kissed her on both cheeks. Up in the gallery, Mr. Rampartap was issuing directions to Madhoo. He seemed a bit peeved. I recalled Radha's remark that he was able to find a use for every-thing—twist it and twist it, she had said—and I wondered at the arrival of his daughter here in the estate. From the car, Rob, mimicking Madhoo's high-pitched voice, screeched, "C'mon, uncle. It's time to go." Mr. Rampartap turned around and went into the house.

For most of the journey Cynthia sat close to Rob and spoke to him in a voice too low for either of us in the front to hear. From time to time, Rob would lean forward, close to Madhoo's ear, and ask about some mansion or factory or dilapidated building. Once Cynthia told him, "Stop it, Rob," as if he had been teasing. After that he was quiet.

Madhoo was relieved and I suspected that he was either intimidated or outraged by Rob's boisterous manner. As we approached the mountain range on the northern coast, he told me, "All these road on this side get build by American fellas. They had a base in Chaguaramas around the war-time and they put up one setta road and building and thing. They had money to burn and they was to be all over Port of Spain running down jamette and drinking and fêteing. But some prime minister or the other, I can't recall which one, tell them that they was getting too big for they britches and start electioning against them until they had was to go. But watch how the road still remain. Cutting right through the mountain. Good tough road, just like the American and them."

While Madhoo was expressing his admiration for Amer-icans, I reflected on the gossip I had heard at Ecclesville School. Mr. Philip hated the Americans so much that a rumour had circulated of his younger sister being seduced into prostitution by an American soldier at the base. According to the story, she was previously a quiet country girl, but, dazzled by the easy money and the glamour, she was living a wanton life on the base. Mr. Philip had brought the campaign to rid the island of the Americans into class: he ground his teeth, he railed against their presumed debauchery and he grew purple with rage at their arrogance. Another rumour, more believable than the first—because he had, to the best of our knowledge, always lived alone in a small, brightly painted wooden house—was that he had been turned down repeatedly in his quest to get a green card.

"All right, fasten allyou seat belt," Madhoo said jokingly because there were no seat belts in the car. The road wound its way through the ridges of the mountain where jagged trees hung precariously from the slopes, and water from springs high above trickled over lichens and small wiry shrubs with orchid-like flowers. After a mile or so, it cut into a narrow cavern where the trees, immortelle and poui and clumps of bamboo, confused by gravity, grew at unusual angles. Now Madhoo was telling the familiar stories of maroons hiding in these forests, and more recently, of criminals from the Carrera prison escaping into the mountains and of bandits who had devised an elaborate system of pipe guns to discourage intruders. "Them is not place for anybody to go at all. Every year 'bout half-dozen people does get they tail blow up with pipe gun. Is to protect the ganja field. From what I hear, it have one setta tunnel running through them mountain way the Americans use to spy to see if any Joemany submarine landing. Tunnel cutting through the whole mountain. Maybe is them escape slave what build them." Surprisingly, Rob leaned forward and became very attentive.

Then, suddenly, the magic was gone. We passed a sign reading, "Welcome to Maracas," and written beneath it in big, black letters were the words "And Leave Fast." A few kilometres on there was a group of men and women by the roadside, bedraggled and surly, arguing with a police officer who was leaning against his jeep. Rob made a remark about "looking for stuff," but Madhoo grew silent and a bit edgy. As we drove by I saw that the officer had his self-loading rifle propped before him, and that behind the Jeep were four small logs and a few truck tires.

Two more Jeeps were speeding towards the lone policeman. "What's happening?" I asked.

"People blocking the road to get water and 'lectricity. Nearly every fortnight now on this side."

"Does it work?"

"Must be. The papers people like this sorta confusion. This *koochoor*. I sure it have one or two of them peeping out from behind the bush with they camera. Look! Look, you see. I didn't lie." He removed a hand from the steering wheel and pointed to Bhogerattie, his neatness and his size setting him apart from the protesters.

"Careful," I cautioned, because to the left was a sheer drop of about a hundred feet.

As we sped by, Rob shouted, "Charlie Chaplin," and I turned away so Bhogerattie wouldn't see me.

"Oh God, Tarzan. I don't want to land up in the papers, you know."

"Why not, uncle? What secrets are you hiding?" Rob was not serious but Madhoo turned ashen and as we drove downhill towards the bay, I noticed his fingers drumming the steering wheel. He swung into some sort of recreation facility, a squat concrete building with a signboard at the side proclaiming Bar, Change Room, Urinal and Toilets. "I go hang around in the bar. This foot didn't design much for swimming."

"More of a weather clock," I said, to shake him out of his edgy mood.

Rob slipped off his jersey, pulled down his shorts and bounded off. I was surprised he didn't wait for Cynthia, who before she went into the changing room offered a curt apology. "Sorry about Rob. He's out of control sometimes."

"It's okay. He's just enjoying himself." She glanced at me incredulously, then looked to the sea, at Rob wading through a group of young women, splashing water over them, their shrieks of feigned annoyance audible from the shore. He was an expert swimmer and as he went further in, one of the women, tall and well built, followed him.

Cynthia walked away. I felt sorry for her and asked if she needed company but she shook her head. I wondered at their relationship; my first impression of her had been of a young woman who, though not unpleasant-looking, had inherited too many of her father's features. I assumed that it was because of this resemblance that I had been more sympathetic towards Rob, but as I watched him showing off to his attractive admirer, indifferent to Cynthia walking alone on the shore, I realized that he reminded me of another thoughtless young man, seventeen years ago.

The scent of the salty water and the booming waves evoked a more recent memory, and, reflecting on the two months I had spent with Shakira at Mayaro, I considered how much of the maturity we claim for ourselves is just a pose to explain and varnish the constant changes into which we are bludgeoned. Then I remembered Radha's more gracious and considered view that these alterations, the injuries we suffer, are responsible for many of our virtues, our compassion and tolerance.

In some ways they were alike, these two women. Bitter experiences had pressured both of them to fashion a private dogma of retribution and redemption, and find hope in their belief that there was a pattern and a meaning in all the arbitrary incidents of their lives. Was this a secret strength of all women, even unlikely candidates like my own mother? And what about Cynthia, some distance ahead, walking slowly; how soon would she too be able to fashion, from her humiliation, the expectation of revenge? Could it apply also to men who had witnessed their lives stolen by those who were bolder and more resilient? And children, seven or eight years old, drawn into a world of secret fantasies and private resentments?

We never discover the rules that indirectly regulate our lives until it is too late. How would Rob, for instance, respond if I told him I saw him repeating my mistakes? Most likely, he would consider the advice as boring and irrelevant. I watched him diving, surfacing behind the young woman and grabbing her legs, hoisting her in the air, the two of them falling backwards in the water.

Cynthia would not have seen this. She was some distance ahead, among the scattered families, the young couples and solitary foreigners. I decided to catch up with her, and because the beach was rather crowded I walked close to the shore to avoid the tourists basking in the sun and the locals sheltering beneath their umbrellas.

Cynthia was now completely lost in the crowd. I remembered Madhoo drinking his beers all alone and, more worrisome, later driving back along the precipices. I entered the bar.

Sitting at a table, stirring a drink with his thumb, perhaps counting the bubbles, was Angus.

"Oddballs," I blurted out.

If Angus was surprised to see me, he certainly did not display it. "Fancy meeting you here, old man." He raised his glass. "This is my second. Forty-two sips in all." He drank. "Forty-three. The revolution's coming, you know. All the indicators are there." He tapped a ledger on the table. "The polls tell me everything." He uttered this dire prediction with a barely restrained relish. "The monkey turns on its tail."

"What?"

But he was finished with me. At the far end of the room, Madhoo had arrayed three empty beer bottles on his table. "I didn't know you was so popular, uncle." He sounded slightly tipsy.

The monkey turns on its tail? Perhaps it was one of Angus's silly word games.

"So you not going for a li'l swim self? Way you leave the bossman daughter?"

"I believe she went for a walk."

He raised the bottle. "With Tarzan?"

"No. Alone."

He drank and wiped his lips. "Fellas like them don't last too long down here, you know."

"He will get . . . wiser as he grow older."

"If he get the chance. The bossman don't like people messing with he daughter 'cause is only one he have."

"What about Dulcie?"

"Dulcie? What about she?" He finished his beer.

He was such a bad liar I decided to play his game. "Don't you see the resemblance? I'm sure everyone knows the minute they spot her."

"Nah, man. Don't tell me that. How come I never notice it before?"

"It's because you are used to seeing both of them. But to a stranger it's obvious."

"So you know all the time?"

"The minute I spotted her. We journalists are trained to notice these things." I added casually, as if I were discussing some item of clothing, "It's almost impossible to keep any secret from us. Like the old man who was murdered." He looked at me incredulously. I leaned over and whispered, "Your bossman might be protecting the killer."

"How you know that he know?"

"He knows everything that goes on in the estate. Spies spying on spy." The waiter, a tiny man who from a distance could have been mistaken for a boy, came to our table, but Madhoo waved him away, leaned back, and with both hands helped his bad leg over the good one. At the other end of the room, Angus was bent over his ledger probably indulging in his word games. He squirted out a string of smoke and in the same motion glanced at our table; I smiled and looked away.

"Spy spying on spy? You sure that is not something you writing in one of you book? It sound so to me." He laughed anxiously.

Once, I had overheard the bartender at Palm Village telling the European couple, "It have a story below every rock in this place." I repeated the statement to Madhoo. This got him even more worried.

"So you know who poison up the old man?"

"I have my suspicions."

"Mr. Choo?"

I shook my head.

He recited a list of names: Sankie, Joe, Lopez, Ashton, Pillooki, and one that was unfamiliar. Zorro.

Because the name was unfamiliar, I inquired, "Zorro?"

He uttered a little shriek, like an asthmatic sensing the onset of an attack. "Zorro? You know him?"

I nodded and I saw him calculating and assessing, then a moment of clarity. "Yes, yes. You was they in the camp that day. Was the day before you leave, not so?"

I remembered the thin Indian boy stepping back and kicking the old man, then grinding his boot over his face. "Yes. A thin Indian boy." I tried to remember some details. "Long hair. Red eyes. Not so bad-looking but a little crazy."

"That is he self." Inexplicably, a look of relief crossed his face.

"So did you know the old man well?"

"Corkie? A real troublemaker. A rumcork." He pulled on a strand of beard and I felt he was going to continue his description, but he looked over at a group of men and women in varying shades of brown entering the bar. One of the women brushed past us and I saw him gaping at her wet clinging bikini, which revealed more than it hid.

"So what about him?"

He grinned. "Ain't you ask me that very same question a while aback? Well, the answer didn't change yet. A rumhound who shoulda remain with he family instead running down other people rum."

"He had a family?"

He scratched his head. "Well, that is the funny part because as far as I could recall was he and he alone."

"What about Ramirez? Dulcie's stepfather?"

"How you know all these people, uncle? But the two of them was anything but friend. In fact, you could say they was enemy."

"But Ramirez is a cripple."

"And guess who responsible for that?"

"The old man?"

"Who else? In them days he was to work for the bossman."

"Who?"

"Aha! I catch you they. I thought you know everything." He pushed his tongue into the gap between two teeth. I waited. "This is not a bad place to hang out, eh. Every size and shape and colour. I gather enough material to last me one whole month." He laughed, a phlegm-tinged yak which ended in a fit of coughing.

"What sort of material?"

He went into his coughing fit again. A dribble of spit hung from his beard. "Material for when I have nothing else to do."

These private disclosures, offered in the Trinidadian manner with an erratic levity, always made me uncomfortable. I felt obliged to smile and I smiled. He was watching me with a shrewd, lopsided grin, expecting me to match his confession, to reveal humorously some personal aspect of my own life. Instead I asked him, "Do you have a wife or a girlfriend?" He stared at me in incomprehension and I repeated the question.

The grin froze, constricting like a mask. His eyes grew tiny. The drop of spit fell. "Wife? Girlfriend?" With a sudden move, he grabbed his bad leg and unloaded it on the table, where it lay, limp like an exhausted macajuel. "You think wife or girlfriend want a man with a dead foot? Feel it."

"No, it's okay."

"No, no. Feel it. Touch it."

As I reached over, he twisted his body and the leg writhed away and dropped to the floor. Startled, I pulled away my hand. "You know what they was to call me in school? Eh? Hopman. With he special Hopmobile and all he nice Hop-powers."

I was about to apologize when he added, "One morning, I chase down a group of them with a divider in me hand and behind me half the school bawling, 'Don't let them get away, Hopman. Fling out you foot and lasso them with it.' That evening, when I tell me father that I fed up with school, he put a serious licking on me. But me mind was make up. Every morning instead of school I start heading down by the weighing scale in the canefield, watching the crane pick up them big-big bundle and fling it on the tasker truck. You understand? Every day as a rule, sitting down on top a concrete bridge and watching all these tractor and them offloading cane and on top the hill, the harvester moving like a war tank and me pretending that was I driving and mashing down everything in me way. Then I start bringing a fishing line, hiding it in me bag every morning so when the workers see me fishing they wouldn't think I is a idle little locho breaking *l'école biche*. That is way I first bounce up the bossman."

He lit a cigarette and inhaled deeply. "He start asking me why I not in school and about me father and if I does sell the fish I catch and because he was so big and strong like the wrestler Dara Singh, I start crying. I thought he was going to lock me up."

He flicked his cigarette and slowly dusted the ash from the table. "He sit down on the concrete bridge right next to me and . . . watch how all the hair on me hand does stand up when I remember this." He moved a hand from elbow to wrist. "He sit down right next to me and tell me that how he too was to catch fish at the side of the road and how people passing from they car was to spit on him and some of them underpay him because he was a small boy who couldn't check good. Then he offer me the job in the estate. A broko-foot little boy like me. Nearly twenty years now. 'Cepting for a little time at the airport, I still working for him."

I had never seen Madhoo like this; he seemed close to tears. "People say all kinda thing about him, some true, some lie, but one thing I could tell you is that he always willing to help out people who willing to help theyself. I hear him say this and that about poor people, how they lazy and don't know the value of hard work and only good at making excuse, but the minute one of them make a attempt to pull theyself up he right on the side pulling too and mad like hell if they ever slacken. I remember one night we was driving back from a Ramayan, one of these seven-night prayer meeting way he had just donate flour and rice and money too and he start telling me that he had to fight for what he have every step of the way. Selling fish, working in a road gang for fifty cents a hour, buying a van and transporting these Texaco people here and there. Saving and saving until he could afford a dump truck, saving and saving until he was able to buy this estate."

He stubbed out his cigarette. "But I really don't think was the money he was really interested in. I really don't think so."

He grew silent, observing the men and women going into the change room or drinking at their tables. The waiter was removing bottles from a nearby table and I called him over. "A beer for me and another for my friend."

"Okay. Two Caribs." He returned with the beer and I paid him. Madhoo gazed at the beer, then finished half in one gulp.

"Thanks for the beer."

He sipped slowly now and kept the bottle close to his lips. "I don't think was the money at all because on that first day on the bridge he say something that keep ringing in me ears ever since. He tell me how he was to swim every day in the Caroni River, a few feet in the beginning, then quarter mile, then half mile and later on, how he start lifting weights. Not real one cause he couldn't afford that but old train wheel that he find throw away in some railway. And then he take up wrestling with a old fella from India who teach him something call a hammerlock and how not to show when he in pain or losing a fight and thing like that. And all that time, he teaching he own self to read. You know why? For nobody to spit on him again or to tief him the way they tief this li'l boy selling fish at the side of the road."

He drained his bottle and set it next to the others on the table. "You know that he land-up in parliament too? And that even the prime minister did 'fraid him? He coulda be a millionaire by now but as I say wasn't the money he was interested in. Not like he wife." He choked back a dry, accusatory laugh. "The minute she set foot on the estate she start ordering around everybody like servant. Bring this, bring that. Fix this, fix that. And quarrelling on top of she voice about how she didn't leave she nice fancy palace for this mash-up place. She even start saying how people want to poison she. Then she fire Dulcie mother who was a housekeeper at the time."

"I'm sure there was a good reason for that."

He was too deep in his defence of Mr. Rampartap to acknowledge this. "Finding fault with everybody and everything. In the beginning, I was to hear she and the bossman

quarrelling and the next morning, she bag pack to go back
to she mother and father. That was to happen every weekend as a rule, but the talk I hear was that they get fed
up and tell she that she married now and this stupidness
have to cut out. Things shoulda get better then but it get
worse.

"When it wasn't somebody trying to poison she, was
somebody else putting a light on she head. Obeah. These
Spanish people, the *coco panyols* who was to work on the
estate, the minute she spot one of them she was to fly back
inside the house and lock sheself in a room, bawling about
how they watching she strange like if they want to sacrifice
she or tief she soul. Now you have to understand that these
is real quiet people, eh, uncle. They living here donkey
years now and they prefer to keep to theyself but it not
right to interfere with them so or to accuse them of this and
that because it have a old saying." He paused, smoothing
his hand.

"What saying?"

"I don't like to talk about these things, eh, but the saying is that they could turn the thing you 'fraid the most
'gainst you."

He went silent, a tremor of fear crossed his face, and I
realized that he believed all that he was saying—Mr. Rampartap's old-fashioned virtues verging almost on nobility,
the wife's disdain and even the revenge exacted by the *coco
panyols*—and because of this I hesitated before I asked him:
"But she was locked up in the old house by the cemetery.
You told me that yourself. That is no way to treat a woman.
Or anyone else for that matter."

His answer, more than anything else since I had left
Canada, more than the violence inflicted on the old man in

the camp, more than Shakira's account of her ordeal with her husband, more than the hole into which Lalchan had fallen, more even than the finessed bullying of Calvin and company; his answer, so simple, so guileless, spoken with the sincerity of the unsophisticated, marked my distance from the land of my birth. He told me, "How else you expect to treat mad people, uncle? People with jumbie in they head. How else? You have to fight fire with fire." And after a slight pause, "Was for she own good."

On the way back, Cynthia gazed out of the window and Rob whistled unaware of her pique. Next to me Madhoo was uncharacteristically silent. I thought about my decision to prolong my stay in Trinidad, and my suspicion that Mr. Rampartap was responsible for the death of the old man, and I realized how much I had lost touch with Trinidad. I had been thinking like a foreigner, like the travel writer from the plane or the European couple at Mayaro; outsiders drawn to the allure of an imperfect little place, driven by a presumptuous naïveté and possessed by the urge to hack away at the confusion, alter and simplify the foreignness, reduce the chaos to order. I had forgotten too much; I had forgotten the uneasiness that had driven me away and that must have clutched at my father until he died in his mid-fifties, the same age as my mother.

I should have seen that the old man's death was probably not because of a complicated vendetta, but had likely been carried out with little awareness of the consequences and when replayed in the murderer's mind would stir no guilt, no regret. Seventeen years earlier, I was a witness to buoyant savageries I had chosen to forget. In a society without boundaries, rules were formulated and broken at whim, and the excuses, always unsatisfactory, frequently boastful, came much later. I had witnessed it in the rumshops, in the warden's office, during visits to friends, walking along the streets. A young woman molested to the point of tears; a father boasting of the savage beating he had inflicted on his son; an old man turned away from a doctor's office because he could not afford the fee; lives lost for the most absurd of reasons.

Seventeen years ago, as I walked along the streets of Rio Claro, I imagined a stranger calmly planning his escape and relieved of complicity because of his *decision* that he was different. I had chosen to forget because, more than I cared to admit, I had been shaped by this turbulence. But I could neither turn away from it nor, like my wife, seek redemption in camouflage. I had seen this pretence among other immigrants in Canada, people who, aware of the fragility of their pose, were afraid of scrutiny, suspicious of compliments and fell apart when criticized. They were like Madhoo's reptiles, shedding their skins each night and artfully applying the polish, but the next day fear made them weak and pompous and abusive. They were equally nervous of exposure as they were of revelation, and because they were forced to suppress knowledge they were squeamish and stupid. But they were frequently wealthy, which made it worse, and usually successful at their jobs; I was both envious of and repulsed by them. My own disguises were private, meant for no one else. It was the camouflage of the secretive and timid; it was thin and vaporous because it was a mood rather than a mask. And now this mood, always under threat, had fallen apart. But it brought release of a kind.

At the end of my two months at Mayaro, during the week I had spent alone, I was afforded an insight into a man I began to consider a stranger because so many of his faults were beyond comprehension and also because nothing in his early life hinted at the distress which would later conquer him. I had seen a man driven by loneliness and retreating into the only option he saw as available: selfishness. Selfishness, the other face of detachment, comforting, consuming and self-destructive. This insight was humiliating, in some ways redemptive, but it was unbalanced; now I felt that I had gotten a glimpse at the other side of the equation.

A memory of my father. It astonished me how much I could now remember of those early flippant years, how much their worth had increased. A thunderstorm, rain tumbling on the aluminium roof. My father was sitting in a wicker rocker, reading a story. My mother entered with two cups of warm green tea. She sat on a wooden settee with a fibre cushion. A clap of thunder, and Varun ran into the room and climbed on her lap. My father finished the story, removed his spectacles, and after a long period of silence, said, "We can never understand ourselves unless we first understand other people."

This memory of my family was so moving that I turned my face so Madhoo would not see the tears. But perhaps it was embroidered; perhaps the rain, the tea, the clap of thunder, and Varun running into the room were details I invented. I had no other recollection of my father wearing spectacles.

Looking outside, I saw in the distance a swirl of sparks flashing upwards like holes in the blackness and in the humid tropical night, where odours become alive, I smelled the sweet sticky aroma of burning cane. Madhoo, silent during the entire journey back, said in a slightly breathless voice, "Canefield on fire. And is not even crop season yet."

TWENTY-SIX

Mr. Rampartap, always unreadable, saved his most impressive act for the end. Throughout newspaper reports of bridges being burnt, of cathedrals and temples defaced with black paint, of a dog's bloated carcass slung on the flagpole at the parliament building, of marauding gangs of teenage looters from the hills descending on the farmers of central Trinidad and the farmers vowing that they would finish what they had not started, of a young woman, the daughter of a government minister, raped by men she could only describe as "demons in human form"—in all of this he displayed no interest. Where I had expected a satisfied grin or long lectures on the naïveté of the government, instead there was silence.

At first I felt that he was trying to avoid Rob but as the sporadic acts of violence increased, his withdrawal grew more baffling. Even when correspondents from the BBC and CNN interviewed the prime minister, an ascetic-looking man who spoke with long pauses, his hands, frail and bony, touching each other as if in prayer; and following him, the leader of the opposition, built like a boxer, with a boxer's calculated swagger, sticking to his lines and repeating a few choice phrases like, "Is time to take a stand," and "You could see today but you can't see tomorrow," Mr. Rampartap offered no gloating comment.

He held his peace when the foreign correspondents conducted their interviews with a few fanatical-looking men with wildly waving arms—"Ordinary men in the street"—and misunderstanding the Trinidadian's flair for drama, located in the riots an Islamic connection, a Hindu revivalist connection, a Shango connection and an ethnic cleansing connection. When the correspondent who had located the ethnic cleansing connection, a small, bald man sweating in his loose floral shirt, intoned gravely about biological weapons designed to eliminate Arabs, and others targeting Chinese, black and Slavic people, Mr. Rampartap passed the twelve-inch television Radha had installed on the top shelf of the bookcase, and I was sure he would make some comment or at least linger to watch, but he just continued on his way to the gallery.

Exactly four days after the violence began, he unfolded a weekly newspaper and asked me to take a look. At last, I thought. But the article was about a former parliamentarian posting bail for an accused murderer. Just three paragraphs, hidden between the reports of car-jackings and lynchings, it was written by A. V. M. Bhogerattie in a style that borrowed from fiction and made liberal use of the local dialect. It was surprisingly easy to read.

"Read it aloud," Mr. Rampartap said. Radha, Cynthia and Rob were watching television and Cynthia got up and turned down the volume.

I read:

With all this confusion that going on in this place, making Trinidad, I tell you, look like one of these places that we only know from the news, you know the kind of place I am talking about, Rwanda and Bosnia and Guyana, places where the cry of race is an excuse to commit all kind of atrocities, it is comforting to know that there are still men like Edwin Rampartap around.

Yesterday, Mr. Rampartap, braving all the hooligans who have emerged from their little holes, calmly walked into the Chaguanas police station and posted the bail for his former employee, Mr. Dangley Chew. But the man was a wrestler, and in case people forget, because the short memory of Trinidadians is legendary, he was once described as "passionate and fearless."

In a brief statement to this reporter Mr. Rampartap said that in spite of all that was happening, all this mayhem, which I tell you make a mockery of the struggle for independence, the man watch me in my eye and say, "The business of the people have to go on."

To put it in a nutshell, we need more people like him. People like Mr. Rampartap should not be allowed to fall in the cracks of this once proud nation, cracks that appearing on all side and because of this it behoves me to say, here and now, that I intend to write a biography of this son of the soil. The business of the people have to go on.

Rob laughed as I began the last paragraph but Mr. Rampartap paid him no attention. He took the newspaper and folded it carefully, leaving me to wonder at his purpose. Was it a rebuke? A polite way of disclosing that he had no further use for me and that I should leave? But he must have known that a state of emergency had been declared the previous night, and that all flights had been suspended. Up to that point, I had been thinking of leaving. I realized, though, that the withdrawal of his hospitality was not unreasonable because I had overstayed my welcome. "I plan to leave once the state of emergency is removed."

"Fraidy cat," Rob said.

Radha got up and reached over for three glasses on the coffee table. She glanced at her daughter and both of them looked at me. She hesitated, then went into the kitchen. Cynthia leaned back on the sofa. Mr. Rampartap appeared pensive. I wondered whether he had seen this interplay between his wife and daughter.

"I have been thinking of writing about the riot for the newspaper in Canada. It might be a good idea for me to stay in a hotel in the meantime."

Radha, returning, heard this and seemed confused, as if she had missed something. "Are you crazy? Staying in a hotel at a time like this?" Once more, she glanced at her daughter.

"There's no need for that," Mr. Rampartap said in a sombre voice.

I hurried downstairs.

The thought of writing had come the day before. It grew out of my restlessness and impatience at being secluded in the safety of Rougeleau, while throughout Port of Spain— and, if the newspapers were to be believed, parts of Arima, Tunapuna, San Fernando and Princes Town—buildings were being burnt and stores ransacked. I was also confused by the orderliness of the protests in Tobago: a few well-attended meetings, thoughtful speeches and respectful audiences. By contrast, Trinidad was chaotic. Apart from a back-to-Tobago movement centred in the university, whose spokespersons issued statements about the distinct nature of the Tobagonian culture, there seemed to be no clear idea why riots had broken out. Because the population of Tobago was mainly of African descent, a few black politicians from

Trinidad had entered the fray, likening the oppression of Tobagonians to that of the blacks who lived in Port of Spain and the northern fringe of Trinidad. Columnists on either side of the divide poured scorn on those who didn't share their views and the host of the call-in radio program labelled all journalists a "cavalcade of wild mules."

Downstairs, my impatience worsened. I thought of all the people I knew. Shakira would be safe in Rio Claro, away from the action. Lalchan was probably watching television alone and muttering, "Faggin' savages. Poosies." Doggie and company might be enjoying a fish broff lime and shaking their heads at the stupidness of the town people. Thankfully, everyone I knew was either dead or lived in the safety of villages. Then I thought of my wife's family.

That night I listened to the scurrilous host of the call-in radio program lambasting the "dull-witted vandals" and the malkins who denied the value of Plato and Coleridge and were "hell-bent on wreaking havoc on this bonny land," screaming too that the government had proven "through its ineptitude that it is nothing more than a conglomerate of vermins, idlers, stoats, jackasses and fowls. No less complicit than some of these bigboys hiding in their holes like zandolies and raining dollars on the troublemakers in Tobago."

An opportunity for escape was granted the next morning. Bhogerattie had been attacked by a mob and Mr. Rampartap was going to visit him at the Mount Hope Hospital. For the first time since the rioting, he was visibly disturbed. He slammed the door as he got into the car and I saw that his face was swollen with anger. And because of this, as the car moved out of the tranquillity of Rougeleau, past the shaded fruit trees, the men walking slowly on the asphalt road and occasionally waving to him, I expected the worst. I expected smouldering buildings and overturned vehicles and gangs of looters stalking the streets, but the only indication of the state of emergency was the police patrolling in their new Cherokee Jeeps. Throughout the journey, he remained silent, one hand on the door and the other on his knee, but as we approached St. Augustine he said, "Take that road to the hospital."

The hospital's waiting room was packed with dejected-looking men and women, though recalling the overcrowded clinics in Rio Claro I judged that this might be a normal situation. As we made our way to the second floor I smelled the antiseptic, and from the rooms I heard anguished screams. A man walked past us, holding a stand from which an intravenous bag was suspended; the fluid flowed into a tube that ran under bandages into his arm. On a bench, a shabbily dressed man sat rubbing his head, while next to him a woman was weeping into her handkerchief. Two young interns, imperious in their white coats, emerged from a room. They sidestepped the patient with the stand and walked briskly down the corridor, unaffected by a flat, baying sound from a nearby ward.

I had always hated hospitals and I felt like getting out.

"Ward twenty-four. We reach," Mr. Rampartap said, opening the door. A female intern with a plump, prissy face seemed set to make some disapproving remark, but at the sight of Mr. Rampartap, big, swollen and angry, she shrank back. There were four beds in the room and I immediately spotted Bhogerattie, his bony knees poking from beneath the coverlet. Beside him was Pillooki, in an old grey jacket, and Tack, looking at his feet and shaking his head. Bhogerattie saw us and levered himself up with his elbows.

"Stay there. Don't get up," Mr. Rampartap said.

"How they could do this to the man? A respected journalist like him," Tack moaned.

"You know who do this?" Mr. Rampartap asked. "You could recognize any of them?"

Bhogerattie shook his head sorrowfully. He looked even tinier and oilier than usual. "It happen so fast. One minute I snapping pictures and the next minute I on the ground with me camera gone."

"He camera gone and kick in he ass. How they could do this to a respected journalist?"

"Were there witnesses?"

"No, Mr. Rampartap. None that I know of. It happen so fast."

"Somebody, please tell me, how?"

"Are you absolutely certain?" Pillooki asked.

"One minute I on me foot and the next minute I on me back."

"Oh, God. You hear that? A respected journalist flat on he back. How, man, how?" I suspected that Tack was searching for anger, for his Clint Eastwood disguise, but he just appeared demented and slobbery.

"I think we should sue," Pillooki said in a grave voice.

"Sue?" Bhogerattie started to laugh. "It have nobody to sue."

"The publisher of the newspaper."

"He not responsible for what happen. I went on me own."

Pillooki leaned closer to Bhogerattie. "Sue the prime minister then."

Bhogerattie attempted to shift away and uttered a soft, painful shriek. "He on the receiving end too."

"We will check the station," Pillooki persisted. "To see if you recognize any photographs."

"Is only four pair of black foot I could recognize." Bhogerattie, surprisingly, was trying to make light of the situation.

"It had any mark on the foot and them?" Tack asked. "Anything different?"

"Then we should sue the police. They should have taken the requisite steps to prevent this."

"Look, Mr. Pillooki, I don't want to sue nobody. I was just doing me job and I get in the way and that is all."

"Then you are nothing but a jackass. A complete jackass. Tomorrow you will get kicked again."

Tack, looking startled, squinted at Pillooki, but Bhogerattie smiled broadly, his cheeks puffing out. I was beginning to believe he was enjoying this. "They could kick me again tomorrow but the freedom of the press must never be compromised. The business of the people have to go on."

"Oh, lord, oh, lord." Tack wiped a dry eyelid. "Allyou seeing the quality of this man? Somebody tell me how Babwah could say this man mad? How, man, how?"

"Call if you need me. I'm a busy man." Pillooki strode off. Mr. Rampartap followed him to the door.

In the bed opposite, an old woman was listening to a bald man in a faded green jersey, and although his back was turned to us the agitated shaking of his head suggested that he was scolding her. Then he relented and placed his brown hand on her greyish-white arm. On the other beds were two men, one middle-aged, the coverlet pulled to his chin, and the other slightly younger, with baggy eyelids and loose flesh hanging from his chin. They were both gaping at us with the unflinching boldness of the infirm and the abandoned. The man opposite was becoming excited once more. I heard him hissing, "You don't know the kind of things I had to put up with." She patted his hand and with her face turned to the side and a cheek pressed against the pillow, her attempted smile seemed leering and mocking. The man's head bobbed up and down. He said, louder now, "We don't belong here. This place is for black people. Black people and Indian. I don't know why we didn't leave after the Black Power foolishness. You don't know the kind of things I have to put up with."

Bhogerattie, observing my attention, beckoned with a finger. "The man is her grandson. The woman had a heart attack. I believe she here for the last six months."

"Oh." That surprised me.

Mr. Rampartap, who after the departure of Pillooki had been conferring with a bosomy nurse, returned. "I just had a little chat with the matron to make sure you have everything you need. And if you remember anything at all, let me know."

As we were leaving, I glanced at the man opposite. He was younger than I imagined and although he was light brown, he had the facial features of a black man.

In the corridor, Mr. Rampartap, calmer now, said, "Madhoo doesn't like hospitals. They wanted to cut off his foot but his mother started to scream and bawl down the place." Then he added, "Sometimes, that is the only way to get people attention."

On the way back, he seemed distant and meditative, but I needed to ask a question. After some silent phrasing and rephrasing, I asked him, "What would you have done if Bhogerattie was able to identify his attackers?"

He answered immediately as if he had been thinking all along about it. "Under normal circumstances, I would have reported them to the police and allowed the officers to perform their duties. But these are not normal circumstances and as you see, the police have a lot on their hands to bother about a little journalist getting beat up."

"And?"

Still looking outside, he said, "This world is not run by thinkers, you know. Thinking and wondering and gauging and guessing. Is a weakness, if you ask me. All this useless information could just pull you down. Act according to your conscience and act decisively."

"And what if you are wrong?"

He laughed. "You see what I mean?" And after a while, "If you are wrong, you suffer the consequences, learn your lesson and move on."

"Like these people who are rioting?"

"The difference is that they have no clear idea why they are doing this. They have no idea what they hope to accomplish." He sounded disappointed.

"They have no leaders, you mean?"

"Could be."

"Your wife said it would blow over."

"I believe she was talking about the little village protests. For water and electricity and things like that. But the government have things under control, it seem," he said moodily. He may have been thinking about my earlier question because after about five minutes or so, he added, "You know what my definition of a fool is? A man who believe his faults are other people mistakes." He was in an unusually sombre mood and I noticed him staring at the small, wooden houses as we approached the estate. We passed the stretch where Madhoo had run over the manicou, and then the house on the hill where I had seen the middle-aged woman who, Madhoo had confessed, was Mr. Rampartap's "craft."

When we arrived at the estate, Madhoo opened the gate, and Rob, who had been standing with Cynthia in the gallery, bounded down the stairs. "Hey, buddy, guess what was in the news? The emergency has been called off."

"You're joking."

"No. It's true."

"How come?"

"Well, you wouldn't believe this," he said, grinning.

TWENTY-SEVEN

That night the prime minister, managing to appear both pious and wounded, surrounded by several dejected foreign correspondents and a few nettled local journalists, reiterated, with lengthy pauses, that the state of emergency had been lifted because of information gathered earlier, that the whole issue of secession had been organized and funded by a few Trinidadian businessmen who were furious that the contract to build an airport in Tobago, a contract they had lobbied hard for, had been given instead to an American firm. He said these aggrieved contractors had also received help from "one or two political troglodytes." At the end of the news conference, he said, "The honourable leader of the opposition has been shouting all over the place"—pause— "about time to take a stand."—pause—"I think he should take his own advice." The local journalists began to giggle, politely at first, then louder, louder, until they were almost uncontrollable. The foreign corespondents, though managing a few stiff smiles, looked more disappointed and bewildered. They may have known of the opposition leader's marital woes with his third wife, a former fashion model twenty years his junior, but they would not have understood the prime minister's clever sexual reference; to take a stand: a local phrase meaning "to have an erection."

And so it ended, in a manner satisfactory to all Trinidadians. The sponsors of the disturbances, the Trinidadian contractors, were all Indians, the rioters mostly blacks. In the rumshops and the government offices across the island, in the parlours and street corners, the irony would be converted into a cause for celebration and the prime minister's cleverness would be matched with cutting *mauvais-langue*, scandalous gossip.

It would end as it began: in confusion.

The protests, the casual assaults, some version of the discontent would continue, but for less opaque reasons. The disgruntled foreign correspondents had departed hurriedly in search of some more reliable trouble spot, annoyed because they had misread the riot and its aftermath; they couldn't see that the true romance of backward societies has less to do with their dark mysteries and their elusive secrets than with their refusal to recognize injury. The basis of so many myths, so many fantasies, so many excuses. My homeland.

I thought of a bloodied, flailing boxer, misunderstanding the extent of his incapacity, stumbling up again and again, and even as he totters to the canvas once more, still locked into his fantasy of himself as a lithe, skilful athlete, dancing around the ring, feinting and jabbing, impervious to hurt.

The article would be written, but humorously, so that Trinidadians would not be offended and everyone else would be amused and reassured.

The prime minister saved his coup de grâce for the following night. When it was announced in the day's newspapers that he would be addressing the nation in a special televised broadcast, I assumed that it would be a routine self-congratulatory affair, but everyone, it seemed, had underestimated him. Looking like an aged movie star, his white hair combed backwards, his make-up and the lighting smoothing his wrinkles and giving his face an even orange tint, he announced that the organizers of the Miss World Pageant had selected Trinidad as the next venue. In an impromptu panel discussion after the prime minister's announcement, a group of elderly, scholarly-looking men discussed the best location in the island for the pageant. One of them, a professor, suggested Chaguaramas for its historic value; a columnist wondered aloud about Mayaro and Maracas with their under-utilized but "pretty-pretty" beaches; and a government senator, with a shining face and ghastly, milky eyes, offered Tobago. The other participants accepted defeat.

The debate resumed in the next day's newspapers. Mr. Alto Jackson complained that these beauty pageants were unfair to black women, who represented a different, "and apparently unacceptable kind of appeal," and an Indian columnist boasted that beauty pageants were held in Indian palaces centuries ago.

I sat up late that night to write my own article for *The Caribbean Crossroad*. The next morning at breakfast I saw Mr. Rampartap glancing, from time to time, at the folder I had placed next to my cup of green tea, but he said nothing, eating hurriedly and staring at the crumbs on the table. He got up abruptly and I followed him into the gallery. "I wrote my article for the newspaper in Canada. I thought you might like to see it."

He placed his hands on the railing and remained silent. I felt he was thinking of what he should say. Finally he told me, "Put in this if you want: Mr. Rampartap withdraws lawsuit. A little exclusive for you." He attempted a laugh but his face was grim and sullen.

I took my folder downstairs and put it in my suitcase, then walked to the front of the house. As I was opening the gate, Rob came running up. "Skipping out on us?"

"I want one last look at this place."

"Mind if I accompany you?"

"Not at all. Where's Cynthia?"

"With her mother. Did they speak with you?"

"No. About what?"

"Not sure." He skipped away and plucked off a sapodilla and threw it to me. The aroma of the sapodilla reminded me of Shakira, of the fruits she brought each morning to Palm Village, the taste syrupy in her mouth. Rob finished his sapodilla and twisted off a navel orange. "Man, I could live in a place like this. I don't know why you're going back. Oh, yeah. Your daughter."

I laughed. "Do you prefer it to Canada?"

"Are you crazy? This place is a paradise."

"Even with the riot?"

"What riot? Did you see the prime minister in the address?

Gandhi with a smirk. I wish the referendums in Quebec were that much fun."

"It's the price you pay for living in a civilized society."

"Oh yes, Daddy. I understand, Daddy," he squeaked in a child's voice. "It's exactly the thing my father would say. *Boring.*"

"Is he happy in Canada?"

Now he switched to a gloomy mystic's voice. "I have been asking myself that question since the day I was born."

"So?"

"I don't know. I really don't know. Maybe, but he gets crazy sometimes about these parties . . . fêtes and limes he calls them, that he used to go to. Usually, I think he is just teasing my mom but sometimes . . . What are you smiling at?"

"Nothing. How old is he?"

"He's an old guy." He punched my shoulder lightly. "Sorry. He's in his fifties. A year or two older than my mom." I wanted to ask him: are they happy together? "They are a good team." The word *team* from Rob, so unexpected, saddened me. "What about you? How long have you been separated?"

"It varies from time to time."

"Come again?"

It had been three weeks since I returned from Mayaro. "About a month or so."

"Lucky."

Now it was my turn to be astonished, but I thought, only the young say things like that. "What about Cynthia?"

"What about her?" he repeated, pretending not to understand.

"Are you two serious?"

"She is. I think she inherited that from her father."

"Oh, come on. You know what I mean." He offered no response, so I continued. "That day on the beach. She seemed a bit bothered."

"Yeah?"

Was it possible that he had not noticed? "I think she was jealous."

"Hey, I didn't do anything. If she was jealous, that's her problem, not mine."

I saw him quickening his steps, hurrying away. I wanted to warn him. To *save* him. For the briefest of moments, I saw him as a callous little idiot. What could I possibly say to him? He would laugh if I tried to explain Shakira's belief in equivalent punishment. Then he said something that gave me hope. "Things should work out in time. We learn something new every day."

We walked silently for a while. Then I said, "Do you know what her father told me the other day?"

"What? Did he lay down an edict? No laughing? No fooling around?"

"He said that only a fool believes his faults are other people's mistakes."

"Hmm. Was that a confession? You know, people down here say the strangest things. Like if they're quoting from an out-of-print book or something. Or a really old movie. All these proverbs and aphorisms."

I reflected on his observation. "Schools here are a bit different from those in Canada."

"How so?"

"We memorize things. Intelligent people can quote an entire ballad."

"I see. So that explains it." He raised an eyebrow like a hammy inquisitor.

"You've seen too many bad movies in your film course."

"Most were good, actually." He thought for a while, then added, "You know what I would like to do someday? I would like to come back here and do a documentary."

"What sort of documentary?" I asked, interested.

"I would go to one of those old rumshops that my father talks about. Somewhere in a quiet little village. And I would sit somewhere in the corner and secretly choose my character. An old man. Tired or bored or frustrated but ordinary in every other way. I would focus on his fingers holding the glass and the shape of his mouth when he drinks. Then I would follow him to his house, filming his boots hitting the road and the way he swings his hands as he climbs the stairs. What he says to his wife and children. How he sits at the table. What he is eating."

"There are laws against this sort of thing," I said, laughing but relieved.

"Yeah. And it wouldn't draw massive crowds. What about you? You are a writer. What would you write about?"

I thought: I would have liked to write a book like your documentary. Ordinary people; quiet, uneventful lives. But I had met Shakira, Lalchan, Doggie and company, Dulcie, Mr. Rampartap, Radha; and each of them had revealed an aspect of his or her own life and uncovered something of mine. "Something about the way people change over time," I told him.

He thought I was joking. "A collaborative effort between you and Charlie Chaplin? Where are we going anyway?"

"We're here."

As we climbed the steps, concrete bricks sunk in the

mud, he pointed to the vines weaving around a latticed fence at the side of the house. "What's that?"

"Passion fruit."

"Wow."

Afterwards, sounding like Madhoo, he told me, "I think I misjudged you, old guy." He muttered something else, but I was still thinking of the last twenty minutes. Dulcie, offering us orange juice, had blushed at Rob's attention and thrown little sidelong glances his way; her mother, flattered but embarrassed by the visit, had quickly collected the basin of peeled yams and tannia from her husband in his sturdy high-back cedar chair, putting it away out of sight. The husband gazed at us, curious at our presence but too polite to ask questions. It was the kind of house I had visited so many times before. The floor covered with linoleum, and on the wall, pictures of Mary and a calendar with a painting of Maracas Falls. In the corner an old safe with oversized hinges, and in the centre of the room a square table with a vinyl cover. I could imagine the neatness of the kitchen and the sparseness of the bedrooms. A typical family; a typical setting. But they were not typical: more than twenty years earlier there had been an affair, a child, and a brutal assault. Rob was still muttering but I was thinking: there are no ordinary lives, just lives of contained frenzy. "I have an idea for your movie. You can make the old man in the rumshop an ex-con."

"A jailbird." He waved his hand before him. "I can see it now. Ernest Borgnine or Jack Palance. Uh-oh. They've made that movie already." As we approached the house, he told me, "That girl . . . what's her name?"

"Dulcie."

"She reminds me of someone." He jumped over the drain to pick an orange. "I wonder if she has a boyfriend?" He came back running and repeated the question.

After a while, I told him, "You never know."

At the dinner table my last night in Rougeleau, I was determined not to be drawn into the tension. I said nothing, even when Mr. Rampartap, smouldering, broke his bread in narrow strips while his wife was revealing her intention to accompany her daughter back to Canada; even when he pushed back his chair, his plate clattering to the floor, the daughter pleading, the wife looking at me expectantly, as if I could somehow solve their problem.

Then Rob's little surprise was sprung: his plan to extend his vacation in Trinidad. Now the daughter was in tears, the mother bewildered, and the father, his sudden rage diverted, brooded over his broken bread. A moment of silence, then once more the pleading, the screaming, the hysteria. I felt overwhelmed, besieged. These people had no right; I was a visitor. Now I too felt like screaming. Creating a scene.

Creating a scene. I had never realized how fake and contrived the phrase was. I almost laughed. But I stayed calm. Calm enough to say to Rob, "Forget the old man in the rumshop. I have a better idea for your documentary. You can set your camera there." I pointed to the bookcase. "You could call it *A Family Dinner*. Or maybe, *The Reunion*. A nice, happy, ordinary family." They each glared at me, then Rob began to grin.

I wanted to hurry away the next morning, but I knew I had to see Mr. Rampartap. Madhoo was in the car, waiting. "Help the man, nah, Tarzan. You standing they like a statue and watching him dragging that suitcase with a car engine inside."

"Coming right up, uncle." They sounded like old pals. Rob tugged away the suitcase. "Give it, give it. It's mine. I saw when you made the exchange."

Radha came down the stairs. "Thanks." She hugged me and when she moved back, I saw that her eyes were red. She pressed her palms against my cheeks, like a mother, and I turned away.

Cynthia was at her mother's side. "Are you okay?" she asked, a little surprised.

"Yes, yes." I shook her hand and when she stepped away, I had recovered enough to tell her, "Don't worry about Rob. He's going to be all right."

Her mother took her hand. "You go back to your country. Don't worry about us here." She hesitated. "Did you tell Edwin goodbye?"

"I'm going to." I felt for the envelope in my pocket.

Mr. Rampartap was sitting on the couch, cradling a glass of juice and staring at the television but at that time of the morning the only programs were soap operas.

"Nice show," I said in a light voice.

"I'm trying to catch up with the way of the world. I don't want to be left behind." He too had spoken jokingly but I felt that it was the kind of casual statement made by desperately lonely people.

"I have something for you."

I was standing at the side of the sofa. He glanced at the envelope in my hand. "What's that?"

"The money you gave me. For the book."

"Keep it."

"I have no intention of keeping it."

He got up, his glass slightly aslant, some of the liquid tipping over to the floor. I felt sorry for him, this man who from our first meeting had both intimidated and disgusted me. His preparations for power—commissioning a biography; sending for his daughter and rehabilitating his wife to create the semblance of a normal, stable family; launching a lawsuit against the prime minister; providing financial support to the secession movement—were so thorough, so precise, they could have been brilliant. And he had no enemies, no one who could embarrass him with slanderous allegations about his past.

As he lowered the volume and walked back to the couch, an image formed in my mind: of him leaning on the balcony's railing, staring into the darkness of his estate at the land, the trees trapped by the shadows; his own image of himself as a powerful and compassionate man who had single-handedly challenged the prime minister and had emerged, in a destabilized country, as a kind of saviour.

But he had underestimated the prime minister and over-estimated the population. The rebels were entranced by the prospect of looting rather than by a nebulous message and the general population, briefly intrigued by the secession drama, had been seduced into a greater spectacle by the prime minister.

In losing, Mr. Rampartap had lost everything. He had lost control; perhaps he had lost his family.

Madhoo sounded the horn.

"I never take back something I have given." He sounded proud and confident now. I started to protest but he cut me off. "One day you will write the book. Keep the advance. You just have more time. Use it wisely."

I realized he would be humiliated if I didn't accept his money. Madhoo sounded the horn again. "Well, thanks for everything," I told him. He gazed at the soap opera, at an old woman with the ravishing figure of a twenty-five-year-old.

When we were leaving, Rob shouted, "Tell the premier I said hello."

"Who?"

"John Wayne."

"John Wayne is the premier now, uncle? I thought he did dead?"

"He was joking."

On our way out of Rougeleau, I spotted Tack squinting over the wheel of a Toyota van, and next to him, his head slumped against the backrest and his eyes closed, a tiny man who might have been Bhogerattie. We drove in silence for a while, then Madhoo said, "Could be, uncle, could be a joke, but I don't know. Them place and them have plenty secret and miss-tree. Not every story is a lie."

EPILOGUE

In the Bel Air Hotel at Piarco, the quietness and orderliness and sterility of the room reminded me of my destination. I sat before a table, empty but for a glass of water and a Bible, and wrote a long letter to Vanita. I slipped the letter in an envelope and placed it in my travelling bag.

There was just one more thing to do. I called a taxi and showed the chauffeur the address I had written on a page from the hotel's notepad. He wanted me to be more specific, but I told him that the only information I had was the family's name and that I couldn't tell him the exact location either. I was willing to pay for his time though.

As we crossed the Eastern Main Road, with its long lines of traffic, pedestrians strolling across the street, and a few irate drivers honking their horns, some of them shouting insults, I noticed a store's broken showcase, the only sign of the riot I had seen so far. "Lay me see the paper again." The chauffeur swung into a crowded bar. "This is Pothound place. He know everybody business." He returned about ten minutes later, wiping his mouth and looking worried. "You sure this is the correct name here?"

"Yes."

"Okay. If you say so. Right over they." He pointed to a hill. The road, sloping upwards, narrowed by a landslip, suddenly dropped down; it was almost like falling into a hole. "You feel that? Aeroplane ride. That is the place they. I go stay in the car."

A broken window, reattached with thick electrical wire, now slackened, was suspended over the front entrance. A loose sheet of aluminium banged against the eave. In the yard, cluttered with tires, a barking mongrel strained against a leash attached to an overturned hammock. From inside someone shouted at the dog, "Why you don't keep you ass quiet, Cooblal." A middle-aged man, dark and lanky, his trousers slung low on his bony hips, emerged a bit unsteadily and fired a kick at the dog, then noticed me standing by the taxi. "Yeah, mistah? Anything I could do for you?"

As he was standing by the hammock, I walked towards him. "I'm visiting from Canada."

He stroked the dog's head. "Yeah? That nice."

"I have a message."

"Why you didn't say that all the time." He shouted, "Mammy," and I smelled the stale alcohol in his breath. "Somebody here from Canada." A woman with a big head and tiny arms, short and misshapen in her sari, danced Indian-movie-style out of the house. But she was too young to be his mother. "She think she is Mala Sinha. One of them Indian stargirl from the cinema." The man twirled a finger over his ear. "Tell Mammy it have somebody from Canada here to meet she."

"Canada?" She danced closer and I saw that her hands, short and flapping, were deformed. "My sister living in Canada too. She married a doctor and a lawyer and a magistrate." Congealed mucus caked her moustache.

"Houri! Get inside fast and call Mammy. Mammy!"

Houri. A Persian word referring to a voluptuous maiden. Perhaps she had gotten it from one of her Indian movies. She danced towards the door, singing to an Indian tune, "Pappy is a bad man. Pappy is a bad man."

Pappy?

From the house, a maniacal scream. "Shut you mad ass before I put a licking on you too."

Now, a woman with an *orhni*, a veil, covering her head came out. "Yes, *beta*? You have a message?" She had the sweetest smile I had ever seen on anyone and I felt she didn't belong in this dilapidated place.

"Your daughter said to say hello."

"And the *bacha*? The little one?"

"She too."

"You see them often?" She was still smiling sweetly but I noticed she was staring at me from head to foot.

I shook my head and made an excuse. "I have to go now. The taxi is waiting."

She glanced at the taxi. "You want anything to eat or drink?"

"No, I have to leave now. My flight is in a little while."

"Okay then, *beta*. Tell she, if you see she again, that everything is the same. Thing don't change much over here."

"And remind she that she have a brother. A few Canadian dollars wouldn't hurt." He laughed, an alcoholic's dry, choking cackle. The aluminium sheet drummed against the eave. The middle-aged man grasped one of Cooblal's ears and spat into it. The driver lowered the volume on his radio to hear what the woman was saying to me. He craned his neck and squinted when I reached into my pocket. A pickup van rattled up the hill, the gears grating and grinding.

Three hours later, I was awakened from my light sleep by a persistent tapping. The man in the adjoining seat was attempting to open his bottle of fruit juice by knocking it against the foldout tray. "You missed your drink," he told me. "The stewardess just passed. This bloody thing." He redirected his attention to his fruit juice. "Could you hold this newspaper for me?" He swept the weekly onto my seat.

I flipped through the newspaper, reading of a man murdered with a pickaxe, and on another page of a woman smeared with hot oil. In the centre pages, I saw the results of a poll, painstakingly broken down into racial and religious categories, and the pollster's extrapolation that a sizeable segment of the population believed that intermittent acts of violence were inevitable, and a smaller group maintained that these riots were not necessarily harmful. I closed the newspaper and on the last page, I saw the headline, "Portrait of a Family." There was a photograph of Mr. Rampartap and his wife standing together, and seated before them, his daughter and Rob. I stared at the photograph and even though it was reproduced in grainy, yellowish paper, I felt that people unwittingly reveal a great deal of themselves when they are locked into poses. I had never previously noticed the quality of exhaustion in Mr. Rampartap's determined, brutal face, nor the self-assurance in his wife's wary eyes.

The woman across the aisle was telling her son that they were now in another time zone. The boy, about ten or so, was wearing oversized glasses that made him appear birdlike and slightly unstable. He asked her whether they were now younger or older. The mother, who had an open magazine before her, continued reading, then told her son that such a small unit would not make a difference.

I glanced at my watch with its sea-blue face, then turned once more to the photograph. I wondered how they would all look five or ten years from now. Would Cynthia still have that hopeful expression and Rob that rakish grin?

"So are we going forward or backward?"

The mother flipped a page impatiently. "It doesn't matter. Now, sit back and try to sleep. I will awaken you when we arrive."

"Will Daddy be there in the airport?"

She closed her magazine and leaned back. "I'm not sure, dear." Her voice was softer now. "What did he say to you when we were leaving Canada?" The boy pushed up his glasses with his thumb and forefinger, then glanced down at a pillow in his lap. "Try to remember, dear." Suddenly her voice was tinged with uncertainty. "Concentrate."

"Tell she that she Pappy does still get vex all the time and pelt everything he could lay he hands on, and that Krish,

that is, she brother, still wasting he time in the rumshop."
She had pulled the end of her *orhni* over her shoulder,
studying the minuscule, transparent beads which, in the
sun, twinkled like tiny fishes' eyes. "No, don't tell she all
them things. That was always to upset she. Running in the
room in the back and locking the door when Pappy and
Krish start fighting and when Houri, that is she sister, start
bawling and screaming." She had glanced back anxiously at
the house. "Tell she that I happy that things working out so
well with she own family."

She must have seen the confusion on my face.

"Yes, *beta*, she does write sometimes, but not too often,
and tell me how she husband had a nice teaching job and
then he startup working with a big-big papers in Canada.
You know him?" She had once more gazed at me speculatively, running her fingers through the loose folds of her
orhni, but she didn't wait for a response. "I hear that the little *bacha* growing up so pretty and bright and only asking
these smart-smart question about Trinidad. I so glad she get
happiness in that place so far-far 'way."

She smiled then, caught in some memory. "But I did
always expect that. Since she was a little child walking
to school alone with she little bookbag on the other side
of the road so these little hooligan wouldn't trouble she
about she Pappy and about Houri. Walking alone and
frighten in case she meet Krish coming home drunk from
the rumshop."

Krish, who had been stroking Cooblal, shouted, "Ay,
mistah. Don't worry 'bout all these chupidness that Mammy
telling you. Just tell the blasted woman when you meet she
to send down some Canadian dollars." Once more from the
house, a barking, rasping scream.

Without thinking, I had reached into my pocket. "She sent this for you." She studied the envelope I had intended to give to Mr. Rampartap and wiped away a tear with her *orhni.*

"Mmmm. I can't remember."

"Never mind, dearie. We will see when we arrive." She fluffed the pillow in his lap. "It's a long flight. Nappy nap."

"Mom!"

The man next to me was still struggling with his bottle cap. "How do you open this bloody thing?"

"Twist it and twist it and twist it," I told him.

I reread the final paragraph of Bhogerattie's article.

And so Mr. Rampartap has ended his long association with the island's politics. Already people are speaking admiringly of his decision to dedicate the rest of his life to building a temple on the bank of the Red water which we all know was a sacred place to our forefathers from India and indeed from Africa too. One unconfirmed rumour playing around the town is that Mr. Dangley Chew, who was recently exonerated from some tragic suicide business involving a troublesome dipsomaniac (may his soul rest in peace), has developed a plan to utilize the natural gas from some nearby mud volcanoes to provide power for the temple. But the real power behind this temple, I tell you, is none other than Mr. Edwin Ramayodha Rampartap.

The man next to me glanced at the article. "It have a name for people like that, you know. Changing at ease."

"What?"

He leaned over and whispered in my ear, "Shape-shifters. Lagahoos."

I wiped the side of my face. Finally, he opened his bottle and took a long drink, gurgling and purring. "So what you going to do when you get back to Canada?"

I leaned over and whispered in his ear, "Lagahoo."

He jerked back, shut his bottle tight and crossed his legs.

I looked out of the window at the small volcanic islands, just brown smudges from the distance. Then the plane ploughed through a cloudbank and was swallowed up by an amorphous whiteness.

Acknowledgments

I would like to thank my agent, Jennifer Barclay, for her encouragement and faith. There were others who helped along the way: Brinsley Samaroo, The Naparima Alumni Association, Stan and Imogen Algoo, my parents and Laurel Boone.

I'm grateful to the Canada Council.

And finally, thanks to Diane Martin, my editor, whose patience and guidance steered this novel through all its stages.

Rabindranath Maharaj's first novel, *Homer in Flight*, was shortlisted for the Chapters/*Books in Canada* First Novel Award and broadcast on CBC's *Between the Covers*. A previous collection of short stories, *The Interloper*, was nominated for the Commonwealth Writers Prize for Best First Book. He lives in Ajax, Ontario.